STILL NOT YOURS

AN ENEMIES TO LOVERS ROMANCE

NICOLE SNOW

ICE LIPS PRESS

Content copyright © Nicole Snow. All rights reserved.
Published in the United States of America.
First published in November, 2018.

Disclaimer: The following book is a work of fiction. Any resemblance characters in this story may have to real people is only coincidental.

Please respect this author's hard work! No section of this book may be reproduced or copied without permission. Exception for brief quotations used in reviews or promotions. This book is licensed for your personal enjoyment only. Thanks!

Cover Design – CoverLuv. Photo by Danny Flores Photography.

Website: Nicolesnowbooks.com

DESCRIPTION

**Pretend engaged. Total opposites. So wrong it hurts.
Now let's pretend he isn't driving me insane...**

I'm on my last nerve.
 And I'm supposed to *marry* him to save my skin.
 Riker Woods might be God's hottest contradiction.
 Perfectly damaged. Stubborn soul. Moth to flame gaze.
 Single dad. Fierce protector. Kind...when he thinks no one's looking.

Then along came little old me.
 The pesky fiancée he never wanted.
 A hot mess in his neat, broody, oh-so-serious world.
 Thanks, witness protection geniuses.

If only the men who want me dead were my biggest problem.
 Nope, it's falling for Jekyll and Hyde.
 We're too close. Too tense. Too inevitable.

We're finding new reasons to fake kiss before you can say *uh-oh*.
He's whispering reckless things that sound so right.
I'm helplessly addicted to playing house.

We're crossing lines like electric fences when it hits me.
Maybe pretending to be Riker's girl isn't the worst.
It's what happens next.
What if I dare to say that magic, fatal word – *yours?*
What if I want us to be real?

I: LITTLE WHITE LINES (OLIVIA)

You never know which day will be the last day of your life.

I'm pretty sure this is the last day of mine, right now, as the sound of gunshots whites out the world around me into nothing but reverberating echoes, then splashes that emptiness with blood.

My ears are ringing.

My heart hits my ribs, racing so fast, running on pure adrenaline and moving at Mach speeds.

Jesus, there's a dead man at my feet.

I don't know him, never met him. But I know if I live past this frozen, pulse-stopping moment, I'll never forget his face.

I'll never forget his strange look of shock, eyes wide, like he's not really dead. Just frozen in time. Caught in the moment he realizes the two men leaning out of a nondescript, matte grey van outside my sister's palatial mansion are pointing their guns *right at him*.

Only, that was fifteen seconds ago. Now, he's crumpled on the sidewalk, and those guns are pointing at *me*.

I can feel the sights of the weapons like they're touching me, reaching across the motionless space between us to caress the vulnerable places of my body and make them quiver, tremble, tighten up with frightened chills.

Everything goes loud. It's not just the surrealness either.

The men are shouting something, but I can't make out the words.

I can't make out anything but the rattle of my own breathing. Then one word repeating over and over in my panicked brain.

Run.

Ask me later, and maybe I'll tell you I made a calm, calculated decision, took a risk, and did something badass to save my life.

Ask me now, though, and the only thing I can say is my mind isn't moving but my legs are, my lizard brain taking over and deciding the best option out of fight or flight is *flight*. No contest.

I don't look where I'm going. I'm just airborne, so fast and frantic I can't feel my feet touch the ground.

The only direction that matters is *away* – away from the dead man, away from the danger, away from the van full of men with guns. I don't realize I'm fleeing right out into the busy street.

Until I almost die for the second time in less than a minute.

I'm lucky the cab driver saw me coming and slowed down.

His front bumper only jolts against me, just hard enough for the pain to slap me out of my daze of animal panic. I tumble against the taxi's hood, clutching the metal to keep from falling, my feet wobbling under me.

For half a frozen second the taxi driver and I stare at each other through the windshield, his eyes wide and ringed in white, my face feeling like a frozen mask caught mid-scream.

Then a gunshot rings out behind me, loud as an explosion, and I fly into motion.

I scramble around the side of the cab, grabbing at anything I can reach until I feel a handle. It's not even the right door, but I don't *care*. I yank the front passenger side door open, throw myself inside, slam the door shut behind me, and immediately duck down below the dash.

"Drive!"

"But –"

"Listen, I'll double your fare, I don't care, but if you want to get us out of here alive – just *drive!*"

The driver stares at me for a second too long, an eternity where I feel my heart stopping and restarting all over again. Then he slams down on the gas so hard, he nearly throws me against the dash.

I barely catch myself, flinging my arms out and smacking them against the glove compartment hard enough to form bruises.

I can feel everything, honestly, my senses ramped so high by adrenaline that just the tickle of my own hair on the back of my neck is like claws and feelers raking over me, making me want to scream.

Shaking, I push myself up and grab the seatbelt strap,

though I can't bring myself to move enough to actually put it on.

Staring in the rear-view mirror, I see traffic scatter around us as the driver rockets down the street. I don't see the van anymore.

I don't see anything but annoyed people honking at us, flipping us off, and my sister's front gate receding rapidly in the distance.

Not rapidly enough.

I don't think *anything* is fast enough to put real distance between me, them, and what just happened.

"Miss?" the driver ventures tentatively. The violent vibrations of the car around me ease a little as he lays off the gas as we get deeper into traffic. "Miss...I think you should call the police."

"Yeah," I manage shakily. "Yeah, probably. I don't...I don't know what that was. Why they..."

Words die when my stomach suddenly revolts. I clutch harder at the seatbelt strap until it's just a scrunched up ribbon in my hands. Everything turns sideways, wrong-ways, and my gut roils and my head is swimming and my mouth floods with a terrible salty taste.

"Pull over," I gasp.

"But Miss –"

"Pull *over*, I said. I'm going to be sick!"

The driver goes pale. The tires screech as he wrenches toward the curb, rocking me wildly enough that I almost lose it then and there. I can feel sweat against my spine, and everything smells too sharp.

He barely bumps up against the sidewalk before I'm bolting out the door, my world on fire.

What happens next isn't dignified. It isn't graceful. It's not anything I ever pictured happening to me, bent over crying and expelling my fear until my throat aches and my chest hurts, and I still don't know what's going on.

I only know I feel *awful.*

This...this whatever it is, it's all wrong wrong.

This isn't what happens to Olivia Holly.

Not to a girl who's always had servants and a father who's in the one-percent's one-percent. Not to a girl with a world famous sister who has fifty million Instagram followers, and who's been around more celebrities and billionaires than most freaking private jets.

Oh, but ready or not, here I am.

Sicking it up in a gutter on the side of a busy Seattle street, with a dead man's blood on my four-hundred-dollar shoes.

Life can't possibly get any worse.

Then, naturally, it does.

* * *

I DON'T HAVE to wait long to find out how wrong I am.

My life definitely gets much worse.

Okay. So, maybe my decision-making processes aren't the best right now.

So, maybe I should've had that cabbie drop me off at a police station so I could immediately go into protective custody. Instead, I had him take me to the Seattle Edgewater, because I felt safer surrounded by a lot of people in a very secure hotel where Daddy's credit card buys me, at the very least, the illusion of being protected in a top-floor locked room while I wait for someone in my family to come get me.

But that illusion is shattered now as I answer the door for a very timid-looking bellhop with my room service order. If I'm being honest, it's mostly an attempt at normalcy when I can't stand the idea of food right now.

Especially because he's shown up with more than the cart. He's got a crumpled piece of paper in his hands, cut down the middle with a slash, and all I can see is black and red ink. But from the way his shoulders are hunched, I know what it means.

More bad news.

He fidgets then offers me the page. "I think this was intended for you, Miss Holly..."

I don't want to take it.

I hold back, hovering, my fingers curled against my chest, my heart doing that scary jitter that makes me feel like it's going to stop mid-beat. "Oh. Thanks. Did you see who left it?"

"N-no." There's no mistaking his fear – his eyes too wide, beads of sweat on his forehead, and he keeps sucking in his upper lip.

He's holding the page like it just might burn him, and his voice drops to a strained whisper as he says, "It was stuck to the service door in the alley." Lower still, eyes widening further. "With a *knife*."

There it is.

That moment when my heart truly stops and my chest feels too tight.

We stare at each other. It's like a standoff, him holding the letter, me not taking it, both of us so scared it's like a silent scream between us.

I *knew* it. I should've called the cops. I should've...

Honestly, I don't know what I should've done.

This isn't my world, or my life. My life is living in my sister Milah Holly's pop starlet shadow, following Daddy around to all his rich functions to make him look good with his meek, pretty daughter on his arm, and not doing much of anything with my day that involves making a single decision for myself.

I'm not equipped to know what to do when a man gets shot to death in front of me.

And I'm not equipped to know what to do when someone leaves me what's clearly an ink-scrawled threat, either.

But this won't end, this standoff, until I really look at it. Take it in, figure out what's going on, and make a choice about what to do. I *need* to do this.

I need to be an adult and figure out how to handle it, instead of staying paralyzed in the doorway with this poor boy who shouldn't even be involved with whatever misfortune has landed at my feet.

The paper crinkles far too loudly in my hand as I pry the page from his clenched fingers and smooth it out. My name jumps out at me in black ink: Olivia Holly.

I'm at the bottom of a list that makes everything inside me twist up in pain and fear.

Alec Holly.

Milah Holly.

Olivia Holly.

My father, my sister, and me. All three names written in black ink and slashed through with red Xs crossing us out.

It doesn't need to say another word to be a proclamation of doom, loud and clear, screaming almost as shrilly as my pulse.

The man who died on the sidewalk wasn't a mistake. It wasn't a simple, nasty case of *wrong place, wrong time.*

Someone wants to kill my family, and they're still after us. I don't understand why. I don't know what's going on.

God, *why* would anyone want us dead?

I lift my head. "You're *sure* you didn't see –"

Too late. The bellhop is gone.

It's just me in the hallway with the room service cart, feeling far too exposed and alone when even this high security luxury hotel isn't safe.

I'm not sure the kind of safety I need is anything money can buy.

Crap. All I wanted was a day away from Daddy hovering all the time.

Spending the weekend at Milah's Seattle place seemed like a good idea. My party girl older sister at least knows how to relax, even if she's not good at much else but singing.

I should've known I was biting off more than I could chew. Most of my weekend was spent keeping Milah from tripping into the pool and drowning herself while drunk, and then searching her a little too extensively for my liking for any little white baggies.

I know she's trying to kick her habit. She's in a twelve-step program for cocaine addicts especially, but I wish she'd told me she was in need *before* I was flushing a dime baggie of cocaine down the toilet and rocking her in the shower through withdrawals.

Another relapse, a little less ugly than the last. I thought I'd gotten her settled, finally, and was fully prepared to go home and just resign myself to another week of being the perfect shadow daughter.

Only to walk outside, into a nightmare straight out of a mafia movie.

I need to get inside. I'm suddenly convinced no one's coming, my father and sister are dead even though I just heard their voices on the phone twenty minutes ago, and then the panic hits.

"Liv!"

I hear my own name. Just once. Loudly.

Let a girl scream, okay?

Look, I'm not Lara Croft or Bayonetta or even Princess Peach. When I was little, I used to daydream about being the first female Starfleet captain in those kicky little boots and cute A-line uniform dresses, but that all boiled down to wanting to look pretty while shooting lasers at bad guys.

As most little girls do.

I didn't grow up a fierce, unstoppable warrior heroine.

I grew up into a spoiled, bratty, rich girl's younger sister, and spoiled, bratty, rich girls' younger sisters *scream like hell when you scare the crap out of them.*

I'm one second from bolting back in the room when I get a glimpse of hot pink and my anxiety ramps down in a heartbeat.

No assassin ever would show up in a pink mohair tube top that's at least a decade out of style, even if it's so *Milah*, it'll probably bring the fashion back.

Sis comes tearing around the corner of the hallway, her eyes too wide, her hair in a wild disarray of highlighted gold, her mile-long legs tottering on platform boots. She looks as scared as I feel, and all the worried frustration I'd felt over her weekend backslide melts away when I realize she's honestly afraid for me.

Milah and I are as different as night and day, but we're still sisters.

She loves me. I love her.

I'm just not a fan of her life choices.

She slams into me so hard she nearly cuts the breath out of me. I can tell from the strength of her grip that she's sober. But while her hands are steadier than normal, it's her voice that's wavery when she demands, "Oh my God, Liv. *Oh my God.* Are you all right?"

"No," I whisper, then burst into tears.

Let a girl scream. And let her cry, too.

I'm not used to being the little sister, not feeling like one, even if I'm two years younger than Milah – but for once instead of me taking care of her, she's taking care of me.

She holds me in her spindly arms while I cry, then ushers me inside and sits me down on the edge of the bed to carefully peel me out of my bloodied clothes. She's brought me a change of clothing, and with a little too much practice, she carefully lays out the dirty things on a chair.

"Don't touch them again. For the police," she says gently, then settles down next to me and plucks the crumpled note from my trembling hands.

"Holy fuck-a-roo." Her brows knit as she scans over our names. Then she shakes her head, looking at me with her wide blue eyes pale, worried. "How'd this happen?"

I sniffle, rubbing at my eyes.

Maybe I feel a tad better now that I'm not wearing that outfit. I hope the police burn it when they're done with it, but I'm better able to speak, to pull myself together, and I tell Milah everything.

"This black car pulled up to the curb right when I was leaving your place," I say. "This guy got out and started asking me about you. I thought he was paparazzi and was just going to blow past him, but then he said something about how you owe him for a 'special delivery' and that you'd remember Vancouver. I...I didn't even know what he was talking about. But then this van comes roaring down the street and these other men lean out and next thing I know there're gunshots and a dead body."

"Two," Milah corrects, her voice ragged at the edges, almost a croak. "There were two dead bodies."

"What?!" I feel the blood drain from my face. "Two? No...no, I only saw them kill one..."

"The driver," she whispers. "We found them both out front. They shot the driver while you ran."

"The second gunshot." I swallow back the thick, awful feeling in my throat. "I was running and heard a second gunshot. I thought they were firing at me, but..."

"They would've." Milah lets out a worried, fretful sound, pressing her fingers to her mouth, then just buries her face in her hands, her shoulders shaking. "Oh, fuck. Fuck, Liv, this is all my fault...there was a show in Vancouver. Several tours ago. I don't remember much of it, I wasn't really myself –"

Wasn't really myself. That's Milah code for *on another coke bender.*

"But listen, hon, I know I fucked up. I wanted to impress a lot of people up there and I blew a lot of money on some really good stuff. Like, really pure, best I've ever had." She breaks off and gives me a guilty look. "I don't mean it like that, I guess. Just that it was expensive, and I guess I must've borrowed from the wrong people. I'm sorry, Liv. I'm so, so *sorry*, I can't believe what a fuckup I am. I'm trying to do better, but this stuff just comes back to –"

"Milah." I try to keep my voice gentle. Here we are, back to being the older younger sister. "You owe people drug money?"

"Maybe." She gets off one word and then she hangs her head.

Mutely, she nods, her little-girl pout drawn and trembling. I sigh, pressing my fingers to the bridge of my nose.

"Paying them off isn't going to work. People are dead now. We're calling the cops. Maybe even the FBI."

"No!" She goes pale, shaking her head frantically, her ponytail bobbing. "The freaking Feds? We can't!"

"Hey, you were the one preserving evidence over there like it's an episode of *CSI: Miami.*"

"That was *before* I knew what this was about." She bites her lip, turning the full force of those pleading baby blues on me. "Going to the police will just make it worse. Trust me, Liv...they may even arrest me for possession."

I tense. "What? Are you carrying right now?"

"No!" She knots her hands together. "Just, you know, past stuff. What if they take these guys down and I go with them?"

I roll my eyes. "Then I'm sure Daddy will be standing by with a legion of lawyers to bail you out."

Groaning, I flop back against the Egyptian cotton sheets. Suddenly I'm less afraid of these men with guns and more resigned to whatever mess Milah has gotten herself into now.

"Can't we just get this over with? Tell Daddy to fix everything like we always do?"

"Daddy won't need to," Milah says almost triumphantly. "Because I know just the thing. And the *man.*"

II: LITTLE TOO MUCH (RIKER)

When I tell people I'm married to my job, I don't mean it so damn literally.

That's just how it feels right now as my daughter gets out of the back seat of my Wrangler with a chipper little wave, and my phone starts blowing up with one text notification after another.

No rest for the wicked? Maybe, but work can wait another ten seconds. There's one thing that can't.

"Hey, Em, you forgetting something?"

I ignore it until she looks back, sighs, then comes around to the driver's side, leans in, and pecks me on the cheek with her bright, impish little smile that she wears so bravely every morning to hide just how shy she is.

She's so tiny you'd never guess she's in her teens, this pixie with forest-green eyes and long brown hair – and you'd never guess how smart she is, either.

So smart she gives me a run for my money daily. So smart the goddamn NSA is already sniffing around for scholarship submissions to get her fast-tracked through cryptography.

She's only twelve.

Older and brighter than most people will ever be, but her heart is still a child's.

I can't help but want to pull her back into the car then.

Just pull her away from school, shut off my phone, and shelter her from the day I know that's coming, when she'll be making her way out into a world I can't save her from.

She's always so guarded, though, her shyness more a shield and a defense than any fear. I know when she comes home tonight, she'll smile and tell me school was fine, but her shoulders will be heavy and that careful withdrawal in her eyes will tell me everything I need to know about how lonely her days in class are.

I'm not sending her into a training center for the frigging government. She isn't ready. Even if it'd cover college expenses that are coming up way too fast for my bank account.

"Have yourself a good day," I say, nodding my head.

I can't keep her locked up forever, though. I can't even keep her locked up today.

All I can do is watch her go with a final wave and a smile when she says, "It's your turn to make dinner tonight, Daddy."

Meanwhile, the phone loses its mind, vibrating like a loose grenade.

Fuck.

I never thought I'd see my life like this. Having a daughter young enough to still call me Daddy, but old enough that I'm already thinking about how the hell I'm going to manage without her when she's all grown up.

Not until her first bell rings and she disappears inside the school building with a last flip of her hair over her Spock backpack do I bother with my phone. Texts have changed into ringing off the hook – two phone calls – but that's always been my rule for working at Enguard.

Family first, even if it means letting Landon work himself into a foaming lather while I see Em off to school.

Once the third call starts rumbling, I fish my phone out and lean back in the driver's seat, draping an arm over the steering wheel while I swipe the Answer button.

Through the windshield, Jenny Cavanaugh's mother catches my eye and flutters her fingers at me with a syrupy little smile. I force a thin smile back – she gave me food poisoning with her tuna salad at a PTA potluck, and I hold grudges – then murmur into the phone.

"Yeah? It's Woods. What's the emergency?"

"Just get your ass down to the office," Landon says. He sounds more exhausted than annoyed. "We've got hell on our hands, and it's probably not something we should discuss over the phone. Even on a secure line."

Awesome.

I strap on my seatbelt, jack the Wrangler into reverse, and then back out of the parking lot one-handed. The other's busy transferring the phone to my dash holder and flicking the Bluetooth clip in my ear. "Not going to give me even a small clue?"

"Milah," Landon says grimly. "Milah Holly."

Triple fuck.

Luckily, there's always a silver lining. James is going to owe me a drink.

We've had a running bet since Skylar got her niece back – that either we were completely out of the woods on catastrophic clusterfucks this year, or we were just getting started.

First there was that mess with Crown Security and a firefight that nearly took the police to break it up, not to mention Milah Holly getting poisoned at her own concert. Then there was Skylar's niece getting kidnapped, missing for months, and Sky herself nearly ending up another victim to a deranged madman who'd do anything to keep that little girl.

My buddy, James, thought that was the end of our chaos streak.

My old man always taught me fortune comes in threes, both good and bad, and I've only counted *two* disasters so far.

Sometimes, I hate being right.

Even if it means getting an entire bottle of aged Glenfiddich as my reward.

Fine scotch can go a long damn way to taking the edge off whatever price I have to pay to win my bet.

Sighing, I pull the Jeep into traffic and set course for the office. "Are you calling everyone or just me?"

"Everyone else is already here. But this job's specific to you, Riker."

Me? There's an edge in my boss' voice I don't like.

My hackles raise, put up their dukes. I can't help it.

I'm a senior security adviser, dammit. Sometimes the muscle, most often in charge of firearms training, safety, and certification for all our field agents. I don't usually have specific jobs assigned to me. I'm more like the team's backbone.

"Landon," I ask, "what the hell are you getting me into?"

"You'll see," he says. "Drive faster."

* * *

I'm almost tempted to "accidentally" get stuck in traffic.

But before long I'm pulling into my parking spot outside Enguard Security. Landon's right – the whole team is here already, earlier than usual, their cars lined up in the lot.

From Sky's junky old Buick to Landon's Impala to Gabe's Dodge to James' sleek Camry. When I walk inside, the command center looks like a war room – everyone gathered grimly around a projector screen where Sky's laptop beams up a bunch of collected tabs with a map, a route, several open dossier files, and a photo of a waifish, fragile-looking blonde girl who most definitely isn't Milah Holly.

Though I think there's a distinct resemblance...

She looks like the kind of girl who attracts danger, from her wide, startled eyes to the subtle tremor captured in a single soft parting of her pink, articulated lips.

She looks like the kind of girl who could drive a man to lose his mind with the need to protect her.

She looks like a siren call to self-destruction.

She looks like trouble, in neon beauty, and I have a feeling she's about to become *my* problem.

Before I even get a chance to ask a question, Landon's passing around handouts.

I skim the blocky chunks of text and photos. Olivia "Liv" Holly, barely twenty-one, daughter of some investment and business incubation mogul, younger sister to pop queen Milah Holly. I catch mention of a gang called the Pilgrims, and flip through a police report with two dead bodies before Landon starts up.

"This is a protection job, pure and simple," he says, "but not quite like any protection job we've done before. We're basically taking this girl into witness protection, but it's a private operation. Not even the cops will know where she is."

Gabe – hovering over Skylar protectively as always – props his shoulder against the wall and asks in his low Southern drawl, "Don't make no sense for it to be us, does it? Don't the cops have setups for this kind of thing?"

"They do," Landon says. "But this girl witnessed a hit. I'm thinking organized mob, the Pilgrims from the looks of it – and you don't work with the cops if you don't want to cross the Pilgrims. They're run by this asshole who calls himself Lion, and he's got his fingers in everything. The cops, private security, maybe even CIA. They'd hang her out to dry in a second if he wanted her."

James frowns, folding his arms over his chest, and somehow never manages to even crease his impeccably pressed suit. "What makes you so certain it's the Pilgrims?"

"Let's just say we have history." Landon's mouth sets in a grim line, dark blue eyes flashing. "When my father ran Crown Security, he had connections in some low places. Dallas' father had some even worse ones." I can tell he tries not to shudder mentioning Dallas, his old rival.

He leans over and taps a few keys on Sky's laptop. The projector screen changes to show an image of a tall, grizzled man with a thick mane of hair half-in, half-out of wiry blonde braids, his beard wild around a grim mouth, the clench of his scarred fists as brutal as the coldness in his eyes.

If he weren't so brutally smart, he'd look like a homeless psycho. More like a modern day pirate than any kind of pilgrim, but I've never had to name a gang.

"I'd see Lion around the office sometimes. Usually looking for people to shore up his protection racket, wringing local businesses for cash to keep them safe from rival gangs. He makes a lot of enemies." Landon looks at us, making sure we're staying sharp.

I've been silent, taking it all in, fighting against the growing sense that this is something I don't want to get involved with, but now I can't help but speak up.

"So, what, you think two crime syndicates may be involved?"

"Bingo. Milah doesn't know the two dead men, and her sister claims they were asking after Milah and a debt before they were gunned down. I saw the forensic photos." Landon folds his arms over his chest. "I think the Pilgrims were after Milah Holly for drug money, and a rival gang shot them up while they were shaking down her sister. The motive, that's less clear."

My heart sinks. Em's little face pops into my head.

I'm getting a bad feeling about this. A very bad fucking feeling about this. I grind my teeth, turning things over, while Sky speaks up.

"There's the old lodge in Eugene," she says. "Where we do field practice. We *could* convert it into a safe house, boss."

"That would be far too obvious," James interjects in his usual refined tone. "From what we know of these Pilgrims, they specialize in finding people in hiding places few expect. I believe for this job we need something more...unorthodox."

They're all looking at me. Waiting. Looking right at me, like they're some hive mind having the same devious thought. I tense, fingers curling into fists until the handout's pages crinkle.

"What?"

"I think you need to get remarried," Landon says.

"*No.*"

"Not really, of course." Landon sighs, fighting at a smile he bites back. "Look, it's not like we're enjoying this. It's just the most obvious solution, Riker. You say she's your fiancée, finally coming to meet your kid, and she moves in with you. You slot her into your home, play house for a while, and keep her safe while we partner up with the FBI and do the dirty work. You'll be her chaperone while we're hunting down everyone involved, making sure they never threaten anyone again."

"Meet my kid." I mirror the words back slowly and precisely, a bitter echo. The dread inside me crystallizes into something cold and dark. "You want me to endanger my daughter by bringing Milah Holly's problems into my house? You want me to prioritize her sister over my own child?"

The entire office goes dead silent save for the faint clicks and whirrs of Sky's laptop. Everyone is watching me in a sort of tense, frozen silence, like I'm a block of C4 waiting to ignite and blow the entire room to kingdom come.

I can't move. I'm too pissed off.

Stillness is the only way I can control my anger, my rage, and keep my training from taking over until I sink away into a dark place where I become someone no one here wants to deal with.

These people are my crew, my friends. But today, dammit, they're really testing my nerve.

Landon's watching me with something almost like sympathy – no, that's not quite it.

Trust.

"I want you to be who you truly are," he says softly. "The only person here who has the strength and the skill to keep them both safe. I trust that you can do it. I know Emily does, too. She's an angel, and I'd never do anything to endanger your daughter. Olivia Holly needs someone like you. It's cover, Riker, nothing more. What happened to the younger Holly isn't her fault, and you're the best one to protect her. The story behind it doesn't matter."

"It matters to me." I'm feeling so much, I can't express anything at all, everything evening out into this flat, dead tone. "You want me to bring another woman into my home and just...tell my daughter to accept her? That's seriously what you're asking?"

"Emily's a brilliant young lady, isn't she?"

Landon pauses until I grudgingly nod my head. I can't deny that part.

"Then she's smart enough to understand. Wiser than her years. It's only temporary, and again..." A sigh heaves Landon's chest. "I'm not asking you to do this out of the goodness of your heart. I'm offering a hazard pay bonus equal to one year's salary. The company will cover the cost of the necessary security upgrades to your house. Whatever you need to feel comfortable and keep safe. We'll turn the damn place into Cheyenne Mountain."

I almost want to quit my job right now. Turn around. Walk out.

Never look at Landon Strauss or any of these people watching me with expectant eyes ever again.

Landon's just put a price tag on my family and my pride. A year's salary.

Fuck.

And the worst part is, a part of me knows it would be a smart idea to accept, when that money could mean everything for my daughter's future.

Landon doesn't know it, but he's dangling a carrot on a stick – and a whole year's extra salary would be enough to get us out of debt. Crystal's been gone for four years now, leaving just me, Em, and a pile of chemotherapy bills that I've been battling the insurance company on even when I didn't have the fortitude for it. All because those relentless bastards want to take us for everything we have and leave us penniless.

I grew up that way. Clawing tooth and nail for everything. Eating fried bologna sandwiches for lunch and dinner.

I *won't* have that life for Em.

Em will have everything she needs, from love to a safe and secure home.

No matter what I have to do to give it to her.

With money like that, I could pay off the chemo bills and round off Em's college fund. Not that I think she'll need it when she'll have schools lining up to offer scholarships, but I've got to think ahead and plan for *every* contingency. She's too bright. Too good. Too likely to make this world a better place.

She only has me to rely on, so I can't have even one

slip, one moment of carelessness. Not one failure as her father.

Which means I can't fail if I take this job on.

Christ, I can't *believe* I'm considering this. Closing my eyes, I massage my temples, trying to pull myself out of that cold, angry, unfeeling place. "You're sure it has to be me?"

"I'm too obvious, after what happened with Joannie," Sky says. "And I can't really pass her off as my kid sister."

"And since me an' Sky come as a unit..." Gabe adds, slipping his big arm around her shoulder.

James thins his lips, side-eyeing me. "Do I look like the sort to rush into a headlong whirlwind engagement with a woman I have just met?"

"So I do?" I snap back.

Landon shakes his head. "You're the best choice, Riker. Plain and simple. My place is too high-profile. It's you, or nothing at all."

Nothing at all, I want to say, but I'm backed into a corner, and I know it.

I have to do this, to secure my daughter's future and give her the life she deserves.

But I have no idea how I'm going to explain it to her.

Or how either of us will deal with having a woman in the house for the first time since her ma passed away.

III: LITTLE BIT OF THAT (OLIVIA)

My head is still reeling by the time I step out of the plane and through the gate at San Francisco International Airport.

My father hovers so close at my back he's practically smothering me. I hadn't expected him to show up to chaperone me from Seattle to San Fran, but he's been this mute, glowering presence in a fine Italian wool suit the entire time, ignoring me for his laptop and tersely muttered calls.

The phone calls give me tiny heart palpitations even though I know that thing about cell phones messing with the flight controls isn't true anymore...mostly.

I should feel safer with Daddy around, but mostly I feel like I've been tossed through a whirlwind.

Just three hours ago, I was still in my Seattle hotel, while Milah made a dozen phone calls and furiously helped me throw my things into my luggage. She wouldn't even let me go home for my own stuff.

It should probably disturb me that my sister knows

this much about running from the mob, but honestly, it's a comfort that *someone* knows what to do.

At least she remembered to grab my notebook.

Milah's a lot of things, not all of them great, but she remembers the little things. She knows what's important to me. And it's those small, subtle details that remind me my sister is still there behind her struggle with addiction.

Right now, though, I've got to think about my own struggles – and this man I'm supposed to be meeting from the security agency, Riker Woods.

I'd tried to write on the flight, but I was too keyed-up remembering yesterday. The sound of gunshots, the way blood smells both hot and crisp. Struggling with the horrid feeling of being completely alone with my father right there, yet so far out of reach.

I should probably remember the details of the attack for my book, but right now it feels so raw and real that I can't really think about writing it down.

And I can't think about what I'm walking into when Milah's set me up to stay with someone from Landon Strauss' security agency.

Yes, *the* Landon Strauss – husband of *the* Kenna Burkenow-Strauss, my writing idol. She's an international bestselling romance author.

I doubt I'll get to meet her, of course.

But that doesn't shake how I've been fascinated with her since the documentary on what happened to my sister, and I've read all her novels. I think, *before I watched a man get shot at my feet*, I was firmly in my "I want to be Kenna when I grow up" phase.

Who knows, maybe writing novels could give me an

independent life of my own. Something I earned for myself instead of –

"Miss Holly?" A rough voice cuts in.

I'd been busy scanning the crowd without really seeing anyone. Now I'm standing at the gate with my suitcase propped on its wheels and dangling from one hand, my father next to me with his hand on my arm, like I'm going to run away if he lets me off my leash.

His grip is a little too tight, hurting me just a bit, but I don't have it in me to say anything right now.

I'm lost in my thoughts, detached, because there's a scream building up inside me and I can't let it out in the middle of a public airport terminal. But it almost bursts from my lips as a deep, gravelly voice to my side speaks my name, calling me *Miss Holly* as if he's addressing royalty he isn't quite sure he particularly likes or not.

I turn slowly.

I'm expecting to see some big, bald guy in aviator glasses and a tank top, tattoos and muscles everywhere. Probably a huge belt buckle. Or maybe some kid my age, clean shaven, first job fresh out of college, bouncing around like a puppy and eager to please.

Instead, I find this man's quiet, searing green gaze looking into me.

It's as clear as sea glass and just as intensely translucent, set against a dark tan of weathered skin creased into lines around deep-set, thoughtful eyes. He's tall, so tall it almost hurts my neck to look up at him, but he has a certain grace in the way he carries himself, with his button-down shirt sleeves cuffed to his elbows and casually tucked into neatly pressed slacks that frame long legs and strong hips.

The arcs of dark hair along his brawny, hard-set arms are the same chocolate brown as the neatly combed sweep of his hair and beard, touched with silver at the temples and the chin.

God, he's handsome.

The kind of *whoa, mama* handsome that makes you stop and look again because it seems too effortless to be real.

The kind that makes me think of a stern teacher whose dark, smoldering looks promise there's a dirty secret under his uptight demeanor.

The perfect kind of *screw the world* edge in his stance that tells me Riker Woods is about to make my world even more complicated than I ever dreamed.

Not what I was expecting.

Not at *all*.

Though there's nothing consciously smoldering about the way he looks at me right now. He studies me like I'm a particularly puzzling package he doesn't quite know how to open, before he repeats, "Miss Holly? You are Olivia Holly, yeah?"

"Um, yeah." I'm at a loss for what to do in this situation, and my lips try to tie themselves around each other. My cheeks burn, and I offer a hand. "Liv. You can call me Liv."

He looks down at my hand. His own are both tucked into the pockets of his slacks, his hips cocked with a sort of devil-may-care assurance.

He doesn't shake my hand, doesn't even take his hands out of his pockets.

I let my hand drop.

O-kay then.

What the hell did Milah get me into?

"Mr. Woods, I presume?" My father breaks the icy silence first.

His voice is cold in a way I've never heard before, and when I glance back at him, he's watching Riker with his blue eyes narrowed, like Riker just spit on his priceless antiques or six-figure platinum watch.

Riker says nothing, looking past me to my father. I can almost see the calculation in his eyes, the way he takes Daddy's measure in a silence that feels electrically charged.

I get the feeling that Riker isn't a man to be spoken to like a lackey, or commanded in any way, even if he's technically on my father's payroll.

And honestly, after a lifetime of seeing people too afraid to stand up to my father...

He's fascinating.

Riker takes his sweet time before he finally answers. "I am."

Two simple words.

My father sniffs. He's got his Fortune 500 Corporate Mogul face on right now, looking down his nose like he's royalty assessing a peasant. "I trust I don't need to remind you how much I'm paying for you to look after my daughter," he says, and I cringe, hunching into myself.

What's my price tag, then?

How much did it take for Daddy to pass me off to another man like nothing?

"I trust," Riker responds coolly, "that you don't need to tell me how to do my job. That's Landon's gig." His gaze then returns to me, skewering. "Car's this way, Miss Holly," he murmurs, and turns on his heel, his powerful stride carrying him across the terminal floor like he owns the freaking airport.

Holy hell.

Daddy's brow clouds over, lightning gathering in his eyes, and oh God he's about to lose his temper and have a *do you know who I am?* moment.

I've got to head it off. Quickly, I rest my hand on his arm, stretch up on my toes, and kiss his cheek. "Love you, Daddy," I say. "Let it go. I'll be okay. Thank you for doing this for me."

Under my touch, the tension in his arm relaxes some, though not by much.

But he tears his gaze from Riker's retreating back and looks down at me. Looks through me, preoccupied and not really seeing me, the ghost I've always been extra transparent today.

At last, he dredges up a distracted smile, and leans down to kiss the top of my head.

"Of course, dearest," he says. "Money's no object when it comes to you."

I don't know how to tell him that money is never what I wanted from him.

So I don't say anything.

Just squeeze his arm, force a brave smile, and murmur, "I'll see you soon when it's all over. You be safe too, okay?"

He doesn't even answer me, other than an absent nod and patting my hand.

He's already on his phone, frowning to himself while he flicks through emails. It's not hard to tell.

He's just waiting for me to leave. Buzz off, so he can get back to his business and his oh-so-important obligations.

If I had the time and energy to spare, I'd be angry.

After being tied to him by apron strings or tie clips or whatever for my entire life, having him suddenly so *indifferent...*

It's like the whole world pulled out from under me, and I'm in free fall.

I'm still feeling like a chastised child as I bow my head and trudge after Riker, dragging my suitcase behind me – only to yelp as he's suddenly *there*, standing in front of me, blocking my path.

Jesus. Do I need another set of eyes to keep tabs on this guy?

I'm not very good with jump-scares. I can't even watch PG-13 horror movies on a good day, and him materializing so close in front of me that I can smell the deep, smoky scent of his cologne is enough to get me stumbling back with that stifled scream I'd been bottling up squeaking out.

My heel turns the wrong way.

I start to tumble, windmill, fall.

Then that brawny arm is around my waist. I land there with an *oomph.*

It's like being captured by a steel cable surging with heat. He jerks me upright like I weigh less than a flower petal, handling me easily, pulling me against a feeling of strength and safety and power that bristles through his neat, straight-laced clothing.

I'm not sure what lights my cheeks on fire more: almost impacting the floor flat on my face or being in this man's arms.

"You okay?" he asks.

I nod. Or rather, I try. I can't peel my eyes off him.

It's like someone dressed a feral panther as a man and told it to act civilized. And maybe something primitive in me reacts to that hidden animal and all his strength when he's holding me like prey, looking down like he doesn't know if he wants to protect or devour me whole.

One word comes to my *what-the-hell-is-happening* mind.

Forbidding. That's a good word for Riker Woods.

Everything he is, from the stiff set of his shoulders to the hawk-eyed way he looks at me, says *stay away*.

But here I am, clutching at his arms to keep myself standing, my entire body arched closer than close while I try to process what just happened.

"You're okay then?" he echoes again. "Tell me you haven't gone deaf."

"Right. I'm fine. Think my shoe just caught in all the excitement. Um, sorry." It's hard to form words.

He says nothing. He doesn't seem to like to talk much.

He just leans down – bringing him close enough that his stubble grazes along my cheek, rasping and rough – and sets me carefully on my feet. He holds me just a second longer to help find my balance before he pulls away.

Then his face tightens, and those eyes are like daggers.

"Don't apologize. Let's go be fine somewhere that isn't this terminal. We're late."

For the briefest moment, his hand rests on the small of my back, thick fingers long enough that the heel of his palm touches one hip and his fingertips touch the other, making my stomach flip over wildly.

Then he pulls away, dips to catch the handle of my

suitcase, and turns to drag it behind him, and I realize that's what he wanted all along.

The suitcase. Duh.

Not me.

I'd ask myself why that stings, but I already know.

He just wants me to move my feet.

My emotions are all over the place. I'm already way too curious about him, and acting totally foolish.

This is real life. I'm not some insta-love little girl from Kenna Strauss' romance books.

I'm *not* anything to Riker Woods, and he damn sure isn't anything to me except more trouble.

It's got to be this state of mind.

I'm scared out of my wits after what happened last night, and I've never been without someone to shelter and protect me. I've always had someone to stroke my hair and say *It'll be all right* over even the smallest situation, and this most definitely isn't a *small situation.*

I need someone right now. I'm desperately craving some kind of human warmth, someone strong who cares that I'm frightened and would offer even a single kind word to help ease the fear.

Instead, I have a sister who can't be there for me. Not this time. Not now, between her own demons and the necessary distance.

Instead, I have a father who brushed me off like I was nothing and handed me over to a man who looks at me like I'm the one who's done something wrong. As if I've somehow ruined his life, or at least like I'm one more burden.

As if he's angry with me, and I don't even know why.

***

THE SILENCE in the car is almost more than I can handle.

Riker drives one of those big, rugged, modernized Jeep Wranglers, the kind of vehicle that can survive a hurricane or go skimming across the sand on a fun beach weekend. I don't want to admit it, but the car makes me feel safer.

It's not like the Lincolns, Escalades, and Teslas I've spent half my life in. It's solid, sturdy, an enclosed space with blackout windows that mean no one can see me. And I'm riding alone with the one person I can trust who won't hurt me, if only because he's getting paid for it.

We've been weaving through highway traffic for a while. I'm leaning my head against the sun-warmed window and looking outside when he speaks, breaking a silence ruled by the Wrangler's rumble and the snarl of other cars around us.

"One golden rule," he says. He has a sort of clipped way of speaking, like every word has to be excavated out of the gravel bed in his throat and pried free. "And only one. No matter how crazy things get, follow my lead."

I lift my head, turning to look at him. He's all eyes on the road and graven stone, that flinty green stare impossible to read.

I frown. "That's it? Don't question, just follow? Sorry, but I guess I expected –"

"Asking questions when people are throwing bullets is how you get shot. One rule, Miss Holly. If you can't follow it, this won't work."

There it is. Pointed and sharp.

"Fine," I mumble, slumping down in the passenger

seat. If only because I, you know, don't actually want to get shot.

But I'm being petulant. I know it.

I should just swallow my pride and listen. He has to know better...right?

I can't help my second-guessing. My entire life, I've been following everyone's lead.

Of course, I want to test the boundaries the one moment when following the lead of the man safeguarding my life makes every bit of sense.

Call it the legacy of a lifetime in Milah's shadow. Even now, I don't even have my own problems.

I have *Milah's* issues, and I'm being pushed around at her whim, doing this to make Daddy feel better that I'm somewhere safe. Away from what he, on the drive to the airport in Seattle, ominously called "cleanup."

That isn't the fault of the beast-man in the driver's seat.

So I try a different tactic – offering a faint smile. It can't hurt to be friendly.

"Aye-aye, captain. One rule. Got it. If all goes well, I shouldn't be your problem for long. Just have to convince my sister it's safe for us both to testify to the FBI. She's afraid they'll drag her in by association."

"And in the meantime, the longer you wait, the farther we get from any hope of catching the people who did this," Riker says grimly. "The Feds are your best shot. Local police may have handled the scene, but they can't be trusted. Not with hardcore hit men."

I bite my lip. *Hit men.* Like I need the reminder.

"I...I know that. And believe me, I want to testify ASAP. I'm supposed to, as soon as I'm ready, I just..." I shake my head. "I know Milah's worrying about nothing. That it doesn't work this way. She's scared for her career and her past catching up to her. But she's my sister and I don't want to hurt her."

"Does she have the same consideration for you?"

I flinch. My hands hurt from where I'm clutching at the seatbelt.

We've all heard of Captain Obvious. Is Riker Captain Blunt?

How is it that this man only met me half an hour ago, but can already see things like that about me?

How does he have the balls to throw it in my face?

And hell, how does he see *me*, really see me, when it feels like he looks right through me as though I'm not even there?

Wetting my lips, I look away, out the window again. "She didn't mean to create this problem."

"But she did."

"She's gotten clean!" I shoot back. Now, I'm getting angry.

My eyes are burning, blurring, and I rub at them with the heel of my palm. "Look, it's not your business, what goes on with her and me. It's the past. Ancient history. We'll fix it, we'll make it through, and it'll go away."

"Just like that, sweetheart? Interesting. You don't even have a guarantee that if you testify, the police will get the right criminals. Not with *two* groups involved."

My heart sinks for several reasons. Mostly because I let this royal prick break my fall, and before I knew better, I liked it.

"Thanks for the reminder. Is there anything *else* you want

to tell me about how wrong I am?" I fire back. "I get it. I'm in over my head. I don't know what I'm doing. I'm not all uptight and badass and I've never held a gun. So I should just listen. Swallow your advice. And my options are...what again? Do nothing? Just shut up and let you call all the shots?"

He says nothing. But the air in the car shifts subtly, and after a few icy seconds, he glances at me contemplatively, that hard glass of his gaze no longer quite so impenetrable. "Right now, don't worry about it," he murmurs. "You're under a lot of stress. We'll worry about the details once you've had time to calm down and feel safe."

I arch a brow. The shift in demeanor surprises me.

I think this big rock is actually trying to comfort me.

He turns his gaze back to the road. I lower my eyes, tangling my fingers together in my lap and picking at the hem of my sundress. "Okay. Yeah. I guess I'm not in the best place to be making decisions right now."

"Likely not. Stress and trauma affect the logic centers of your brain." The rumble of the car shifts around us as he eases toward the off-ramp. "But I also need us to not discuss this any further until I say."

I frown. "Why?"

"Because we're picking my daughter up from school, and as her father, I decide how much she knows."

His daughter. *Right.*

I gulp, twisting my fingers harder in my dress. This man makes me prickle all over with nerves, but I'm suddenly ten times more afraid of meeting his daughter.

She's twelve, I was told during the briefing...and I'm just supposed to pretend to be her new stepmother-in-progress, engaged to this walking brick who barely spares me a glance.

Right. Somehow, bullets no longer seem so bad.

"Fine," I whisper. "I won't say anything I shouldn't."

"Thank you."

I don't know what to say.

So I don't say anything at all.

Not even when we pull up outside a two-story brick school campus, and a petite little bundle of energy comes rocketing into the back seat with her Star Trek backpack in her lap and adorable clip-on communicator earrings. She freezes in the middle of shutting the door, staring at me in the rear-view mirror. I look back, feeling like I've just been caught doing something wrong.

"Um," she says. "Dad? Who's she?"

"Just close the door," Riker answers flatly. "I'll explain when we get home, honey."

* * *

I THINK I'm going to start hyperventilating.

I'm sitting in Riker's living room. I guess for now it's technically *my* living room, since that's the story we're going with.

A cover story that makes me feel like I've been turned inside out.

Quick rundown: we're in love, whirlwind courtship, and now Riker wants to integrate me into the family so his daughter and I get used to each other before our actual marriage.

His house looks like the perfect place a woman in love would want to come home to.

It's small, cozy, rustic. Nothing like the spacious mansions I'm used to, and everything like what you'd imagine an Average American home would be, with all these fatherly personal touches and little bits of *them* everywhere. From a shelf lined with dog-eared sci-fi novels to an open door giving me a glimpse into a workshop where a ship in a bottle sits on a desk, waiting to be finished.

This is their place.

And I shouldn't be here, screwing up their lives.

They're in the kitchen now. I can't tell what they're saying, just a low murmur of voices, but no one sounds upset.

The daughter – her name is Emily, and I hope she won't get mad at me for calling her that – just sounds curious and thoughtful. She talks a little bit like her father, like she's got a lot to say but she's trying to condense it down to as few words as possible.

But there's a more youthful openness to it, too. While Riker seems more closed off, a glacier of a man, I can't help wondering if he was more like her as a boy.

I shouldn't be wondering anything.

I'm not part of their lives. It's just pretend.

There's no real bond between us, and it's nothing but a formal arrangement. We're a business transaction. Nothing more.

I don't know them. I don't know anything. Like where Emily's birth mother must be, or why Riker even *agreed* to this when he clearly doesn't want to have me here.

I guess it's his job, and maybe the boss made it an order?

Here I am, being someone else's burden again.

All I've ever wanted was to learn how to stand on my own, but it feels like now that'll never happen. Until the FBI catches the people after my sister, I'll always be looking over my shoulder.

Heck, maybe always spending my life shuttled from safe house to safe house and false identity to false identity. I don't know what's going to happen to Milah if this gets worse. Her life is in the public spotlight, and she can't just disappear. Though she also has practice navigating this mess of personal security and personal threats from random nutjobs.

It's also a lot harder to get to her *because* she's so famous.

I'm the one who can disappear all too easily, with no one even noticing.

When the voices in the kitchen move closer to the living room, I'm half a second away from standing and bolting and just...hiding away in a dirty dive hotel. Somewhere no one will ever find me.

But even then, I know I'm not thinking realistically. Not like someone self-sufficient, because the only money I have is Daddy's credit cards. And the second one of those flags, anyone watching can hunt me down.

See? Useless. Hopeless. Burden.

And frozen in place, too, as Emily steps into the living room and then stops, staring at me uncomfortably. She slowly wraps her arms around herself and looks away and down. I'm not sure who feels more awkward.

Riker's massive shape fills the doorway, watching, brooding. I glance at him helplessly, but there's no guidance there.

He's just this silent, protective papa bear. I know it's

usually the mama bears who protect their cubs, but trust me, looking at Riker right now?

You wouldn't want to cross his kid. *Ever.*

Not if you want to keep your head intact.

Oddly, that makes it easier to speak. Because someone who cares that much about his daughter can't be a snarly, scary brute every hour of the day.

He's human, somewhere, under his stony façade.

It's not his fault I've been thrust into his life, either.

So I make another effort, mustering a smile. "Hi there, Emily –"

"Em," she corrects softly.

"Em. I can do that." I take a deep breath. "If you're Em, then I'm Liv instead of Olivia. Listen, I'm sorry I'm barging in like this. It's only temporary and it's just...your dad and I have to play pretend for a little while. Once the coast is clear, then I'll be out of your hair and –"

"Lady, it's okay." Em gives me another look. A shy one where she's watching me from under her lashes, but the look is long and thoughtful. A sort of considerate maturity that makes her seem older than twelve, even if she's so small she could pass for nine or ten. "I get it, you know," she says quietly.

She steps closer, then settles down on the couch in the far corner from me and unzips her backpack to start pulling out books and notebooks and a tablet with matter-of-fact movements. "Daddy already told me. There are bad guys after you, and we're helping keep you safe. It's okay. You'll be all right here."

There's something humbling about having my situation explained to me so bluntly by a twelve-year-old who actually goes out of her way to reassure me.

God. I almost feel like *I'm* the child here, and it's overwhelming.

I can't focus right now. So I watch her without staring, trying not to intrude as she flips open a massive textbook and starts scribbling in a notebook full of something that isn't English.

I guess I'd call it Greek but then it wouldn't be sarcastic. I'm pretty sure some of those math symbols are actual, honest-to-God Greek.

It's so alien it looks like hieroglyphics. Pure cuneiform. Last I remembered, twelve-year-olds stuck to math where the only symbol more complex than one through zero was x.

"Is that...algebra?" I venture.

"Calculus," she responds primly, and I stare. Then immediately look away. I'm sure she's used to people staring at her for being so smart, probably treating her like some kind of freak, and I don't want to be yet another bystander making her uncomfortable.

But I don't know calculus from camembert, so I fish for something else, then land on her backpack and reach out to lightly trace the tip of one of Spock's pointy ears.

"Old school Nimoy, huh? Not a fan of the new Quinto?"

Her pencil's scratch stops, and she glances, measuring me, but I can see the spark of interest in her eyes. "They're both pretty cool. But I like Zachary Quinto because he's hot and Leonard Nimoy because he'll always be the *real* deal."

I grin. "You're right about that. Though I've always been a big Uhura fan, too. I dressed up as her for five Halloweens straight when I was your age."

Emily perks. "Really?" Then she shoots Riker a peevish look. "Daddy won't let me because he says the skirt and gogo boots are 'too much.'"

Riker's brows lower thunderously. "They *are* too much."

"But –"

A firm rap at the front door stops us all in our tracks. A waiting stillness settles over the room, a prickling silence as the three of us exchange worried looks before Riker steps forward and toward the door.

"It's just Landon," he says. "I've been expecting him."

He pauses in passing and rests his hand lightly on top of Em's head, his voice, his gaze gentling so much, rough fingers so careful as they tuck her hair back. "Go upstairs, love. We need some privacy."

Em quickly gathers her things with a nod, stretches up on her toes while Riker bends down to meet her for a kiss on the cheek, then patters upstairs with a last curious glance at me.

Awkward turtle disaster averted. Maybe.

I curl my fingers against my clammy palms. Now, I'm wondering about the door.

I trust that it's Landon Strauss, but I can't miss the fact Riker just sent his daughter upstairs – where it's extra safe.

Riker strides to the door, gripping the handle lightly and leaning swiftly to one side to glimpse the other person past the front curtains, moving with a tension and wariness born of practice.

Satisfied, he nods, then he flicks the lock with his thumb and pulls the door open, relaxing slightly as the tall, dark-haired, tattooed man I've seen so often on TV walks inside, wary blue eyes cutting around as if he's checking the place for snipers.

Wow. He's not quite my type, but I can see how he'd inspire a writer like Kenna.

Landon's gaze lands on me, and he offers a brief, distracted smile that I guess is supposed to be reassuring. "Miss Holly," he says. "Glad you made it safely into Riker's hands."

"And living room," I offer with a lame little laugh.

Neither of them laughs back.

Lame.

"He'll take good care of you," Landon says.

Riker sinks down in the deep recliner at the other end of the couch, his body moving with powerful ease, slouching into a sort of lazy, careless grace. Landon remains more tense, still standing as he smacks his knuckles into his fist.

"All right, here's the plan. We're keeping this off the books even though Enguard is cooperating with the FBI. Just in case Lion and the Pilgrims have deeper connections than we think, technically, you don't exist anymore, Olivia. No one knows where you are, and for all Milah knows you got scared and ran away."

I frown. "Will anyone actually believe that?"

"It'll work. Just long enough to keep them spinning and slow down any search efforts they may have going," Landon says. "But even though we're doing this off the books, just in case we have to make sure everything is on the up-and-up as far as legal witness protection standards. We can't do anything that may invalidate your testimony at a later date."

"What about my family?" I ask. "Is Milah safe? And my Dad...his wife..."

Charlotte may be Daddy's fourth wife and no relation to me, but I still don't want anything to happen to her.

"Milah's got herself under control." Then he grimaces, an expression I'm all too familiar with, and for a moment, it almost feels like he's part of the family. "In this, at least. She learned a lot about personal security after our last incident with Crown Security."

"The people who are after you," Riker cuts in quietly, "they go fast and hard. They operate in the shadows. In silence. Targeting your father openly is nearly impossible. Alec Holly's an international household name. Taking out a Fortune Five Hundred presence like him could do them more harm than good."

There's something odd in the way Riker speaks, something almost like...resentment?

Maybe even contempt.

I wonder if maybe he hates me more for being a spoiled little rich girl than he does for disrupting his life with an unwanted job. But even though I'm watching him, he's not looking at me.

I guess this conversation is supposed to make me feel better, but it just leaves me numb with a block of ice in the pit of my stomach. The man who's supposed to be keeping me safe won't even acknowledge I'm in the room. Not beyond a few more words about details.

Yet when he speaks again later, although he's looking at Landon...I feel like his words are for me.

"There's nothing to worry about with me." There's a confidence in his voice that runs far deeper than anything I've ever felt in my life.

I can't help admiring him. He's a quiet man who doesn't mean to brag, but that doesn't mean he's not certain of his own power – and of the promise he offers when he says, "Nothing's happening. That, I swear on my life. Anyone who wants Olivia Holly will have to go through me."

IV: JUST THE LITTLE THINGS (RIKER)

I thought I was ready for this.
And I was dead wrong.

It's strange to have a woman in the house again. There's just a different energy in a home when a woman settles into it, especially when over the past four years, Em and I have learned to work around each other like clockwork.

We know which gears to turn to keep our lives running smoothly. Now there's another cog in the wheel, someone else turning those gears, and I have no idea how to fit her in without the entire machinery of our household seizing up.

Especially when I'm constantly reminded who she's *not*. It's a relief, really, and that relief feels like a betrayal, when it shouldn't.

I don't need those reminders.

I don't need someone teasing old shadows of grief and pain.

Fuck, if Olivia were anything like Crystal, then it might *feel* like having a ghost in the house.

But Olivia's so very different – from my dead wife, from her plastic-accented sister, from anyone I've ever known, and she fills the space so uniquely it's like she transforms everything she touches.

I don't know how to handle that.

Not when after all this time, I've gotten used to the way I am, and I don't know how to change myself around someone else.

Especially not someone this *young*, someone from a world so different from mine; it's like some asshole threw this delicate, soft-spoken angel out of an ivory tower. Just left her glowing in the middle of all my darkened spaces, lighting up all the uncomfortable things I try like hell not to see.

Or hear, at barely five o'clock in the morning, when I'm dragging out of the shower with my hair dripping in my eyes and my brain about two hours behind my body.

Apparently, Milah's not the only one with vocal talents because Olivia's soft voice trills up the stairs in low, sweet lilts that sound almost like subdued opera.

It's not hard to tell she's trying to keep herself quiet so she won't wake anyone, but despite the things that have happened to her there's a brightness around her she can't keep contained.

I don't want to admire that about her, when she's just a problem I have to deal with until the danger she brings is as far away from my daughter as possible.

But I do.

I shouldn't be thinking about this shit.

I'm half-asleep and I don't know where my mind is going. Then I hear it.

The second a sudden, alarming squeal rises from downstairs, I'm wide awake and bolting down the steps, nearly vaulting the banister rail into the living room with the towel around my waist flapping. I bolt into the kitchen, heart hammering, ready to pry Olivia from the hands of a masked intruder.

Only, I find her standing there covered in spattered coffee grounds, dripping wet, her short, silk bathrobe clinging to her body in translucent patches. The kind that make it crystal clear whatever she's wearing underneath is paper thin, enough that her skin swells in soft, curving mounds against the soaked fabric.

She freezes, staring at me guiltily. I stare back, caught between surprise at finding her here half-dressed and stunned confusion at why the hell my Keurig is smoking on the kitchen counter.

Her cheeks flush. It's funny how when women blush, their cheeks turn the same color as their lips – and hers are a sort of velvety strawberry, natural red without any lipstick.

Liv bites her lower lip, then ducks her head sheepishly, lacing her fingers together behind her back and peeking up at me through her lashes with her shoulders hunched.

"Sorry," she mumbles, scuffing one foot against the floor. "I just wanted to help, but I've...I've never done this before. This thing just exploded everywhere. It's usually Julia, our live-in housekeeper, you know, and she makes the best French pressed –"

"Enough."

I don't want to hear about this.

Nothing about this pampered life she had growing up with a silver spoon in her mouth, unable to even make coffee for herself.

I *especially* don't want to feel sympathy for her over it, when I should be disgusted.

Hell, whatever else I should be feeling, there's one thing I know damn well I *shouldn't*.

I can't stand seeing this woman in my house, under-dressed, looking at me sheepishly in that flimsy little robe. I can't be here, hyper-focused on this beautiful, too young, dick-hardening mess while we should be sweeping up the real mess she's just created.

Swallowing a growl, I tear my gaze off her and stalk past to a cabinet.

I'm just going to help her and then get out.

And hope like hell she doesn't burn my house down with me and my daughter in it.

There's an old Moka pot in the cabinet, one from before I replaced it with the Keurig. I pull it down and set it on the stove. "Over here. You're going to learn how to make your own coffee," I say. "Chateau Woods doesn't come with espresso service or turn-downs."

She laughs a bit shakily and leans in to watch. "Okay, fair enough. What's that thing?"

"Moka pot. It's a little different from a normal coffee pot, but the same result. Here." I open the pot and ladle in grounds, then run it under the sink to fill its well with water. "You just fill both compartments – don't forget the filter – then put it on the stove and keep an eye on it." I set the pot down on a burner and turn it to medium high heat. "Try not to explode this, too."

Rather than sulking at me like I'd expect a spoiled little

rich girl to do, she lights up with a smile, like this is some kind of inside joke between us. "What's the harm? The kitchen's already ruined."

I just arch a brow.

Turn away.

And pull the broom off the hook by the back door, thrusting it at her without a single solitary word.

She blinks at me like I've just tried to give her a live snake before she reaches out tentatively, her slender fingers grasping loosely at the broom, soft skin brushing against mine with a tingle that raises the hairs along the backs of my knuckles. I let go quickly, and she clutches tighter, catching the broom and then pulling it against her. Her wide eyes look up at me, blue as a clear morning.

"You...you want me to sweep?"

"You made the mess," I say. "You clean it. House rule."

I wait for the whine. The protest. The demand that *I* be her servant and do it myself, like witness protection is a luxury five-star hotel and she's just here for us to wait on her hand and foot.

Instead, she only gives me a fierce, determined little smile, looking almost happy about the prospect, and whips around.

Her robe flashes to the side for a moment, and I catch an edge of scalloped pink lace and a taut, curving cleft. My dick jerks under my towel. She grips the broom firmly in both hands and starts pushing the patch of coffee grounds on the floor around, gathering them up clumsily, and...whistling.

The girl is *whistling*.

Even more, I recognize the tune from some of the DVDs Em used to watch when she was a little girl.

It's *Whistle While You Work*.

"Playing Cinderella now?" I ask, leaning against the counter next to the stove and just watching. She's doing something, all right. Not sure I'd call it cleaning, but she's *trying* determinedly.

She stops for a moment and flashes me that fierce little smile, oddly self-contained in how she expresses herself. "It's Snow White, but thanks."

"Whatever. I'm not a dwarf."

I almost *swear* the look she flicks over me lingers, that it isn't just amusement, right before she suddenly looks away. Back down to watch the broom scoot across the floor, her cheeks reddening again. "Maybe not, Riker. But you're sure as hell Grumpy. Don't you want to go put some clothes on?"

Not really.

My house, my space, and I'm comfortable here. I keep my mouth closed and just watch her as she putters around with the broom.

She's making much more work of it than she has to, but Snow White here seems determined to get the coffee grounds into a single pile. It's mostly working. The water splattered everywhere, not so much. I don't quite have the heart to tell her there's a mop that will do that, or paper towels.

Because it's actually kind of adorable, watching her determinedly try to sweep water into a single puddle in the center of the floor.

She keeps peeking at me in the silence, though, past the fringe of soft honey-blonde hair that falls over her shoulders and into her face. It's the color of summer wheat.

I grumble to myself, then look away, glaring toward the window, where the sun is coming through the curtains in soft, misty wisps.

Fine. Small talk it is.

"Why are you up so early, anyway?" I ask.

It's Saturday, for one – and while my tension had me up early today, normally I like to sleep in on Saturdays. Before Em turns into a little tornado, dragging me over every hill. For two, I expected her to be lying in bed until noon, a sleep mask over her eyes.

She blinks, then straightens, leaning on the broom. "Oh, well, I normally get up before everyone else. It's the only quiet time I can find to do some writing without people hovering over me or wanting my attention."

Writing? I tilt my head, folding my arms over my chest. "What do you write? Landon's wife writes these chick flick reads –"

I've never seen someone light up so fast at the very mention, like a teenager coming face to face with a music idol. She's practically got stars in her eyes. "I know! I love Kenna's books. She's what made me want to try writing. If I could write as well as she does, maybe I could..."

She trails off. An odd glow flashes over her features, wrinkling between her brows, and she stops the broom's regular sweeping.

I know I shouldn't ask, but she looks so damn vulnerable. Hell, she looks so damn vulnerable all the time, and every time I want to snarl at her for fucking up my life this thing inside me yanks me back because I can't stand to bruise or crush fragile things, especially when this situation *isn't her fault*.

So I make myself ask her, bridging the quiet between us. "Maybe you could...what?"

She says nothing, until she shakes herself and flashes that soft, self-contained smile at me again. "Nothing. I don't really write like Kenna, anyway. I write more Nicholas Sparks type romance. Ugly cry books for masochists in love. Love over all, fighting through tragedy together, natural disasters, lost kids, dying wives."

Dying wives.

Fuck. You'd think it wouldn't hit so hard.

But it does, like she picked that broom up and jammed the handle right into my solar plexus.

I let out an odd wheezing sigh before I'm aware of it, then turn away quickly. The Moka pot saves me with its low cry, and I push everything out of me until there's nothing but the simple robotic actions needed to pour us two steaming cups.

My jaw won't unclench, though. I can't get words out. I can feel her watching me, and the silence between us is far too heavy for two people who just met the day before.

Finally, she ventures softly, "I'm sorry." A pause, then a faint, worried sound. "Riker, I didn't mean...I know Em's mom isn't around. I don't know what happened, but if I was insensitive, just know –"

"It's fine." I can't stand to hear excuses.

Can't stand to hear her tiptoeing around invisible land mines. Unspoken traps I've put over this topic so that rather than ever having to look at it, I'll just raze it to the ground if anyone treads too hard.

I don't have time to dwell on the past. There's no fucking point.

I take a deep breath, remembering how innocent she seems.

"Don't apologize. *We're* fine. It's been four years and we're good. You don't need to say anything. I'm not some wounded beast with a fucking thorn in its paw."

"Wrong Disney film," she offers with a sort of weak, gentle humor that has more understanding in it than I can deal with right now.

I can't be here. With her.

This soft, young, lovely woman in my home, making herself fit in like she's the last bit of color to make a stained glass window complete. It's wrong.

Once, that window might've been beautiful on its own, but broken, missing shard changes the entire shade of everything. I'm not looking for a replacement.

I'm not ready for how different things look when something and someone new is introduced into my life.

Without a word I turn and walk away from her, heading upstairs.

I'm not running away. Escaping, I'll admit that. And I almost run smack into Em.

I'm so wrapped up in my own gloom, I don't hear her coming out of her room, and only stop half a second before plowing into her.

Christ. I manage to pull myself back, and take a shaky breath before offering a smile. "Morning, love."

"Morning, Daddy." She's scruffy in pajama pants and a Lord of the Rings nightshirt, rubbing at her eyes, her tangled hair everywhere. "Are you ready to go?"

I blink blankly. "Go? Where are we going?"

Em frowns slightly. "It's the first day of class? Remember?"

Class? Oh.

Oh, shit. That's right.

The new self-defense classes at the expensive studio that just opened up down the road.

The martial arts classes we can't really afford, but when Em said she wanted to learn how to take care of herself, how to be tough, the last thing I could do was say no. Besides, she needs a physical activity to keep her body working as well as her genius mind.

It's a reminder why I agreed to let Liv into my house, so I can give Em the things she wants and needs. It helps me center myself and calm the hell down, and I offer a smile to the lovely little girl who's growing up so fast, I'm more than a little freaked that soon I won't be able to keep up with her.

She's got a brilliant enough head on her shoulders to know what she wants. Who am I to deny her?

I'm counting on this place to provide the safety gear they said.

Because if they let her brain get knocked around too much in class without the right protection, a few more people are going to need to learn to protect themselves from me very fast.

I pull her into a hug.

"Em, it's barely morning," I tease, ruffling her hair. "Class is tonight. I know you're excited, but we've got time. Go shower up. Our guest is downstairs making a mess of the kitchen, and we've got to salvage it for breakfast."

"Okay, Daddy." With a tight squeeze, she bounces away and into the bathroom, leaving me standing there just staring after her, wondering what the hell I'm doing.

How the hell I got here?

And what this raw, heavy feeling is in my chest, when I've been fine for years and yet suddenly *fine* feels like a pathetic front thrown up just for Olivia.

Just so I'll believe I'm as okay as I say I am.

Fuck it.

I'm *not* okay. I'm a single father whose work could mangle or kill him any day, with a daughter who depends on him and him alone, and now suddenly she's grown up enough to want to know how to fight for herself instead of relying on her old man to protect her.

Everything's changing too fast. Em's growing up. We have a woman in this house again.

And she's brought all the painfully distracting things I notice. Everything from the softness of her skin against mine to the way her clothing clings to her curves, as if it has an obsession with that soft, smooth flesh to rival mine.

Goddamn it.

Get a grip, I tell myself.

I can't, I won't let this tear me apart.

* * *

I'VE NEVER BEEN MORE uncomfortable in my life than I am now, sitting next to Olivia, with the word "engaged" hanging over our heads.

We've been avoiding each other all day, me outside fixing a rain gutter that came loose in the last storm, her holed up in her room doing her thing. Whatever it is she does when she's alone.

And now we're officially *engaged.*

I still can't believe I said that out loud. To my daughter's new self-defense instructor, too, a man roughly my age named Mike whose wiry build and spry way of moving makes me think of a chipmunk that can never quite hold still.

I just stood there, shook his hand, and told him Liv was my fiancée, we were engaged.

Then I watched the other moms, none of whom know Olivia and very few of whom know me, swarm her with congratulations and excited exclamations and questions about where's the ring, before I was chided with stern looks about poor planning when you *never* propose to a girl without the ring.

Why is this my life?

And why do I now have to stop by a frigging jeweler's soon to find a ring that'll make this bull convincing?

On the bench next to me, Liv looks away from watching Em wrap up her cool-downs and studies me from the corner of her eye. I don't know how to feel about the fact that on day one, they're teaching my daughter how to disarm a man with a knife – but I know even less how to feel about the woman watching me as if she wants to say something but is just trying to be *polite* and not bother me.

She's trying so, so hard not to intrude on my life.

Why does that annoy me?

"Talk, Liv," I mutter from the corner of my mouth. "If we're engaged, people will have a lot of questions about our relationship if you look like you're afraid to even speak to me."

She frowns quizzically, then blinks as it clicks.

"Oh," she says softly, looking down at her knees. "I

hadn't thought about that, it's just...you don't seem to want to talk to me."

"I never want to talk to anyone much. It's not personal."

"I get that. I mean, like you said, we're supposed to be engaged. It isn't easy."

Easy?

I've forgotten what this is.

Not when we're having a conversation in sub-vocal whispers, making eye contact sidelong, set off far enough away from the other parents for some privacy.

Not when she curls her little arm in mine, her fingers so warm through my shirt sleeve. There's a soft hiss of skin and fabric.

She tends to like these wispy, short little dresses, I've noticed. Whatever looks loose and light and gauzy until she moves, and they pull tight and translucent against her curving, delicate body. The pale blue sombre of her dress does just that now, molding against the outline of her hip, deepening into a starker curve as she draws her legs up next to her on the bench.

And she leans into me, tucking her body against my side and resting her head on my shoulder.

My blood ignites and my pulse drums like mad. A strange, wild thud, the lead shocks before an earthquake. *Fuck.*

I know it's only an act. It's pretend. It's nothing.

And it's been a long goddamn time since a woman leaned against me in a gesture so sweet, so trusting, that the simple act becomes so *intimate.*

Her hair tumbles over my shoulder and down my chest. She bites her lip, peeking up at me.

"We should act like it's easy," she finishes softly. "At least in public."

"I know." I try to make myself relax. "You're right."

Part of me wonders if I should put my arm around her, rest my hand in that deeply enticing curve where her hip meets her waist, but she looks comfortable and I don't want her to move from where she is right now. "I was thinking of getting you a ring," I growl.

My voice sounds tormented. Technically, it is, judging by the insane hard-on that's turning me into a poorly conditioned animal.

She laughs softly under her breath. "Isn't that going a little far? And aren't rings expensive?"

I tense, feeling like a boar with its hackles raised. "What? You think I can't afford it?"

"No, Riker." And there's something so *innocent* in the way she says it that I believe her.

I believe there's not a single bit of silver spoon condescension, that she doesn't even think about how her money and family history make other people see her because she's been too sheltered to understand how bitter the topic of money can be.

She flashes me a faint, sweet smile. "Just thinking it's not worth spending that on me when I'll be gone soon. We don't need to go that far with this game, surely."

Sheltered or not, there's a subtle undercurrent on *it's not worth spending that on me* that speaks to a cynicism and worldly bitterness that has me more curious than I should ever be.

I grunt under my breath and lightly jostle her with my shoulder. "Jewelry stores take returns. Engagements fall through all the time."

"Is that your story when I'm gone?" she muses lightly, shifting her gaze back to Em. "That our engagement fell through?"

"It's the easiest."

"Will it be hard on her?"

I frown. "What do you mean?"

"Em." She actually sounds worried, and her fingers curl tighter in my shirt. "I know we're faking, and she knows, but I'm still going to be a part of her life for a while, and then suddenly I'm gone. Won't it...hurt her? Even more when she has to lie about why?"

What the hell? Is this woman actually worried about my daughter's well-being?

Olivia Holly is alarmingly good at inching past every line I meant to lay down between us, and damn it, I don't want to like her, but I'm starting to.

After working her sister's gigs, I expected another Milah – rich, reckless, self-absorbed, well aware of her status, expecting others to worship her.

I would say Liv is like everything soft and sweet Milah once shed to become the monster she is, but that'd be wrong. Liv's her own person. I can see it in her contemplative silence, in the way she always restrains something behind her smile.

She looks like the untouched, virginal innocent from the outside. Meanwhile, she holds a piece of herself tight and fiercely guarded, deep down, somewhere no one else's demands can take it from her.

Just like me.

Damn.

I can't let her get under my skin when I'll be ejecting

her from my home as soon as the Feds and Landon say it's safe.

Growling to myself, I mutter, "Em's managed before. She'll manage again. She's a strong girl."

"She is." Olivia's smile is warm, her eyes crinkling at the corners, while she watches Em. "I kind of want to be her when I grow up. Do you think I should take lessons, too?"

I snort at the joke. "You? Why?"

"You never know what might happen in this situation. I might need to defend myself."

"So you think I can't protect you?"

She blinks. "No, I just thought maybe I want..." She deflates without finishing. "It doesn't matter what I want, does it?"

"When it comes to keeping you safe, no. It's not about what you want. It's about making sure you don't get hurt, Liv," I say. "What Em's learning helps a person fight off a drunken idiot, or maybe a mugger or two. A few lessons on how to knock a gun out of someone's hand won't save you from people like them. They're smart. They know how to fight dirty, and in groups. The Pilgrims are killing machines."

Her smile is sad yet soft. I realize that this conversation wasn't about the danger from the Pilgrims at all. We're talking about two things, but we're only saying one out loud.

"But you'll protect me, right?" she whispers.

"Yeah," I answer, throat dry, as Em breaks away from her instructor and comes barreling at us with her eyes bright and a dozen *Daddy, did you see*s on her lips. "That's my job. Taking care of you."

* * *

EM IS a buffer between us for the rest of the evening.

Over a quick dinner of burgers and fries, she tells us all about learning reverse chokeholds and disabling grips and other beginner self-defense 101 things.

Whatever worries I had with her getting into this ease. I love seeing her glow like this.

So excited. So focused. So alive.

Liv seems curious but restrained. I see her open her mouth several times as if to join in Em's enthusiasm before retreating back to silence again.

Not just her. We make eyes across the table several times and let Em do the talking.

Once my little girl's showered and collapsed into bed in an exhausted heap, there's no more avoiding it.

It's just me and Olivia.

I finish tidying the kitchen – Liv tried, but it's not actually clean – then step into the living room to find her curled up on the couch in a little matching cotton tank top and shorts set that barely covers her chest or her ass. The shorts are powder blue, clingy, and a stark contrast to the bright pink toenails that wiggle with absolute concentration as she stares firmly at a notebook with a pen clutched in her teeth.

Somebody say a prayer for my cock.

I need a damn distraction, stat.

"I think," I say, leaning against the doorframe, "you're using that pen the wrong way."

She looks up, blinking owlishly, then lets the pen go and catches it in her fingers. The middle has teeth marks on it, making white divots in the pink plastic. "Writer's block. Can't think of what to say tonight," she says, glancing at me, then back at the notebook with a frustrated frown. "Usually my brain's more active at night..."

I don't know what to say to that.

I don't know what writers do, how that magic in their heads works when they take this idea and put it together into words that recreate the same image in someone else's head.

I don't even know if it'd be appropriate for me to point out that she's just undergone a traumatizing, shocking experience that's obviously going to affect her creativity.

I'm about to fall back on offering her a drink before bed, something to either loosen up her thoughts or let her set it down and sleep, when she looks at me again. That little wrinkle appears between her eyebrows, right up top above the bridge of her nose.

"Riker? How long are we really going to do this?" she asks. "We talk like it'll be over in weeks, but I'm not so sure. And I'm not sure you are, either." She makes a distressed sound, wetting her lips.

I say nothing, guilty as charged.

"Is it ever even possible for me to be safe? Can they really figure out what happened and catch who's responsible, or am I just..." She shakes her head. "Am I going to *keep* being someone else's burden forever? What if someone else gets killed in front of me? Jesus. Those two men are *dead.* I saw, I watched one get mowed down right in front of me...I..."

I think I realize it's going to happen before she does.

First her voice cracks, trembling, her lashes shivering, and I push away from the door and settle down on the couch next to her just as she makes a choking sound, jerking like she can't believe all that spilled past her lips. Then she bursts into tears.

It's a dagger straight to the heart.

Look, I may not want this woman in my life, but I can't sit here with a stick up my ass when she's vulnerable and fragile and feeling so unsafe. So I slip an arm around her shoulders, and give her somewhere to hide. I give her someone to hide in.

Me.

Liv's so light, shaking like a leaf, and she makes the smallest bundle as she burrows herself into me and just sobs. It's one of those ragged, full-body breakdowns that makes someone sound like they're breaking. I only hope that having me wrapped around her is doing something to help her keep all the shattered pieces in one place until she can pick them up and fit them back together.

They damn sure won't fit the same way they did before, no.

Still, this kind of release can be cathartic, and what's left behind might be even stronger than what broke. Someday.

That, I know from experience.

It feels like an eternity while she cries against me, until slowly she goes quiet, her heaving breaths slowing to shallow whimpers, then a tired, drooping sigh. Sniffling, hiccuping, she rubs at her eyes and nose. It's not hard to see she's trying to pull herself together.

She stays huddled against me like I'm her only port in a storm. I should pull back, tug my arm from around her.

I don't.

We remain locked for some time in burning silence.

Me and this stranger, this girl, curled up and tangled around each other like we know each other.

Like we mean something to each other.

I don't want to admit it eases something inside me, something ragged-edged and tired, to at least be able to do this. To offer shelter, even if there's not much else I can do now but keep her hidden away from the people who want to hurt her. But finally, she shifts against me, her shoulder against my side, her cheek against my ribs, as she takes a deep breath to speak.

"I'm sorry," she murmurs, her voice husky and low with tears, but before I can tell her not to apologize, she continues, "I'm...I'm always burdening someone. Milah, my Dad...now you. Here you are stuck coddling me like a baby, when it's my bad luck that put you in this situation."

"Your bad luck did," I point out. "You didn't. What happened isn't your fault."

"But I wasn't able to fix it myself, was I?"

I can't help a faint smile. "Bull. Having the mob after you isn't something most people can fix on their own, Olivia."

"Liv," she murmurs.

"Liv," I say. It rolls off my tongue like a madness.

"Sorry. Daddy calls me Olivia, and it's wrong." She grimaces. "It makes me feel really...small. Invisible. Liv sounds like a name for someone strong enough to stand on her own. That's who I want to be."

"Well," I point out, "your old man isn't here now. You are. And if we're going to make this work without anyone suspecting our ruse, we're all going to have to pull together. You've already shown you're smart and can think independently. You're the one who remembered people would expect us to act like a loving couple in public. Not me."

Halfheartedly, she pokes my ribs. "Whatever. You look like the type who needs his fiancée to pick on him until he relaxes and remembers how to laugh."

"Is that my type? Really?"

"Yeah. And glowering at me isn't changing my mind. You're busted, Riker."

I hadn't even realized I was glowering, but now I snort. "I'm not a type. What I am is here to protect you. That's my job. You focus on making this work and on writing your book. Treat this like it really is your life now. All yours, and no one else's."

"But it's just a lie in the end," she points out softly.

"So are stories. Guess what? Those still have value. Ask anyone who's ever bought a book."

She doesn't say anything. Just looks at me like she's seeing something new and strange, and I don't know what to do with that. Don't know what to do with this moment, either.

From the second I met her, I had every intention of keeping her on the outside where she belongs, just a client and nothing real, this paper doll cut out of another picture inserted into all the wrong places in the chaotic photograph of my life.

And from the second I met her, I've been unbending in so many small ways for her, because I can't bring myself to hurt someone who's already been hurt so much.

It creates an uncomfortable dichotomy between the distance I want and the closeness in the silence between us, in the warmth of her body against mine, in the softness of her flesh where my hand has somehow ended up splayed against her hip. My fingertips just graze the edge of those tiny shorts and come so close to touching naked skin. The air in the room suddenly feels too thin, and I only barely remember to be gentle in disengaging from her and letting her shift to rest on the couch without dropping her, before I'm up and crossing the room to the liquor cabinet.

"Have a drink with me?"

I don't wait for her reply, but I can see her nodding from the corner of my eye.

I take down two tumblers and dump out two fingers of Jack into both, then bring them back to the couch, settle down an appropriate distance from her, and offer her the second tumbler.

She takes it, looking down into the whiskey, then offers me one of those sweet, strange little smiles turned all the sweeter on her swollen pink lips. "Should we toast to something?"

"You have any ideas?"

She considers, then says, "To things that have value...even when they look like they don't."

"I'll take that."

I clink my glass to hers, then take a sip – while she tosses hers down in a single breath, not even choking or gasping, before wiping at her mouth. She catches me staring, then blinks and blushes.

"What?"

"Nothing," I say, and hide my smile behind the rim of my glass. "I just like a girl who can hold her liquor."

V: MAYBE JUST A LITTLE (OLIVIA)

I've daydreamed about being a lot of things. A starship high commander. A princess at a school for magical fighting fairy warriors. A sailor girl in a short skirt with bows everywhere and a moon crescent tiara. A world famous author.

One thing I've never daydreamed about, though, is the life of a stay-at-home author and soon-to-be stepmom, integrating into her new home.

Riker's wood-frame house is nice, but my father's ten-car garage is larger than this entire building.

Yet I'm finding, as I've settled in over the past week, that I *love* this little house more than I could ever love the sterile hallways of Daddy's sprawling mansion. This feels like a *home*, a real one, while Daddy's and Milah's extravagant palaces just feel like properties.

It feels like it could be my home, even if I know that's just a temporary illusion. Something to strive for one day myself, maybe.

Before, I never really noticed how constantly

surrounded I am by people. Whether it was Daddy's aides or just the household staff, cleaners, gardeners, it was never quiet. I was never alone.

There's something really freeing about just having space, being *alone* during the day, when Riker's at work and Emily's at school. You'd think I'd be afraid being by myself, but the fact that Riker feels safe with me alone in the house, while he keeps up the illusion of normalcy by going to work, says it'll all be okay.

I keep calling him Grumpy or Beast just because the Disney references amuse me, but right now, I feel like Giselle in *Enchanted*: completely enthralled by the most normal things.

Last night I did *laundry* for the first time ever. And managed not to screw it up, even if I only washed my own things. I couldn't risk Riker's or Em's.

I'll admit I was picturing the usual rom-com disaster with the helpless rich girl: soap suds everywhere, the washing machine exploding a mess all over the laundry room.

Turns out, if you just read the back of the box, the instructions aren't that hard.

Maybe I shouldn't be proud of that, but I am.

And I was proud, this morning, of making breakfast before sending everyone off to their day.

I'm not really the 'little woman' type, but I'm totally here for the functional family unit where everyone pulls their weight. Riker's been making breakfast so far, but every day I've been asking to help with little tasks.

He has this way of looking at me, measuring me, not like he thinks I can't do it, but like he's not sure he wants to give up enough control of his life to let someone help.

But then he steps aside. Puts whatever I need in my hands and shows me what I have to do, guiding me sometimes with a light touch to the back of my hand.

I like it.

Maybe more than I should.

And I loved the baffled look on his face today when he came downstairs to find me shaking powdered sugar over perfectly edible French toast with coffee already going in the Moka pot and a steaming plate of cheesy scrambled eggs waiting to be dashed with pepper and divvied up.

You'd think money could've bought me a million times more happinesses than this, but somehow I'm only finding contentment here. Where I'm hiding for my life and figuring out how to crack an egg on a skillet without getting shell bits into the whites.

Right now, though, I'm staring at my notebook, chewing on a pen and figuring out how to fix a plot hole. Turns out writing a book isn't just splattering random, overexcited words on a page.

Except...

Okay, it is. It totally is. But making those words actually *good* is hard. Making them fit together into a real, thrilling story instead of just my own random fantasies is harder yet.

Like, I've been writing fan fiction for years, but figuring out how to get past an alien's seven-year mating gap is way easier than figuring out whether or not my hero should have some dramatic tearjerker death in the end, or if I want to give them a happily ever after.

I'm not sure if I'm worried what readers will think, or if I'm just not really a fan, right now, of stories that end in death.

I'm leaning toward some last-minute Hail Mary play that will hold readers in thrall until that critical final second...

Then my phone rings in my pocket, pulling me from my all-important staring at the page. The ringtone's one of Milah's peppier songs, meaning it's Milah herself and the jingle I set for her.

It's kind of my way of remembering happier times, a happier sister, so that even when I'm dreading another phone call needing me to drag her out of some dive where she's wound up half-naked and barely-conscious?

I still smile whenever I hear that song.

When I pick up, though, rather than the inebriated slur I'm dreading, Milah's crisp, calm voice gives me another reason to smile. She's *sober*. I know I get frustrated when she backslides, but she's trying with all her heart and soul, and that's what matters.

"Hey, baby sis," she says. She sounds breathless, probably from practicing a stage routine. "How are things?"

"I'm good, for now. Working on another dance number?"

"No, just hitting the treadmill. It helps with the –" She stops, but I know what's left blank. *The cravings.*

Whatever she needs to cope. Now in the background I can pick up the mechanical sound, the whirring, her feet hitting the track. "I'm in Toronto for the week for several shows and just rented out a villa with a private gym. You sure you're okay down there in dumpsville?"

"I'm good, I swear. I'm trying to get some writing in, and Riker's taking good care of me."

"I hope Riker's less of a stick in the mud than Landon. Total straight-edge bore, that one, but he knows his stuff."

I catch a wet sloshing sound, I think a water bottle, then, "Just sit tight. He'll take care of everything, and Daddy's got all the costs covered."

I don't have a reply for that. Not one I want to say out loud anyway, when I feel so sick and frustrated inside.

I should just be grateful. Say the right words, tell her how glad I am that she and Daddy are taking care of me, putting me in the hands of people who will wrap everything up nice and tidy while I don't have to lift a finger.

Instead I just feel like someone else's problem.

Always someone else's problem, never part of anyone's success.

"Liv? You there?" Milah says into the silence, then starts muttering to herself. "This fucking Bluetooth, it never holds a connection –"

"I'm here!" I blurt, then fall silent again. I can't find words. I love Milah, but we've never been up for deep conversations and long soul-searching exchanges.

Finally, I say, "You know, sis...I might stay here, after this is over. In San Francisco, I mean. It's nice. It's *different.*"

She makes a scoffing sound. "Different from what? Don't tell me you're falling for that fog on the Bay and Silicon Valley nerds jogging around."

"Well," I hesitate. "Life." I shake my head, clutching the phone closer. "The life I had at home, the *non-life* I had at home, I should say. I feel like everyone's problems are mine and I'm everyone's problem, but I'm not even enough of a real person to *have* problems of my own. At home, I can't. There's always somebody ready to come rushing to the rescue."

I can almost hear Milah's wince. "Sorry, Liv. I never

thought you'd wind up in this. God, I thought I *paid* those shit-rats..."

"I know," I say softly. "I know, Milah, I don't blame you. So you've had some things in your past, but they were the ones who took this so far. It's not your fault, Mimi."

The childhood nickname chokes a tired, pained laugh from her. "Who knew being good could be so hard? You always made it look so easy."

"Not sure I was ever good," I say with a shrug. "I just wasn't bad. I wasn't anything."

"So that's what you're looking for out there? Your chance to find out if you're good or bad or somewhere in between without Daddy hovering around and checking your every move?"

"Something like that." I smile, and it hurts. "I never understood why he watched me so closely."

"You didn't? Really?" Her voice gentles. "He was afraid you'd turn into *me*, Liv. Trouble. I may be his biggest financial success, but I'm his disappointment as a daughter."

"No way. You're *not*," I say fiercely. "Milah, you're...you're my sister and you just need help. You're not a disappointment. That's crazy talk."

"You sound like my twelve-step coach." Her laugh is bitter, and I can feel the subject change coming even before she forges on brightly, "Sooo...how about that walking pile of sexy Daddy issues? Is *he* part of this sudden need to flex your wings? Baby bird want to fly up that tall gorgeous tree? I tell ya, the older guys, they know a thing or two about how to pry a lock real good and –"

"*No!*" I splutter, before taking a few deep, shaky

breaths and resting my hand over my heart. "It isn't like that."

I'm amazed I haven't had a heart attack over the past week with how many times it's gone off the rails with wild rushing beats, but for once it's not beating in terror. It's a light, rainy patter of thrills running through my chest.

"Mmm-hm. Next I guess you'll tell me you've never snuck a second glance? Not even if he steps out of the shower wearing nothing but a freaking towel?"

Damn it, Milah. My brain instantly goes to the image of the great coffee disaster. I got a nice, long look at Riker Woods then. Shirtless, ripped, inked, and magnificently hard.

"Don't make it weird, Mimi. Riker's a professional. He's my *bodyguard*. You're full of it."

And so am I, when late at night after everyone's asleep...

I think about the thick corded strength in his arms, and how they held me so easily.

I think about how hot his hand was curved against my hip, searing me through my thin pajama shorts.

I think about the dark ink branded on his chest, shaping and defining the hard, worn-in ridges of muscle that have been chiseled and chipped into raw power by time, age, woe.

All the weathering of years and pain and wisdom that's made this man incredible.

And I *can't* be thinking about these things.

But I can't get them out of my head, and Milah isn't helping one bit.

Especially when she lets out another teasing laugh and

says, "I am not. He's almost as gorgeous as Landon. Maybe not my type, but you..." She snickers. "Why not have a little fun? Get some tension out. Riker looks like he could use it, too. You're both too uptight."

"That doesn't mean we need to fix that with each other!"

Milah starts to say something that sounds sly and teasing. I can't take it when I feel like my head is going to pop from all the blood rushing to it, so I just hang up the call and drop the phone, staring at the little slim rose-gold plated iPhone like it's going to bite me.

Fun.

With Riker.

I doubt he'd even look my way, but I hate that she put that idea even deeper into my head.

I need to do something to take my mind off this. Anything to get my brain away from the memory of Riker standing in the kitchen in a towel and nothing else, his wet-slicked hair raked back from his brow, that thick, tightly trimmed beard framing the hard, stern set of his mouth.

It's his mouth that really gets to me. There's something about it, something commanding, something vicious, and yet sometimes he speaks to me so gently and –

"Oh my God, Liv." I moan, cutting off my thoughts, and bury my face in my hands. *"Stop."*

Dinner. I should make dinner.

Flex my newfound culinary skills and keep helping make Riker's and Em's lives easier by pulling my fair share of the weight around here. I unfold myself from the couch and slip into the kitchen, opening the fridge to see if I remembered to put any meat out to thaw this morning. I may or may not want to try a recipe I saw on *Julie and Julia*, but I'm probably going to mess it up.

Just as I lean in to peer at a saran-wrapped carton of beef, though, a sudden *crash* reverberates up through the house and right through me, shocking my entire body to the bone.

I freeze. Somehow, I've risen up on my toes, like I'm going to take off running but the rest of my body didn't get the memo.

So I'm just poised there on the balls of my feet, breathing shallowly, my eyes so wide I can feel them drying out while I just *listen* and hope I'm not about to flirt with death a second time. I already turned that date down once.

Another crash comes rocketing up from downstairs. And another, louder, steadier – almost like someone's hitting something.

My mind conjures up visions of someone breaking in through the basement storm door, hacking at it with fists or a crowbar or whatever else they can use to get it open.

Crap. Crap, crap, crap, crap, *crap*.

Taking a shaky breath, I snatch up the giant shallow stir-fry pan I'd just put out on the stove, clutching it by the handle.

I should call 9-11. Get the cops out here as fast as possible while I find a safe place to hide until someone can come.

Come rescue me.

Like some kind of damsel in distress.

Like I've been all my life.

Okay. I know this is the dumbest chain of thought I've

ever had in my life, and the worst time to decide to be brave.

I know I'm about to probably get myself shot or worse, just because my sister had to say something that got me all caught up in my lack of independence.

I know I'm about to be the dumb girl who gets killed in the first scene of every horror movie, and we don't even find out her name until the end credits and it's usually "Moron Girl Who Didn't Run Away."

But heaven help me, I'm creeping toward the basement stairs anyway, holding the skillet like I'm standing at bat, ready to swing a home run.

The crashing noise is still coming from down there, rhythmic and echoing.

Just a steady, machine-like *thud-thud-thud.*

If there's someone trying to break in, they're having a lot of trouble, I guess. Good.

Maybe I can use it to my advantage. Hide behind the storm door. And when they come barging in, brain them with the skillet and *then* call 9-11 before they can get away.

I think, as I tiptoe down one step at a time, I may be doing things in the wrong order.

But it's too late to turn back now. I round the corner of the stairwell, peeking out carefully, ready to jerk back before anyone spots me.

Only to come face to face with a shirtless Riker, right before a swinging punching bag slams me in the face.

I don't know what drops first, me or the skillet. I'm not even sure if the ringing, reverberating crash I hear is my skull, or the pan hitting the floor.

All I know is, one minute I'm staring at rivulets of

sweat glistening and pooling in the deep grooves of Riker's chest, and the next a hundred pounds of hard-packed leather smacks me right between the eyes before everything goes white, then black, then a million colors all at once as I tumble to the floor.

"Liv? Shit, Liv!"

I vaguely hear Riker calling my name.

The throbbing in my head is louder, but suddenly the world leaps into sharp relief as his arms slip around me and he lifts me up. He's kneeling next to me, I realize fuzzily, and suddenly the powerful lengths of his thighs are underneath me, supporting me, while his arm stretches along my back and he props me against the overwhelming heat of his chest.

I'm awake.

I'm very awake, and Riker smells like the most primal, dizzying thing I've ever breathed.

He scowls down at me, lines forming around his eyes as he presses his fingers to my throat, then moves my head from side to side, looking me over critically. "What the hell were you doing? Are you all right?"

"I...ow." I wince when he touches a tender spot right on the tip of my nose. "I'll live. Nothing's bleeding. Just a little bump." Then I scowl right back at him, trying to ignore how I'm in his lap and my entire body feels like it's made for fluttering. "You couldn't warn me before you started making all this noise down here?"

"Warn you? It's just my evening workout routine and – oh." He looks past me at the skillet on the floor. "You thought someone was breaking in?"

"Maybe. Because *someone* didn't tell me he'd be down

here banging around when I was trying to make dinner for his sweaty, rude, overprotective butt!"

I'm not sure where the sharp words come from. I'm not even mad at him for being overprotective, really. It's his job, after all.

But they're out, and I can't believe I'm sitting here with his body wrapped around me in all this delicious heat, and all I want to do is shove away from him and cry. Especially when he seems to turn to ice against me.

All that radiant body heat shuts off until he's just motionless stone, looking down at me without any expression except a tightening of that stern, arresting mouth that seems to say so much more when he's silent than it ever does when he speaks.

But I almost wish he'd stayed silent when he bites off coldly, "That won't be necessary. Dinner's my job, Liv. We'll take care of ourselves."

Then he lets me go, arms falling away until the only thing keeping me close to him, keeping me in his lap, is gravity and my own will. The message is clear – he's only giving me a choice to be some kind of gentleman.

I'm not feeling very ladylike.

But I muster strength, pull myself up, and separate from him, standing on shaky feet. The ground feels too far away and my head hurts, my eyes not quite focusing right, and my face burns as much with the impact of the punching bag as it does with mortification and hurt. I square my shoulders, looking for a little dignity. Even one scrap.

"I'll go lie down then," I say. "Until I feel better."

Still, he says nothing.

So I just leave.

I go, dragging myself up the stairs, fighting the urge to run. He's so frustrating. I can't figure out what the hell's truly up with him.

And I'm not sure why I want to.

* * *

I FEEL bad when Em comes to get me for dinner and I tell her I'm not hungry, and I just need to rest.

I feel too sick to my stomach. If I'm being honest, it's worse than the fading headache and stinging in my face. More than anything, I'm avoiding the little reminders that I'm not really part of their family and I'm not wanted here.

The way Em's face falls makes it even worse. I really, really like her, and not just because we've taught each other more Klingon vocabulary than we ever knew alone.

Ugh.

I wait for Riker and Em to split off to do their own separate things before I slink out with my tail tucked between my legs, quiet as a church mouse as I make a sandwich and then exile myself to the back porch with my notebook and plate. I ignore both, though, as I curl up on a faded, floral-patterned chaise and stare up at the sky, watching the stars come out against clouds that turn the broad expanse into a soft blue-purple haze.

I lose myself watching the stars.

It's easier not to think that way. Easier to just enjoy the quiet and the calm, and the way at night it still feels just as warm as day but the colors of everything turn the temperature down just a few soft, soothing notches.

Slowly, as I let my tension and melancholy bleed out, I

start to let my mind drift back to my story. My tortured hero, broken and bruised inside but still so strong, and the heroine who gives up everything to show him love only to lose it all when a car accident takes his life. Or her life, maybe. Nearly. Or not so nearly. Maybe. I still don't *know*.

And I feel like I don't like this girl I've written, who only exists to give things to other people and has no dreams for herself.

I want her to *want* something. To need something. To yearn for something so deeply, and I don't want it to be something the hero can give her. I want her to reach for it with both hands and grasp it herself, then draw it close and never, ever let it go.

I just don't know what that thing is.

Too real? Hell yeah.

I'm pulled from my thoughts by a loud creak – the second sound to startle me half out of my skin tonight. I jerk, but this time manage not to injure myself, though my blood feels like it's going to split out of my veins, it's roaring so fast.

The back gate is open.

I shoot to my feet, pen clutched in one hand, fingers crumpling my notebook into a near-ball with the other, breath caught in the back of my throat. This time I know it's not Riker, or Em.

Em's in the garage practicing, and I can hear Riker in his workroom doing something with an electric saw. I know the gate was closed before, almost invisible under the festooning tangles of closed-up morning glories pouring over the fence, the backyard completely enclosed in a little box of twilight.

But it's swung open on the narrow swath of grass

between the fence and the backyard of the house on the next block, only there's no one in sight. I scan the yard quickly, darting my gaze left to right – only to scream and clutch my pen and notebook to my chest with a shrill little squeak as someone lets out a calm, quiet "Hi" at my elbow.

I jump.

So does a gangly boy with sandy hair and kind eyes, rawboned with just that hint of muscle that promises he's going to start growing soon. He stares at me warily. I stare back, only to let out a sharp breath as I realize I'm freaking out over a *kid*.

I slump, then offer a sheepish smile. "Sorry, a little jumpy."

"Yeah," he says, though it's not hard to tell he's trying not to laugh and piss off the grown-up. "Might want to take a breath. Um. You're Em's mom, right?"

"Soon-to-be stepmom," I say with a wry smile, hating how easily the lie falls off my tongue. "Are you a friend of hers?"

"I'm Ryan," he says, then at my blank look, adds, "My dad runs the studio where Em takes lessons? We live in this neighborhood, too. We just moved a few weeks ago."

"Oh!" It's easier to smile then, relaxing and tucking my hair back. "Want me to go get Em for y—"

"No need!" Em chirps as she comes rocketing out from the side door to the garage. For someone so shy and reserved, when something catches her attention she's this wildly animated ball of energy, and that energy is radiating everywhere now as she tumbles toward Ryan, her cheeks flushed.

She doesn't even look at me. Only him, her eyes glittering, her smile a bit tentative but so broad it's like she can't contain it if she wanted to. "Hi."

He makes a flustered sound, breaking into a smile. "Hi," he answers, then fidgets and looks away awkwardly, clearing his throat. "I, um, thought you might want to practice. Like, defensive holds or something."

Em lights up even further, asking "Yeah?" breathlessly, then, "Cool. Let me ask my –"

"Dad says it's fine." Riker appears out of nowhere, materializing in the kitchen back door, his chiseled bulk taking up the entire frame.

He's got a rugged mountain man's physique, imposing but somehow still lithe, and he seems to define the space around him rather than the space defining him. He wipes his hands on a towel, looking Ryan over, before offering a brief, warm smile to Em. "Just remember to be careful and stay on the mats. You know where the first aid kit is?"

Em half rolls her eyes, half smiles. "Over the torque wrench set, where it always is. I do listen sometimes, Daddy."

"That's my girl."

Em grins, then tosses her head at Ryan and takes off for the garage. It's like the light she brings with her snuffs out the instant they vanish inside, leaving me and Riker alone in a silence filled only with crickets, cicadas, and unspoken words.

I stand there helplessly, just looking at him. He returns my gaze expressionlessly, still wiping his hands on the towel, yet I feel like I'm starting to get a read on him because it seems like he's just trying to keep his hands busy.

But he's not walking away.

And I feel like something's waiting to happen between us, but I don't know what, and I don't know how to broach this. So I tear my gaze away, then settle down to sit on the chaise once more, drawing my legs up and tucking my notebook into my lap, staring down at my fingers as I pluck at my pen and turn it over and run my fingertips along the ridges my teeth have left in the plastic.

Riker lets out a rumbling sound, almost reluctant, then mutters, "There's moo goo gai pan left for you. If you're hungry..."

I gesture weakly at the sandwich resting on the little side table. "I made something for myself." But I can't help but bite back, "I could've made you more than moo goo gai pan. Something healthier."

"With your Martha Stewart cookbook?" he fires back.

"Julia Child, thank you, and yes." I glower at him. "I'm not *that* helpless, Riker. I can follow simple instructions. I do fine with breakfast, and you ate it right up. So why's dinner such a big deal?"

His jaw tightens subtly. It's always *subtle* with him, but every action speaks so loud, and I wonder if it's because I'm listening so hard or if it's just because on some deep, strange level, it's like I *feel* him, all the things he doesn't say.

But I'm not sure where he's going with this as he cuts his gaze toward the garage and asks neutrally, "Do you hear that? Do you hear my daughter laughing?"

It's hard not to. Em's laughter is shy but lovely, this bright, unrestrained thing, effusive and sweet, and the boy's laughter is just as youthful and exuberant, completely unashamed of his happiness, unlike the shame and self-restraint we're taught as adults. As if being happy is something wrong, and we shouldn't be too loud or too joyous about it, or else we'll make other people miserable and angry.

"Yeah," I say softly. "Yeah, I hear her."

"Funny. I haven't heard her laugh that way in years. Fuck, at this age, her life should be nothing *but* laughter." There's something grim in his voice, dark and determined. "This is a job, Liv. You know that. You're a guest in my home, and a client. I don't want Em to get confused that this means anything else. I don't want her thinking you'll stay, only to lose the laughter in her life when you go, and she doesn't understand why someone else had to leave her behind. She's finally making friends, and that's not easy for her when bratty high school kids in her advanced courses don't want to talk to the precocious monster making better grades than all of them combined, or they want to treat her like a pet and a mascot when she's too proud for that. Finding balance for Em is damn hard. And I don't want your presence here to tip her in the wrong direction. That's why I said no dinner. Understood?"

I suddenly feel smaller than ever.

Like I'm so ready for a hole to open up under me and pull me under.

Again, I'm someone's problem. Something to be dealt with, and I shrink down into myself, plucking at the spiral rings of my notebook. Any desire to fight has gone out of me. "It was just dinner. It didn't have to *mean* anything else."

"It's never 'just dinner,'" Riker says. "It's never 'just' anything. So I don't want to have any drama, complications, or misunderstandings. This is strictly business. If my boss even thinks there's anything inappropriate happening here, it could ruin the entire operation."

Anything inappropriate? I shake my head. "I still don't get what's so inappropriate about me making dinner."

He just looks at me, the towel stopping between his hands, twisted and curled tight between his knuckles.

Then he turns and walks away, leaving me alone as the first chill of evening starts to sink in, seeping into my bones with a finality as harsh as the kitchen door slamming shut.

I don't understand what just happened.

And I don't understand how a man who's so kind and gentle with his daughter and real in his pain can be such a massive jerk to me.

VI: GIVE JUST A LITTLE (RIKER)

I'm starting to realize my house isn't big enough for the three of us.

It was just fine with me and Em. We coexisted, and we found balance. I was her friend when I could be, her father when she needed me to be, her protector always, but we fit in and out of each other's intertwined lives with the balance only a father and daughter could have.

We could occupy the same space and have it be *our* space, or go to our separate corners. Either was fine.

What isn't fine is the bizarre dance I keep doing to avoid being alone in a room with Liv. And it's a necessary dance when this girl is a natural at doing dark, confounding shit to my body and mind.

The only relief I ever have is at work.

It's odd to do my job at the office and also have a full-time protection gig waiting at home, just taking up space. Enguard's HQ is a sanctuary of sorts. A safe harbor where I can be the man I thought I was before Olivia Holly.

There, I'm not noticing how thin and gauzy her little

dresses are, or how the sun shines through them so that every time she moves, her body becomes a silhouette in pastel shades.

I'm not noticing how whenever she forgets herself, she hums these tuneless little melodies that are really just her working through soft, thoughtful rainbows of sound.

I'm not escaping every room she's in, shutting myself in my workshop and trying to find the concentration needed to fit a masthead to a miniature ship through the neck of a bottle. And failing every damn time.

I'm not wanting to pull that pen out of her mouth and replace it with something warmer, softer.

I'm not torturing myself with how fucking bad her very presence makes me *throb.*

I remember what it was like to relax at home. Building wooden ships – the precision, the expertise, the delicacy necessary – used to be my way to unwind. My Zen place.

Now it's pure frustration. Because every time I try, I find myself stopping and listening to the sound of laughter coming from the living room while they talk about star-something or X-Men or I think, this morning, Tesla. Em's always had a fascination with electric cars, and apparently Liv is, in her words, "Here for it."

If you held a magnum to my head, I couldn't tell you which is worse: my daughter's authentic happiness with Liv, or the siren call to self-destruct that woman puts in my blood.

I'm not here for this. Her, getting comfortable in Em's life, only to abandon her and go back to her own once there's no longer a need for us and the convenient illusions of our world.

Or me, lashing out and doing something incredibly

stupid the next time I catch a glimpse of Liv's lush little ass, something that'll win me a pink slip from Landon and possibly a lawsuit from her uptight CEO prick of a father.

"Riker. Hey, Riker?"

It takes me a minute to realize Skylar's been calling my name, probably for a while. I pull myself from my blank stare out the window and swivel my chair around toward her. "Sorry. Yeah?"

She frowns, tilting her head. "I was going to ask if you had inventory numbers for ammo clips, but now I just want to know where the hell you were right now."

I frown. "Where I...was?"

"Yeah." She shifts her pixie-like frame around to straddle the back of her chair and folds her arms over it, watching me with knowing eyes.

Somehow, we're the only people left in the office, burning the evening oil, though I know she'll be leaving soon to make her way home to Gabe. He always leaves before she does, just so she can come home to someone warm and welcoming with dinner already waiting so she can settle down and relax.

I wonder what that must be like.

I wonder if I want to wonder.

"See?" she says. "You're doing it again. Drifting off. Daydreaming. And that's not your MO, man."

With a scowl, I glance back at the map I was supposed to be studying. A blueprint, actually, of the auditorium for tomorrow's easy job: afternoon security for a speech by a Tibetan religious leader. "I'm not daydreaming. I'm thinking."

"Not about work, clearly. What's really on your mind?"

"Nothing," I deflect, when the real answer is *everything*.

"Just work, Sky."

Because *just work* is why I avoid her further questions. Of course. And *just work* is why I stay even when she goes with one last light, affectionate tap on my shoulder, leaving me brooding at the screen when there's really nothing left for me to do but wrap it up and go home.

Em will be waiting, anyway. She'd texted me she was catching a ride home from school with that boy she likes, Ryan, but she'll still wait for me to get home and order in so we can have dinner.

Rather, so she can have dinner with Liv while I carry my takeout container to the workshop and try once again not to hear how happy Em sounds when talking with this stranger who was thrust into my life.

Fuck. I pinch the bridge of my nose, then force myself up and gather my things into my briefcase.

Home. Home is just another extension of work right now, but this isn't permanent.

I don't *want* it to be permanent.

As I'm locking my briefcase, the door swings open. Landon steps in, caught in the fading colors of sunset. He blinks at me, frowning.

"Shouldn't you have left by now? Who's got Em?"

"Caught a ride home with her self-defense instructor. He lives a few blocks away." I shrug into my suit coat. "Are we any closer to leads on the Holly case?"

"No. It's been bizarrely quiet, but I missed a call from Milah while I was driving." He grimaces. "I can't say I was really sorry about that."

"What? She's still flirting with you?"

"No, but that doesn't stop my wife from wanting to murder her." He smiles and spreads his hands. "Trying to keep the peace. But for now, I need to lock up, so go home."

I don't want to say how reluctant I am to go home.

Or how, despite my reluctance...something's pulling on me anyway, drawing me out the door and to my car.

I haven't felt this much of a chaotic tangle inside since I was a teenager and first in love. That's how I know I'm well and truly fucked.

I don't remember her name now, but I remember this shirt she'd wear, spangled with blue glitter and seeming to just burn with the brightness she brought into every room. I always thought falling hard, falling fast, was for kids like the boy I was then, while as adults you took things slow and reasoned, followed the formula, took one step after another to progress at a sensible pace.

That's how it was with me and Crystal. And maybe that's why things got messy before she died.

There's nothing slow, reasoned, or formulaic about the way everything in my head gets scrambled up the moment I'm within sight of Liv.

Liv – who, when I pull into the garage and step into the house, is angrier than I've ever seen her.

She's pacing the living room, iPhone pressed to her ear, her hair lashing around her, her eyes snapping. Every line of her body is so tense she's practically having trouble walking because her muscles are locked so tight. "Fine," she snaps, her soft voice hard-edged and trembling with a restrained edge of fury. "Just do whatever you have to do."

Then she hangs up, rounding in a frustrated whirl – only to freeze when she sees me. She blanks, her eyes widening and sort of looking through me, before skittering away. "Oh. Hi, Riker."

I eyeball her, especially what she's hiding. Her defensive body language, the flush of anger in her cheeks. "What happened?"

"Nothing," she bites off sullenly, and suddenly I see the resemblance to Milah Holly all too well.

It just doesn't annoy me as much as it should.

"Liv," I start, then sigh. I know I've made this distance, this tension, and right now might not be the best time to prod at it, but dammit, I need to. "What happened? If there's something I need to know, tell me. Was someone threatening you?"

"*No*," she says firmly, then breaks off as Em comes running downstairs in her gym pants and protective gear.

"Ready?" she asks breathlessly, that light in her eyes, completely oblivious to the stifling miasma between me and Liv.

Whatever this is, we can't finish it now. Not in front of my girl.

"You know it," I say, and toss my head to both of them. "Come on."

* * *

AT EM'S CLASSES, Liv and I have developed a routine.

We sit far enough from the other parents so that we seem lost in our own little world, soon-to-be newlyweds too wrapped up in each other to want to engage with anyone else. Nobody questions it.

She curls her hand on my arm and leans her head on my shoulder. I lean subtly into her, and we murmur to each other about the case while people think we're whispering sweet nothings.

Only today, it's different. Everything's different.

Liv sits stiffly away from me, her arms folded over her chest, and while she's watching Em, her eyes are glassy and lost and distant. Lover's quarrel, anyone would think.

I probably did or said something shitty.

They'd be right, I think, but I know my coldness isn't why Liv is like this right now.

And I'm surprised how much I miss her slight, sweet warmth against my side. I miss the delicate torture of her soft young skin on mine.

I glance up, watching Em a few minutes. She's absorbed in learning about ankle holds and doesn't even remember I'm in the room. She'll be fine for a little time without us.

Standing, I lightly brush my fingers over Liv's shoulder. She glances at me sidelong, watching me from the corner of her eye but saying nothing.

"Hallway. Need a few words," I growl. When her mouth tightens, I add, "Please."

She's good at talking with silence, and right now her quiet says that while her mood might not be wholly because of me, I'm not helping. But after a pointed moment, she stands, following me out into the hall.

Why the hell does this guilt leap up and bite me?

I know why. I can't let this go on any longer. And the moment the classroom door closes behind us and we're alone in the dim gray-white fluorescents of the hall, I spit it the fuck out, "I'm sorry."

She stills, looking at me like she's never heard those words in her life. "Excuse me?"

"I said I'm sorry." I take a deep breath. "I always tell Em that part of growing up is being willing to apologize. So I need to set an example. And I'm sorry, Liv. I shouldn't have shut you out. I'm sorry if I made you feel unsafe while you're dealing with all of this. You didn't mean a personal insult when you offered to make us dinner. I get defensive for bullshit reasons that aren't your fault, and I shouldn't have taken it out on you, or pulled this cat and mouse shit when you just wanted to help. How else can I say it? I fucked up."

She eyes me warily, folding her arms over her chest, but then sniffs, her mouth twitching at the corners. "Bravo. I guess you win Dad points for this one, but I've got to tell you...you're a *terrible* fiancé."

I crack a small smile. "Yeah. Fair."

"Guess I'll let you off the hook. But *only* if you stop hiding during dinner, Riker. Em misses you. She's actually getting tired of takeout. And maybe...me, too."

I don't ask whether she means the takeout or me. It's obvious and complicated.

"I'm not hiding," I bite off, sinking my teeth into my own tongue. I can't even get that lie out straight. "All right."

"Thank you." She glances back toward the classroom door. There's an even silence around us, save for the enthusiastic shouts drifting through the walls, before she says tentatively, "That was my sister earlier. When I was on the phone."

That sets off alarm bells, knowing Milah tried to call Landon and then wound up arguing with Liv. "What happened? Is everything all right?"

"She said I can come home." Her mouth goes from a soft, lush bloom to a bitterly twisted bud, tight and closed. "Just like that. Like I can't tell Daddy's behind it, when it's all talk about how he can keep me safe in Seattle now or at one of his vacation houses. I guess since I'm not around, she's his new mouthpiece. Don't ask me why the change of heart, when he pushed this witness protection thing in the first place. I just don't understand..."

I don't either, and I don't fucking like it.

I'm also not liking Liv's father much. Didn't seem possible my opinion could fall any lower after seeing how he shoved her off to me and stopped just short of asking me to shine his shoes at the airport.

Plus, I'm liking the idea of her suddenly disappearing even less, and that makes *zero* damned sense when I should be rejoicing to have this problem out of my life.

I try to keep my voice neutral. "If it fits Enguard protocol and common sense, it's your choice. Have you made up your mind?"

Technically, it's Landon's. I can't believe he'd sanction her to go back to Seattle with a bastard like Lion still itching to take her hostage, but who am I to say? Her old man could hire her a small country's army for protection.

"Yeah." Liv smiles this fierce, strange smile that I'm starting to realize is her way of coping when she's hurt. "Bad news, Riker..."

Bad news? My balls crawl up into my throat. Fuck, it shouldn't bother me so much, but it does and I'm barely listening when she continues on.

"You're not getting rid of me that easy. I feel safer with you than I do at home with Daddy. He'll throw money at the problem like that will make it go away. But you and Em...you actually care."

Fuck yes.

I do.

I care about keeping this strange woman, with her bizarre mixture of naivete and weary worldliness, as safe as possible.

I care about being the man to see with my own eyes that she's made it through every day safe and sound, protected and within arm's reach. So I can stand between her and anything that tries to hurt her.

I care about the fact that she changes the energy of the house when she's there – hell, my whole life – and it'll seem duller and grayer and uglier when she's gone.

I care about her because I don't understand what the hell's happening to me.

I'm saved from having to answer that question – or Liv's shining eyes – when the classroom door bursts open and Em spills out like an overexcited puppy. The other students are behind her, that Ryan boy slipping out and hovering shyly a few feet away.

For once, though, Em's not focused on the boy I'm pretty sure she has a crush on. She's latched onto Liv. That makes me take even more notice.

My daughter isn't someone who touches others easily. During family counseling after Crystal's funeral, I was warned that one way Em would try to guard herself against fear, pain, and loss would be to physically retreat from others. To trust very few with contact.

It's one more reason why I was happy she wanted to take martial arts, cost be damned, because it means she's working past her tendency to flinch away from the slightest contact with anyone but me.

But it's amazing to see her so casually wrap her hands around Liv's upper arm, leaning into her for a moment before putting her entire tiny weight into it, dragging Liv toward the door.

I fight back a smile that hurts in the strangest way.

Then Liv laughs her lyrical laugh, as that brightness she has in spades unfurls for Em. "Hey, now! Where're you taking me?"

"You promised!" Em says. "That you'd come spar with me. Remember? Class is over. It's open gym!"

Liv looks down at herself, at the shimmery, flowing dress that skims her thighs. "You're right. It's just...I'm not really dressed for sparring matches."

"Sure you are!" Em grins. "Master Mike always says you have to be ready to defend yourself on the playground or in a fight, because no one's going to give you a chance to change your clothes or warm up. So it's better if you learn in the clothes you normally wear."

Liv lets out a mock sigh. "Smart advice. Well, if I end up flashing half the class, it's your fault."

My brows lower.

I shouldn't want to growl at the idea of that breezy skirt flashing aside and giving anyone else a glimpse of that sweet place where her panties dip between her thighs from the back, molding up into the inner curves of her ass.

I've seen that tempting little glance of flesh and lace too many times, with her fondness for short robes, short shorts, and short skirts.

I've seen it and sworn it's already mine even though that'd be a mammoth fuckup.

Shit. I'm not going to be able to watch this.

Not without wanting to fight any asshole who looks at her a little too long.

Not without fighting my own body if I see her bent over, writhing, showing too much skin.

Fuck!

But I let myself get dragged back inside the gym by both of them, Liv catching one of my arms, Em catching the other, both of them already planning – without even asking me – to stop for ice cream after.

Maybe it's for the best. We'll all need something cool and refreshing after this for very different reasons.

Somehow, my life has gone from being ruled by one irrepressible woman to two.

As they split off, though, I make my way to the back of the class and take up a position near the other parents and students milling around. Everyone watches the free sparring while the instructor calls out pointers.

Mike circles the room, and eventually makes his way around to me, clapping his hand to my shoulder. I try not to jerk away from the uninvited contact.

Em's not the only one with issues being touched.

Odd how I don't even think about pulling away when it's Liv.

But it's not just that. This guy has a certain vibe around him. Like one of those try-hard New Age fitness freaks who also thinks he's God's gift for – what does he call it? – 'nurturing bright young minds.'

It's hard not to cringe when Mike flashes his too-wide grin at me. "Em's an incredible student, Mr. Woods," he says. "One of my best. And I'm glad she and Ryan are getting along so well. I was worried about him making friends here after the move."

I nod, only halfway listening "Yeah. Good."

Whatever. No matter how idle and neutral I try to keep

my gaze, I end up drawn back to Liv again and again, watching how the dress swirls, clings to her, makes rippled patterns over the curve of her hips and rides up her thighs to tease and taunt and never quite satisfy until my mouth goes dry, waiting for that one special glimpse that keeps promising and never quite delivering.

Fucking hell.

And hell is right because Mike's still talking. Still saying something about Tacoma and moving for Ryan's education.

I force my attention from Liv, barely, and glance at him. "Yeah," I say, though I can't muster much interest. "Picking the right school's always important."

"You said it, almost-neighbor. Now, if you'll excuse me, I really should make the rounds. That boy over there, Joey, he likes to imitate the wrestlers on TV who are far too big into power slamming for my liking..."

He doesn't stick around for more small talk, and I'm glad.

I've never really been the PTA super-dad type. I'm less interested in being friendly with the other kids' parents and more interested in protecting my own little cub.

Said cub turns into a bouncing bundle of triumph, though. With a sudden, sharp maneuver, Em flips Liv down in a tumble of limbs and golden hair and pale fabric to spill her onto the floor.

"I win!" Em proclaims.

Liv groans, though it's more a resigned laugh, and pushes herself up on her elbows. She's a gloriously disheveled mess, as if she's just been tumbled into bed, and she tosses me a wry, rather charming grin. "I'm totally going to say I let her win."

"Naturally," I say, marveling at how easy it is to smile back at our little joke. "Keep telling yourself that, sweetheart. C'mon." I cross the mat and offer her my hand. "You've earned an ice cream for your beating."

She slips her hand into mine then. Her fingers clasp mine so tight it doesn't even feel like show, this act we keep up in public.

Her skin feels so delicate. Soft and light as a new spring leaf, and her warmth soaks into me.

Then she just looks up at me with those wide, hopeful eyes, full of so much emotion and a sort of lovely, unguarded laughter. I forget I'm supposed to be helping her up, as I linger on the way her hair teases her face in honey-colored wisps against her lips and tumbles around her bare shoulders.

I'm stuck there like a fool, savoring how small her hand is in my palm as I fold my fingers around hers. My heartbeat is a strange and distant echo.

Good thing Em's voice is plenty loud, snapping me from my reverie, as she tugs on my arm. "Come *on*, Dad. Ice cream shop's gonna close soon."

Right. I shake myself, and for a moment Liv and I exchange an almost wondering look before I pull her up and she laughs, rolling gracefully to her feet. She's flushed, and I think my blood is too, so I smile slightly and look away, tossing my head to the girls. "Let's go."

Still holding Liv's hand, I start to lean down to kiss her cheek.

We're in public. We seem so easy and natural, and I need to keep the façade up.

Were we actually engaged, it'd be completely normal for me to kiss her so casually for everyone to see after a playful little moment that brings us closer together as a family.

But I don't realize she's had the same idea, stretching up on her toes to kiss my cheek, until we both miss the mark and somehow – sweet fuck.

It's lips to lips and my breath stiffens.

It's chaste. Soft. Brief.

Just a little accident, but goddamn does it *hold* as we both freeze, our eyes locked, our lips pressed close.

I've never known any woman's mouth as pliable and yielding as hers, like she's a sigh made flesh and you just want to melt away with her. My heart thunders.

My cock surges, hot and throbbing, as the softness of her mouth makes me aware of how soft she is everywhere else. Her hand still curled in mine. The teasing swell of her tight body on mine, tits resting lightly against my arm.

Her scent, creeping into me. I'm caught here, entranced, held in the thrall of this fake kiss that feels all too fucking real.

We might have stayed like that forever if not for Em.

She's my lifesaver, my...I don't know, because I don't know if I want this to stop, but people are starting to stare, and Em gives us a reason to break apart when she grins and starts chanting, "Daddy and Liv, sitting in a tree, k-i-s-s-i-n-g..."

I suck in a breath. Liv and I rebound from each other sharply, both of us almost panting, and God if she's that red then I can't be any better. Not with how hot my face is.

Our fingers are still linked until we both seem to realize in the same moment and jerk back. The air between us is too hot. It's Liv who breaks eye contact first, turning away and ducking her head, tucking her hair behind her ear. She glances at me shyly once more from the corner of her eye, then turns her attention to Em and gives her a light, playful shove.

"Oh, come on," she teases. "Nursery rhymes?"

Em shoves her back, the two of them playfully tussling. "You're so PDA."

"I don't think PDA is something a person can be," Liv laughs. "It's something you do."

They keep teasing like that.

Somehow, things feel natural still, despite the memory of Liv's lips on mine, breathless and hot and forever stamped on me. Despite the dark, animal urges they've sent into my blood. Despite the need that's still building in me every time I lay eyes on my pretend wife-to-be.

I manage to smile despite the ache in my chest and turn to head outside.

They fall into their usual chatter as they trail me out toward the parking lot. I'm pretty sure they're speaking another language, and it's not human, something from one of their sci-fi shows.

As we step out into the darkness, I can't help letting my senses range out far, tuning them out to focus instead on our surroundings. I know this parking lot by day and by night, every crevice and cranny and vulnerable point of attack where someone could catch me off guard and possibly hurt Em – and now, Liv, too.

It's natural for me to position my body so I make a shield for them as we cross the lot toward the Wrangler. I'm on alert for anyone creeping around in the shadows.

So I'm really not expecting someone to be brazenly

hunched over my driver's side door, fiddling at the lock with a wire hook.

My blood goes cold and dark. I snarl, striding forward.

"Stay back!" I throw at Liv, barely catching a glimpse of her positioning herself protectively in front of Em before my vision narrows on my target.

I make it three steps before the man – dressed all in scruffy black, a mask over his face, lank hair trickling from under the cap – realizes I'm almost on him.

He jerks, looking up with his eyes wide through the mask. They're brown.

I mark those eyes, in case I ever see them again, in case he hurts either of my girls and I have to pull them from his sockets. But in another split second, they're turning away from me as the man bolts for the side alley leading into the lot.

It's only his head start that lets him get away. I take off after him, pouring all my strength into the chase, but he's already vanished into narrow side streets and rushing traffic where it'll be impossible to find him, especially at this busy time of night.

I stop at the mouth of the alley, staring out into the main street, searching, my adrenaline a thing with teeth demanding that I find and end anyone and anything threatening what's mine.

But I don't like having them out of my sight right now, and after a few more searching moments, I turn, making my way quickly back to the lot.

Liv and Em have retreated to the outside wall of the building, huddled next to the door. It says everything to me how Liv has Em wrapped up in her arms, how she's moved to shelter her even though I'm pretty sure Liv was the one they'd be after.

"He got away," I say grimly. "Let me check the car, and then we'll file a police report. I'll let Landon know, and then we'll go home."

They're both wide-eyed, silent, but almost eerily calm. I wonder if they're in shock or just holding it together until this is over.

I do a thorough inspection of my Wrangler, but I can't find any signs of tampering other than the attempt to jimmy the lock, leaving a few scrapes on the paint and the window. The intruder had been wearing gloves, so no likelihood of prints.

Maybe not the Pilgrims. Looks more like a random break-in, the kind that's inevitable if you've lived enough years around the Bay.

Sighing, I text it to Landon anyway, then call 9-11.

It's a short wait for the cops to show, and I stay close to my girls until the patrol car pulls up. Both of them lean into me while I talk to the officer, and it feels entirely natural to wrap one arm around them both and keep them close against my side while I run through the details with the cop.

Just an act, I tell myself.

Just an act, soothing my so-called fiancée.

I'm cagey on details with the cop. Landon's warnings about the Pilgrims' connections make everyone suspect.

For all we know, it could've been a random prowler and a crime of opportunity.

That's a little too much coincidence for me, but it's all the cop needs to know. Before long, we're let go, and I usher them into the car.

My first instinct is to take them home and lock all the doors, but I don't want to scare them more. Right now, the illusion of normalcy might be the best thing after all.

There's just enough time. So, ice cream it is.

And two very subdued girls who keep giving me and each other worried looks over mint chocolate chip and fudge ripple waffle cones, though they're still clinging to each other and talking in hushed whispers while I focus on my phone.

That quick text I'd sent to Landon wasn't enough, and I'm locked up in my own head, texting my boss more details and plotting out patrols for James and questioning where the hell Milah Holly disappeared to when she never called Landon back.

Then a sandaled foot nudges me under the table.

I look up. Liv is watching, her eyes dark and worried. Em's more focused on her own phone, and I bet that boy's on the other end of her texts. But it's Liv who captures me, watching me intently, then reaching across the table to touch my arm, just the barest brush of her fingertips.

"Hey," she asks softly. "Are you okay?"

How the fuck do I answer that? It's an even tougher question than usual.

People don't ask me if I'm okay. They trust that I can handle myself, always, and rely on me to be the one making sure *they're* okay.

I'm not sure what to do with the genuine, deep concern brimming in her eyes, or the fact that she sees me enough to realize I could even be shaken by an intruder getting so close to the people I need to protect most.

I take a deep breath and manage a smile – for her and for Em. I don't want to worry them.

"I'm fine," I say. "Just taking care of business while it's still fresh in my mind, and keeping Landon updated. Company procedure. He's got some questions about your father suddenly wanting you home."

She frowns. "Is that weird?"

"It raises questions." I glance at Em.

I don't like talking work in front of her, bringing the dirtiness of my world into her innocent life, but she's so completely absorbed in her phone I don't think she even hears us. "It's odd, is all. Why make such complex arrangements to set you up with Enguard, then abruptly change his mind? Why'd your sister call Landon and never call back, then call you the way she did? How is it that two separate criminal groups showed up at Milah's house at exactly the same time and pulled off something so well orchestrated in the middle of a busy street?"

Liv tilts her head, poking her spoon into her ice cream and turning it into mush. "I hadn't thought about all that." She shakes her head. "I'm so used to going with the flow that I don't really question the whys, just whether or not I want to do them." She makes a face, scrunching up her nose. "Pretty sure the answer to the last part is 'no' for most of this past week and a half."

"Not enjoying your stay at Chateau Woods, then? Will you be leaving a bad review on Yelp?"

She laughs, short and quick and startled. "You know what I mean."

It's damn strange that I like making her laugh, like my chest is a locked and rusted vault that's slowly starting to creak open. Em glances at us both in disgust, rolling her eyes.

"You tell the *worst* jokes, Dad."

"I don't mind them," Liv says, eyes glimmering. "And I don't mind the accommodations, either. Even if the concierge's a bit grumpy. I meant whatever's going on with Daddy, of course."

"Just for that," I say, "you're cooking dinner for the next week."

Liv lights up. "Can I?"

I can't help but groan. I can never anticipate Liv's reactions to the most common things, and it's bizarrely charming and endearing. "Maybe not. If you're on dinner duty, I'm on dishes."

"Could make Em do them," she counters. "For being on her phone at the table."

Em sticks her tongue out. "You're not my stepmom yet."

Yet.

Just like that, the air sucks out of the room, and we're all quiet, realizing what she just said.

I purse my lips and look away. Liv stares down at her ice cream. Em winces, then adds haltingly, "I mean, it's a match made in heaven, right? You even like the same ice cream."

I hadn't even noticed. Both of us with cones of mint chip. I know Em's just trying to break the ice and clear out the awkwardness, but it can't really ease the tightness in my chest, that vault trying to slam shut again but catching on something and nearly crushing it.

"Yeah," I say, playing along listlessly, digging my spoon into my ice cream. "That's how you can tell we're soul mates."

VII: A LITTLE THORNY (OLIVIA)

Would it be weird if, once this is over, I wanted to hire out as a housekeeper?

I'm just saying, I've really got this whole morning thing down now.

Riker doesn't even have to help me with breakfast anymore. I'm up before either him or Em, stealing an hour to jot down some more words each day before the sound of Riker's bedroom door opening prompts me to start the coffee brewing and figure out what I want to make. I've been tearing through online 'cooking for beginners' blogs, and it's fun to figure out what I can make with the ingredients on hand.

This morning it's crepes in warm strawberry compote. My crepes aren't exactly gourmet, and I can't really get them as fluffy and smooth as they should be, but I'm a little distracted from cooking anyway by the sounds from downstairs.

By now, those rhythmic thuds that scared me so much

the first time are commonplace, something I almost anticipate.

Because they mean Riker's downstairs in the basement he's converted into a gym, working himself into a sweat, straining every muscle in his feral, inked body against that punching bag.

I shouldn't enjoy those glimpses I get every day so much.

I shouldn't, but I *do.*

He goes running or takes his frustrations out on the punching bag, then comes up shirtless and drenched in glistening lines that make his entire bronzed, weathered body glow.

Pure wild. Pure heat. Pure man.

I'm not used to feeling this way.

I can't lie, I haven't really dated. Or kissed. Or anything.

Daddy kept me so sheltered. I never really had a chance to go out with boys or even let anyone get close to me. It wasn't long before I realized that anyone who tried was more interested in either Daddy's money or Milah's fame than *me.*

Once, I let this skeezy blogger with boyish good looks buy me a couple dinners in Seattle. It lasted three whole dates before I wanted to gag myself with a spoon. Our last date was nothing but him feeling me out about my sister's antics. Oh, and he didn't even pick up the tab on the way out.

Disappointing. Humiliating. Typical.

Is it really so surprising, this silly crush on Riker?

That I'd turn to a grown man? Not another little boy.

Here I am, the eternally wistful virgin, in way over my

head. Lost sneaking peeks at a man twice my age and wondering if I'd ever be brave enough to let him break me the way I know he could.

I just...

I just want to know what he *tastes* like.

All that ink and muscle and darkness.

Just one taste of his skin when he's a mess like I know he is right now, like I can visualize in my mind's eye. Just to find out if his skin feels as rough as it looks, with that taut, weathered texture stretched so tight over hard muscle.

If his body would burn my lips with its heat.

If I'd like the taste of sweat licked from the chiseled edge of his pecs, heady and dark and hot and wild, and maybe then he'd catch my chin in his hand and tip me up into a kiss that says, *fuck yes, sweetheart.*

"Smells good," Riker actually says from the doorway, and I jump, nearly screaming out loud.

My face goes volcanic with heat, realizing the very man I'd been fantasizing about is standing over my shoulder, the tart scent of the very sweat I'd wanted to taste invading my senses.

If I were the heroine in my book, *Eden in Alaska*, this is the moment when I'd take a risk.

I'd lean back into him, like scripted characters do.

Close that distance between us, let myself feel the fire of him soaking through my robe, the dampness of sweat filming us together until we fuse in skin-on-seething-skin.

I'd say something soft and flirty, because I can't even lie that I've been writing Riker into that damn book and trying to turn Eden into everything I'd want real life to be.

Now's my chance to take those daydreams from paper to reality.

Now's my chance to ask Riker if he could ever see me as more than a client, a job, a burden. Now's my chance to say *something*.

Too freaking bad this is real life, where nothing goes according to plan.

"Uh." I get out one mushy syllable.

Real smooth. And then the smell of burning crepes hits me.

Oh, crud, the *crepes!* I've left them sizzling too long, and I hastily flip them out onto a plate and flash him a sheepish smile.

"Sorry, caught me off guard, but I don't think I burned them too bad," I rattle off a little too quickly – like I'm trying to talk fast enough, loud enough, so my thoughts can't seep out on their own and go arrowing off into that way too perceptive brain of his. "Still trying to get the fluffiness right, but they should taste okay even if they're flat and probably too thick."

"It'll be fine. You did good, Liv."

Oh, but I want to do so much more.

He's already moving around me, reaching up to open the cabinet over my head, and my stomach drops out and does a few backflips when he's barely an inch away, his raw heat radiating, my entire vision filled with the hard stretch of muscle flowing down his arm to his shoulder to his chest and waist and then those jackhammer hips as he pulls down plates and cups.

I can't remember to move until he's pulling away with a stack of dishes and moving to set the kitchen table. God.

Then I steal a glance over my shoulder at him, holding

my breath because I'm afraid if I let these sharp, shallow things out, he'll hear me panting. My toes are tingling, too. I feel so stupid right now because he has no idea all he has to do is stand close to me to turn me into this trembling inexperienced mess of *want*.

When he speaks again, though, it jerks me from my reverie.

I whip around quickly to face the stove again and gather up the plate of stacked flat crepe wraps, the bubbling pot of strawberry compote, and the tubs of whipped cream and cottage cheese.

"So," he says, moving around me with an almost familiar fluidity as I start arranging breakfast on plates and pouring out compote and cottage cheese, "I don't have to go into the office today."

"Oh?"

I glance over my shoulder at him. He's spooning sugar into coffee cups.

It makes me bite my lip at how he remembers I like mine with a whole six spoonfuls of sugar, and a hefty dash of milk. He finishes splashing in the milk and retrieves the Moka pot, catching my eye once again as he works.

"We're between jobs right now, other than you. Landon's out scouting some new contracts and everyone else is either doing field work or taking downtime." He finishes pouring the coffee and then opens the fridge to retrieve a bottle of orange juice. "That includes me. Everyone's up on their firearms certifications and we're not due for a mandatory refresh day at the range. I can't go scouting with Landon because we can't risk the Pilgrims spotting me and tracing me back to you. So he told me to stay home. Keep an eye on you. Once we drop Em off at school, it's just you and me for the day."

"Oh," I say again, more faintly.

Just him and me.

I don't know what to do with that. I'm not sure if he wants me to do anything. I'm not even sure how to survive it.

Riker's such an enigma, this calm wall of withdrawal who only occasionally demonstrates mild irritation and allows nothing through but his love for Em.

He's occasionally given me a moment of gentleness, of softness, when I needed it most – but right now I can't tell at all how he feels about spending an entire day alone with me when I'm about to spin apart into a thousand showering threads of nervousness.

I can't decide if this is an invitation or a warning.

He might just feel like he's babysitting. Might even disappear into his workshop and leave me alone to write all day, both of us lingering in our separate corners.

How did I ever get *this* emotionally invested?

One day, I was frustrated at being in this situation, and the next I'm somehow blending into this house until it feels so right and wonderful and easy and simple for the two of us to move around each other. We're here in the kitchen in perfect sync, as if we've been living together our whole lives and know each other so well we can read each other's minds. Like we're the front and back covers of a love story without all the chapters in between.

I don't know when I started wanting those chapters.

I don't know when I started wanting this act to be real, but that wanting builds inside me with such intensity, it takes up all the space I need to breathe.

And I can't help but wonder if this is infatuation, damsel-in-distress syndrome. Something.

Something about falling for the man protecting me, the man taking the place of my father in my life to become my shield.

Or is it just that there's something about *Riker?* And I'd be helplessly drawn to his quiet, stony magnetism even if I'd met him on the street somewhere on a normal, idle day?

He glances up from pouring orange juice. Intensely sharp, green eyes capture mine, blazing into me, and I realize I've stopped moving. Ducking my head, ears burning, I start ladling compote onto the crepes I've laid out on each plate.

He remains silent for long moments, then asks, "You want to go somewhere, after we drop Em off?"

I almost drop the pot.

I do drop the spoon *in* the pot, and scramble to catch it before the handle slips down into the sweet-smelling strawberry goo. "Go somewhere?"

"Yeah." He slides past me, his body almost brushing mine, and my toes curl. Completely oblivious, he starts sorting utensils out of the drawer. "You've been stuck in this house day in, day out. Thought you might want to get out for something other than Em's classes. With an escort, naturally."

"S-sure." Act natural, I tell myself.

Act natural, don't turn into a flustered, giggling dork...

I put all my focus into the crepes. Cottage cheese, strawberry, fold, more strawberry, whipped cream. Keep it together. "Where did you have in mind?" I ask coolly.

"Don't know, sweetheart." Powerful shoulders shrug,

muscles rippling in tanned, ink marked lines. "Coffee shop. Do you need to do any shopping?"

I bite my lip. I've *been* biting it since hearing that rough edge in his voice when he says *sweetheart.*

"Maybe. I kind of want a new notebook and some colored pens so I can make some color-coded plot charts."

"For your book?"

"Yeah."

"There's a little strip mall about a mile from Em's school." He sets the orange juice down, folds his arms over his chest, and leans one angular hip against the table, watching me while I focus obsessively, almost manically, on a stiff repetition of cheese-strawberry-fold-strawberry-cream. "There's a café and an office supply store. We could stop by."

"Sounds good!" I flash a smile that feels almost plastic. My eyes feel too wide, my lips stretched. "You going to put a shirt on first?"

"Eh?" He glances down, as if he has no clue what he's doing to me. "Oh. I was waiting for Em to finish her shower."

I glance up. I can hear the water shutting off, the squeal of the faucet, pipes draining. "Sounds like it's your turn. Hope she left you some hot water."

Not even a half-smile. He just gives me another of those penetrating, unreadable looks, then pushes away from the table. "Yeah."

I have no idea what to say to *yeah*, but I don't have to.

He's already walking away, ducking out into the living room and toward the stairs. And I'm left standing there, clutching a pot of warm strawberry compote to my chest like it's a life preserver that can stop me from sinking deeper and deeper into this wild, breathless feeling I get around him.

I'm going to spend the day alone with Riker. Oh.

Oh, crap, I think I'm going to hyperventilate.

***

THIS IS *NOT* A DATE.

It's nothing, just a simple shopping trip out.

So why did I go out of my way to look pretty?

Like, I even spent half an hour on my makeup to get that natural, wet-dewed look that most guys can't tell is makeup at all, pairing it with "windswept" hair courtesy of the cool setting on my blow dryer. It's all wrapped up with a double-layered sleeveless slip dress, one sheer sheath of gauzy white over a pale-blue linen underlayer. Add in strappy cork wedge heels with flowers on the ankle ties, and I look like I should be lighter than air.

Instead I feel heavier than a stone, as I sink down in the passenger's seat and watch Em disappear into the school with one last wave over her shoulder.

I know I'm making too much of this.

Riker's completely calm in the driver's seat, eyes locked on the road, as he drives the Wrangler out of the school's lot. I'm trying to remember the last time I felt like this.

All I remember is being seventeen. Going to junior prom at my academy alone and standing against the wall watching Matt Anderson dance with Milah because I was too afraid to ask him out and Milah was never afraid of anything at all.

She'd already *graduated* and yet she'd somehow still managed to upstage me without even trying.

I never resented her for it. I've always admired how brave and messy and wild and open and free Milah is, even if it gets her into a lot of trouble

That night, she'd spent hours making me look so pretty, in a soft white silk dress that poured all the way to the floor and made me look like mist when I walked. She'd dusted my shoulders in sweet pearl shimmer and taught me how to purse my lips until just by breathing, I looked like I wanted a kiss.

And then she'd been my prom partner and shone so bright in her slinky gold dress she'd completely eclipsed me. I don't think Matt even saw me when he came over to ask her if she'd like to dance.

I've never envied how brightly Milah burns. She's the sun, and I'm a tiny star.

I just want to meet someone who thinks the quiet and distant stars are beautiful, too.

"Something on your mind?" Riker asks.

I jerk from my thoughts and bite my tongue on the obvious answer.

You.

Because Riker, quiet as he is, seems like someone made for secret starlit nights, not bright and blazing days.

I clear my throat, straightening in my seat, and glance at him. He's as crisp as always in that mix of dress-up and casual that suits him so well; a tailored shirt in palest blue with darker gray pinstripes outlines the power and elegance of his frame, the collar open, the sleeves cuffed to let those burly forearms bristle free. Even on a day off he's wearing slacks, his shirt neatly tucked in and belted, long muscled legs spread beneath the steering wheel. But rather than dress shoes, he's paired them with a pair of biker boots that makes me wonder if he rides, or if it's just a style thing.

Maybe because my brain *cannot* handle the idea of him straddling a motorcycle with his thighs spread wide and taut with all that power quivering between his legs.

Okay, Liv. Out of fantasy-land. You're supposed to be talking like a normal human being.

"Just stuck on a plot point, I guess," I tell him. "I've been trying to work it out for days."

"You need to whiteboard with someone?"

Not with him, I think. Not with the way he looked at me when I talked about the kind of stories I write.

Not when that brutal, unanswered question about Em's mom is still there, and it feels like it would be cruel to ask Riker, of all people, whether or not I should kill my characters off for some tragic effect when happily-never-after must be very real for him.

"Maybe later," I deflect with a smile. "I don't think my thoughts are organized enough for that right now."

"Okay. Fair enough."

And that's it.

We don't say another word to each other, not even when he pulls in to park not far away at this charming little collection of shops that's less a strip mall and more a small village of uniquely designed stores clustered around each other. Even in the coffee shop – a warm-toned place in different shades of wood and amber cooled by tall, leafy ferns everywhere – we're silent, standing next to each other stiffly.

We look up at the menu while the sounds of brewing

coffee bubble around us and we're wrapped in the thick, heady scents of coffee beans and sweet things.

The only time we speak is to place our orders – a minty frappe for me, a strong dark black Arabica for him – and he stops me when I reach for my debit card, his hand electric and rough on my wrist.

"I've got it, sweetheart. Sit."

My heart skips a beat, my pulse spikes, but he only shakes his head subtly and lets his hand fall away before fishing out his own card from his wallet and paying for us both.

Such a simple gesture, and not a dull kindness.

He may have just saved my life.

Right. I can't use my card. Because we don't know how sophisticated the Pilgrims' tracking is, and God only knows if they might ping me using my card somewhere.

Right then and there, I vow I'm going to track down every penny Riker spends on me and pay it back in full.

I sneak a peek at the receipt as he pockets it. $4.63 for my frappe. I make a mental note.

I feel numb. And not just because his simple generosity reminds me of the danger I'm in.

The energy is different. Every breath, every second, every glance. I'm staring at this beautiful, broken man holding up my whole world and losing my mind.

It's gutting.

It's extreme.

Heck yes, it's even kinda ridiculous.

But it's one of those things where my only choice is react. Feel. Savor.

While we wait for our drinks, milling around, not looking at each other, I take advantage of his inattention and dig out the pocket scratch pad I keep in my little purse and jot down that amount.

Come to think of it...shouldn't I be thinking about what it's costing for Riker to feed an extra mouth, too? I haven't been going with him on the grocery trips he's started making since I've started cooking, and if I'm being honest, I've never been grocery shopping in my life.

Google, I decide firmly. I'm going to Google how much food costs and work out an average of what I owe him.

God, how did I end up so sheltered I can't even guess the cost of a loaf of bread?

No matter where my life goes after this mess is over, there are *so many* things I need to change.

So many things I need to learn. I can't just keep bouncing between people who want to take care of me, without knowing how to do anything for myself.

"Liz?" penetrates my thoughts.

"Liz!" Someone calls louder.

Its not until Riker bumps me with his elbow that I realize they mean me, and the barista had written down *Liz* instead of *Liv* on the coffee cup. The paranoid part of me says that's a lucky accident, because I'm not even sure I *should* be using my real name in public. Who knows who might overhear and rat me out to someone who wants to kill me?

Look at me now. Liv Holly, international spy.

I fetch my frappe, and Riker's right after me with his Arabica.

We find a little booth right by the tall floor-to-ceiling windows, letting us look out over a sunny day, a palm-lined street, and beyond the road's safety barrier, a sloping hill leading down to a sandy shore and a glittering stretch of reflective blue.

If this were just a normal day out, it'd be gorgeous. The water's never so bright and sparkly in Seattle, more of a muted slate blue that's calming but doesn't quite have the same breathtaking brilliance as these California seas.

I can't help but watch, letting the shimmer of the waves hypnotize away my worries. A welcome distraction from the tense silence stretching longer and longer while Riker and I sip our drinks and look anywhere but at each other.

I want him to look at me, though.

Want him to look at me so much, to *see* me, and it takes everything in me to risk a glance at him before offering a shy smile and murmuring, "This is awkward, isn't it?"

He pulls away from watching the other people in the café and blinks at me, then offers me a rarely vouchsafed smile – easy, dry, a wry and charming realness that changes his entire face and brings warmth to those cool eyes.

"Yeah, sweetheart. It is." His eyes crinkle around the corners as he chuckles, sliding one hand back through his silver-streaked hair. "Glad you said it first."

He's got to stop doing things like that. He's *got* to stop giving me these little freaking bits of what makes him *human* when I just know the second I get too close, he'll pull away again. Tentatively, I offer, "I'm sorry you're stuck with me."

"Wrong," he growls, and he's not smiling anymore. But he's not closing off, either, a hint of cynical humor lingering around his lips that diffuses my nervousness.

"Stuck, that is. I'm just trying to figure out how to make this easy."

"Easy? What do you mean?"

Riker says nothing but idly drums his fingers against his thigh several times, his knee shifting restlessly.

For such a still, quiet, immovable man, there's a disquiet under his skin, a tension that makes him seem slingshot ready to snap whenever he has to sit still. Only in public, though, I realize.

At home – can I really call it home? – he eases off, but in public, it's like he's always on the alert for any danger that might come near.

Finally, though, he says, "I'm talking 'bout how we relate, Liv. We're not friends. We're not lovers. You're a client, but you're also someone occupying a space in my house – but damn if you're not more than a guest, too. You've made yourself part of our daily lives. Here we are, pretending to be engaged. We touch, we hold each other, we fake all those little things for show." The flat, matter-of-fact way he recites it shouldn't hurt, but it's like little needles sinking into me. Only for his gaze to suddenly hit like daggers, slicing into me as he looks at me head on. "And we know nothing about each other."

I blink. Surprised. Not what I expected.

My voice stays calm, hopeful, but calm when I ask, "Do you...want to get to know me?"

He's still looking at me in that sharp, piercing way that sees everything. Like how nervous I am.

Like how easy he can make my heart race and my skin prickle and this deep, drawing, wonderful feeling start deep in my stomach before it melts lower, pooling in this tiny, sweet point like happy pain, throbbing and hot. It's almost embarrassing.

How much I want to know him.

How afraid I am to ask.

"Something like that," he says slowly, warily.

"It doesn't have to mean anything, Riker." I wet my lips, then reach across the table and tentatively cover his hand with mine, praying he won't jerk away when we're still supposed to be engaged. "We can be friends. Just friends. It's okay. I mean, I think it'd even be easier for Em if we were."

"Friends?" His entire body stiffens like a gargoyle turning to stone in the sunlight. His hand curls into a clenched fist under mine, but he doesn't pull away. "Why are you bringing Em into this?"

"Because I adore her. She's brilliant, funny, sweet, and you're so lucky to have such an amazing daughter. And I'd like to think she and I are friends already, even if you and I aren't."

Even if his fist is a coiled knot under my palm, I still curl my fingers against it, trying to coax, to soothe, just asking with the softest touch for him to loosen up and let me in just the slightest.

"I'm not trying to convince you. But you know how smart she is. You know how perceptive she is. You can't think she's missed how tense you are around me, or how unhappy you are to have me in the house. How do you think she feels, when you're so stiff all the time and obviously disapprove, but she still wants to be my friend?"

His eyes narrow. "She shouldn't want to be your friend."

"Why?"

"Because you're leaving," he says, and for a moment his voice fades into a soft growl as he looks away, glaring out the window. "Em can't take more people leaving her."

If I weren't studying him so closely, it might come off rude.

But there's so much pain in the tense line of his shoulders, in the harsh knit of his brows, and I can't help but wonder.

Em can't take it...or you can't?

Gently, testing, I stroke my thumb along the side of his fist. "Just because the job will end doesn't mean I'll stop being Em's friend when it's over." I cover his fist with my other hand, then cradle it in both. "Or yours."

He shifts another tense glance back, just barely looking at me. But he's still not pulling away, and slowly that tight-curled fist is relaxing, the hard ridges of his knuckles easing.

"If we can all be friends," I add softly, "the next few weeks will be that much easier."

A grunt. And then he turns his hand underneath mine. Every warmth in the world rushes through me like a flooding wave as he curls his hand around mine.

I bet for anyone watching it looks like we just had a lover's spat before I talked Mr. Grump down from his sulk. But they aren't in my world.

No one will ever know what a leap that hand capturing mine is. No one will ever know what it does to me, or how deeply it melts me. No one on Earth can measure the speed of my heart.

And it's nothing compared to the insane second he finally – finally! – admits, his voice raw, "Don't know how to be your friend, sweetheart. But I'll try."

A smile lights me up inside. "Trying is good." I let my fingers tangle with his and remind myself to *breathe*. "And if you mean it, may I ask you something personal?"

"Only if it's not mandatory I answer."

"No." I shake my head quickly. "I just want to know, but I won't get angry if it's too much for you."

He heaves a deep sigh, less exasperated and more patiently tired, and cocks his head toward me. "Too much? I'm over that. You want to ask me about Em's ma, don't you?"

Oh, Jesus. Busted.

I cringe. "Is it that obvious?"

"Not so much that you need to turn *that* shade of red." His faint smile makes me redder. "We've just been talking about why I don't want anything confusing Em. Can't be hard to guess her mother's the one who left us and that's why I don't want her to feel that pain again."

Then I take a deep breath and drop the inevitable. "How did she leave you, Riker?"

"Cancer," he answers simply.

Nothing simple about it.

That one word is a gut shot, like every letter is made of cruel barbs meant to hook and hurt the speaker and the listener. My heart wilts before he even speaks another word.

"Four years ago. But she was already leaving us before that, if I'm honest, I..." Riker pauses, a fresh scowl on his face.

For a second, I'm worried it's meant for me. But then I see it's clenched, pointed inward, and I hurt so bad for him. "Fuck, Liv. It just didn't work. What else can I say?"

He'd started off answering like it was just cold, empty

data. Now, he trails off, and his fingers clench again – only this time they're wrapped up in mine and he's holding my hand so tight, so *tight*, and I wish with all the world I could give him strength through that touch, strength enough to ease the rough and aching edge to his words when he drops the next bomb.

"We were about to divorce, Crystal and me, when she got the diagnosis. We just weren't right for each other and while we tried not to fight in front of Em, it was still hurting her. And then Crystal...we didn't know until she was already stage four. It was in her lungs, her lymphatic system, and I couldn't leave her that way. She was the mother of our girl. Once, when we were younger and different, I loved her more than life itself, even if that love was gone by then." His throat works, a hard swallow, his voice thickening. "I couldn't fucking do it. I couldn't walk away. I wasn't going to leave her to die alone."

Oh, Riker. It's a physical burn in my chest.

My eyes are brimming, but I blink hard, trying to shove the stinging feeling away. Trying to be strong for him while he cuts himself open and bleeds.

This isn't my pain. I'm not going to make this about me when he's baring his soul.

I only hold his hand tighter, stroking both my thumbs over his weathered skin and coarse hair on the backs of his knuckles, leaning in close to listen.

"It was the right thing to do," I whisper. "And it's not your fault. It can't be."

"Maybe not." His jaw is hard, a jutting line of self-recrimination. "But I feel like I did everything wrong. I couldn't save Em from the hurt. And I couldn't save Crystal from dying. And I couldn't save myself from realizing that I'd thought I was ready to let her go...and I was wrong. I was powerless."

"Riker." I want so much to leave this chair and go to him, wrap him up, comfort him, but we're in public, and this hushed conversation is all low seething words and secrets told in the open air. "Sometimes there are things in life you can't save anyone from. But I think it's part of who you are that you tried. You gave everything."

"Trying isn't shit. I *have* to save Em from more pain. Don't you get it?" He's still so tense, but there's something almost desperate in the way he looks at me. As if *he* thinks I have the power to break *him*, instead of the other way around.

Holy hell. And now, he's almost begging me not to. "Well, we're trying now," I tell him, twirling my hand in his. "Trying to get to know each other. I don't know you that well, not yet, but I know two things: you're a good dad. And a good man."

"You want to know who I am, Olivia? Really? Truly?"

Those words come like three neat, savage gunshots. They don't stop me from nodding fiercely.

"I'm an asshole trying to keep his head above water with way too goddamn much weighing him down. I've got room for two E-words in my life: Emily and Enguard. Not entanglements, not emotions, not extra baggage. So if we're going to be friends, I need you to get why I draw lines. Not for me. For *her* sake."

I won't lie: that hurts.

It hurts so bad, crumpling up that fledgling hope inside me, that sweet quiet wanting, before it even had a chance to bloom into something beautiful.

I'm not even sure what he's trying to guard against

when really there's nothing between us but my own wishful thinking, and yet it feels like he's saying if he wasn't so afraid of me, wasn't so afraid of me leaving, or confusing his daughter...

There could be.

Only there won't ever be.

Because Riker's a wall I don't know how to scale and I can't bring myself to hurt him more by trying to batter through his defenses. He's equal parts infuriating and irresistible.

Make that unattainable, too.

So all I can do is smile. *Smile, damn it.*

Even if it feels like a sickle cutting through my heart, I do, and I squeeze his hands reassuringly. "It's okay," I say softly. I'm proud my voice doesn't break when I feel like I'm going to lose it any second. "I understand. I won't do anything to hurt either of you. You have my word. My promise. Friends don't let each other down.."

* * *

It's nothing but quiet after that, but it's not the same hostile, defensive quiet as before.

I don't know if everything's changed or nothing has at all, but when Riker voluntarily asks me about my story for the second time, I'm willing to tell him a little more.

All about an innocent girl named Eden who's shipped off to Alaska for work as an assistant museum curator, and although she thinks she's going to Juno or another big city, instead she's dumped off in a tiny town only accessible by private plane.

One where people are expected to fend for themselves

on generator power and with plumbing that doesn't work half the time, where people subsist on hunting and fishing and gardening without easy access to grocery stores.

City born and raised, she's helpless. Completely dependent on her host – the very man she's been sent to coax into selling a priceless antique heirloom her employer wants for his museum collection.

By the time we finish our coffees and move on to browsing the office supply store, I can see Riker trying not to wrinkle his nose when I describe the hero as a handsome, rugged lumberjack of a man with brown hair, silver streaks at the temple, and the wounded snarl of a bear with a thorn in its paw.

Yep, my book boyfriend is a beast-man. *Surprise.*

It's not hard to tell he wants to say something but keeps holding back, and it makes me restrain a smile.

My voice stays as bland as possible as I tell him how the hero tries to chase Eden out, but instead a life-threatening blizzard leaves her trapped there, forced to learn how to fend for herself and stand on her own two feet when it's all hands on deck to make sure everyone in town weathers the blizzard safely.

Of course, my heroine and enigmatic hero fall for each other desperately, passionately, trapped together day in, day out.

Riker outright rolls his eyes with an amused snort. "Typical romance. It's too neat, sweetheart. Shit like that never happens so clean in real life."

I grin and sail right past my dilemma with the ending as the checkout counter gives me a convenient moment to break off. I have to say, I'm pleased with myself.

I know I said I wouldn't make any complications, but

I'm pretty sure I just turned describing my book into flirty banter, and...and Riker actually seemed to find it funny.

Even in a ridiculous, dry way. He cracked a smile. He *cracked.*

Flirty banter with a friend isn't crossing any lines, right?

Things seem easier, at least, on the drive back home. I have a new day planner that I'm going to turn into a plot blocking workbook through colored pens and sticky tabs, and Riker seems more comfortable with me now that he's told me why he's so careful and I've said I understand. I guess now that he knows where the lines are, I'm not so dangerous anymore.

Was I dangerous before?

Am I awful now for wanting to know if maybe, just maybe, some small part of him saw me as more than just a job and a nuisance?

That's still on my mind as we pull up to the house – but we can't pull into the drive because there's a car already there.

Riker's tension comes back immediately, like a third presence in the car, wary and battle-ready.

Thankfully, it's not a total surprise.

I already know *this* car. No one else on the entire West Coast drives a pink Bugatti Veyron, because no one else can *afford* one – and that's saying a lot considering we're sharing a demographic with Hollywood.

Even before we park the Wrangler on the street and get out, I know who'll be waiting for us, even if I don't know why.

Milah.

She's standing on the doorstep, *completely* exposed and alone.

As if two men didn't die trying to get to her and a lot more aren't trying to murder us both out of some weird blood grudge. She's there, tapping her sparkly translucent pink heels impatiently and filing her nails. As Riker and I open the gate, she glances up, then lets out an exasperated sigh and curls her hand on her hip.

"Oh my God, *finally!*" she calls, twisting her lips in a pout. "I've been waiting for ten minutes."

"Your life must be over," Riker says flatly, while I scowl.

"What are you even doing here?" I ask. "Where's your escort?"

"Waiting at the airport for both of us, duh." She flicks Riker over with an appreciative look. "You too, if you want to come. And the kid."

I'm too shocked to ask questions.

Riker folds his arms over his chest in his way that makes a huge bulwark out of him, as if he's settling in and prepared not to move no matter how much anyone pushes at him. "Where exactly would we be going?"

"Vancouver," Milah chirps. "My other *other* vacation house. I was going to take Livvie on a little girl-on-girl sisters' getaway for some stress relief, but we could make it a group thing. Landon said it was okay."

Riker looks distinctly unimpressed by Milah's double entendre. I'm just embarrassed and wondering if she's drunk, high, or in the mood to make trouble because she's bored.

"I don't think so, sis," I say. "Doesn't seem wise. I'm supposed to be in hiding. Not jetting around."

"Actually," Riker says grudgingly, "one of the best ways to keep you hidden *is* to move you around. I'm just not sure one of Milah's houses is a good idea. They'd be watching them."

"Not in *Vancouver*," Milah says sourly. "C'mon, Riker. I'm blonde. I'm not stupid. We're talking international borders, even if it's just Canada. No one's going to fuck around with that. Plus, we'd be taking my private jet, so no passenger manifest or TS-Asshole tracking."

Riker and I exchange skeptical looks.

It's not hard to tell we're both thinking the same thing: this could be a great idea or a disaster.

When neither of us say anything, Milah flounces off the front stoop and over to me, wrapping both her arms around one of mine and *pulling* with a sulky little whine.

"Come oooon," she keens, dragging me off balance. "It's just two days! And I really need the company to keep from going stir crazy."

I know what that means. *Stir crazy* is like code for when the withdrawals start to hit, and none of her employees or handlers are willing to risk their jobs standing up to her when she starts fiending – and her groupies will just enable and possibly even supply her.

What she's saying without saying it is that she needs me. I sigh, leaning into her and meeting Riker's eyes over her head.

Please, I mouth, and he sets his jaw, then makes an annoyed sound.

"Fine," he says. "But I'm not pulling Em out of school early. You can wait."

Milah pouts harder. "But –"

"*Wait*," Riker repeats tightly, sweeping past Milah to

unlock the front door with sharp, jerky movements. Milah sticks her tongue out at his back.

"Asshole. It's always the Daddy types," she says, and I bite back a faint, fond smile.

He's not an asshole, I think to myself.

He's just a beast, and you're the newest thorn in his paw.

VIII: LITTLE WHITE LIES (RIKER)

I can't believe Milah Holly actually owns a private jet.

Even harder to believe I actually agreed to this trip, when I haven't even had a chance to go over security at the Vancouver house yet.

How the hell am I supposed to protect Liv when I can't even control the environment?

And why does this all feel so damned fishy?

I almost wouldn't believe Landon approved this, if James wasn't settled calmly in one of the lush bucket seats. He's ice cold as ever, this human razor made of all elegance, sharp edges, and frosty blond slickness that makes him look more like a candidate to play 007 than an enforcer at a small-time security company.

James is the type you don't ask about his past. All I think I know is he was a government spook, FBI or CIA or something, and while he's friendly enough and I'd trust him with my life...

I don't ask questions.

Not when James looks at me with slitted eyes like a snake's, like he's calculating exactly how much pressure it would take on my jugular to kill me. Just in case.

Right now, though, he's all cool, cultured charm as he leans over a table with Em and duels her through one chess game after another. They've both won two rounds each.

Meanwhile, Liv watches and cheers Em on, trying to distract James from his utmost focus with wiggling fingers and random noises to give her a home team advantage. It doesn't work.

It'd take a hammer to the head to pull this man away from anything. She keeps at it anyway, grinning when James doesn't even crack a smile, his lips thin and pursed.

It's hard not to just watch them together and feel a sense of warmth, but I can't forget it's temporary.

And I can't miss how Liv goes tense every time she looks at her sister, while Milah smiles innocently and avoids making eye contact.

There's something going on here.

Something I haven't been told about, and I don't like being kept in the dark.

I try to distract myself by going over the plans for Milah's house and nearby grounds. It took half an hour of arguing to even get her to put me in touch with her security team so they could forward the details to my email. Now I'm distracted, brooding over it even as I stare at my screen and mentally note points of entry and exit, possible emergency escape routes, blind spots, vulnerabilities.

Milah doesn't seem to be taking this situation seriously. Shocking, I know.

The Pilgrims are after her life. Plus the lives of her father and little sister, all because of her drug habits coming home to roost. The Pilgrims blame her for some mysterious third party involved in their members' deaths.

That alone would have any other pop starlet taking up refuge in another country at some foreign vacation spot with the best security money could buy, but Milah's continuing to tour around the West Coast and flit around her vacation homes and show up at my house without even a damn security escort.

Does she know something more? Or is she just this young and reckless and irresponsible?

I shift my gaze to Liv.

Liv is two years Milah's junior, yet she so often seems like the older sister. If youth makes Milah so irresponsible, Liv must've missed the memo.

It's strange. Even if she *is* a spoiled little rich girl, she takes full accountability for that and dives in with both hands to learn the things she never knew before. She tries like hell not to be a burden on anyone.

Yeah, I'm biased. I've never been fond of assholes born with silver spoons.

Maybe it comes with the territory, from growing up the only child of struggling parents, a latchkey kid living on dollar store snack packs and always peeking through the chain lock before letting Mom in at midnight after a sixteen-hour double shift, sometimes not seeing my father for days when he'd steal a few hours of sleep on the job between killing long hours. The kind of upbringing Milah and Liv had, I can't imagine.

I'm not sure I'd even want it for Em, if I had that kind

of money. I want her to have a good life, a comfortable life, a safe life...

But anyone with the kind of money Alec and Milah Holly have tends to make me wary, because it generally disconnects them from the reality normal people live through, suffer, and fear.

Is that why Milah doesn't understand fear? Why she lacks common sense?

The life she's had has insulated her so much that she just assumes if she keeps throwing money at this problem, it'll go away?

Fuck.

And is that why Liv is so different, when she's never had money of her own? When she's looked that fear straight in the eye, stared down the barrel of a gun?

I don't realize I've been watching Liv intently until she glances up, catches my eye, and offers a sweet smile that turns her eyes into warm, glimmering crescents.

Her bare shoulders shrug up around her jaw in a cute little quirk of hers as she cocks her head questioningly. I jerk awake and flick my fingers, beckoning her over.

She lifts both brows, then touches Em's shoulder with a smile as she stands to edge around her, moving carefully and barely bumping the chess table with her hip.

But as she crosses the aisle to me, I can feel Milah's eyes on us, watching us closely.

Liv starts to aim for the chair opposite me, but I shake my head, shifting over into the window seat to leave the aisle seat next to me free, gesturing her toward it. She looks confused, before her cheeks flush a doll-like shade of pink and she slips into the deep, plush chair.

That flush deepens as I lean in toward her, bending to speak in her ear.

Harder than it sounds. I'm momentarily distracted by her scent.

It's something soft and breezy and cool with a faint, sweet undertone, like clean skin and quiet coastal nights. There's a rock-hard tension in the pit of my stomach, my solar plexus turning into an iron core, as if as long as I keep myself tight, I'll keep the heat in my gut from traveling any lower and turning into something I didn't ask for.

Business. Right. *Focus on the damn business.*

I exhale like I can eject her scent from me, but I can't miss her shiver as my breath stirs her hair in soft, golden waves against her neck. "Liv, we need to talk," I whisper.

She watches me from the corner of her eye. She's toying at her rosy little lower lip with just one tooth, making it swell and plump and dent, reminding me how her mouth melted against mine in that one forbidden kiss. Fuck.

Then she leans in with a playful little mock-whisper and a teasing smile.

"You're too worried. Everybody here knows we're not engaged," she says, while I'm struggling with the sudden prickle of fire and heat as her warmth brushes me. "You don't have to put on this act and pretend. Not here."

"I don't want everyone to hear what I'm saying, and there's not exactly anywhere private to speak on an airplane." I keep my lips close to her ear, voice low, and even if this is for secrecy, I can't escape the intimacy. It's just us and the vanishing distance between us, close enough so I'm a lone breath away from kissing the soft shell of her ear, the slope of her bare, slender throat.

That's what I want to do, yeah, but that's not what it's about. She doesn't get it.

I force a wary gaze on a watchful Milah Holly over Liv's shoulder, reminding myself why I'm here. Why I'm doing this. And that we're not alone, and I'm not sure we can trust our host. "Tell me something, Liv. How much does your sis really know about those two murdered men?"

Liv frowns, puzzled lines furrowing her brow, before she turns her head.

Her cheek brushes mine, all peach-fine softness and silk. That fire in my blood turns my veins into smelters, turns me into a simmering pool of something dark and heavy that I most definitely should not be feeling. Not with this danger, this mystery, this damn enigma.

"Liv?" I prod her, but she's not answering, rubbing her cheek.

Too much? I wonder, holding my breath as she leans in, trying not to inhale her scent, but when her throaty, lilting voice caresses my ear, it's like the curl of her breath strokes every inch of my body and licks right down to my cock.

Fuck me.

I never should've asked her about Milah.

Never should've told her anything about myself.

Never should've let her in. Because now it's getting harder and harder to shut her out.

She's talking again. Damn.

I was so focused on those soft sounds stroking against me that I missed what they were actually saying, and have to rewind to replay and parse what she actually said.

"I don't know," Liv whispers. "She says they were after her for some money she owed after a wild night on a Vancouver stop. That's all Milah's ever said."

"So the other men who killed them just saw it as an opportunity to take down a rival syndicate while they were out in the open? Hit and run?"

She makes a soft, confused noise. "I dunno, maybe? Is that strange?"

"Very. Especially that they'd gun them down in the middle of a busy street in a nice part of Seattle. That's either deliberate for a reason, or the mark of amateurs."

Liv shakes her head subtly, and her cheek moves against my jaw in a velvety way I feel pouring all the way down to my balls. "And you think Milah has something to do with that?"

"I think Milah's acting strange as hell for someone who's the prime target. I know her reputation, I know she can be reckless and thinks she's invincible, but..."

But, fuck, she's still watching us. Right now.

Even as I drug myself on Liv's intoxicating, dick-teasing scent, I can't miss the pinched, nervous look around Milah's eyes. It's not hard to tell she's wondering what we're whispering about, why we're sitting so close, and her interest is suspicious in and of itself. "Listen, I'm not casting doubts on your sis. I believe she loves you enough not to endanger you. Showing up on my doorstep when we're supposed to be hiding out and someone could be tailing you? That's dangerous. And a waste of the money your old man's spending to keep you safe. So why the sudden field trip to Canada?"

Liv says nothing. She's got no answers, and I can't blame her.

Suddenly, the silence between us is different, her head ducking, though she doesn't pull away from me. All I can see is the long slope of her neck right now, teased by tendrils of honey-gold hair slipping free from a messy twisted-up clip, each soft strand licking at her skin the way I want to right now.

My lips throb in time with the movement of her pulse against her throat. I already know she'd taste like sweet things and silk. Know she'd moan like a dove under me, enough to drive me bat-fuck mad.

But I also know she's hiding something, too. She knows more than she lets on.

Because Liv Holly is as transparent as a window in her emotions, and her silence says there's something she doesn't want to tell me, but she doesn't know how to get around it.

Finally, she whispers, "I'll ask her about it later. Promise."

"Later?"

"When I can talk to her alone."

I nod, suddenly hopeful that we've got a prayer of figuring this out.

I can't think of anything else to say. I should pull away, put distance between us, remind myself of the boundaries I laid down like law.

Instead I let my gaze linger, following the curving slope where her neck blends into her shoulder, tracing over the fine articulated ridges of her collarbone, slipping down to follow her pale skin over the soft, warm swell of her chest peeking up over the neck of her dress. It's just enough to flirt, to entice, to make me want to delve deeper, to discover creamy, virgin flesh.

Up this close, her skin has a subtle mottled texture. Like how a pearl looks smooth and white from far away, but when you look more closely, it's swirls and subtle grains and beautifully random.

"*Hey!*"

Milah's voice snaps over me like a whip, sharp-edged and biting and too damn loud as her shadow falls over us. My eyes snap up, trying to hide my irritation.

She slaps her hands on the back of Liv's seat and the opposite facing seat hard enough to make them bounce and grins down at us. I jerk back from Liv, one last brush of her cheek against mine before we're separated.

I tell myself I'm imagining it, that she's flushed. I tell myself it's not because of me that she touches the place on her jaw where our bodies connected.

Milah grins down at us just a little too widely, her eyes almost manic. "What are you two lovebirds up to over here?"

Liv tosses me an uncertain glance and a fleeting, shallow smile before glancing at Milah and standing. "Nothing," she says, her voice low. "We were just planning a surprise for Em. Can we keep it down?"

Strange. She lies to Milah so smoothly, but telegraphs everything with me.

And there's something significant in the way she looks back at me, even as Milah hooks her arm in hers and drags her back across the aisle, chattering all the way.

I don't want to take my eyes off Liv, but I have to. Have to remember the lines I drew, and Liv's not the only one who needs to stay on her side of them. But as I return my gaze to the laptop screen and the blueprints, I can't help but wonder:

What the hell am I *doing?*

* * *

From the moment we step off the plane, I can sense that something's wrong.

Milah's personal Dassault jet touches down on a private airstrip just north of Vancouver, set in a broad field and ringed by trees. It's nearly midnight, the sky mostly clear with a few low-hanging clouds making muted gray silhouettes against the stars. The evening air has a hint of pine instead of the ocean breeze I'm used to.

There's a subtle tension, too.

I'm expecting an escort waiting for us, a car, but there's no one in sight beyond the fenced exit at the end of the airfield's service road – and from what I could hear from the cabin, the tower had gone strangely silent on our final approach.

I'm the first off the plane, overnight bag banging on my hip, James bringing up the rear, the two of us forming a protective shield. I glance over my shoulder, catching his eye.

He nods subtly. He senses it, too.

I can see danger forming the lines of his body with the same lethal, menacing smoothness as a sword sliding from its sheath. Milah starts to strut out ahead of me, her ponytail swinging, but I snap my arm out to block her path and shake my head.

"No. Stay behind me," I murmur. "All of you, stay back."

"Emily," James says softly, a steely note of command in his refined voice. "Please hand me your bag."

Em frowns curiously and slings her backpack down to pass it over. "Why?"

"I don't want you hindered if we need to run."

Em sucks in a soft breath but says nothing. I've taught my girl well. In these situations, you save the questions for later. It's more important to listen and be ready for anything.

We're too exposed, out in the open like this. I want us in a sheltered place before we try to figure out what's happening.

I don't like the wide-open space with no cover, and I like the tree line obscuring sight beyond the edges of the field even less. Right now, the plane's our only cover, and it makes me uncomfortable to move away from it.

Still, we can't huddle here all night, and the door is already swinging shut and sealing, the pilot heeding my advice to lock down.

I do a slow, careful scan of the perimeter. Nothing.

Then, glancing at James, I gesture toward my eyes with two fingers, then flick them toward the air traffic control tower, which is less a tower and more a small concrete outbuilding attached to a hangar barely big enough for a small prop plane.

We'll regroup with the air traffic control personnel – safety in numbers, a defensible position, and access to outbound communications with the authorities – and then take it from there.

Another nod from James, and he spreads his arms, ushering our charges forward. "Everyone as quickly as possible, please. Keep your heads low, precisely half an arm's length between you."

Milah scoffs softly. "How am I supposed to know –"

"Just come on," I bite off, then bolt across the tarmac at a tight clip, staying just far enough ahead to lead them, but close enough to defend.

I'm grateful for James. He understands tactics, can plot coolly in a tense situation, and knows how to keep the civilians just informed enough to save their lives without confusing them or weighing them down. Why half an arm's length between everyone?

So we're not a large enough cluster to make an easy target, but not so far apart that they can pick out individual bodies for a clear shot, either. I've always planned for the eventuality that I would have to protect my daughter from being shot.

That doesn't mean I don't want to kill the person or people who put her in this situation.

I can't let myself be distracted by Em right now, or by Liv. The best thing I can do, the best way I can care for them, is to keep myself focused and tight.

I'm not Em's father right now, or Liv's fake lover. I'm a hunter seeking prey, scanning for any hint of movement, waiting for that one rustle in the grass or tell-tale sound that marks a fatal mistake and shows me where to close in for the kill. They thought they had cornered, defenseless victims.

They're about to find out how wrong they are.

We're a few yards out from the air traffic control tower when that sense of something *wrong* redoubles. Through the windows, the low outbuilding is dark, as if it's unoccupied – but I know I heard voices communicating with the pilot on descent. Even if there's only one person manning their lonely station, someone should be inside with the lights on, consoles up.

The hairs all over my body prickle, rising up as if sensing for another presence. I move in a quick, silent sidestep to flatten myself against the wall next to a window, and gesture quickly for everyone to follow. James herds them in and lines them up along the wall, ushering them down below the windows and out of line of sight from inside. I slip my hand inside my leather jacket, curling my hand around the grip of the Beretta slotted into my shoulder holster, and lean carefully to the side to catch a glimpse inside the building.

Only for three men to step out from inside the hangar behind us, the first gunshot zinging loud, whizzing over my head like a furious hornet.

Instinct takes over.

I don't even feel my body move. I'm just flattened against the wall one second, and the next I'm between them, my people, my *family*, and these punked-out assholes in their ripped jeans and torn jackets, holding their guns like they learned how to shoot from a decades-old mafia flick.

I trust James has them covered – he's already herding them forward at a crouching run, around the corner of the building, Milah's scream echoing over the night, Liv and Em almost worrisomely silent – but it's my job to keep them *safe*.

I'm their shield, even if it means using my own body.

And as I step out into the open, all emotion leaves that body. There's only the slow-time tracking of my arm as I pull my Beretta from its holster and aim. Only the knowledge that it doesn't matter if I'm hurt, if I bleed, if I die, so long as I fulfill my mission to protect them.

This is who I am, under the skin.

This is why Crystal drifted away long before death ever took her.

Because she couldn't look into the eyes of a man who didn't fear death, and not fear him instead.

A pound of pressure on the trigger. The slightest squeeze of my finger. The recoil in my hand, sharp slow motion, the burst of smoke and spark of fire and the bullet flying out.

Time crawls, stops...then races forward as the bullet strikes one of the three men in the shoulder and he drops with a scream, his shot going wide and far afield. Even as the other two swing guns on me, I'm aiming again. Victory in a firefight requires calm. Detachment.

The pure and focused intent to make sure every hit is a kill shot.

You don't win shootouts acting like some crazed asshole spraying bullets everywhere and hoping.

A bullet zips past my shoulder, close enough where I feel the force of it through my jacket. I sidestep, ever a moving target, and once more sight down the barrel, taking aim.

Calculating. Processing. Focused.

One cold, methodical decision after another in a chain of events that ends in my finger tightening on the trigger once, twice, recoil and bodies dropping and blood that looks black as it sprays against the darkness of the night.

I wait just long enough to make sure they're not getting back up – I don't care if they're dead or alive, just that they can't hurt my people anymore – before turning to follow James and the others around the building's side.

James has gathered everyone to one side of the door, and flattened himself against the door's very edge. I sweep a quick glance to make sure no one's injured. Em's face is white as a sheet, but she looks calm, composed, even withdrawn. Like father, like daughter.

Milah's cheeks are apple red, likely from screaming against her sister's palm, her blue eyes wide and streaked with tears. Liv trembles, but holds steady, muffling Milah's nonstop screams against her hand, her eyes dark and liquid and lost.

For just a moment our gazes meet, and something strikes that emotionless emptiness inside me, some dark and terrible pang.

I can't read her. I can't see myself reflected in her eyes. I can't fucking do it now.

I can't even tell if she still sees a man, or a demon darkness wearing human skin.

A sound from inside tells me I don't have time to wonder. I take up a flanking position on the other side of the door. James has his Ruger drawn, cocked and ready. On my nod, he kicks the door open and comes in hot on my heels as I shoulder into the room gun first.

It's pitch black, save for tiny power lights on the edges of a few consoles, but someone's here.

I feel them. Breathing. Waiting.

It's like I can hear the trickle of sweat pouring down their spines, the nervous fear chilling until it's like a cold kiss on the back of their necks. I can taste the sourness on the air.

"James," I whisper, and the lights flood on in a sudden burst as he flicks the switch.

I'm ready. The man standing over the shaking air traffic controllers with a pump-action shotgun isn't.

He winces, swinging the shotgun toward me with a cry, squinting against the light and swearing. One of the air traffic controllers, huddled in her chair and bent over her console with her hands on the back of her neck, lets out a trembling whimper.

I shoot Mr. Shotgun in the thigh without a second's hesitation, the recoil vibrating and stinging against my palm.

The other air traffic controller screams, his eyes rolling back in his head as his body slumps from the chair to the floor in a dead faint.

I drop down and check his pulse, then check Mr. Shotgun's. He's still breathing, but unconscious. Losing a lot of blood from his femoral artery, spreading in a red sea across the floor.

I want to question him, but he won't be waking up for a while.

We can't risk taking him with us when that could bring an entire army down on our heads. But there's a tattoo on his neck. I know it, a gang sign, subtle enough to pass off as nothing unless you recognize it.

Three neat dots arranged in an equilateral triangle. The three corners of a Pilgrim's tricorne.

I guess Lion's a history buff.

We kidnap a Pilgrim, we'll be dead by morning.

If it were just myself, I'd risk it for the intel alone, the answers – but it's not just me.

I have three non-combatants on my hands, and that's what makes my decision.

Standing, I catch James' eye again. We have an unspoken rhythm that comes from familiarity, each of us knowing what we're best at, and right now, it's James' cool composure in the face of even the worst danger, the way he has of exuding a sort of icy killer charm, that's needed to manage the task at hand.

James inclines his head, then steps over to the shaking woman behind the console. His Ruger disappears into his suit coat, and he offers a brief, formal smile. "You'll have to pardon me for intruding, Miss. Are you hurt?"

The air traffic controller shakes her head. "N-no..."

"Excellent. Then I'll need you to do me the courtesy of calling the local authorities, please. We won't be staying, but here's my card so the police can get in touch with us for a statement."

He retrieves a business card from his breast pocket and holds it out to the woman with two fingers. She stares at him as if he's grown a second head, while he lets out a dry, patient sigh.

"You'll want to hurry, Miss. Without paramedics, the man we just shot may die. Two others outside are likely in similar condition. I'd really rather not have to testify in a self-defense case."

The woman reaches out, taking the card in wavering fingers, her mouth quivering like she's about to cry. "Wh-who are you?"

James' thin smile returns. "Enguard Security." He sweeps a brief, mocking bow. "Pleasure to make your acquaintance."

I roll my eyes and slip my Beretta back into the holster. I don't think we'll see any more Pilgrims, or the gunshots would have brought them running, but I can't shake the sense of alertness that says we're not out of danger yet.

I turn back to Liv, Em, and Milah. Milah has flattened herself against the wall inside the door and sunk down it, hugging her knees to her chest. Liv is crushed against the wall as well, but she's got her arms around Em – and Em clings to her like a baby monkey, burying her face in Liv's side, while Liv gently strokes her back and whispers wordless things and watches me with that same unreadable, wide-eyed gaze.

Fuck.

I can't *do* this right now.

There's no room for the ripping feeling inside me.

I sink down to one knee in front of Milah. She's not quite looking at me, she's more looking *through* me, her eyes vacant with shock.

I take both her hands, trying to get her to focus, trying to ground her, speaking slow and steady.

"Milah." When I say her name, she jerks sharply, her pupils constricting and locking on me, but she says nothing. "Where are your people?"

She starts to make shaky sounds, but then stops, her lips tight. She shakes her head, eyes welling, fingers clutching at mine, and I squeeze them back gently. I don't have words of reassurance in me when I'm like this, but I can at least promise with touch *I'm here, I'm protecting you, you're safe. I have you, and I'm not letting go.*

"Milah," I repeat. Keep her focused with her name. "I need you to be calm right now. I need you to concentrate. You arranged for a car to meet us here, didn't you?"

It takes long moments before she answers. She nods slowly, rigidly, then stammers out, "Y-yes."

"Can you call them again? Find out where they are?"

Again a delay. She's in shock, and she's going to need time to recover from this.

I have a feeling, despite my suspicions about her motivations, that this is the first time the blood and danger truly became real to her. After her run-in with death last year, she must've thought the worst of it was over and she was invincible.

I never thought I'd find myself feeling sorry for a diva like Milah Holly, but even divas are allowed to be scared.

But she must have some inner reserve of strength, because something snaps in her eyes and she nods a bit more firmly. "O-okay. I'll call."

Then she pulls her hands free from mine and fumbles inside her jacket until she pulls out a Motorola in a hot pink case. With clumsy fingers, she stabs at the screen, then lifts it to her ear. Distantly, I hear the ringtone repeating.

But I also hear something else, faint and far away – a hint of melody, and I lift my head, turning it toward the window.

Milah pulls the phone away from her ear, the call dead-ends, and that thin hint of sound stops. She shakes her head. "Nobody's answering."

"Try again," I murmur, this time straining to listen even harder.

There: a repetitive jingle, some snatch of a pop song, stopping and starting over and over again, outside. Not close by, but not too distant, either. Maybe on the deserted road running alongside the airstrip. I glance over my shoulder at James.

"You hear that?"

He's already striding toward the door, meticulously adjusting his cufflinks. "On it."

As James slips out into the night, I transfer my attention back to the three girls in front of me. Em's finally peeking out from where she's buried herself in Liv, watching me with dark, questioning eyes asking more than I can answer right now.

This is the second time, though, that Liv immediately moved to protect Em over herself, even though my daughter's not even a target. This time, too, she extended her quiet strength to Milah, one hand even now rubbing her sister's back while her inquisitive gaze seems to ask me what the next step is like a soldier awaiting orders.

There's a hidden iron core inside this girl. Untested, maybe buried so deep she's not even aware of it herself, but it's something born not of hardship or experience but a certain strength of character.

Liv isn't nearly as helpless as she thinks – and I'm grateful to her for being there for Em when I'm too deep in mission mode to take that on.

"We're going to get out of here," I say, keeping my voice in that same even tone. Keep calm, and the others will too. "The men who attacked us are Pilgrims. Either they're more reckless than we thought, or they've got connections. This isn't a place we want to be, in case more of them show up before the police do. The cops can always come to us. I've looked over security at Milah's place, and it should be enough to keep us safe until we can go back home."

Em pipes up, "Why can't we just get on the plane and go home?"

"Because I don't know or trust that pilot, love, and we don't have air clearance. We'll go home once people I do trust are here to escort us."

"Mr. Strauss?" she asks softly, and even when I'm empty inside I can't help but smile.

"Mr. Strauss," I confirm. "But until then, we'll lock down Milah's place and stay low."

The air traffic controller speaks tentatively at my back. "The police and an ambulance are on their way."

"That's good," I respond. "I want you to tell them what happened here. My friend and I are with a private security company and licensed for concealed carry both in Washington state and British Columbia. We acted today to defend our clients from criminals in a violent attack. Please tell the police to use the number on that card to get in touch with us."

The air traffic controller still looks like she'll pass out any second, but she nods a little too quickly and clutches the card to her chest. "Okay," she whispers, then adds tentatively, "And...thank you."

I don't understand what she's thanking me for, until my gaze catches on the man bleeding out on the floor, the scent of his blood a cold, sticky metallic hint in the air conditioned room.

She's thanking me for saving her life.

I'm still clueless after all these years.

Don't know what to do when someone thanks me for hurting someone else, even if it's for the only reasons that could ever be the right ones.

I'm saved from figuring out how to respond by James,

who ducks back inside with a look of weary exasperation, straightening his tie. "There's an SUV parked outside, roughly fifty yards from the exit gate," he says dryly, though there's a touch of a sardonic edge to it. I'm not sure why until he continues, "Two men outside of it, unconscious from blunt force trauma, keys in the ignition." His gaze cuts to Milah. "I presume, since the jumble of letters on the vanity plate approximately translates to 'BAD BITCHMOBILE' –" he pronounces it as precisely and articulately as if giving a valedictorian speech, " – that this would be your vehicle?"

Milah flushes scarlet up to her hairline and shrinks down with a sheepish nod, staring at him.

James' lips curl coolly at the corners. "Excellent. It seems the interlopers subdued your men to prevent intervention, but their injuries don't look particularly severe. We can gather them and be on our merry way."

That's our cue to move. Between James and I, we round everyone up, keeping them tight between us and heading out at a quick, militaristic trot.

We head through the chain-link fence, out to the road, where the SUV sits with its doors open, headlights bright, flooding the night. Two burly men in suits slump against the front and back driver's side tires.

I check their pulses just in case. They're strong.

The bloody spots on the backs of their heads are small, barely breaking the skin, and they're already starting to groan toward consciousness as James and I heft them into the rear storage space and settle them with their jackets folded under their heads.

James takes the wheel, stealing Milah's phone to get her address and borrow her GPS, while I settle in the back seat with everyone else. It's a tight fit with two grown women, one girl, and me, but if anything goes wrong as the car speeds smoothly through the night, I'd rather be close by and able to shield them.

The moment she has her seatbelt on, Em latches onto my side like a burr, curling her fingers in my jacket. *"Daddy."*

I shouldn't crack. I *can't* fucking crack, not until we're behind secure walls at Milah's villa, but this is my daughter, dammit. And she's just come far too close to being shot.

Everything I've repressed blows through that wall of ice in a burst of raw emotion: love, fear, relief, gratitude.

I cup Em's sweet little face in my palms, searching her over, looking for even so much as a scratch, but I'm just as afraid of the kind of damage that can't be seen on the surface when her eyes well and she chokes back a sob.

"Em," I murmur. "Em, honey, tell me you're all right."

She hiccups, eyes spilling over, but forces a smile, brave and bright and wonderful and I'm so, so fucking proud of her. So glad I haven't lost her today.

"I'm f-fine," she says, then sniffles and rubs at her nose. "I promise I'm okay." Her smile strengthens. "You should've let me help. I could've taken one of them."

I can't help a broken, harsh bark of laughter, and I gather her closer, wrapping her up like I can hide her from the awfulness of my world. "That's my girl," I whisper.

Over Em's head, I catch Liv watching me – and for a moment she reaches over, her fingertips resting on my arm, the lightest butterfly's touch. Blue eyes search me over as if seeking something deeper, something more.

I'm sorry, she mouths, and now I finally understand that look in her eyes.

It's guilt.

I didn't think I could ache anymore, but I was wrong. And even though I know I shouldn't care, shouldn't push these lines, I can't help seizing her hand in mine, pressing it against Em's back.

Later, I mouth back, and keep her cool, shaking fingers twined in mine. We'll talk when we're able.

The urge to murder something, someone, hasn't fully faded.

I'm fucking furious at the people who put my daughter in danger. Furious that this sick vendetta has gone this far.

But I can't be furious with Liv.

And I can't let her blame herself for this. Lion's the only one who deserves my fury, my scorn.

My vengeance.

Sooner or later, he'll pay for threatening my daughter, and for threatening Liv.

* * *

MILAH'S VANCOUVER estate is more of a fortress than I expected, even after reviewing the plans on the plane. Electrified fences, double access codes requiring either internal lock activation or Milah's bioprint, security cameras mounted everywhere.

As Milah leans around me and half climbs over James to stick her arm out the driver's side window and press her palm to the bioprint plate, I give her a skeptical look, raising a brow.

She plunks back down in her seat almost sulkily. "What?" she mumbles, shooting me a defiant look. "I don't like paparazzi."

That almost gets a smile out of me.

But I don't feel easy until the SUV is parked in the eight-car garage and we're inside the sprawling, multi-story imitation-Victorian house. Here, the lines are just *off* enough from classical to lean into showy gaudiness, with just enough extra to be so very perfectly Milah.

I'm worried about the size of it, but as long as I can keep everyone within shouting distance, we should be fine.

Milah's on-site staff are either still up this late at night, or very good at rolling out of bed in an instant, as they're waiting to usher us to our rooms.

They adapt quickly when I make it very clear I don't want us scattered, and all of our rooms need to be adjacent, within easy reach of each other. A shuffling of room reassignments later, and I'm promising I'll be there to tuck Em in and see her safely to sleep as soon as I've dropped my bag off in my room and shrugged out of a jacket stained in blood spatters.

But as I open the door to my room, I pause as Liv breaks away from our group to head toward hers. It's to the right of mine, Em's to the left. Liv looks so tired, so small, so forlorn and pulled into herself, as if she's locked herself up in this tiny, fragile bundle of guilt and is holding down hard to keep anything from escaping to hurt anyone else.

Before I know what I'm doing, I'm pulling away from my door and stepping closer, reaching out to rest my hand lightly on her wrist. She stills, lifting her head as if waking from a daze, looking up at me.

"Riker..." she says, as if just realizing I'm here.

The urge to take her in my arms is so powerful I almost can't resist.

I want to shelter her, to stand between her and anything that might make her feel as lost as she looks right now.

But I can't forget the one night I reached for Crystal, after subduing a home invader...

She flinched from me, looking back as if I was the one who might hurt her.

It's that memory that makes me pull back from Liv, shoving my hands into the pockets of my slacks for lack of anything else to do.

For lack of anything else to say, too, when I don't know the words and I'm tangled up inside my own head. It's a raw sharp blow to the gut to realize I don't want this woman to be afraid of me.

To realize I don't want her gone from my life, either.

But it seems like a good place to start, to force out, "I'm sorry you had to see that shit back there. Sorry if I frightened you."

"Frightened me?" Her brow wrinkles, and her head cocks. "Riker, no." She shakes her head. "You saved us. All of us." She trails off, faltering, staring up at me with those wide, pretty eyes, then looking down, her hand curling against her chest. "I feel so safe in your hands."

Such simple words shouldn't rock my world. "You're serious?"

"Why wouldn't I be?"

"Because I just shot several men. Shot them like nothing. I walked into gunfire without caring if I got shot myself. I may have killed them." I don't think it's even apparent to me how heavy this is until I look away sharply, staring down the hall. "Being willing, being *capable* of doing that...it can frighten people, you know."

"It doesn't frighten me."

I blink back my surprise. And then she's so close – leaning into me, resting her hand on my chest, soft and yet so warm, that touch asking me to look at her. Asking me to believe her as much as the quiet earnestness in her voice asks, offers, *gives* so much with warmth and understanding. "How hard is it to do that for a living? To be that way? But you did it anyway, to keep me and Em and even my sister safe." Her fingers curl, tangling in my shirt, fingering one of the buttons. "That doesn't scare me, Riker. It's comforting."

She's not looking at me now, but I can't look away from her.

The way she glances down and off to the side, so shy, so clearly afraid of rejection, and yet putting herself out there to comfort me anyway, to *accept* me.

Fuck. Sometimes it's not force that can break you, but the gentlest touch.

This woman's gentleness will annihilate me, if I let it.

I cover her hand with mine, catching it against my chest. "Liv."

I just say her name, slow, waiting for those eyes.

Her breath catches. Her cheeks warm with pretty washes of pink, and she lifts her head, looking up at me. But before she can speak, James leans into the hall from the living room.

"Riker?"

He pauses as Liv and I break apart abruptly, his keen silver-blue eyes flicking over us both, but his expression remains neutral.

"The police wish to speak with you," is all he says, before ducking back out.

Right. I sigh and glance at Liv, offering her a tired smile as I turn away. But she steps forward abruptly, pressing against my back, this slight figure weighing me to earth, every bit of her imprinting against me.

"Hey, Riker..." Her breath is warm through my shirt, her lips moving against my spine. "Come back soon."

I reach back and catch her hand, squeezing tight in the only reassurance I can offer, before I pull myself away—hating every step between us, and the duty that I have to face.

IX: A LITTLE LESS (OLIVIA)

This is all my fault.

That thought loops in my head as we convene in the living room.

Riker's on the phone with his Enguard crew, arranging for a personal convoy of trusted personnel to take us back home.

Em's putting on a brave face, sitting next to me and pretending to read a book. But over the tops of the pages, she never takes her eyes from the comforting sight of her father.

Milah has isolated herself on a deep, plush divan, curling up in one corner and staring sulkily out the window, refusing to talk to anyone. I know her well enough to know she's angry.

And I know her well enough to know she's frightened, too.

Worse, this mess is because of me.

I know my sister was the original target, but I just made things messier by being in the wrong place at the wrong time. If I hadn't been at Milah's place in Seattle when I was, then her security team would've handled both those groups of men, and this would've been long over.

I'd never have met Riker or Em. Never have become their problem. Never would've put them in danger.

I hate that some selfish part of me can't stand the idea of never having met these two wonderful people, when it's my fault Em is pale with sleepless hollows under her eyes, refusing to keep her promise to go to bed until her father can see her safely to sleep.

It's my fault that little knot of stress and tension wrinkles above the bridge of Riker's nose.

It's my fault everyone was almost shot tonight.

It's my fault we're stuck here, under lockdown in the world's fanciest panic room.

Riker pulls his phone away and drops it into his pocket, then sweeps the gathered assembly with a long look.

"We're staying until Sunday night," he says. "Landon's coming for us with an armored convoy then. It's safer than us trying to get back to another airport on our own, even with police support, and we won't have to worry about walking into an ambush on landing again. But it's going to take some wrangling and paperwork to get that kind of heavy armor and artillery over the border without causing an incident."

Milah wrinkles her nose. "Freaking tanks? Is all of that really necessary?"

The look Riker shoots her is guarded and thoughtful. "Not tanks. Armored cars. Yeah, it is necessary if you want to go home alive. I never should've agreed to this in the first place. Should've known something was up. How did they even know where we'd be? Who told them where to find us, and at just the right time?"

My sister's eyes widen, and she stares at Riker. "What are you implying? That *I* set this up?"

"I'm implying something isn't right," Riker growls coolly, "and that you may have been taken advantage of. No, I don't believe you'd knowingly put your sister in danger. That doesn't mean this doesn't reek to hell and back."

"That's not my fault!" Milah cries, balling her fists.

"No one's saying it is, sis," I soothe. "Look, we're all raw right now. We've got two days cooped up together trying to be as safe as possible. Let's get some rest and maybe in the morning we can talk things through some more."

No one answers. Not even James, the only one of us who seems completely unfazed by the situation, his expression icy calm as he flicks through his phone, the light reflecting from the lenses of his glasses.

It's not hard to see that tensions are high, and we're all a little freaked out, but I just...I just can't stand my sister and this man who makes my heart hurt in all new ways fighting with each other. Not now.

Especially when I need to ask Milah a few questions myself, but I need privacy.

"Daddy?" Em chirps softly. "I'm tired."

I know Em well enough by now to know she does that on purpose.

She's too smart, perceptive, and she knows that as the child here, she can give everyone reasons to back down without conceding ground, because someone needs to take care of her. I flash her a grateful smile. She beams a tired one back at me.

Riker sighs, pressing two fingers against his temple before his shoulders slump and he offers Em a weary smile. "I'll tuck you in, love. We'll talk."

Em nods, closing her book and clutching it to her chest as she climbs off the couch. "Okay."

Riker sweeps us all with a measured look, lingering on me the longest. "After Em's asleep, I need to go tour the property and check for anything suspicious. We'll talk later," he tells everyone.

But I know, from the way he lingers, he really means *me*.

* * *

IT'S NOT LONG before Milah and I are alone. Em and Riker have left, and James excuses himself to his room with a cordial *goodnight*. Milah's still sulking, refusing to look at me. *Sigh.*

"Is there a reason you're pissed at me?" I ask her.

Milah flinches, then scrunches her nose up before hanging her head. "I'm not. Not at you. Just feels like I'm being put on trial here for this entire thing."

"I think that might be your guilt talking, sis."

"Whatever. Probably." She uncurls herself, standing. She looks about ready to drop, and she should go to bed, I think, but she offers me a humorless smile of pure exhaustion and asks, "Hey, wanna go sit by the fire pit? It's a nice night."

"Should we be out in the open? Riker might worry."

Milah actually looks horrified. "You think the fire pit's

outside? Um, do you *know* what a mosquito bite would do to my skin?"

I hang my head, struggling not to laugh.

Same old Milah.

And it's same old Milah when she shows me her custom-designed patio – an entire glass enclosure looking out over the stars, with a few screened panels to let fresh air in and keep bugs out.

This fire pit is an elegant thing set right into the stone floor, sunken into the ground, and the casual seating scattered around looks like it was stolen from the Palace at Versailles. Milah drapes herself dramatically along a chaise. Very Marilyn Monroe.

I find myself a deep upholstered easy chair and tuck myself into it, hugging a pillow to my chest.

"Okay," I say. "Now, what's really going on? Why bring us up here? I thought this was your private sanctum. Not even family allowed."

Milah cringes and flings an arm over her eyes. "I just wanted to talk to you alone, and then when the Daddy train wanted to tag along, I couldn't think of a good reason to say no."

"Phone calls are good for private convos, Mimi. You didn't have to drag me to *Canada*." I study her closely, the way her skin looks especially thin over her inner elbows, blue veins showing.

I hate that I can't tell if the shadows under her eyes are withdrawals or just the shade of her sprawling arm. "Be real with me. How bad is it?"

That's when Milah goes stone-still.

She drops the sulky party girl act, and I get to see my real sister.

There's Milah, the pop starlet, and then there's Milah, my sister – and Milah, my sister, is a quiet and brooding woman, sensitive and vulnerable and full of tortured, self-recriminating thoughts that drive her to extremes. She's always been this way. When we were girls, she'd take bigger and bigger risks to be the center of attention, even if it meant hurting herself.

She'd fall off a stair railing after claiming she could run down it in heels. She'd mess around with dangerous boys who didn't know how to take no for an answer. She'd drink herself into a stupor.

If I had to guess, I'd say she was a junior in high school when she started with the drugs, but I'm not sure.

I just know that once, long long ago, she wasn't like this.

Then one day, when she was ten and I was eight, I found her with her mouth bloody and her dress ripped, sobbing into her skinned kneecaps. She would never tell me what happened. She still won't.

But she became a different girl that day, and it felt like she was trying to take on all the bad things in the world so they couldn't touch me.

Which is why I try so hard, no matter what, to be a good thing for her and, in my own way, protect her right back.

Without her party girl mask, Milah's eyes seem a darker, steadier blue. She bites her lip, flaking off day-old lipstick.

"Feels like it's eating me, you want to know the truth," she whispers. "Goddamn. I thought it'd be better after all this time, but..."

I'm out of the chair in a moment and over to her chaise, settling on the edge, gathering her into my arms. Shaking, she huddles against me, burying her face against my stomach. Her arms are like narrow bands of steel around my hips and stomach. I stroke her hair and kiss the top of her head.

"Remember what your therapist said," I murmur. "It's always going to come and go. It'll never be completely gone, but the important thing to remember when it comes is that it *will* go again. It'll pass. It won't hurt forever, Mimi."

The wretched sound she makes nearly breaks me.

"I need you home, Livvie," she sobs. "*Daddy* needs you home. It's just...it's not the same without you, it –"

I stiffen. That's when it all makes sense. That's when it sinks in.

Daddy set this up.

He used Milah and her withdrawals to get at me because he knows I can't resist my sister when she's in pain. He's manipulating her to manipulate me into coming back home to Seattle, and to him.

I should be furious, but there's one question I can't get past.

Why?

Why go through all this trouble to pay Enguard to keep me safe, then play these weird games to get me to come home?

Is my father more involved in this than I realized?

I know he's one of the targets, but I always thought it was just tertiary to Milah. That she was the main focus, and we were just collateral damage to scare her and even the score for their two dead men. Maybe I've been around

Riker too long and I'm absorbing his suspicious nature and jumping to too many conclusions, but now?

Now, I'm not so sure.

Jesus. When did I become so mistrustful of my own father?

Then again, when he's always looked right through me...

Did I ever really trust him in the first place?

"Milah," I say carefully. I don't want to set her off. This whole thing may be a farce, but her pain is too real. "Did Daddy ask you to bring me home?"

She whimpers, her hold tightening on me. "Please. Don't be mad."

It takes everything in me not to explode.

"*Why?* People are still after us. Home's the easiest place to get all of us together in one place to take us out together. It doesn't make sense."

"It does, though!" she protests. "It's safe. It wasn't safe before, but Daddy's put in new security systems and hired an entirely new security team. There are armed guards *everywhere*. It's okay now. It's okay to come home."

"What if I don't want to?"

Milah blinks, lifting her head, looking up at me with confused, tear-streaked eyes. "Huh?"

"I mean, what if I don't want to come home? What if I'm enjoying life without having everything handed to me?"

She looks puzzled, staring blankly. "Sooo, what? You mean you want to keep playing house with Senor Daddy Issues?"

"I feel safer with him than I would at home."

I feel *seen* with Riker, too. I feel appreciated. I feel alive.

But I can't say that to Milah.

She pouts. "Daddy's really falling apart without you, Liv. You keep everything together in one piece."

"So hire a secretary. Hell, hire ten."

"He has a secretary. It's not that. Logistics, I mean. It's more –"

"I'm a piece of furniture to him," I say. "A prop. I might be his favorite chair, but I'm still a chair, Mimi. I'm tired of being invisible, but essential. Sick of being kept."

Milah flumps against me sullenly. "Look, at least you aren't the one he parades around like a show poodle on a leash. You should consider yourself lucky. You *get* to be invisible."

"I don't *want* to be invisible!" I flare. "I don't want to just stand around doing nothing. I want to do things. For myself, for other people. Daddy's acting like a kid who lost his comfort blanket. When your role in someone's life can be replicated by a fetish object, you're not really part of their life at all."

"Oh come on, Livvie, don't be that way –"

"*What* way?"

I can't be here. I feel for Milah, I do. She's as dependent on Daddy as Daddy is on me, this weird triangle of emotional crutches.

And I know she's shaky, but right now she's in the safest place she can possibly be without being in police custody, and I'm ready to scream. I don't know where this sudden rage and frustration and pain and tension are coming from. Maybe it's over twenty years of bottling up every emotion to be the passive, meek, perfectly invisible daughter.

But if I don't get out of here, I'm going to say some things I'll regret – and possibly hurt Milah beyond repair.

I peel away from her clinging embrace, shaking off her clutching hands and doing my best to ignore the instinct to cave to her wounded look. I rise, backing away a few steps, toward the glass door leading out onto the lawn.

"I'm not being any kind of way, Milah," I say. "And I need you to understand that. I'm being *me*, and it scares me that I'm this old, and I don't even know who that is. I want to find out. I want to find out what kind of spark is inside me and if it could ever burn as bright as a flame, before Daddy smothers it enough to snuff it out."

I can tell by Milah's stare that she doesn't understand.

Of course she doesn't. I don't think she knows who she is, either, but she's spent her whole life exploding everywhere trying to find out, while I've just curled smaller and smaller inside myself.

Before she says anything else, I turn and walk away.

My name floats after me, echoing off the glass walls of her glittering cage as I dash through the door and out into the night.

* * *

I MAKE it to the tree line before a stitch in my side reminds me this is likely the worst in a long string of bad ideas.

I slow down, bending over and catching my breath. My sandals weren't made for running, and it's dark and I feel like the biggest idiot in the world.

My father likes to tease me about how I was such a quiet baby. I never cried, supposedly, never threw tantrums.

Now I feel like I'm making up for lost time, acting like a little girl who didn't get her way.

No. No, I'm not.

I'm acting like someone who's been locked away forever but couldn't even see the gold bars of her prison – only to finally recognize them and start rattling and screaming to be let out.

I'm not going back, I realize.

Not to that life. I can't stay with Riker and Em forever, sure, but I'm going to make a life of my own one way or another. Maybe I'll do something with my books. Or maybe I'll end up waitressing in a dirty dive and renting a single room in a shared apartment with four other strangers I'll love one day and hate the next. It doesn't matter.

All that matters is that I get to choose.

I straighten, staring into the darkness, the trees.

Milah's property is massive enough to have its own forest even inside the electric fence, and I can just make out a dirt jogging trail slipping between the trees.

I need air. I need to clear my head, because I know I'm thinking crazy. I'm stressed, scared, running on fumes and adrenaline, not even close to processing the shock and trauma of getting shot at.

So while I might be firm in my resolve...I think I need a walk to calm down before I go back to that house and have a real talk with my sister.

My heart trembles just a little as I head down the trail, but honestly, I'm too tired to be afraid.

Riker's out checking the perimeter. There's only so much that can happen in one night. I can't help but feel the dark closing in on me as I make my way over loose gravel and silty dirt, but I don't think anything out there can scare me more than the thoughts inside my own head.

I'm so wrapped up in my brain that I only halfway notice the trail starting to slope down through narrow, swaying pines that spear up against a clear night sky. I subconsciously adjust my stride, reaching out for an overhanging tree limb to brace myself as the path takes a sharp turn.

Then a large, loose rock slips under my heel, and suddenly the world goes tumbling away.

I let out a sharp scream as I hit the ground with a *whoosh*, the night tilting by and my breath punching out of my lungs. Mother Nature's not done with me yet.

This slope is steeper than I thought. Suddenly, the gravel's a conveyer belt, speeding me down the hill.

I shriek, pulse slamming, everything flashing by as I grab on desperately for anything I can, but it all slips through my fingers: twigs, brush, fallen branches, dead leaves, grass.

They're scraping my palms raw in a hot burn of pain but nothing else.

My life flashes before my eyes in all its wondrous, dull monotony. I realize I'm about to die with my greatest accomplishment in life being learning how to smile pretty and stand just far enough behind Daddy, when the ground drops out under me and gravity yanks my stomach down with my body not far behind.

I'm going to die at the bottom of a cliff, and it'll be weeks before anyone finds my body.

Another shriek rips out of me as the fall drags me down, and I'm already bracing for long seconds of terror – only to slam up hard after barely half a second, landing on soft earth.

"Soft" doesn't stop it from jarring up through me hard enough to make my teeth snap together and my skull jolt, whipping back on my neck. I lie there groaning, pain throbbing through me like a heartbeat, a full-body bruise. A sharp twinge in my leg tells me I've probably sprained it.

Ugh. Carefully, I push myself onto my back so I can look up.

I'm at the bottom of a shallow pit. I can hear water nearby, a big stream, probably something dug by fishermen or loggers long ago. It's not too deep, but I don't think I can get out of it on my own with my ankle like this. The sky is a circle of blue overhead – blue and little twinkling lights, like a bowl full of stars. I count them as I catch my breath, waiting for my head to stop spinning.

Welp.

At least I didn't die.

Riker's going to be so mad at me.

"—iv? *Liv!*"

I smile because I must've hit my head harder than I thought.

That's Riker's voice, calling my name with a stark desperation, ragged with emotion I'd never thought I'd hear from anyone. Not for me.

"Liv, fuck! Hold on. I'm coming."

It's really him. Not a hallucination.

My heart leaps – with relief, I tell myself, *only* relief and nothing else – as I strain up on my elbows.

"Riker." Too soft. I choke and spit out dirt, taking in a deep breath and swallowing before trying again. "Riker!"

"Liv!"

"I'm over here. I'm over here!"

I hear something crashing through the brush like a bear.

Holy hell. Please, please don't let it *be* an actual bear. That's more than I can take right now. But I can hear Riker mutter to himself, cursing with those crashes, and I realize what's happening too little, too late.

"Riker, don't, there's a pit!"

He's undaunted. I get one glimpse of his tall, thickly powerful body silhouetted against the night before it comes hurtling down right on top of me.

I'd never realized the weight of a man could be so *heavy* – this thing of stone crushing me, only stone isn't this warm and sinewy and doesn't smell like Riker, that deep smoky scent that wraps me up as much as his heat, mixing with the sharp, crisp stinging scent of crushed pine needles.

Somehow, his arms are around me, as if by lifting me into his bulk he could minimize the bruising force slamming into me. Somehow, he's buried his face in my throat, his beard teasing against my skin and tracing the sensitive hollow where my collarbones meet.

It hurts. It hurts where his weight digs in, but I don't care, because nothing could possibly hurt more than the raw, desperate burst of longing for the man tumbled on top of me right now.

Pure stillness, save for the rasp of our breathing, the chirp of crickets, and the whisper of my beating heart, slowed down to a soft and almost frightened thing. I *am* afraid, right now. Afraid of what I'm feeling. Afraid of getting my heart broken.

Afraid of the heat surging through me in wild, sweet flares, leaping through my veins, as Riker pushes himself up on his elbows, and the shift in position molds his entire body intimately close to mine.

The tip of his nose brushes mine as he looks down. His chest heaves with shallow, swift breaths, pushing out to crush against my breasts, dragging my dress and my bra against my flesh and suddenly making me aware of my body in a way I've never known before.

As I look up into darkened green eyes, I feel like a *woman.* Not just a thing of limbs and bone that happens to breathe on this earth.

I feel how soft I am compared to his masculine hardness, how small I am compared to his bulk.

I feel every nerve in my body tingling, radiating waves pouring out to the very tips of my fingers.

I know the weight and fullness of my breasts and how they seem to ache for his touch, and I know the swell and softness of my stomach, leading down to a tightness between my legs and a tension in my thighs.

I know a gnawing, hard pull inside that whispers how it might feel to just spread my legs to either side of Riker's hips, and to discover just how hot and delicious it'd be if he moved against me just right.

And I know him as a man, too, when he shifts on top of me and I feel something hard, something thick, something hotter than even the fire building between us rubbing against my hips and stomach.

I breathe in sharply, air licking over my tingling, sensitive lips.

Riker still hasn't said anything, his body tenses, bulk hardened into steel, and I struggle to find something, *anything* to break the stillness between us before it shatters into a scream.

"Are you all right?" My voice is raw inside me, breaking, throaty, coming from somewhere deep that seems to give away secrets I'm afraid to tell.

Riker's gaze drops, watching my lips as they move on the words, and the warmth inside me spreads further, deeper, in a liquid flush.

"Don't think I broke anything," he whispers, a low growl under the words, all fire and wild. "You?"

"My ankle," I breathe. "I don't think it's broken, but probably sprained."

"Which ankle?"

"Left."

I expect him to lift off me, to check my foot, but he doesn't move.

He's so close I can make out the faint flecks of gold against the green of his eyes, glimmering like fireflies in the dark.

So close his every breath lets me taste the hint of coffee he drank on the flight here, mingling with his natural cologne of everything intensely masculine.

So close his body heat melts through me like he's a hearth on a cold winter night.

And then that melting turns into something like napalm pooling between my thighs until my panties cling to my skin and I catch a scent that I think is *me*, creamy and soft and sweet and with just enough sultry-hot musk to whisper the forbidden.

I want this man so much it *hurts*.

Riker's nostrils flare. He senses it too, this mating call turning animal between us, pure primal call and response, and a low growl begins to rumble in his chest and roll through us both.

His head dips toward me, closing that last distance, and my lips part in yearning, in need, in hunger, and in every question and answer that's ever waited inside me to be found.

"Riker?" James' cool voice calls over the woods. "I heard shouting, a crash...you need backup?"

Riker and I both freeze.

I expect him to close behind that familiar mask, but instead he lets out a low, self-mocking laugh that's half groan and all thrill when it feels like he's letting me in on the joke between us.

His head drops between his shoulders, resting on my collarbone for just a moment, his lips and beard moving so close to my chest that my entire body tightens.

It's an oddly intimate moment, sweet, and I want so much to wrap my arms around him. Want it so bad, but I restrain myself.

Barely.

He lifts his head, looking up toward the edge of the pit, and calls, "Could use a hand, James, but nothing to worry about."

James' voice sounds closer. "What the hell happened?"

"Was doing a perimeter walk and heard Liv scream. Looks like she slipped on the path and fell in a gravel pit." He glances at me with a questioning lift of his brows. I nod before he smirks and continues, "Dumbass that I am, I fell in after her."

James' exasperated sigh carries over the night, before

his head appears over the side of the pit, looking down at us with flat disgust. "What am I going to do with you?"

Riker rocks back, pushing himself up onto his knees, practically straddling me – then shifts to roll off me, before those strong, thick arms I love so much slide underneath me and lift me up against his chest.

"Just take Liv," he says, lifting me higher. "Mind her left ankle. I'll get myself out."

There's a flash of vertigo as I'm lifted over Riker's head.

I feel like I'm going to fall again, but then James slips his arms under me, pulling me against his chest. It doesn't feel the same as Riker – colder, sharper, James' suit scratching at me – but I don't have to stay with him for long.

In a powerful heave of muscle, Riker hauls himself out of the pit. Even in the darkness of night, he's beautifully dirty, his shirt streaked with earth and the top button popped off to expose a tuft of chest hair, a scratch bleeding down his cheek and mud smudged along his sweat-glistening throat and jaw.

He takes a minute to shake his body out, not even looking fazed by the fall, before he's there, taking me from James with a look that howls possession.

I have to be imagining that.

I hit myself too hard.

Right?

But I'm not imagining how close and tight Riker holds on as he cradles me against him and flicks James a look. "Go on ahead and ask the house staff for a first aid kit. I'll be right behind. Don't want to jostle Liv too much."

James responds with one of those heavily skeptical

looks, then just snorts and turns away. Like a shadow, he melts into the woods, leaving us alone.

Riker looks down at me for the better part of a minute, something like a promise glimmering in his eyes, before he curls his arms tighter and sets off toward the trail.

"It'll be all right," he murmurs. "I've got you."

I tuck my head under his chin – and he lets me.

I can feel his heart against my shoulder, and it's beating so wild, as manic as mine. I hurt all over, but I hardly feel it when this warmth is stronger, brighter, louder.

"I know," I whisper. Then I close my eyes and sink into him.

His hands are strong, seeming to promise they'll hold me together.

No matter what comes next.

* * *

I DON'T REMEMBER FALLING asleep. But I must have, lulled by the gentle rhythm of Riker's strides, because the next thing I know, I'm waking up in the dark with the softness of a bed under my sore, aching body.

I can feel something tight and grainy on my ankle. Probably a bandage or a wrap, but the compression feels good against the dull, steady pain.

I crack one eye open. I'm in a large, lush guest bed in a darkened room that's not mine.

My shoes are gone. I'm nestled under the covers, still in my dress. I'm clean, too, the feeling of grit and dirt wiped away. My scratches sting, but not as much as they could.

And I'm not alone.

A mountain breathes next to me, quiet and slow. *Riker.*

He's sprawled out shirtless, thick corded muscle rising and falling in weathered, tanned swells, his normally-combed hair a tangled mess against the pillow, his lips parted on quietly grumbling, drowsy breaths.

His chest is a swarthy plain of hard chisels dusted with deep-brown, curling hair and fatal tattoos, and I think if not for the heavy, burly arm pinning me in place and making it hard to move, I wouldn't be able to resist the urge to run my hands through that pelt and tangle my fingers in it.

Oh my God.

I'm tucked up against Riker.

He's *holding* me.

And my entire body feels so hot, so electric. If I move, I'm sure I'll shower sparks.

If I don't pull away from him right now, I'm going to do something rash and reckless.

I feel like being wild, like letting my hair down for the first time in my life, but throwing myself at Riker isn't the best way to do it.

I want to talk to him first, to know if I'm misreading the way he touches me, the way he looks at me, the way he's holding me right now. But I don't want to wake him, either.

I need to get this energy out somewhere, assuming I can even walk.

No way to test but try, so I very, very slowly wiggle my way out from underneath him and replace my body with a pillow, nudging it underneath his arm.

He snorts a little, then settles, sighing.

I linger for a moment, fondly watching his sleeping face, then slip my legs over the side of the bed and stand gingerly.

There's a twinge from my ankle, but it holds my weight and I barely even limp.

It's just a mild sprain, probably hurt more when it happened. With one last look at Riker, I pad to the door and step out into the hall.

Immediately, the sound of my father's voice beckons me from down the hall.

I get a crawling chill that I can't quite explain.

What's going on? Daddy? *Here?*

No – his voice is crackly, too distant to be natural.

He's on speakerphone. His voice is coming from the master bedroom suite down the hall. I see the door cracked, light spilling out, and I hear Milah countering, her voice agitated and shrill.

I shouldn't eavesdrop, but I'm still upset and confused over this whole mess with my Dad and Milah conspiring to get me home like this entire angry crime syndicate thing isn't happening.

I need to know what's going on. I creep closer to the door and lean against the wall, taking the opportunity to take my weight off my ankle. Just inside I can glimpse Milah pacing back and forth, her hair swinging like an angry cat's tail.

"Look," she says. "I've tried everything. She doesn't want to listen, Daddy. And no, I don't get what the big deal is. Why do I have to do this? Livvie's an adult. She can do what she wants. Last I checked, we were more worried about who's trying to kill her, not who's babysitting."

Our father's voice barks back from her phone speaker. I can just barely see it glowing on the nightstand. "Have you forgotten everything I've done for you, Milah?"

His voice is cajoling, coaxing, the kind of tone that makes it hard to focus on what he's actually saying even as the guilt trip hits you in the gut like a sledgehammer. He's good at that. "All I'm asking is this one tiny thing from you, and it's *too much?*"

Milah's pacing stops. She drops into baby girl voice, syrupy and sulking. "But Daddy..."

"You can 'but Daddy' me, babe, but remember that doesn't work on me any more than it worked when you were begging for another hit. I covered for you, Milah. I paid for rehab. All in the hopes that someday you'd get better. You are better now, aren't you, baby girl?"

I've never wanted to hit my father so hard in my life.

I'm going to be sick.

You don't *do* this to recovering addicts. You don't pressure them to magically get *better* or treat them like their recovery status determines if they're worthy of basic human consideration.

If this is what Daddy's been doing all this time, then it's no wonder Milah backslides so hard, so often.

No wonder she breaks down out of the blue when it really does seem like she's making progress.

No. Fucking. Wonder.

Yet this clicks together with a dawning realization, too. I knew something wasn't right with our father, and it's not hard to see now that he has some kind of end game in mind.

He wants me home for some reason other than what's

being said, and I have a feeling he knows more about the incident with the Pilgrims than he lets on.

Why else would he be so calm when the two daughters he supposedly loves more than anything in the world are on a mob hit list?

God, maybe I'm just being paranoid. I don't know.

My head's spinning in too many directions. I don't know what to think when I feel like I'm looking at a puzzle with half the pieces missing. I'm losing my mind.

Milah's still talking, though, and I pull myself out of my swirling thoughts to listen.

"Yeah...I guess I'm better," she says, her voice small. Weak, submissive, totally not my world-famous sister. A thing that hurts me to hear when I don't think she's even aware of it, unlike her pouty baby girl act. "I can try, maybe? I mean, I don't think she'll listen, but..."

"Of course she'll listen to you," Daddy oozes out. "You're her sister. Do your best, baby girl. I'll be waiting."

The call ends, the phone emitting a little *bloop*.

I hear a groan, then a rustle of cloth, and peer around the door carefully to glimpse Milah slumping into a chair next to the bed. An open, half-empty bottle of champagne sits on the nightstand, and she swipes it up by the neck and takes a long, mournful pull, tipping her head all the way back.

I can't stand to see her like this, but I'm not sure if I should intervene.

Until she opens the drawer of the nightstand and pulls out a little clear baggie with fine white powder in the bottom.

No.

She's barely shaken it, barely torn it open to start

laying out a neat line of bone white on the dresser when I have the door open, barging in without thinking.

"Mimi, *don't.*"

Milah jumps with a little squeak, the baggie flying.

She snatches at it, but I dive across the floor.

Okay, so I'm not exactly an action hero here. I trip on my bad ankle and get lucky.

Our hands collide, grasping for the baggie, but I'm the one who manages to grab hold of it, even if I get my face and hands dusted with white powder for the trouble. I immediately snap my hands behind my back with the baggie clutched inside. Milah tries to reach around me, keening softly, grabbing.

I take a step back, out of reach, and square my shoulders before saying firmly, "*No.*"

Milah stares up at me like I'm some new species she's never seen.

Then she just crumples, drooping forward with a whimper, pressing her face against her thighs, small and forlorn with her kimono-style robe draped around her. "Goddamn it, Liv, just once. Just this *once* to make it stop!"

"You know it won't make anything stop," I say. "Why do you want it so bad now? Is it because of Daddy? Does he make you feel so bad you need it?"

Milah says nothing, turning her face to the side, staring dully across the room. That scares me.

It scares me more than I want to admit.

Because maybe, just maybe, as bad as I thought I had it with Dad, Milah's had it *worse* all these years. And maybe I never noticed because I was invisible to her, too, and as long as I didn't look too close, it didn't have to hurt when she didn't look back.

I bite my lip. "Milah...please. Tell me the truth. What's going on with Daddy?"

I can already tell by how her mouth twists that she's not going to tell me.

Not everything, anyway. She wraps her arms around herself, shaking her head.

"He's just being proud, that's all. You know how it goes. He thinks he can take care of you better than Enguard and he's really getting hung up on it. You know what he's like when you take a hit at his ego."

I'm not buying that for a second, but I don't know what else to say, do, or ask.

I just sigh and limp across her room to push the bathroom door open and step inside. The plastic baggie splashes in the toilet, then swirls away with a whoosh.

When I step back out, Milah's hunched down, her shoulders practically touching her ears.

"I'm sorry," she says, staring at her knees. "I just...when the craving hits..." Her eyes brim, fat wet droplets pooling on her lower lashes. "Why am I so broken, Livvie? Why can't I just walk away from this?"

"You aren't broken, Mimi. And you can't walk away because if it was that easy, we wouldn't have addicts at all." I'm still so mad at her, but I can't be cruel to her right now.

Leaning down, I rest my brow to hers. "Your body's just confused, that's all. It thinks it needs something it doesn't need like it's life or death, so it's sending you the wrong signals. We're going to ignore those signals and look for the right ones, and what the right ones say now is that your body needs sleep."

Milah nods mutely and lets me help her to her feet.

It's times like this she's almost childlike, letting me help her into bed and tuck her up close. I take the bottle of champagne into the bathroom and pour the rest of it down the sink so she can't gateway herself into going for another fix again, then sit with her, stroking her hair, until she falls asleep in a shaking, clammy knot of miserable whimpers.

I don't doubt that she's in real, genuine pain. Real need.

But I can't let her have any more of that mess that was ruining her life.

And the second she's asleep, I pull off what has to be the first completely silent room shakedown in history.

Tiptoeing everywhere, I check in and under drawers, in the closet, even under the mattress, creeping a hand in to keep from waking her and making her go all Princess and the Pea on me. I peek under boxes, turn out her purse, even look inside the toilet tank.

Nothing.

I'm hoping that was her last stash, but just to be safe, I check the areas of the house she frequents, too. I'll have to do a more thorough check tomorrow since my ankle is starting to hurt like hell and it's well after midnight.

I took care of my sister. Now I need to take care of myself, too, and after the last twenty-four hours, I need the kind of sleep you can only have when you've nearly died twice and can't remember if you even ate dinner.

I should go back to my room, but I don't want Riker to wake up and worry when he finds me gone.

Yes. That's my excuse, and I'm sticking to it.

That's my reason why, after a few minutes in my own room to change into a clean nightie, I creep back into his room on silent mouse feet, crawling back into the me-shaped space left in the bed's wrinkles.

That's my reason for easing that pillow out of the space between his arms, and gently inserting myself back where I belong.

That's my reason for curling up and burrowing into his chest, letting his warmth and smoky scent completely surround me until I feel sheltered and safe and so deliciously hot.

That's my reason.

Not because Riker's world taming arms are the best place to hide from the terrifying thoughts that threaten to permanently destroy my life.

X: A LITTLE MORE (RIKER)

The last time I woke up with my body this twisted up and hot, I was in the throes of puberty, tossing and turning every night through dreams of my classmates' uniform skirts swishing against the backs of their thighs.

I was thirteen then. I'm in my forties now.

And my dreams go a fuck of a lot farther than an inch of naked thigh, especially when I'm waking up with desire itself pressed so close, I can practically feel the texture of her skin through her thin nightgown.

Liv.

Delicate. Soft. Beautiful.

I don't understand how someone this frail and small can give off so much heat, but everywhere her body touches mine, it's like a raw hot iron brand taken from the forge and pushed against my skin until it sizzles.

I can't peel my eyes off her.

Not when half my dreams were dick hungry obsessions, remembering her body under mine, the way we tangled, and how her softness yielded.

Yielded just perfect when my cock swelled against her, and I couldn't ignore the way she looked at me, the way her strawberry lips parted...

That was half my dreams.

The other half was terrified replays of every bullet fired, every splash of blood, that moment when I found her in the pit and thought her splayed body was lifeless and broken instead of just tired and a little bit dirty.

She'd fallen asleep so trustingly in my arms after I carried her back to the house.

The entire time, I couldn't help thinking how close I came to losing her, when I've never actually had her. I don't know where my mind is right now.

I'm the asshole who said no emotions, no entanglements...aren't I? No confusion. No temptation. No insanity.

Yet, I'm the one aching to kiss her awake.

To touch her softly and coax her into opening for me until she sighs herself lucid enough to open her eyes and pull me deeper and deeper into her.

To go on a rampage between her legs, biting the last moan off her lips while every hard inch of me strokes her to heaven.

I can't help but drink her in. Her nightgown feels paper thin. It's that same pale, almost pearl blue she wears so well in everything, only so sheer the color of her skin turns it sweetly cloudy. Her limbs show through it like mist. Her curves outlined so clearly, I can see where the delicate lines of her panties bite into the lush flesh of her hip, where the pink rises of her nipples darken her tits.

Fuck.

I tell myself I'm taking in every spare detail to remind myself she's safe, down to every last scratch and bruise that does nothing to mar her near angelic beauty.

But if I'm honest with myself, I'm being selfish. Letting myself look to appreciate her for once when those wide, sweet eyes don't prompt every instinct I've ever had to kick in and shut her out before I can hurt her.

No.

Before she can hurt *me.*

Angry teeth sink into my lower lip. That's what this is really about, isn't it? Hurt.

My first marriage was just the pain of that look in Crystal's eyes, the careful distance around me, and then suddenly more distance damn near unfathomable.

It wasn't my wife looking at me like I was some kind of monster anymore, but instead my wife looking at me across a chasm as deep and black as the River Styx. And there was no way I could cross it because fate already decided she belonged on one side of death and I belonged on the other. Fate didn't give us time to sort shit out, file for divorce, or do anything.

Fate moves on its own fucking schedule.

I'm not angry at Fate, or her for the pain, the confusion, but I'm angry at *something*.

Life, maybe. And I've been brick-walling so hard in that anger, stewing, trying to keep out anything that could ever cause that kind of torture again.

Like a pretty young woman who looks up at me and tells me I don't frighten her.

That I make her feel safe.

Her hand rests so trustingly on my chest, curled into a

loose fist. I give myself the luxury of covering her slender hand with my own – only to frown as I feel something grainy and fine on her skin, almost like sugar or sand under my touch.

I pull back a little, looking down. There's a fine dust of white on my chest, passed from her hand to me, and more streaked against her fingers. Both her hands.

What the hell? My brows slam together when it hits me.

I don't need to sniff or taste to have a very good idea what that is, considering whose house we're in.

No. Not Liv. She fucking wouldn't...would she?

There was *nothing* in the file Landon gave me on her. No hint when she was living under our roof that she was hiding a habit. No sign of her jonesing for anything but a friend.

But shit, if she's got a secret habit...if I'd known, I'd have –

What, exactly?

A month ago, my answer would've been *I'd have put her as far away from my daughter as possible.*

But now, all I can think is that I would've found a way to help her, if I'd known.

Like I need to help her now, to make sure she's all right.

She took a hard fall and might've hit her head. Mixing drugs with even the mildest concussion can be fatal, and I feel sick inside at the thought of seeing Liv through so much only to lose her to something like this.

I sit up, blood rushing to my ears. She's breathing steadily, resting easy, but better safe than sorry.

Catching her face gently in my palms, I stroke my thumbs over her cheeks, coaxing.

"Liv," I murmur, then a bit more firmly, "*Liv*. Wake up. Please."

She makes a drowsy noise, protesting, and just screws her eyes shut. Carefully, I jostle her, repeating her name a bit louder. "*Liv*."

"Nnh." Liv yawns dramatically, then cracks one eye open, one hazy, dark eye peering at me without much recognition. "Hmm?"

What I can see of that eye doesn't tell me much. It could be dilated with stimulants, or just dilated because of the darkened room.

"Sweetheart," I say, keeping my voice low and soothing. "I need you to wake up for me. Need you to tell me how much you took, and how long ago."

That sparks a touch more clarity, her other eye opening as she looks at me in sleepy puzzlement. "How much I...took? Huh?"

"Liv, your hands are covered in what I'm pretty damn sure is cocaine. You fell earlier. Might have hit your head. I need to know if I should get you to a hospital."

Liv blinks. Then just blinks again, suddenly wide awake, and flinches back from me, looking down at her white-streaked hands and arms and my chest.

"Cocaine? Oh my *God*."

I arch a brow. She's way too lucid. "You're not high at all, are you?"

"*No!*" With a groan, she curls her hands helplessly. "Oh God, no. No, I – Milah almost – I had to stop her. And I did. It kind of spilled out everywhere. Then I was so tired after searching the house for her stash, I guess I just didn't notice it was still all over me."

Milah. Of course.

I shouldn't feel so relieved, but Milah's already in recovery while Liv would've been a whole new problem.

Wait.

Milah's in recovery.

Or Milah's *supposed* to be in recovery, at least.

I frown. "Milah's still using?"

Liv winces. "Sometimes. She backslides, whenever things trigger her. Her counselor said it's bound to happen. We just deal with it and try to help her as much as we can."

Now I get it. The secretive behavior. The almost manic need for Liv to come with Milah.

The way Liv dodged my suspicions before. She wasn't hiding anything to do with the Pilgrims.

She was keeping her sister's secrets, trying to protect the family she loves.

"Is this what you haven't been telling me?" I ask softly.

"Yeah." Liv lowers her eyes, staring down at her knuckles. "Milah's trying so hard. She just doesn't need the world to know she's still struggling. All her fans rallied behind her when she opened up about her problem a few months ago, you know? And she doesn't want to let them down. She'll get there. She *will*. If she trips a little on the way, it's her business, and no one else's."

She's so earnest, in her belief in Milah. Even after everything Milah's jerked her through, Liv's still there, still saying *she can do it, I know she can*. And the only thing for me to say in response is, "You're right."

It's not my business.

Not to judge, not to tell.

All I can do is support Liv, and it stuns me down to my core to realize that I *want* to.

That I want to be the one to hold her up while she's struggling to carry everyone else.

She looks up at me with her eyes so clear and startled, as if she'd expected everything but those two words. "Thank you, Riker," she whispers, her smile radiant. "Thanks for looking after me."

"You don't have to thank me."

"No?" A bitter note enters her voice. "Do you have any idea what life's like growing up with someone who doesn't respect even the smallest hint of your freedom? Who makes all your decisions for you? Do you know how it feels when someone suddenly *does* respect even one tiny thing that you might want? My own freaking father...he's why this happened. Everything that's bad for Milah, and for me."

Before I can answer, she pushes away, still shaking her head. It's so abrupt I let her go without realizing it, and she tumbles out of bed, still clutching her hands to her chest, carefully held away from her skin and nightgown. She swallows hard, then offers me a wan, tense smile.

"Sorry," she whispers. "Let me go wash this off. Who knows if absorption through skin contact is a thing?"

Then she's gone, disappearing into the attached bathroom.

I'm left lying there, cocaine dusted on my chest, staring after her and wondering just what the hell is happening right now.

I don't know if she's upset, angry, or happy.

I don't know if I want to protect her, get her as far

away from me as possible, or tear that flimsy nightgown off and devour her from the inside out.

I listen to the sound of running water from inside the bathroom.

Have to close my eyes when she emerges, a dripping wet towel curled in both hands, and splatters of water all over her gown. The little babydoll nightie was already translucent, but now it sticks to her in transparent spots that make me want to seal my mouth over them and suck every bit of moisture from her flesh.

If I open my eyes, I won't be able to look away.

Fuck, even with them closed, she's seared on my vision. Every dark spreading stain of water branded on my mind's eye.

The splash over her left breast, molding over the upper curve in that plush, perfect swell leading in toward her nipple. The soaked spot against her stomach, just below her navel, sealing fabric to her skin and drawing my eyes to the temptation of her panties, swooping low beneath the subtle curve of her belly and leading down to the lush flesh making a warm, inviting mound against creased fabric.

What would that pussy be like under my tongue?

Would it burn right down with her clit in my teeth?

Would it come real sweet, even sweeter than she moans?

"Riker?" I hadn't heard her footsteps, but her voice sounds closer, almost to the bed. "Here. So you can – *oh!*"

My eyes snap open at that cry.

Just in time to watch her come crashing down onto the bed.

Fuck. Her ankle, it must've –

Everything in my brain cuts off, short circuiting, as the wet towel slaps down coldly in the center of my chest...followed by a much, much warmer body, tumbling down on top of me.

Instinctively, I catch her arms to steady her, before I freeze, my entire body locking up with painfully intense awareness of *hers*.

It's not Liv's ankle at all. It's not a mistake, a misstep.

I couldn't mistake what's happening now for my life.

Her tits are soft wells of heat pushing against my ribs, nipples hardened, wrapped in silk and stroking in twin points of fire over my skin. Her stomach rests over my hips, yielding to the growing, hardening rise of my cock, her slim, soft thighs anchored along my legs.

She pushes herself up with a stammered apology.

Then she freezes as the position makes her legs slip to either side of my hips. I'm not wearing much, just a pair of loose, thin cotton pajama pants, and she's wearing even less...and suddenly it feels like pure skin-on-skin when her panties drag against the painful hardness of my cock.

It's like tissue paper on fire, and yet no fire could ever be this *wet*.

She's been so quiet, so subtle, I hadn't even realized until she's straddling me, pressing down, and soaking into the fabric separating us until we're slicked together and I have to hold my breath against the thick, sweet scent of her – or else I'll turn into a complete fucking animal.

More of a beast than I already am, I should say.

She's breathing slow, but shallow. Like she's having to control every one, holding perfectly still, her hands braced against my stomach.

Neither of us move as the towel slides slowly off my

chest and crumples to the sheets against my arm. I can't tear my gaze from her, and her eyes are locked on mine, seeming to beg me for something, a silent shivering plea building in the trembling tension between us.

I realize I'm still holding her arms, trapping her on me, and loosen my grip.

"Sorry," I force out, throat dry.

But before I can fully pull my hands away, she curls her hands against my forearms, just below the elbow, brutally insistent.

"Don't be, Riker." Soft, breathy, and trailing into a hitching, agonizingly erotic sigh of my name as she shifts tentatively against me and her panties make a soft, damply rasping sound as warmth slides over me enticingly, through me. "Riker, please."

Fuck. No one's said my name that way in years.

No one ever *should* say my name that way, when I'm so pent up I could explode and this snarling, furious creature inside me that wanted to protect Liv is now throbbing with the need to *possess* her.

I can't breathe. Can't speak. Can't think.

It's all I can do to hold still when my cock strains toward her, pulsing between us, and if I move, I'm going to do something we both might regret.

When she looks at me with such gentleness in her gaze, despite how *young* she is, somehow I feel as though she's the wiser one.

The one who knows what she wants, and who knows what I'm thinking, what I'm struggling with, without me having to say a single word.

It's in her smile, in the way she leans, in the way her

voice softens and warms with quiet, coaxing understanding.

"It's okay," she says. "Whatever this is, I feel it, too." She smiles faintly. "God, right now it's the only thing I can *stand* to feel. Everything's so wrong with all of this. My sister, my Dad, these people trying to kill us. Make me forget. Even if it's just for a few amazing hours..."

When she reaches out, I grab her wrist, fisting it. Her eyes widen and another lightning strike coils through me.

Wrong is the biggest understatement on earth for all this. Damn if it means I'm going to be able to stop, what's taking on a life of its own as I search her near naked body. "Liv..."

She doesn't care how strained her name sounds on my lips. She just smiles.

Little minx. Must know this is nothing but a one-way express ticket to hell, but fuck if the ride isn't worth it for one night.

My grip loosens.

Her fingers trail up my chest, stroking, seeming to awaken every dormant nerve ending she touches. Then there's just a stark awareness of her skin, of mine, of everywhere we come in contact.

She bows over me, her hair tumbling down over her shoulders to curtain us both, trapping us in our own secret darkness. Her delicate fingers find my throat, then stroke up through my beard, into my hair, making me quake with a groan.

She presses her lips to my jaw, and leaves sensations like droplets of burning rain melting into my skin as she trails kisses up toward the corner of my mouth.

"You're the only thing that feels right," she whispers. "Is it so wrong to ask you to feel right with me?"

It's completely fucking wrong, and she knows it, but damn if I can even hope to remember why. "Liv..."

"Please." Shyly, she kisses the very edge of my mouth, a flirt and a promise and a tease that only makes me crave the real thing. "It doesn't have to be real. It just has to be right now. Can't we have one thing that feels good?"

It doesn't have to be real.

I don't know how to tell this beguiling little slip of a girl that for me, it's already real.

That every time I've tried to push her to the edge of my world, it's not her I've been fighting.

It's myself. The instant, insane *pull* I felt the moment I saw her face looking up from that dossier photo and knew that Olivia Holly was someone I needed to protect with all my heart and soul.

If I thought this could hurt her, there's no way I could ever give in. But when I realize how much she needs this – a kind touch, a moment of comfort, a night to forget, to lose herself in passion and fire – and that the only one who'll end up hurting is me...

"Liv. Fuck."

I curl my hands against her hip then and tumble her back, rolling over to spill her to the bed half-against me, beneath me, our legs tangled and her curves fitting perfectly against my edges.

She makes a startled sound that trails into a shivering gasp as I curl my hand against her hip and stroke over the sheer fabric turning smooth skin into silk, my thumb dipping in to trace the line of her panties along the crease where her thigh meets her hip.

Her lashes lower in a demure sweep, her eyes averting as she starts to reach for me, then stops, pulling back and curling her hands against her chest, her lips parted on words that don't come.

She's so sheltered. So *new*. And I realize, from those shy, hesitant reactions, so virgin.

"Sweetheart. Have you ever –"

That actually prompts a laugh, and her blush is the most enticing thing I've ever seen. "Am I that obvious?" She tucks a skein of her hair behind her ear. "No, I've never. But I want to. With you." The look she gives me is the kind that could shatter a man. "I trust you to make me feel safe, Riker Woods."

That's one-part terrifying – but also exhilarating. Entirely arousing.

It's not her youth or her purity that turns my blood hot. It's the faith she has that I won't hurt her or turn her first time into a bad memory. It's knowing I can rock her world, shake the dirt off it, make it shine and burn and come undone until it's as beautiful as the rest of her.

I have to fuck this girl.

It's the choice she's making to trust me that seals it, when I'm not even sure I trust myself.

"Liv, yeah," I snarl her name, capture her mouth, tasting her gently and savoring how delicately she opens for me.

It's a kiss made for flirting, teasing, brushing flesh, dipping tongues, testing and exploring and slowly slipping deeper and deeper. Her moan spills in my mouth like warm molasses.

With every moment that passes, she melts beneath me,

until we're sinking into the bed together in a tangle of quickening heat.

I crave her so much, every damn swipe of my fingers on her body, but I make myself hold back, keeping my hands against her back and hip, holding her close, until the moment when I bite at her lip just to test her reaction.

Then she arches against me with a full-body moan, pressing close and trembling, her nipples peaked hard against her nightgown and pressed against my chest.

Carefully, I slip my hand up over her waist, stroking her warmth, caressing her shape, until I can curl my fingers against her round tit. Her flesh is so soft it spills over my fingers, heavy in my palm, its weight making my cock throb.

But it's nothing compared to the sound she makes when I flick my teasing thumb against her nipple.

Liv stiffens, a soft, breathy cry escaping, her hands clutching at my forearms.

I can't help drinking in every tiny reaction, watching her eyes go darker, softer, hazier as I circle her nub with my thumb, kneading her flesh against my palm, feeling every hitching shudder that goes through her as her cheeks flush hotter.

"Any time it's too much, sweetheart," I whisper, "any time you need it slower, you say."

She licks her kiss-swollen, beautifully red mouth and nods, her chest heaving with shallow, audible breaths that turn ragged every time I flick the hardened peak of her nipple again. I can't believe this gorgeous, fey thing wants me. Wants to be owned by someone older and broken and battered like me, scarred inside and out.

If I'm her choice, I'll make damn sure she doesn't regret it.

I steal another soft kiss, a promise to her. Then I slide down her body, savoring her sleekness sliding against me, and take my first taste of her.

First through the sheer fabric of her nightgown – closing my mouth over the nipple I've teased and tormented to sensitivity, wetting the fabric and taking deep, hot pleasure in the feeling of the hard little bud rolling against my tongue.

She sucks in a startled gasp, her fingers hot on my shoulders, gripping and kneading, but she doesn't stop me. She only writhes as I tease and torment her, making these delicious little heated sounds in the back of her throat, like she's trying to hold back but just can't help herself.

I want – no, *need* – more of those sounds. Need to see her undone.

Can't stop from dragging that flimsy, sheer little nightie over her head and baring her naked flesh to my lips, my touch.

She's delicate, yet lush.

Tiny, yet made entirely of flowing curves, her thighs supple and soft, the subtle swell of her belly calling below the narrow dip of her waist, her tits full and heavy and pale, moving like liquid against my gripping palms and tipped in cherry pink as sweet as her lips.

This time, when I take one in my mouth, it's pure skin against my tongue, rough and luscious and making my mouth water with pure greed. I'm ready to devour her.

Every time I suckle harder at her nipple, she gasps, arching, raking her nails over my shoulders and driving me to do it again and again. She makes me frenzied with the way she moves under me, her body like silk against mine.

I can't stop tasting her, nibbling her, like I'm trying to relish her down to the very last bite, and suddenly I want to taste more than just skin. I want to taste that alluring, tart-creamy scent drenching the air, rising off her flesh.

One bite at a time, I taste my way down her body, leaving gentle marks that nonetheless vent the sense of possession inside me, animalistic and hungry.

Her panties are as sheer as everything else she wears. The teasing hint of her pussy that's visible just past the silk arouses me even more, my cock straining and wild and aching against my pajama pants.

But this isn't about me right now. It's about her.

About making sure she doesn't regret this, doing everything I can to make her feel beautiful, sensual, completely overcome. I want to ruin her sweetness so hard she's too numb for a single self-conscious thought.

She makes a low, protesting sound as I hook my thumbs in her panties and draw them down her thighs. Her hands fall to cover herself, cupping over the warm, sweet place between her thighs, and I can't help but smile as I toss her panties aside.

I kiss her quivering inner thigh, then bite down lightly.

Just enough to feel her flesh yield against my teeth. Just enough to make her jerk, one of her hands flying to her parted lips.

"You nervous?" I ask.

She swallows hard, her eyes wide, and nods. "Well, I'm *naked*..."

"And beautiful." I shift, propping myself up on one

elbow, then catch the waist of my pajama pants and pull them down so I can kick them off. "We're even. Now I'm naked, too."

Liv immediately slams her eyes shut. "Riker!"

Laughing softly, I nuzzle at her stomach, just below her navel. "You've never seen a naked man before? I don't believe that. Not unless you've never been on the internet."

"That's different!" she squeaks, but there's a subtle undercurrent of laughter in her voice. "It's not...it's not you."

"So I'm special somehow?"

She bites her lip. "You know you are."

Fuck. My dick jerks, pounds pure madness, overcome with raw want.

"Then show me, sweetheart." I push myself up over her, kneeling between her thighs. "Open your eyes and look at me."

Shyly, she peeks one eye open, then the other. It'd be funny if I weren't so ready to fuck her.

The flush in her cheeks deepens as she just *looks* at me, and the way her gaze drifts over me is like the touch of soft fingers against my skin, until I can feel it in sharp jolts all down my body.

Her eyes dilate, her tongue catching between her teeth, as she traces over my chest, down my stomach, my hips...my cock, resting against my stomach, harder than it's ever been in my life.

She reaches out, starting to touch my chest, then pulls back – but I catch her hand and gently press her palm flat to my chest.

"Do it," I whisper. "It's okay to touch me."

Tentatively, she lays her fingers on my chest, stroking me like I'm a great animal whose pelt needs to be tamed. Then lower, and my gut tightens as she trails her fingers in slow, exploring swirls over my stomach, my hips.

Lower, lower...until her fingertips graze along the length of my cock, and I have to grit my teeth, closing my eyes and fighting to hold back the growl in my throat as my hips jerk forward.

Never has such a gentle touch felt so good, like she's melting me everywhere she touches, and I clench my fists against my thighs and fight to hold still and let her explore.

Every time she strokes over the length of my cock, it jerks against her hand, swelling thicker, throbbing harder, until the pulse of blood throughout takes over my senses.

If she doesn't fucking stop, I'm going to snap.

Especially when she wraps her full hand around it, enveloping me in a tight grip of body heat, and I exhale a rough gasp, dropping my hand to catch her wrist and opening my eyes.

"Slow down, sweetheart," I rasp. "You don't want me losing it just yet."

She looks half guilty, half completely lost, as if she'd been so entirely absorbed in what she was doing – but she's still got that hand covering herself. "Sorry," she whispers.

"Don't apologize." I lean down over her, brushing my lips across hers. "It feels good when you touch me. I want you to like it, and I want you to enjoy being touched in return." I ghost my hand over the back of her palm, gently nudging. "Let me. Hands off, Liv."

She falters for just a moment, then looks away, that

pretty pink blush returning as she slowly slips her hand to one side and lets me see her: all soft flesh and smooth skin, glistening damp. I run my fingertip along the very outer edge of her folds, and she rolls into my touch, her eyes sinking closed on a startled moan.

Smiling, baring my teeth, I do it again.

She barely gasps out a *yes* before she stops speaking entirely, whimpering as I trace my fingertips up and down, again and again, slipping ever deeper each time until wet, hot flesh wraps around my finger and sucks me into warm, gripping lips.

It's fascinating, tempting, maddeningly arousing to learn her by touch.

How her pink pussy layers in its wetness, how she bucks and lifts her hips whenever I trace every soft slick curve, the way she throws her head back when I find her clit and gently circle it with my thumb, making her arch and shudder and moan.

I've got her on the end of a thinly-held tether.

I'm barely holding myself on my own leash.

Every cry, every tortured expression of confused, straining bliss, every scratch of her nails as she claws at the sheets just pushes this need inside me into a desperate craving. A demand.

Every inch of my body needs to know how she feels writhing and thrusting under me, convulsing and tightening, wet and slick and gripping hot against my cock. But I won't ruin this for her.

I'm not pushing her too fast, no matter how much it hurts to control myself. And when I lightly dip two fingers inside her, testing. And the moment she locks up with a frightened little whimper, I pull back.

"You okay?" I ask, reaching up to smooth her hair back from her sweat-dewed brow.

She nods a bit sheepishly. "Yeah. I just...you startled me."

"You'll be tight your first time." I curl my hand against her inner thigh, resting close, reassuring. "It helps to warm you up a little with my fingers." I grin wickedly. "Or my tongue."

Her eyes widen. "Your tongue?!"

"Let me show you."

Her questioning sound trails into a tortured moan as I slide down her body and part her thighs, taking my first taste of her. She's scalding hot on my tongue, yet so sweet I can hardly stand it, the lusciousness of her flesh yielding against the slow, probing licks and strokes of my tongue is more than I ever could have asked for.

But even better is her reaction – going wild against me, clutching her fingers in my hair, gasping "Riker, *Riker!*" as her thighs grip at my shoulders and her hips undulate and squirm and every part of her clenches and clutches and tenses real sweet.

I torment her with flicks against her clit, then lick her clean as every bit of stimulation makes her soaked, drenching her skin with more of that perfect-smelling wetness. And when I dip my tongue inside her, searching deep...

Fuck me.

She loses control, gasping out hoarse, husky, needful cries, wrapping her legs around my shoulders, painting my lips with her wetness as her body arches and thrashes in gorgeous chaos.

I stop, resting on my elbows to just watch her as she

slowly comes down. Her eyes slip open, staring dazed at the ceiling. "Oh," she whispers breathily. "I'm sorry."

I can't help laughing warmly. Of course.

Of course Liv would apologize for that. Turning my head, I nuzzle her inner thigh, deliberately dragging my beard against her sensitive flesh just to feel her shudder. "You've got nothing to apologize for, love."

She bites her lip. "But I was trying not to..."

"I wanted you to come." I press a kiss to the inside of her knee. "It helps. You'll be more sensitive so it'll feel better. Plus, it's hot as fuck when you go off, little rocket."

She smiles, batting her eyes a couple times. "So...it's going to hurt?"

I push myself up to hover over her, fitting our bodies together gently – letting her feel me, the weight of me, my cock resting against her thigh and her belly. Leaning down, I kiss her, tasting her uncertainty, trying to soothe it with soft touches.

"It's natural for it to hurt the first time, but everyone's different, and it might not hurt at all. I'll be gentle, sweetheart."

"Okay." She sighs and slips her arms around me, twining her fingers against my nape and offering me the most lovely smile. "I trust you, Riker. I always do."

Fuck. She knows how to break me with the simplest things.

Here I am, trying to rein myself in because I want to cherish her, treasure her, make this just right for her, and she's tearing me apart with these simple words. I capture one of her little hands and press my lips to her palm, then settle her fingers against my shoulder once more.

"Hold onto me," I breathe, "and remember you can stop me any time."

Liv nods, watching me with those wide, trusting eyes, her fingers curling a bit tighter against my neck and back. I catch the underside of her knee, stroking down the satiny sheen of her thigh and then up again as I spread her open, lifting her up just enough to open her sweet cunt for me.

The slightest nudge of my hips and the tip of my cock presses to her entrance.

Damn. She's so hot, so wet, so everything, I almost lose control right then.

She keens softly in the back of her throat and shifts against me, her nails biting into my skin. There's a trembling moment when I can't move. When I'm completely overwhelmed by her, before my body takes over and I just can't resist.

I try to go slow. I try to be gentle, but the moment I feel her parting around me and that heat enveloping me, I come close to losing my senses.

Clenching my teeth, straining with everything in me, I ease in slowly, letting her get used to me, but she's clenching tight and shaking underneath me and raking her nails down my back, and every point of sensation is scoring through me and branding her on me body and soul until I'll never forget her in this moment.

Liv is more than magic. She's fucking intoxicating, and I'm drunk on her, drugged on her, completely consumed as I sink into the depths of her body.

She's making soft, whimpering sounds in the back of her throat, turning into a low cry as I seat myself fully inside her.

"Shh," I soothe, cupping her cheek, kissing her trembling lips. "Relax for me, sweetheart."

She makes sounds that aren't quite words, but then kisses me so sweetly, and slowly her body relaxes around me, accepting me, welcoming me deep into her body.

When I move, it's like gliding through pure silk, stroking in and out of her slowly, relishing every fold and plush wave of flesh rolling and caressing around me, licking at my cock until I throb inside and out.

"Fuck, Liv," I growl, finding my rhythm, beginning to pound her into the mattress.

Her arms fold tighter around my neck. I fuck her good and deep, loving how she whines, how her brows crinkle, how her eyes start to roll under their lids in pure rapture.

This is how I claim this sweet, young thing.

Even if it destroys me.

My balls churn, all fire and dark, possessive need. There's a crazed, magnum-hot vision where I bury myself deep and shoot off in her cunt. Where my seed sinks deep, finds its mark, and binds her to me forever.

Fuck, I can't let that happen. Even if every irrational, animal thing in my flesh wants a fuck that will end both our worlds. Even if some snarling, psycho thing inside me wants to breed her tender pussy.

When she starts to move with me...that's when I break. When she rises up to meet me, finding a perfect tempo, until it's not me and not her but just *us*, together – that's what destroys me.

That's what makes me lose control, until I fall into her, fall into fire, fall into the perfect wonder of pleasure and emotion and pure, maniacal need.

I fucking need her.

I need her more than I can even comprehend, and it takes me over so completely, I couldn't stop myself from coming if I tried.

"Liv!" She's a roar in my throat as I bury myself to the hilt, her pussy tenses around me, and I'm gone. In the zone. Combusting.

She's there with me, legs around my waist, lips feverish over mine, and I taste my name on her lips.

"Riker!"

One word turns my spine electric, bathes my brain in fire, and my whole fucking body comes unscrewed. I just bury myself in her with a growl, sinking my teeth into her bottom lip, coming so hard it's bruising.

We both go crashing over the ledge to bottomless ecstasy.

We fall to pieces together.

* * *

I DON'T EVEN REMEMBER FALLING asleep.

We've worn each other out fairly well by the time the night takes on the stillness that comes before dawn, and I suppose I must've dozed off after spending myself for the...hell, I've lost count how many times she's gotten me off.

I couldn't tell you how many times I've left her dizzy with every gasping, needy, convulsion. How many times I've ransacked her sweetness, and taken her cherry for life.

We barely stopped our fuck fest to grab something to drink, and to have a quick conversation about her birth control before falling into bed again, chasing each other through climax after climax, again and again.

She's that amazing.

And as the first trilling calls of birds pull me drowsily from sleep to study Liv's gently snoozing face, I wonder how I'll ever let her go when this assignment is done.

Is it wrong to hope she doesn't want me to?

There's something about this woman. Something strange and terrible and magic, and it's woken something inside me I thought was dead, but that I know now was only sleeping.

Just waiting for me to give it enough light and warmth to wake the hell up. My own personal monster.

Because if I were a good man, I'd feel shame right now. Guilt.

I don't, and I don't know how I could ever call this feeling inside me bad when it feels so right, so clean, so pure.

None of which changes the fact that she's a client, her life's in danger, and she's quickly becoming my daughter's best friend.

Never let it be said that I ever take the easy path.

I brush her hair back behind her ear. I don't mean to wake her.

I just can't resist the softness of her skin, the relaxed bliss on her face. But she stirs drowsily, I guess she wasn't as deep asleep as I thought. With a catlike little yawn, she scrunches her eyes up, then opens them, blinking up at me slowly.

She says nothing at first. When her eyes clear, it's with a frank and stark awareness of the position we're in: bodies tangled so close, naked skin on skin, addictively entwined and holding each other close beneath the light layer of a summer duvet.

She ducks down a little, peeking at me with a shy yet pleased smile. An infectious one I'm a sucker for but return. "Hey, sweetheart."

"Hey yourself," she whispers back.

"You okay?"

"Ah?" She blinks, looking confused. "Why wouldn't I be?"

"You know why." I don't say it. Fuck, I don't even know how I'm more flustered about this than her. "I was your first. That's gotta mean something. Heavy shit."

She brightens. "Oh, that!"

I almost laugh. Next thing I know, I'm hugging a bundle of lovely young woman as she nearly throws herself against me, wrapping her arms around my neck and burying her face in my chest.

"It wasn't uncomfortable at all. It was really nice. Really, *really* freaking nice." She angles her head enough for one coy blue eye to catch mine. "Nice enough that I wouldn't mind doing it a whole lot more."

"Brat," I growl, jostling her gently. "Aren't you sore yet?"

"Isn't being sore part of the *fun?*"

This time, I do laugh. "Irreverent little monster. Get some sleep. We've got all day to sleep in if we want."

"Mmhm." She snuggles into me, yawning again, and we both close our eyes, but I open mine again as she asks, "Riker?"

"Yeah?"

"Maybe when we're back in San Francisco...could we go on a date?"

"A date." I arch a brow. "A real one?"

She nods quickly. "No, pretend. Of course a real date!"

"A date," I echo. "Me and you."

My brain needs a few seconds to compute what the fuck is happening.

Her playfulness slips away, leaving a quiet, wistful sincerity as she looks up with solemn eyes. "I'm asking if you want me and you, period."

That's a hell of a question.

One I can't just answer, rolling off my tongue like it's nothing. This could be a temporary thing, just making the best of a bad situation. We have a little fun, then part ways when it's over and hope Landon never finds out or he'll kick my ass up and down the entire western seaboard.

Or, I could admit to myself the earnest, open hope in her eyes speaks to something inside me. That terrible, magic thing that's been starved so long for something *more*.

"I think I do," I answer slowly, carefully. "But I need to think about it, Liv. I don't just make decisions for myself anymore. You understand that, don't you?"

"I do." With a gentle smile, she pushes herself up and kisses me gently. "I promise I do."

Somehow, that quiet acceptance makes my gut sink.

Everything I know about Liv says she's always been raised to put others above herself, and even now she's doing it again. And while I do need her understanding, need her to respect that it's not so easy for me with a daughter to think of...it bothers me knowing Liv would put herself aside, anything she wants and feels, to do what she thinks is right by me and Em.

Sure, it's part of what makes her amazing. Still doesn't mean it's right to just discard her feelings, her desires, as if they never mattered at all.

The better this gets, the more fucked up it is, too.

I feel like I've just complicated her life more, instead of making it better.

But I can find a way to make this work. I know I can.

To balance these lives, to give everyone the attention and care they deserve, and to treat Liv as if she's worth being *first* in someone's life, in mine, without neglecting or sacrificing my daughter.

So I offer her a smile.

"Then it's a deal. Soon as I'm sure you're safe, back in San Francisco..." I steal another kiss, savoring the liquid-soft warmth of her lips, before promising, "We'll go on that date."

XI: A LITTLE DATE (OLIVIA)

I don't think Riker actually knows what a date really is.

And I might almost be offended, if I wasn't having so much fun.

Riker wouldn't tell me what he had planned for our time out. Not for the rest of the weekend at Milah's, and not for the entirely weird, surreal drive back home in an actual armored truck convoy with every member of Enguard armed to the teeth, geared up in flak jackets, and on constant alert.

That night, when Riker told me he'd found the perfect place where he was absolutely certain he could keep me safe, I didn't know what he meant. And that man keeps secrets like a vault – just a long, knowing look and an enigmatic smile and not a word.

Even on the drive here today, when I was poking his arm and pinching his sleeve, he was dressed for a date.

A crisp, expensive pinstriped linen button-down and these slacks that do things to his angular hips that make me bite my lip. He just grinned like the cat that got the cream, telling me to be patient and stop being a brat, I'd know soon enough.

If any other man called me a brat, I'd be hurt or angry.

But Riker...Riker says it with a sweetness that says he knows damn well I'm poking him for attention, and he's okay with it. Because he knows it's just us being playful and warm, and there's nothing bratty about wanting to tease the man you like.

Like?

Is that all this is, just *like*?

I'm still wondering that when Riker pulls up outside a long, flat concrete building, nondescript gray with a fenced-in field beyond, divided into lanes and with...targets on the far end?

I blink, tilting my head, peering at the sign over the glass double doors before sucking in a breath.

"A firing range?" I ask, staring at him wide-eyed.

"A firing range," he says. "I teach here on weekends sometimes, and do firearms certifications. Since you're so interested in learning to take care of yourself, I thought you should learn how to handle a gun."

I bounce in my seat, clapping my hands together. "You mean I get a gun of my own? I like the one James has. It's really sleek and stylish."

"Uh." Riker actually recoils, staring at me, his eyes wide. "Hell no."

"Why not?"

"Because you like the sound of it too much!" he splutters, half-laughing, yet his eyes are almost horrified. "Look at you, woman. Your eyes are practically glowing. Had no idea you were such a violent little beast, Liv."

"I'm not violent! I just don't like being defenseless!" And if I'm being honest, being able to do something so serious for myself like learn to shoot excites me to no end. I cross my arms over my chest and stick my tongue out at him. "Look, if someone shoots at me, I want to be able to shoot back."

I'm practically vibrating, but he stills me with a single touch, his fingers clasping my chin gently and holding me in place. He looks down with that combined sternness and warmth that makes me want to melt for him and go completely belly-up submissive, weak to his every touch.

"The first goal when someone's shooting at you," he says, "isn't to shoot back. It's to get the fuck out of the line of fire and to safety as quick as possible." His thumb traces my lower lip, tingling my skin. "You deserve a chance to defend yourself if you need to. Let's be clear. I'm not training you to be a vigilante assassin."

I lean into him, smiling slyly, and flick my tongue out against his thumb, tasting the masculine salt of his skin. "I'd make a really cute vigilante assassin, though."

Heat kindles in his eyes, and his gaze dips down.

Right over the filmy, breezy, little babydoll dress I'd picked out when I'd thought we were going to dinner or a park or some other typical date night thing.

I can feel his eyes touching me, everywhere the dress clings, where my breasts rise against the lace edging the somewhat modest bodice, and where the hem rides up my bare thighs.

He's raspy and heavy when he murmurs, "Don't know where you'd hide a gun in there. But I'd find it, sweets."

Holy hell. When he looks at me like that, my body burns, and I want to climb right in his lap.

I unbuckle my seatbelt, just so I can reach to brush my lips across his. "I could give you a few hints."

But Riker doesn't need me to give him any ideas.

Not the moment our lips touch and he takes my mouth with a growl, kissing me deep and rough, the hard, plunging rhythm echoing throughout my entire sore, throbbing body with the memory of what he does to me at night.

I've never known I could feel this way. This glowing, sated fullness. Like every part of me has come alive and I burn with this wonderful pulse centered between my thighs as his kiss leaves my mouth hot and swollen and wet.

He draws back only when we're both panting, his fingers tangling a rough handful of my hair, his beard tickling my mouth as we rest brow to brow.

"Fuck, the things you do to me," he rumbles.

"Good things?" I whisper, curling my hand against his chest. His heat bakes through the shirt, and I can't help fingering the top button, the hint of thick, dark ink peeking past.

"Very bad things." His fingers slip down, tracing my shoulder, coaxing sweet shivers in his wake. "Absolutely filthy things. Things I can't do to you in the parking lot of a gun range without us getting arrested."

"Then..." I lean into him a bit more, molding my body to his just because I love the way his eyes darken when I tease him, and they're nearly black as I brush my mouth across his. "Maybe you should hurry up and teach me how to handle your gun so we can get home."

Before he can take hold of me again, I unlatch the car door and slide out, dancing out of his reach and tossing a grin over my shoulder as he growls after me in warning, in amusement, in desire.

He plays at being so gruff, but really he's so complex and subtle and nuanced. What seems like nothing on the surface can convey so many things with this man.

I love that he's starting to let me see more layers, starting to let me understand him.

And I love that he cares enough about me striking out to find my independence to *help* me with that.

I want to stand on my own two feet. But there's nothing wrong with some training wheels while I figure out how not to fall on my face, and Riker's more than just training wheels.

He's everything, in ways I don't know how to define.

Plus?

This is going to be *so* great for my book.

He takes the lead as he steps inside the main building, and he spends a little time chatting with the man behind the counter, a guy named Brandon who Riker obviously has history with. It's good to see him with people he's friendly with in an environment he's comfortable in.

Him and Brandon clasp hands, speaking with familiarity, chuckling as they talk over next month's class schedule and certification tests. Then Riker gestures to me, beckoning me forward and directing Brandon's attention toward me.

"Brandon, this is Liv," he says, and only hesitates a half-second before finishing, "my fiancée."

Brandon's eyes bug out.

He's older than Riker by about a decade, yet he's fresh-faced and friendly with bright, warm blue eyes. Those eyes grow even brighter as he blinks at me, then grins.

"It's sure nice to meet you," he says, taking my outstretched hand and shaking firmly. He's got a bit of a southern drawl, kind of like Enguard's resident giant, Gabe. "You getting on with Em?"

I'm surprised by the bluntness of the question. For a moment, I blink, faltering, before catching myself.

"Uh, I think you'd probably better ask her that," I say, offering a rueful smile. "I love her to death, but she's the only one who can tell you if she likes me. I just think she's amazing."

Brandon arches a brow, glancing at Riker with a knowing smile. "Damn, man. You really know how to find the smart chicks. But I didn't even know you were dating anyone! Where you been hiding her?"

A chill runs up my spine. A question more literal than Brandon even knows.

Riker's looking at me strangely, though. Not bothered by it. More like he's seeing me for the first time.

I can't quite read that look before he's all easy warmth again as he lightly socks Brandon's shoulder. "We kept things secret for a while. That's all. Until we were sure we were serious enough to tell Em. Didn't want to disrupt things for her too much."

"Makes sense, makes sense," Brandon says. "So when's the wedding?"

We both freeze. I nearly choke.

Riker and I exchange stiff, wide-eyed looks that basically say *oh crap* without saying a word. We're so stupid. So oblivious.

How could we have planned out this whole cover story and not covered details like that?

Well...let's be real.

We never expected this to be anything but me holed up in a room in Riker's house. Never thought we'd have to explain anything to anyone besides a few nosy neighbors.

Riker's as quick in his thinking as he is on his feet, though, and he recovers with a self-deprecating chuckle. "Haven't decided on a date yet. I'm still trying to find her the perfect engagement ring, and then we'll talk about planning the perfect wedding."

"Don't sleep on that too long, man." Brandon claps Riker's shoulder companionably, accepting the explanation easily, and I let out the breath currently making my lungs tight as a vise. "You don't hold onto a girl like that with everything in you, she'll slip away. C'mon, Liv. I'll get you set up with the right safety gear, and then old Riker can give you your walkthrough."

Slip away, huh?

It makes me wonder.

Even if we both said this could be more...how *real* is it, when we still have to lie like this to people every day?

But I keep my thoughts to myself as Brandon leads us into the back where there's an indoor range with walled off booths and paper targets with human silhouettes printed on them.

It's exciting when I'm fitted with a little pair of clear glasses and a pair of noise-canceling headphones. There's a smell in the air, sharp and burning and dry, that I think I recognize as gunpowder.

Shots go off in the lanes to either side of us, rhythmic and confident.

Brandon tells me I need the gear because gunshots don't sound the way they do on TV. Up close they can deafen you, and even do serious damage to your hearing over time – and if you're really trying to aim, you're going to be holding the gun up close instead of flailing it around at the end of your arm like actors who've never handled a real gun in their lives.

"Watch out for the recoil," he says with an almost sly grin as he turns to leave. I look after him in puzzlement.

"Recoil?"

"You'll see," Riker says. "I'll make sure you won't fall, but you'll likely be sore once we're done."

I arch a brow at him. "You do remember we're in a public place when you say things like that, right?"

Riker just grins – quick and unexpected. So feral and wolfish it sends chills right through me, then the most delicious feeling in the pit of my stomach. I keep discovering new sides to him, peeling away all these layers of protection to find the man underneath, and if I'm not careful...it'll happen.

I'm going to fall in love.

He distracts me with a warm hand on the small of my back, guiding me to look over several guns laid out on the shelf in front of us with a view beyond, out over the gallery.

I have no idea what I'm looking at, only that all the guns look a little different.

He points to each one in turn. "Glock 19. Ruger SR9. Sig P226. Beretta 92FS. What these all have in common is, they're all nine millimeters. You know what that means?"

"Um...no idea, really."

"That's the size of the bullet. There're different standards for measuring bullet caliber, but we'll stick with nine millimeters because they're the most common and popular right now. Most military and police handguns use nine millimeter bullets, and most self-defense and street weapons do, too."

I tilt my head back, looking up at him. He's wearing safety glasses, too, and we both have our noise-canceling headphones around our necks. "So everyone who makes guns makes them for the same bullet size?"

"Yes. You're not going to win any customers by locking them into your proprietary ammo. They need versatility, choice, and easy access. Now, which one do you want to try first?"

"That one!" I say, pointing at a sleeker, smaller one in silver and black. The others are all these long, intimidating black things that are all barrel, but this one's more hilt and just looks more compact and tidy.

Riker gives me a penetrating look. "Why that one?"

"Well...I recognize it. It looks just like James'. And I think..." I twine my fingers together, biting my lip. I don't want to give a stupid answer but I'm trying to be practical. "It's smaller than the others, isn't it? I have smaller hands. I want to be able to keep a good grip on it when it fires, right? Or I could endanger myself or someone else. It'll be easier to hold a smaller gun."

Riker's slow smile warms with approval. "Good answer."

He picks up the gun I chose and turns it over, showing it to me. "This is the Ruger. It's very lightweight, with a semiautomatic firing function. Means it's a good civilian gun because you have two safeties to deal with before you can fire, instead of just one. Harder to have a mishap that way."

Then he does something to the hilt, and I gasp as the entire inside of it slides out.

"Oh!"

"Here's the clip," he says, and turns it so I can see the bullet resting in the very top. "It's also called a magazine. Rugers use a double-stacked type, so you can fit seventeen bullets in a single clip. If you run out of bullets, you just release the clip, slide it out, and lock a full one in." He shows me by pushing the clip back in until there's a *click*. "Clips can be reloaded with fresh bullets, but if you're in a situation where you need to fire seventeen bullets, you don't have time to refill a magazine. Better to have a spare."

A chill tightens my skin. "I don't want to be in a situation where I even have to fire one bullet. I just want to know what to do in case I have to."

"That's my girl." I don't expect him to ruffle my hair and kiss the top of my head the way he does, but it chases that chill away, leaving his soft, slow spreading warmth. "In an ideal world, guns would be nothing but deterrents. But since people will never be angels...let's teach you how to shoot. Here."

Then his arms are around me and I suck in a startled breath.

He's just *full* of surprises today. Because I also wasn't expecting to be wrapped up so suddenly in his strength and heat, pressing against my back, fully enveloping me.

I lean into him while he strokes his hands down my arms, leaving feather-fine trails of sensations, then clasps my hands and slowly fits the gun into them both.

I expect something heavy and metallic, but instead the handle feels like plastic or some other kind of resin, and it's surprisingly light. Gentle fingers guide me, showing me how to hold it in both hands, folding one hand over the other, then nudging my index forefinger on my right hand to rest outside the loop thing in front of the trigger.

Loop thing? The trigger guard? Even if I was sure, it's hard to remember words right now when his hot breaths wash through my hair, trickling down my skin to find the throbbing mark hidden under my hair. The same place where, last night, he'd held me down on my hands and knees and taken me like some kind of wild animal with his teeth buried against the nape of my neck.

"Keep it pointed away from us," he tells me, angling our joined grips away and down, toward the floor.

His voice is deep in my ear, and I'm all shivers everywhere, sweet hot points all over my body pricking and pulsing. "Get used to how it feels. The safety's on, so you can't fire. But you should make it a habit to keep your finger outside the trigger guard. Only touch the trigger when you're sure you're ready to fire."

I take a shaky breath and just tighten my grip, running my thumb over the back end of the gun, then the side. "There are a lot of little buttons and switches."

"You'll get used to where they are and what they do. The switches right above where your grip is seated on both sides are the manual safeties. They're on both sides in case you're a leftie, but you only have to release one. They keep it locked so you can't pull the trigger. You have to push up." He chuckles gently. "Don't push it up now, sweetheart. Your hands are shaking. Please don't accidentally shoot me in the foot."

"I won't!"

I might.

"I almost believe you." His fingers stroke over the backs of mine in electric caresses. "The button closer to the trigger is the mag release, so you can eject a clip and snap a new one in. The rubber knob on the very back tells you whether or not the gun's cocked with a round in the chamber. The extra lever in front of the trigger is the other safety, so it's harder to squeeze the trigger by accident. Next up, breathing. Short, simple breaths. Inhale before you aim, lungs nice and full. Find your target. Then exhale, natural and calm. You want your lungs near empty before you pull the trigger." He turns his head, beard dragging down my throat, and my knees nearly buckle. "Got it?"

"N-not really, but I'm willing to give it a try." I turn my head.

Like this, our lips are almost touching. It's like our breaths are kissing.

Maybe I shouldn't be thinking about this when I have a weapon capable of killing both of us clutched in a death grip in both hands. "Show me?"

"Yeah. You won't be able to hear me. Just follow my touch."

I don't quite get what he means until he pulls one hand away from mine and gently tugs my noise-canceling earmuffs up over my ears. Then all the sounds around me go muted behind a distant blanket of quiet.

He tugs his up, too. Even though I can't tell what he's saying, he's still talking, his voice a low, soothing rumble that tells me it'll be okay. *I can do this.*

He clasps my hands in his again and guides my arms up to take aim at the target. His fingers tease at mine, showing them how to move. How to push the safety up. How to fit my forefinger against the trigger. And then a slow, careful squeeze.

Crack!

It goes off deafeningly loud even through the earmuffs.

The gun flings me backward, force reverberating up my arm until it's shaking like a plucked guitar string.

I'd probably have fallen over, but instead I just rocket against Riker. His solid bulk catches me before I can shift more than an inch. Safe in his arms, my own still quivering, my hands feeling hot and tingly and weirdly numb, I stare at the hole punched in the black paper silhouette, my entire body crackling like a live wire.

"Holy crap," I gasp. "Holy shit! That was so cool. So cool! I was like Uhura with a phaser."

Riker gently takes the gun from my hand and sets it down, then tugs his earmuffs down around his neck before tugging mine down, too, looking down at me with an amused smile. "No clue what you just said, sweetheart, but I take it you enjoyed yourself."

"Yes!" I bounce on the balls of my feet. "I wasn't expecting it to throw me around like that."

"That's the recoil I was telling you about." He gently brushes my messy hair back. "A bullet can travel at over one thousand, seven hundred miles per hour. That's over two thousand, five hundred feet per second. The force it takes to push that shot forward that fast is going to push the other way, back at you, too."

"Newton's third law? For every action there's an equal and opposite reaction." When he lifts both brows, I grin. "Oh, c'mon. I'm sheltered, but I'm smart. I took physics."

"You are." He chuckles and tugs a strand of my hair. "You want to try on your own or are your hands too numb? The shock can take a little getting used to."

I probably sound way too eager when I gasp, "I want to try!"

"Let me show you how to aim." He picks up one of the other guns – the Glock, I think he called it – and shifts to take up a stance in front of the target, feet spread and braced confidently, arms raised level with his shoulder.

"You sight down your dominant arm. We're both right-handed, so sight down your right and angle your body accordingly. Using the trigger sight on the tip helps, but it's your arm that'll guide you true. The left arm helps brace and hold your aim steady." He lets go of the gun with one hand to pull the earmuffs up again, and nods toward me. "Ears up."

I tug mine up quickly, muffling the world again, but I still hear the sharp sound of the safety flicking off.

Then there's nine rounds firing, booming so fast I can barely hear a pause between one shot and the next.

Riker's green eyes flash like a tiger's, stone-steady and ice-cold as he fires with perfect precision. Every bullet rips through the paper right over the target's heart, making a cluster of holes that nearly shred it to pieces like someone punched a fist right through it.

Part of me can't help how it makes me burn, to see Riker looking so formidable, so self-assured, this lethal beast-man protector who's so strong and capable with such a dangerous weapon.

But the other part of me feels the sound of every gunshot shocking the pit of my stomach, and suddenly there's a man I don't know in front of me, his body exploding in red, his eyes blank and accusing as he collapses to the sidewalk at my feet and men with murder in their eyes aim their guns at me.

Cruel memory.

Gasping, I turn away from Riker and cover my ears. My heart beats wild, but cold and heavy, and I just want that awful sight to go away, to stop *ruining* my time with Riker.

But I still smell gunpowder and that makes me smell blood and I can't breathe. *I can't breathe.*

"—iv? *Liv.*"

I don't realize Riker's muffled voice calls my name until he's pulled my earmuffs off and he's wrapped around me again, pulling me against his chest and reminding me where I am, what's real. He was right – I couldn't be any safer than here.

Only *here* isn't the gun range.

It's in his arms.

I bury my face in his chest, huddling against him, trying to just even out my breaths. He holds me fiercely close, burying his face in my hair.

"What's wrong?" he asks raggedly. "Talk to me. You okay?"

"I will be." I curl up tight handfuls of his shirt, clinging, breathing in his scent and letting it chase away the smell of blood. "It's just, for a second, the gunshots...the smell...I was back *there*. Back in Seattle. When that man got killed."

"Oh, sweetheart. Shit, I'm sorry. I didn't even think –"

"It's okay!" I assure him quickly. "It is. I want this. I want to learn, and it's a really good idea. I just wasn't expecting I'd freakout, I'd –"

"Be human?" he finishes gently. "Trauma responses are normal, Liv. Especially when you aren't trained for something like this. Sometimes things will trigger you, and it's okay to need the people you care about to help you feel safe."

Is that your way of saying you really care about me? I wonder. I'm not brave enough to ask.

Instead, I rest my cheek over his beating heart and whisper, "How'd you get to be so good with guns?"

"Lifetime of use," he answers. "Sniper training, for one. Went through U.S. Army Sniper School and everything."

"You're military like Mr. Strauss and Mr. Barin?"

"Ex-military...and a generation before them." There's warmth in his voice, but also old pain, old bitterness, and as much as I hate that remembering hurts him, I'm grateful he's willing to show those things to me instead of locking them down.

"They're Afghanistan babies. I was deployed to Iraq the first time around." He stops then, and I think he won't say anything else until he continues, more quiet and strained, "Cover ops. Sniper missions, dark runs in Kuwait, you name it. Me and my team went in fast, went in dirty, got out." His voice breaks.

Subtle, but it's there. "We did our jobs. But we always left a mess behind for someone else to clean up. Broken worlds. Shattered lives. All fucked up."

I tilt my head back to look up at him. He's looking somewhere over my head.

His gaze is trained toward the target but I think he's seeing somewhere much farther away, maybe even somewhere that's gone now except in his mind. I reach up to brush my fingertips to his cheek, softly asking him to come back to now, to the real world, *to me.*

"You don't like remembering it, do you?" I ask.

"No." His eyes clear and focus, turning down to me,

and he catches my hand and presses a raspy kiss of stroking beard and softer lips to the center of my palm. "Don't like remembering what it made me."

"A kind man? A loving father? A dedicated, honorable protector?"

His eyes widen slightly. "Is that what you see?"

"You know I do, Riker. Who do *you* think you are?"

"Someone who used to be very dangerous," he says bitterly. "Who might *still* be very dangerous. Who might kill a man like it's nothing, if there's a damn good reason."

"Do you think Em sees you that way? Dangerous?"

He sets his jaw and looks away from me. "No. I've always shielded her."

"Then how could you be?"

He looks almost confused as his gaze jerks back, searching me as if looking for the answer to that question inside me, instead of inside himself. "I don't understand how you can have such faith in me."

I smile and stretch up on my toes to steal a chaste, sweet kiss, murmuring against his lips. "I don't understand how you can't."

"Liv." For all the harshness of his self-recriminating words, his mouth is gentle on mine. When he pulls back, he asks, "Are you feeling better?"

I nod and give him my best smile. "Yeah. I think I'm ready to try on my own." And it's true. I had my moment, but that just means more than ever I want to learn how to defend myself so no one can ever make me feel that powerless again. "I don't want to be afraid anymore, Riker."

"You don't have to be," he says as he picks up the Ruger

and presses it once more into my hand. "Not while you're mine."

* * *

I THINK I just might have an author in me after all.

I just needed a little inspiration – and Riker seems perfectly happy to give me *plenty* every night, so that every morning for the past couple of weeks, I wake up sore as hell.

Walking on air.

Ready to whip up breakfast before waving him and Em off to work and school so I can settle on the couch with my notebook and write. At this rate, I'll have this book completely drafted within a week, if I can just make up my mind on the ending.

I feel like I'm leaning toward that last-minute Hail Mary play for a bit of tension and then a happy ending, but I can't deny it's my own mood making me feel that way. I guess when I was miserable and sad I was more into the idea of tragic heroines, but with the tension gone between us, and me slipping into his bedroom every night after Em's asleep...the giddy, lovesick fool in me wants that 'love against all odds' ending, even if it might turn out a bit cheesy.

I mean, there are lots of people who like cheesy endings. Romance too perfect for this world. All that matters is if it makes them feel good, right?

I won't lie: I'm hoping for a happy ending that makes *me* feel good.

After all these weeks of playing house, pretend engaged, to the point where I'm even helping Riker pick out a long-promised Russian blue kitten for Em after a lot of hinting and outright pouting...

I want to play house for real.

More, I want to settle down into a life like this. No, not a life *like* this.

Just this.

This is the life I want.

It's perfect. So perfect, it feels like every day just squeezes my heart tighter, and I don't know how to let it go. Yet it might end up breaking. Scattering apart any day now.

Because the longer this stretches on, the more chance there is of Mr. Strauss at Enguard finding out we're doing more than practicing self-defense behind Riker's closed doors.

And I don't know what I'll do if I'm the reason Riker loses his job for unprofessional conduct.

He's too proud a man to ever let me help him in that case, or help financially.

Besides, Daddy's money feels too dirty.

But I already owe Riker so much. My little notepad is filled with pages of scribbled numbers, from grocery estimates to every last ice cream trip to the nice dinner he took me to last night at a secluded little oceanside seafood shack, intimate and soft-lit and far enough out of the way that there was little chance of anyone dangerous recognizing me.

Crap. I've stopped writing.

I've been sitting here staring at my page for hours, halted mid-sentence while I chew on my pen and wander off into thoughts of what life could be like with Riker a year, two years, ten years down the road. I take the pen out of my mouth and press the tip to the page.

Right. Back to work. Back to –

A knock rattles the door. I freeze. Even after weeks of relative safety, I can't help how my pulse skips and lurches.

I'm here alone.

Yeah, thanks to Em's classes, I can now flip an attacker twice my size over my head, and I know where the gun safe is, the combination, and where the bullets are, and while I can't hit with any accuracy, I could at least scare someone off. *I hope.*

But it still makes me nervous, wondering who could be on the other side of that door.

"Probably nothing. Just a package or a friend of Em's or..." I swallow all the mundane possibilities, willing them to be real.

I uncurl myself from the couch and creep closer to the door, bare feet silent. I probably look like a cartoon burglar, all hunched over and tiptoeing, then stretching up to squint one eye at the peephole.

Only to slump against the door in relief.

God. I recognize the woman on the other side, even if only barely. She's another Enguard employee.

Skylar, I remember. That's her name. Skylar Barin, Gabe's wife.

Yet, I can't help a nagging worry in the back of my mind, that she's showing up in the middle of the day.

What if something happened to Riker?

I pull the door open before she can knock again and flash what has to be the most manic smile in the world. "Mrs. Barin! Hi."

She's small and stone-faced with a sort of cynical, knowing smile and a perpetually quirked eyebrow that's pointed at me right now as she looks me over. "Morning, Miss Holly. You can just call me Sky."

"Oh, then, um, you should just call me Liv." I'm still smiling like a doll in a wax museum, fixed and frozen and completely uncomfortable with anyone who isn't Riker or Em. Being a shut-in with the same person for weeks will do that to you. "Something I can do for you? Is Riker okay?"

"Riker's fine, besides wanting to kill some of our more unreasonable clients and a new hire or two." She smirks. "Can I come in?"

I flush hot. Where are my manners? I mean, it's not like this is my house so I'm not exactly stepping into the role as the lady of the house, so I really don't have any right to –

Okay. Okay, rabbit brain. *Stop, calm down, act normal.*

I flash another smile, easier this time, and step back. "Sorry, of course. You just startled me, dropping by."

She steps inside. I recognize the look she slides over the interior. It's the same as Riker's look any time we walk into a public space, checking for threats and avenues of escape. But she seems to find the living room safe enough. Sky relaxes subtly, her sun-browned shoulders loosening in her tank top. Her smile is warmer as she plunks herself into the easy chair and tucks her sandy brown, pixie-cut hair behind her ear.

"Sorry for catching you off guard like this. I was just in the neighborhood, running some errands, and wanted to check in with you about your sister."

I reclaim my spot on the couch, relocating my notebook and pen to the coffee table so I can sit cross-legged with my ankles tucked under me. "My sister? What, Milah?"

"I just wanted to know if there was anything we could do to help." Sky shrugs. "I know she's got her own hand-picked security team now, and I think everyone at Enguard would rather drown themselves than be a part of it, but we were still there when that mess went down with her and Crown. We worry about her, and if her team's taking the right care of her. Sometimes, she seems to forget she's a target, too."

"Yeah...she does that." But even if it's resigned, I can't help smiling when I say it because I know my sister drives these people completely crazy, but they still care enough to want her to be okay.

I sigh, tilting my head back against the couch. "Milah and I are only halfway on speaking terms right now, but I think she's okay. She's doing some studio recording in L.A. right now and it's easier for her team to keep an eye on her when she's either in that recording booth or sound asleep."

"Good." Skylar watches me shrewdly. She's a little scary, hard as nails, a small package of dynamite I don't want exploding all over me. "Forgive me if I don't know how to be delicate about this but...how's her *health?*"

I wince. I know exactly what she's hinting at. Landon must've gotten a full report from James about what went down in Vancouver.

"I don't think she's using right now. Even when it was bad, she'd get herself clean for recording sessions because it was hard work and she had to stay focused. Now...now, she's promised me she'll reach out if she's tempted." I smile faintly. "I'm kind of her accountability buddy. Her good luck charm."

"Fair. And what about you, Liv? Who's *your* good luck charm?"

The question hits me harder than it should, if only because I've been brooding so much on how I'm just a token in my father's life, there for a purpose. And even if she doesn't mean it that way, even if I know she loves me, Milah uses me the same way.

It's only when I'm with Riker and Em that I feel real, and know they actually *see* me as that person until they know her almost better than I do.

And before I can even really think about it, I answer, "Riker."

Just saying his name sends a flush of warmth through me. "It's Riker, honestly. I've never felt safer since I met him. He's my luck."

"Oh," Skylar says matter-of-factly. "You slept together."

She could've hit me, and it would've shocked me less. The breath punches out of me, and I make a weird, wheezing sound, staring at her. "Wh-what? No!"

She snorts, mouth twitching, clearly hiding a laugh. "Don't ever play poker, dear."

I bury my face in my palms with a despairing moan. "Oh, God. Riker's going to be in so much trouble. How did you know?"

"It's not really your fault." She chuckles. "James just isn't as subtle as he thinks he is when he starts needling at Riker just to make him sulk. Or maybe I've just known them long enough to be able to read them."

James. Oh, damn it.

I'd almost forgotten...James has this weird thing he

does where he kind of vanishes in the background so you almost forget he's there, observing everything, thinking, noticing things you might not want him to notice.

He's almost a little creepy, but in that reassuring way that makes you glad someone like him is on your side.

Right now, though, I'm not particularly happy that he was apparently observant enough over that weekend to suss us out.

As if we weren't being completely obvious anyway.

I rub my hands over my face, then peek at Skylar over my fingers. "Be real – how much trouble are we in?"

"None." Those sharp eyes skewer me, but her voice isn't unkind. "Landon's so wrapped up in Kenna that he hasn't even noticed. I doubt he'll figure it out if we don't tell him. I don't have any intention of telling him." She arches a brow. "Do you?"

"No. Certainly not." I shake my head, blinking confusion. "But...if you aren't going to tell on us, then why did you ask?"

"I just wanted to see how you'd react." Skylar's grin is practically wicked. "Riker's kind of like a big brother to me. I just wanted to have a real conversation with you, since he's so upside down over you. Plus, it's good if someone in Enguard knows this is going on. Someone you both can trust."

My heart does that delicious clenching thing that happens every time Riker so much as looks at me. "Upside down? Him? Over me?"

"Are you kidding? Who else? He's spacing out at work constantly, dropping things, and he looks like he's ready to murder someone if your name comes up just when we're discussing the case."

"Oh." I shouldn't be so euphoric, but God, I can't lie.

I'm so thoroughly, madly, stupidly in love.

I curl my hand against my chest, trying – and failing – to suppress my smile. "Sorry if I'm causing problems at work."

"We'll manage." She stands, leaning over to gently grip and squeeze my shoulder. "I'm sure the two of you will manage, too. But I've got to get back to the office." With a jaunty little backward wave, Skylar turns and saunters toward the door. "Later, Liv. Thanks for your honesty. Hope to be seeing more of you around."

She lets herself out, leaving me there on the couch, hugging my arms to myself and feeling oddly warm.

I feel like I passed some kind of test. Some weird initiation rite.

It's nice to know the people who care about Riker don't hate me and don't think I'm bad for him.

It's nicer knowing this thing between us isn't going to cost him his career.

It's in that sort of dreamlike cloud where – I won't lie, I'm thinking a little too much about happily ever afters – that I lock up the house, then slip upstairs to curl up in Riker's bed.

Even when he's not there, it's comforting. The bed smells like him. It smells like *us*.

Even though I just washed the sheets this morning, there's still a lingering warmth that reminds me of the way we smell together when we're lying there, damp and overheated and catching our breath, and it's quiet and wonderful and the only sounds between us are two beating hearts.

I drift off thinking about that, slipping into a deep and quiet sleep.

Only to snap awake, my gut tightening, the sound of a footstep creaking on a loose board in the hall.

Riker *never* steps on that board.

He knows where it is and navigates around it without ever thinking. So does Em. I'm the only one who ever trips it.

Someone else is in the house. A stranger.

I push myself up carefully, just as the bedroom door opens.

For half a second, I'm staring at a pair of cold, glittering dark eyes in a ski mask. I can't see his face, but I'll never forget *those eyes.*

I'll never forget the look of cold malice and triumph in them, or the dark and murderous intent.

My mind flashes through a million things in half a second: bone-chilling fear, the box of 9mm bullets in the bedroom closet, the gun safe under the bed, the passcode, whether I can get to it before he does anything, whether I'd survive a fall out the second-floor window to escape.

Then he lunges.

And all thought disappears as I give in to an animal instinct and bolt.

He comes at me from one side of the bed, and I tumble off the other, darting for the door.

I'm almost free, so close to free – but a hand snares my hair.

Scalp on fire, neck whiplashed, he jerks me back into him.

I start to scream, calling for help.

His hand clamps over my mouth with something soft

clutched between us, almost forcing it into my open mouth, silencing me. It smells noxious and chemical, and suddenly my brain is floating.

My body ignites in fear, nerves prickling everywhere, knees wobbly and weak, fingers twitching, but my mind lifts away, leaving me there, alone.

So alone, terrified, and sinking.

Lost in a darkness I don't expect to wake from.

XII: NOT EVEN A LITTLE (RIKER)

Em calls my talent for sensing danger from afar my "Spidey senses."

Well, right now, my Spidey senses are tingling on high alert, even before I take the last turn to my house and see the black car parked at the end of the block.

I know every car on my street, and this one doesn't belong to any of my neighbors.

Sure, it could be a visitor, but something about the ominous, imposing presence it makes crouched there like some hulking black beetle tells me that car is trouble.

I don't care if it isn't in front of my house. It has something to do with me.

And something to do with *Liv*.

"Daddy?" Em says from the passenger seat, looking up from her book. "What's wrong?"

"Not sure, baby," I murmur. "But I'm going to need you to stay with Mrs. Baum for a little bit. Just until I check the house, okay?"

Mrs. Baum is in her garden, her house bumped up to ours.

As I pull up outside her fence, she looks up with a smile and a wave, her blue-washed curls matted with sweat. "Riker," she calls cheerfully as we slip out of the car. "Hello! How are you? I've hardly seen you since that girlfriend of yours moved in." Her eyes twinkle. "I miss being in love like that."

Any other time, I might've spluttered and protested, but right now, there's just my inner darkness.

It slips over me like an oily second skin, into mission mode. I guide Em forward with a hand against her back, offering Mrs. Baum a forced smile.

"You'll have to come by for dinner to meet her some time," I say. "Would you mind keeping an eye on Em for a few minutes? I forgot something important at the office."

Mrs. Baum blinks, then smiles indulgently.

"Of course, dearies!" She beckons to Em. "This way, darling. You're in luck. I've just finished a batch of those cookies you love so much."

Em perks. "Cinnamon swirl?"

But as they head up the walk, Em glances back, giving me a heavy look that says she's still worried about me.

Fuck.

She's worried, she loves me, she trusts me, and she needs me to be careful.

I will, sweetheart, I telegraph silently.

I wait until they disappear into the house before I text our preset code for this – 11324 – to Landon.

He knows that means there's trouble at my place, and it involves Liv. We use numeric codes on different cases when there's no time to explain and we need to mobilize a specific response.

There's no time for a briefing or a breakdown. Not when I need to check on Liv.

I put my phone away and slip off, rounding the other side of my house to the back fence. Mrs. Baum will be too busy feeding Em enough sugar to keep her up all night to notice my car's still parked outside when I was supposed to be going back to the office.

Carefully, I ease my back gate open without the slightest creak, then creep up to the back door and look through the glass insets.

I can only see the kitchen and a glimpse of the living room.

No sign of Liv.

Yet, when I hear a muffled squeal and a thump from upstairs...

My blood runs cold, freezing into sharp and cutting spears, the color of my vision as black as murder.

I slide the key into the lock and turn it soundlessly, then slip it open just enough to let me in before I close and latch it silently. My hand is already inside my suit coat, on my Beretta, as I move upstairs as quickly as I can, missing every loose step and every old board.

I know my house. Just like I know how to move through it quickly, soundlessly, dangerously.

There's another thump as I crest the top of the stairs. My jaw tightens.

If I were capable of still feeling shit after everything in me shuts down in favor of focusing on finding and eliminating a target...

I'd be terrified.

Because that sound is too much like a slack body hitting the floor.

Liv, fuck. Hold on.

Flattening myself against the wall outside my room, I risk a quick glance around the doorframe.

What I see turns my heart to iron.

A man in a ski mask, all in black, dragging a motionless and unresisting Liv across the floor, her heels thumping, her head lolling, a damp cloth clasped against her mouth. Even from here I can smell chloroform.

I'm going to kill this bastard. I *want* to kill this bastard.

Finger on the trigger, I rip the pistol from its holster.

But not before I make him talk.

He's so busy struggling to heft Liv that he doesn't even see my shadow fall over him. There's a darkly satisfying *thunck* as I whip the Beretta against the back of his head.

Asshole goes limp as a puppet with its strings cut, grunting as he tumbles to the side, his grasp on my woman loosening.

I catch her just in time, before she hits the floor, shielding her with my body and letting her tumble against me. She's too light – like some essential part of her has *vacated*, and I have to check her pulse to be able to breathe easily.

She's alive. Thank God.

Just unconscious but breathing steadily. I lift her onto the bed and lay her out gently, then rise to my feet, moving to stand over the prick who tried to take her.

He's conscious. Still groaning, blood leaking from the back of his head, while he fingers the trickle and rolls on the floor.

I take a deep breath, baring my teeth. This raw, real

fury rises up inside me, catches my throat, and I hear something like a shrieking, vengeful eagle inside my head.

This is it.

It's up to me whether or not he gets to live.

And right now, the part of me that knows where to cut, where to strike, where to puncture, where to bend, where to fucking hurt, that part is in control.

It knows every part of his body that can suffer to the point of breaking without killing him, until I'm good and ready for him to go.

His eyes creak open then, and he groans. "What the hell, man –"

He doesn't get a chance to finish.

I press my polished leather shoe down on his throat.

Slowly, deliberately, exerting more and more barely controlled pressure with each passing second.

Gagging, choking, grappling at my ankle, he arches his body, but he can't budge my foot.

Thirty seconds later, the skin around his eyes turns purple and he's wheezing, his look wide and panicked behind the mask. I know those eyes.

I saw them once, brown and muddled, above a mask. The same man who tried to break into my car.

His struggling grows feebler until I finally let up.

He sucks in a hoarse, wheezing gasp. I watch him coldly, then say, "Now you understand the position you're in. As long as you give me the answers I want, you get to breathe. You decide to get smart, you don't tell me what I want to know, you even get a little rude, and breathing suddenly gets optional. Are we clear?"

To make my point, I press down again. Not enough to fully cut off his air, but enough for him to feel the grind of my sole against his skin. Enough to make his next sucking, choking breath very uncomfortable. He rakes his nails against my shoe, my slacks, then nods frantically.

"Good." I ease up again, but keep my foot perfectly positioned. "Take your mask off."

Practically sniveling, he grapples with his ski mask and pulls it off, getting himself tangled in it and stretching it out and blubbering before he manages to rip it away.

There's a flushed, haggard face with pockmarked skin and sunken hollows under dark-brown eyes. He's a sort of pasty-fish pale that says he's got a substance abuse problem.

Not the kind of substance abuse that makes him the kind of shit who'd go after an innocent girl just because their pestilent coward of a leader, Lion, told them to. His lank, greasy, blond hair spreads around his head as he looks up at me, his rubbery lips trembling, his eyes hot with a mixture of defiance and fear.

"Show me your tattoo," I order.

He shakes his head. "Tattoo? I don't know –"

Snarling, I cut him off, shoving my heel against his trachea *hard.*

Almost hard enough to crush his esophagus. He chokes out a gargling, pained sound, his body jerking and twitching, his eyes bulging as he scrabbles and claws. I hold for a good fifteen-count while he wheezes, then let go.

"I thought," I murmur coolly, "I'd made my point? Lie to me, and your air quota drops to nil. Now, fuckhead, tell me very nicely. Where's your Pilgrim tattoo?"

He's slow to respond. Probably from lack of oxygen to the brain.

I give him a second to recover, knowing he's no good to me if he can't talk.

Finally, though, he scrapes back the cuff of his leather jacket, over his left wrist, and thrusts his arm out so I can see the three dots tattooed on the underside of his wrist.

"Thank you." I cock the slide on my Beretta, flick the safety off, and point it right at his forehead.

Right between the eyes.

One shot, and he's a splatter of red. No more Pilgrim.

I meet his eyes over the barrel of the gun, a silent promise between us. "Okay. You're going to tell me why you're in my house, and why you hurt my girl, or you'll never tell anyone anything ever again."

"I wasn't gonna hurt her," he struggles out, voice raspy and broken. I've probably damaged his vocal cords. Fuck if I care. "Lion...he just told me to get her. Honest. I wasn't gonna do nothing else, I –"

"I don't believe you, asshole, considering she's *unconscious*." A touch more pressure on his throat, and my finger slips past the guard to rest on the trigger.

I don't need to say anything else to threaten him. All it takes is one little movement, a wordless statement of intent, to make a man feel like a guillotine is hanging over him on an increasingly fraying thread.

"What does Lion want with her? She's innocent in this. You're after Milah for drug money."

"Fuck the money!" he flares – only to squeak as I grind my heel. He gulps, his Adam's apple moving against the sole of my shoe, and I ease off to let him speak again. He's meeker this time, quieter, as he says, "We don't care about the money. This is about blood."

"Liv didn't kill your men. Neither did Milah."

He stares at me – like I'm the one missing something here.

Like I'm the powerless one, and he's got an advantage over me.

Then he actually *grins*, although I could shoot him with one reckless, careless twitch of a finger. "You really don't get it, do you?"

"No," I admit. "But that's why you're here. Gloat and die, or tell me and live. I turn you over to the police, you have a chance to walk. Break out. Whatever you're going to do. Keep testing my patience, and..."

"You won't kill me," he sneers. "Because if I die, you still won't know shit. So I don't have to say anything, because as long as I'm alive there's a chance I'll tell y—"

His loss.

I calmly reverse the Beretta, flick the safety on, grip it by its barrel, and smash it across his jaw, putting all of my strength into it.

His mouth explodes in a fountain of teeth and blood.

Two of his teeth knock loose and arc across the floor, clattering when they land. From the amount of blood spurting out of his mouth, he's likely bitten his tongue.

He's shrieking, clutching at his face with both hands, a mess of pain it's impossible to feel any sympathy for.

Calmly, I straighten, gaining a proper grip on the Beretta again, and take a moment to meticulously wipe the blood from the barrel onto his shirt. Then I flick the safety off once more, regarding him flatly.

"You're right," I say. "I can't kill you if I want to know what you're hiding. But there are quite a few interesting things I can do to you while you're alive. Did you know a man can survive a Y-incision?" He's staring up at me with blank terror in his eyes, confused.

I cock my head. "I see you don't know what a Y-incision is, do you? It's simple. Basically what a coroner does when they perform an autopsy, my friend. They cut a V from either shoulder to the center of your chest, right over your sternum...and then they cut you open from sternum to navel right...down...here." I trace my free hand down my own chest to mark a path. "Afterward, they generally grip your ribs to either side and pull. They come loose from your spine. That, I'm not so certain you'd survive, but we'd try it. Oh, fuck, we'd try."

I hadn't thought he could get any paler.

I was wrong.

He makes a blubbering sound, his split and swollen lips wobbling, and his tongue lolling and fumbling around words I can't understand.

More like pained noises that meld into each other. I arch a brow, letting him go for a few moments, then stop him by nudging the toe of my shoe against his cheek.

"Slower, now. I understand you're willing to talk, but we'll have to work around these new developments, won't we? Start again from the beginning. Slowly. Tell me what I don't know. If I can't understand you, I'll make you start over. I imagine talking hurts quite a bit now, doesn't it?"

He nods – a small, frightened motion.

Good. He believes me, now, that I'll make him suffer.

He'll tell me anything I want to know.

"A-Alec Holly," he slurs out, contorting his ruined mouth to try to make the muffled syllables come out clear. "It...it's not about M-Milah anymore. F-Fuck her drug money. Alec H-Holly took out a hit on our guys.

He's the reason..." He breaks off, choking a little, then turns his head to the side and spits out another tooth before continuing, glaring up at me with a mixture of terror and defiance. "He's the asshole we want. It's a b-blood vendetta now. Easy. He killed our family. We kill his."

I close my eyes, taking a deep, centering breath.

Because if I don't keep my calm, I'm going to put him down like a suffering animal.

Snap his neck right here and now.

"Who did Alec Holly hire?" I ask as I tighten my finger on the trigger. "Only gonna ask you once."

He shakes his head, waving his hands frantically.

"All right! I'll tell you, I'll tell you!" he blubbers. "It was the damn Runners!"

The Runners. Not a name I recognize instantly, though vague memory tells me they're another underground crime syndicate.

Not as big as the Pilgrims. Not someone we've really needed to have on our radar at Enguard, but they've come up a couple of times on small-time protection jobs for a few other music industry people who had an occasional white powder problem and might need to be on guard for their old dealers. They've never come up as the kind who hired out for assassination work.

That's probably why the job went so wrong and was so fucking clumsy.

I narrow my eyes at the man beneath me and lean down, enough to press my weight on his throat, enough to tap the cold tip of the Beretta's barrel against his nose.

"Let me get this straight," I say. "Alec Holly paid a rival gang to kill your men? And instead of going after Alec and the gang, you decide to target his innocent daughters?"

Maybe I've knocked a few of his brain cells loose. Maybe he's just stupid and suicidal. But he actually grins at me, baring the bloodied remnants of his teeth, separated by black gaps.

"Milah Holly's no innocent," he spits. "I bet her sister's a rich, whacked-out whore just like her."

I don't need to hear more.

I know what I need to know, and he's not getting another word about Liv past his filthy fucking mouth.

Without a word, I whip the pistol across the side of his head. He makes a guttural noise, and his head slumps to the side.

He's out cold.

I flip him over and dig his wallet from his back pocket to check his name.

Scott Richards. Ridiculously fucking ordinary surfer boy name for this pathetic waste of space who'd actually tried to kidnap a defenseless girl.

I pull my handcuffs from my belt and shove his wrists into them, being none too gentle as I snap them in place and leave him trussed up on the floor. I'm just standing when I hear a strangled, upset noise from the bed, and jerk my head up, staring into wide blue eyes.

Liv's awake.

Liv's awake, and she's shaking, staring at me with horror, tears streaming down her face.

* * *

I DON'T HAVE a chance to reach for her.

To comfort her, to explain, to *nothing*.

While we'd stared at each other, frozen, Landon's voice shouted from downstairs, calling my name, as the front door of my house burst open. I'm suddenly regretting giving my coworkers at Enguard the emergency key, but I know I'd be grateful if I'd ended up in a situation I couldn't handle.

I start toward Liv, but she flinches, and I recoil.

That one subtle motion of hers stabs right through my heart. It's only then I realize how many of my defenses I've let down, that she can even *reach* my heart to pierce it so easily.

But then I'm pulled away into low, muttered conversations with Landon, James, and Gabe, while Skylar's got Liv, furiously checking her over.

Liv is compliant, polite, letting Sky fuss over her with the first aid kit, but she keeps her eyes lowered. She won't look at me.

Snarling, I force myself to tear my gaze away, giving Landon a full rundown of everything the fuck on the floor told me. It's hard to form words in this whirlwind.

Cop cars scream in the closing distance, sirens coming. They'll be here soon to take him into custody. Too late to stop the man who showed Liv I'm a violent monster.

Landon falls silent after I finish recapping, stroking at the five o'clock shadow covering his chin and frowning, his mouth set in a thin, displeased line, before he shakes his head.

"Damn it. I thought we might have two organizations in this, but I don't like this one bit. Not knowing it for sure. Two makes things twice as messy. Now we've got two different unpredictable agents to deal with."

"Can we keep Liv and Em safe?" I ask. "Do we need new measures? This fucker was in my *home*."

"We'll make sure of it, one way or the other." Landon looks past me.

I follow his line of sight. Liv watches me now, her eyes wide and liquid with tears, and fuck if she's not melting the walls I've been struggling to keep around myself all over again.

Landon sighs. "Go talk to her. Try to reassure her."

"I don't think she –"

"She knows you," Landon says. "She's been living with you. The rest of us might as well be strangers."

He's right. Too bad it only makes it worse.

The real question is, does she *want* me anywhere near her?

I pull away from Landon and approach the bed, where Liv is curled up in a ball against the headboard, hugging her knees to her chest and staring miserably down at her toes. I sink down to the edge gently, far enough away to keep from making her feel cornered or threatened but offer my hand with a hope I hadn't known I could feel, fragile and trembling.

"Liv," I say softly.

She doesn't take my hand.

She throws herself against me.

Buries her face against my chest and wraps her arms around me with a surprising, desperate strength.

"*Riker*," she gasps, almost a sob.

I hold my arms out from my sides almost helplessly.

James is watching me slyly. Landon gives me an unreadable look. Meanwhile, Gabe is so preoccupied with Sky, whispering something in his thick Louisiana accent, I don't think he even realizes we're in the same room, nor does she.

But even if the others are watching, fuck it.

I can't resist the need to bring her home.

Slowly settling my arms around her, I wrap her up against me. It soothes some animal fear inside me, to feel her soft, slim body pressed so close.

"Still wondering if you hate me, sweetheart?" I growl softly in her ear.

Liv peeks up at me through her tangled, mussed hair. "Huh?"

"That look, back there...thought you didn't want me touching you."

She shakes her head quickly, messing up her hair even more as it whips around, then buries her face against my side with a muffled, "No! I need you, Riker. I need you so much right now."

"I'm here. I'm here, Liv." I stroke her back slowly, trying to calm her trembling body.

I hardly notice when the others tactfully take their leave, murmuring to each other as they file out of my bedroom. If they're noticing this is more than professional, I don't give a damn. I'll deal with the fallout later.

What's really important here is her, relaxing in my arms.

She's alive. She's safe. She's still mine.

"You'll have to talk to the police soon. Can you handle that?"

Sniffling, she pulls back enough to wipe at her tear-streaked face, and offers me the bravest, most beautiful smile I've ever seen, all the more heart-wrenching when she's devastated. "As long as you stay with me, yes."

"I'm here. Promise you I'm here." I brush my knuckles to her cheek, easing away a few more damp trails on her skin. "Are you okay?"

"No." Her eyes well, and her lips tremble with the clear struggle not to burst out sobbing. "This doesn't make any sense. Daddy, Jesus, why would he..."

She can't get it out, and I don't blame her.

"Don't know, Liv. He obviously didn't think this through or realize it'd put you both in danger." A harsh truth that makes my fist hungry for Alec Holly's face.

"Or he didn't care," she says bitterly.

"I hope he cares. You're his daughter."

I gather her closer. I'm still trying to fathom how even someone as self-absorbed as Alec Holly wouldn't care how his actions affect his children.

It's much easier to believe he's too arrogant. So far up in his ivory tower that he doesn't really comprehend the real-world repercussions of certain things. Maybe he thought he was powerful enough. That he could mess with a gang like the Pilgrims and come away clean because he's just that untouchable.

Instead, he set ripples into motion that are growing wider as they spread, aftershocks threatening to shake Liv's entire world apart.

I could never do that. Not to Em. I'm a different kind of father from Alec Holly.

Liv shifts against me, resting her head to my shoulder and hugging close against my side. "Riker? Why would you think I wouldn't want you to touch me?"

Fuck.

I tense. My gut sinks. "Just thought you woke up and saw what I did. To that man, the bastard on the floor, who tried to hurt you."

"I did." Her hand creeps up to curl against the back of my neck, stroking through the tight trim of hair at my nape, a gesture that I suspect soothes her as much as it demolishes me. "I told you before – you don't scare me, Riker. I'm grateful for you." She rubs her cheek to my shoulder in such a sweetly trusting gesture. "I get it. You did what you had to do to protect me. And now we know what's going on, all thanks to you."

"Do we?" I ask. "This entire thing still doesn't add up. Why would your father hire hit men? Especially such clumsy ones?"

"I don't know." She bites her lip, her eyes glazing over, distant and contemplative. "I guess he was trying to take care of Milah, but this isn't really something he's ever dealt with. Organized crime, I mean. Not that I know of. It's a horrible accident. A mistake." She looks at me again, something haunted in her gaze, a tired weariness that so often makes her seem so much wiser and more jaded than her years and sheltered innocence. "That's kind of what Daddy's done our whole lives. If there's a problem, he throws money at it until it goes away. He even paid someone to transfer their daughter to another school when I was eleven because the girl was bullying me."

Her smile looks cynical, with a touch of self-loathing I can't stand to see. "I should've stood up to him, when I couldn't stand up to her. And he's still doing it. I mean, Milah did need rehab, still needs rehab, but the way Daddy handled it was disgusting. It was just paying someone to fix his 'broken' daughter. And I guess he thought paying someone would fix this too, but he just made a bigger mess."

"We'll clean it up," I promise, kissing the top of her head and just holding her, reminding myself she's safe and I got here in time.

I don't know how I'll fix this, honestly.

It's the most fucked up, dangerous situation I've ever seen at Enguard, or when I was overseas for Uncle Sam.

But I know I have to try, for Liv.

For this sweet, fragile, impossible woman, there's no other option.

* * *

IT'S AN UNSETTLING FEELING, worrying about having Em and Liv in my own home. Thinking about how close I came to losing everything here, but I can't leave Em at Mrs. Baum's forever.

Also don't think the Pilgrims will try anything here again once they realize their man is in custody. What's nagging at me, though, as I sit at the kitchen table finishing out the details on a police report, is how they knew Liv was at my house in the first place.

That was the whole point of this endeavor – that she disappear somewhere safe, somewhere we could keep an eye on her but where they'd be unlikely to track her down.

Either someone told them where to find her, or they've gotten more diligent in their search and made the connection between Enguard and Liv.

The possibility makes my guts churn.

I make a mental note to tell the others to keep a tight

perimeter around their own homes, all while half-listening to Liv, Em, and Sky talking over Chinese takeout in the living room.

I'm grateful Skylar stayed after everybody left. She's a strong, calming presence, a bit of extra security helping to nail things down and keep them feeling safe while I'm distracted with the report. I'm careful about what I say, about the use of necessary force.

Was it truly necessary?

Or did the sadist in me just want to hurt the man who hurt Liv for the sheer pleasure of it?

I'm tapping my pen against my lower lip, lost in thought, when Sky comes drifting into the kitchen. She leans her little shoulder against the doorframe and folds her arms over her chest, just looking at me with her mouth slightly pursed and one eyebrow arched. I cock my head at her.

"That look usually means I'm about to get my ass handed to me. What now?"

"You're damn right you are." She glances over her shoulder, then steps closer, dropping her voice to a hiss. "You're screwing a *client*, Riker. What the hell are you thinking?"

Goddammit. I rake my hand over my face, exhaling the fire in my lungs slowly.

She must've gotten it out of Liv, that girl can't lie to save her life.

"How long have you known?" Then I pause, eyeing her through my spread fingers. "And how screwed am I?"

"Not at all. *Yet.* Landon doesn't know, but that doesn't mean he won't figure it out if I did." She rests her hands on her hips, mock-glaring at me. "You're lucky I'm such a good friend."

"You're also a bit of a hypocrite."

"Nah. That's the other reason I'm keeping your secrets, pal." Her grin looks annoyed but affectionate. "Not like I didn't do the exact same damn thing with Gabe."

"It was different with Gabe, though. You're both in the protection business. Liv, she's..."

"Out of your league?"

"*Vulnerable*," I correct with a glower. "Dammit, Sky. The last thing I'd ever want is to take advantage of her. This is more than just a fuck."

"I know. So don't." She leans forward, resting her elbows on the table, that sarcastic façade dropping for an unexpectedly sincere look. "If she's vulnerable, then protect her. Don't take advantage of her."

"What if I can't protect her? What if we're in over our fucking heads on this one?"

"It's not a choice. It's your job, Riker, and it's also what you do for people you love."

"Love?" I whisper the word like it's in some new language.

"Yeah. Your own words, almost, 'more than just a fuck.' Remember?"

I do. *But love? Fuck.*

The unspoken question hangs heavy between us, making a strange throbbing start somewhere below my ribs.

Do I love Olivia Holly?

Sky saves me from falling into that bottomless pit by straightening, slapping her thin hand on the table. "Right now, though, you need to get packing. Your cover's blown, your place is compromised, and you can't stay here."

Another shock rolls through me, turning my blood scalding red. It's worse because she's right.

"I don't think they'd try anything here again. Not a repeat job," I snarl.

"You don't know that. You don't know how reckless or how vindictive Lion is. We have reports of entire families being *slaughtered* in their homes over a Pilgrim vendetta," she says grimly, and the very thought chills my bones. "So, big guy, get your shit together. Literally and metaphorically. Get your girls ready to go, and figure out what you're doing with Liv before you fuck everything up. It'd be better to break up with her than keep stringing her along. She's too brand new, Riker. You don't want to be the first man to break her heart."

"I don't think I am," I mutter, though the things her father did broke her heart in an entirely different way. And I have a lot to think about, but not right now.

Sighing, I sink down in the kitchen chair. "Fine. I'll take care of it. Think I know just the place to take her, where no one will even think to look."

XIII: TOO LITTLE, TOO LATE
(OLIVIA)

Few things drive home how serious this is than watching Riker sit down and have a very quiet, very solemn talk with Em about the fact that we're leaving again.

And this time, we might not be coming back for a very long time.

Somehow, it's more final. More real. It was one thing when it was just scattered incidents, but in the end, once it was over, we were always coming home to a normal life.

No.

They were always coming home to a normal life. This isn't my life, no matter how much I've loved pretending all this time. But they still had that – the illusion everything would be okay, and nothing would change for them, in the end.

Not really.

Riker would still go to work. Em would still go to school. They'd have their friends, their hobbies, Riker and his wooden ships in bottles and his late night drinks and his quiet, broody, irresistible man-thoughts. And Em with her savant-level math and her self-defense classes and her crush on her instructor's kid, Ryan.

I've disrupted their entire lives. Screwed up *everything*.

I was supposed to be in and out and gone once this problem was over, but it's been almost a month now and we only know a little more than we did before. We're no closer to ending this.

I have no idea how large the Pilgrims' organization is. There could be hundreds or thousands of them.

Are we going to have to arrest them all before we can feel safe again?

How are we going to stop this when they can just send an endless wave of people after us? And even if I walk out of Riker and Em's lives right now, they'll never be safe again – and it's all because of me?

I just want to curl up into a ball and disappear, take all my problems with me.

Em, though, isn't nearly so reserved. As soon as Riker finishes explaining that we're going back to "Grandma Em's house," she's all excited energy, rattling off memories of swimming in a creek and learning how to skip stones and how it actually snows and and and –

I almost smile. She's so alive, so courageous, and I really do admire her.

She's an amazing girl, who's going to grow up to be an amazing woman.

She races upstairs to pack, leaving me and Riker alone, sitting a significant distance apart on the couch. He sits like there's a mammoth on his shoulders, bowing him forward, his hands dangling between his legs, and he just stares at them coldly without a word.

I'm afraid to break the silence, but I venture anyway, "There's a Grandma Em?"

"Ah. Her maternal grandmother. She's named after her." He looks up at me with an exhausted smile, and the tired lines in his face nearly kill me. "There's a winter lodge just outside Yosemite, up around the ski resorts. Crystal – my ex-wife's parents – are still alive, but they'd deeded the lodge to her. When she died, I couldn't stand to keep it. So I gave the deed back, but I still have a key. They've told me I'm welcome to take Em up any time."

Nodding, I smile. This doesn't sound half bad. "We can use the getaway."

He shrugs, looking up with his eyes dark and severe. "It's messy terrain, Liv. Hard to get to on foot, impossible to get to directly by car or even prop plane. We'll have to hike about a mile, but it's defensible – and since there's no legal connection between me and Em's grandparents except Em, it's a lot harder to trace through any official records to figure out we might've disappeared to a remote cabin with my ex-in-laws' names on the title."

I want to comfort him so much, so deeply.

Anything to ease some of the misery I've brought to his life. I half expect him to push me away when I scoot over to lean against his side, offering closeness when I don't have words.

But I nearly squeak when instead he wraps both arms tight around me so suddenly. So strongly.

That's when I realize I've done the right thing. This bear of a man is way too proud to ever ask, but it couldn't be clearer...

Riker needs me.

Just as much as I need him.

And I hadn't realized how much I'd needed this until we're holding each other so tight, nearly clinging, and he's rasping soft words into my hair with such raw, pure feeling.

The desperation, the fear, and something even deeper.

"I almost fucking lost you today," he whispers. "Christ. If I'd shown up just a minute later..."

"But you *didn't* lose me." I clutch my hands against the back of his shirt and press into him so hard, it's like I'm trying to melt into his muscle, his ink, his wall of flesh. "You saved me. You always save me. I know you always *will*."

"Liv, yeah." Two simple words, more like thunder than human speech.

He sweeps me up so suddenly then.

It takes my breath away – but not nearly as much as his kiss.

He holds me captive, not with force but with gentle, tender warmth so magnetic it pulls me into an unbreakable hold, compelling me to fall into him.

My lips part for him. For the wonderful, luscious feeling that comes when he slips into me and tastes me and caresses me so intimately from within, making my mouth his with every touch, branding me far deeper than my lips.

He's been inside my body, my mind, my *heart*.

Even if I ran away tomorrow to try to keep him safe, I'd always carry him with me.

Yet I know now, as I melt into him with a moan, as he nips and teases my mouth to a sweet addiction, as he makes me gasp with the sheer intensity that's Riker Woods...

I can't leave.

Not for anything.

Not unless he tells me to go because I'm so deeply in love with this stoic, strange, wonderfully kind man that I don't have the strength to pull away.

He's shown me in so many ways that I have it in me to be strong, that there's a fierceness inside me I never knew I had. But no power, no force of will, could ever compel me to walk away.

I'm his, now and always, even if he doesn't even know it.

We finally break, just barely.

Just enough to breathe.

But we lean so close against each other that the familiar scratch of his beard against my cheek is equal parts comfort and cruel temptation. I don't know who's soothing who anymore, when he's holding me so close and I'm stroking my fingers through his hair until the hard tension in his shoulders eases.

Does it matter?

No. All that matters is that we're here for each other.

"I'm going to find a way out of this," I whisper, tucking my head beneath his jaw. "I'll find a way to fix this. My Dad made this problem. I know I'll find a way to make it right."

"You shouldn't have to, Liv. That's my job."

"Maybe." But there's a firm resolution in me, something growing that even I don't wholly understand.

Only that it's like a steady fire, one that doesn't rage but holds its heat bright and hot and true, patient and waiting. "But I know how to handle Daddy. We can go to Yosemite for now, but once I figure out what to do...I'm going to make sure you come home again, Riker. This place will be safe for everyone again."

I can feel his smile, where his cheek presses to mine. "Damn, sweetheart, so now you're protecting me?"

"I owe you a few."

He pulls back, looking at me strangely, then kisses me with a heartbreaking softness. "You don't owe me nothing, Liv," he says, "other than to be yourself."

Be myself.

But who am I today?

I think of Eden, my heroine in my book, and her quest to answer the same question. I know her journey has been a mirror of my own, but I still can't help but wonder.

Who am I now? Who, really?

And how far am I willing to go to keep this new life I've discovered?

XIV: CRAZY LITTLE THING (RIKER)

I haven't been up to the winter lodge since Em was six years old.

I'm surprised she remembers it so well, but then it shouldn't be that startling. Our last trip here was one of the final good memories we had together as a family.

Crystal was still healthy, carrying Em on her shoulders, as we left the car in the guarded lot a few blocks down from the main trail and climbed, huffing and wheezing in the thin mountain air, up the leaf-strewn autumn hills and rocky crags with our backpacks weighing us down. Em, every once in a while, demanded to get down on the ground and ask about the shape of this leaf or why the air smelled different or would we see any wolves or coyotes, and were they too scared of people?

You know, the usual heart-rending shit kids do.

She'd been such a bright, inquisitive child even then. We'd tucked away happily for a few months to watch the winter settle in and see the first snow fall through windows lit with the reflections from firelight. I want to say it's a pure, happy memory for me, but it's not.

Not all of it.

Because I still remember nights after Em fell asleep. The low, bitter conversations with Crystal, and then sleeping on the pullout couch while they shared the bed.

My wife only tolerated me then because we had to get through this. She appreciated what I did for her, how I swore up and down we'd see this through, how hard we'd fight her cancer. But she didn't love me.

We were too damaged. Too weary. Too wrong from the very beginning, and the years took their toll.

We stayed in this for Em. And if we ever thought there was a ghost of a chance at mending it, at fixing us, it wasn't meant to be.

I'm clenching my teeth as I shift out of the driver's seat and back into the present.

It's not déjà vu I'm feeling anymore as we leave the Wrangler in the lot and load up our backpacks full of supplies.

It's something different as I watch Em and Liv practically chase each other through the trees, while Em excitedly shows Liv the different plant species she can identify and answers Liv's bright-eyed, curious questions about squirrels and caterpillars and the pretty butterflies flitting through the warm summer air, just as eager and inquisitive as Em herself.

It's unmistakable what it is.

Pride.

I'm *proud* to be here with them. Rather than erasing those old memories, it just closes their book and tucks their pages away to the archives, leaving something fresh and new where I can write in another story, another chapter.

A new beginning.

By the time we make it up to the peak of the tree-shrouded slope, though, I'm ready for an ending.

More, I'm ready to sit down. The girls are carrying their own backpacks with their personal effects and a few other things, but I had to be Mr. Big Ox and carry the massive camping frame loaded down with a few weeks' worth of groceries and other essential supplies.

The lodge is modern and has electricity, appliances, and other necessities for comfort, but as remote as it is, it's still helpful to stock up on things in case of emergencies.

I'm sweating down the back of my collar by the time we emerge from a break in the trees to see the peaked roof of the cozy little cottage-style house with its dark shingles, brick chimney, and pale slat siding. Crystal's parents must've been here recently or sent out a caretaker because the garden out back is only a little overgrown, and the blown leaves along the front stepping stones aren't too thick.

Before we let ourselves in, I turn back and look down the way we came.

Nothing but forest. The road isn't visible from here, or the parking lot.

The cottage wasn't visible from the road, either. A sheer cliff rises up the back of the house, with a thin little waterfall pouring down through foliage, running into the pond and creek in the backyard.

We're surrounded on two sides, with only two possible

avenues of approach up a steep, rocky hill that'd make it nearly impossible for a stealth approach.

The direct trail, and a narrow, gentler paved footpath coming from the north are actually harder to use when it winds over three miles from the point of entry on a higher curve of the highway some ways away.

It's fucking perfect.

When we step inside the cabin, though, it's a punch of nostalgia and memory straight to my gut.

Crystal decorated this place a long time ago. It's all homey deep-rose colors and complementary plaids and subtle florals, giving it a sort of soft, rustic look. Her touch is everywhere here.

I look over, know Em feels it, too, when she stops just past the threshold and looks around.

Normally, she's so energetic that even when standing still she always seems to be in motion, but right now she's just arrested, quiet. Her little eyes shift down.

I walk over and grip her shoulder gently. She looks up at me and offers a wan smile that feels like a mirror of my own.

"It's okay to miss her," I say.

She bites her lip. "Do you?"

"In my own way, love."

That question should've hurt, so much. Should've ripped me the fuck open.

I should've known that even at such a young age, Em was aware of the tension between me and her mother. It's a reasonable question to ask. And one I'm okay with answering it half honestly today, when I don't think I would've been before.

As Em pulls me close, burrows in for a hug, I fold her

in my arms and catch Liv's eye over her head, sharing a brief, wistful smile.

Don't have to ask myself who's responsible for my honesty today.

Em's bright again in a matter of seconds, pulling away and flashing us both a smile. "C'mon, Liv! I'll show you where you can put your stuff. We're sharing the bedroom."

"Sleepover style, huh?" Liv hefts her back and flashes me an impish smile. "Where's your father going to sleep?"

I chuckle. "The couch pulls out into a rollaway bed. You two get the room. I know how girls need their privacy."

Even if that privacy – and the structure of the cabin – is going to put a serious damper on our sex life.

We'll find a way, I vow.

Even if I wind up flat on the ground outside with a pine cone up my ass, rolling around in needles.

The thought shouldn't amuse me as much as it does, but even being able to laugh in the midst of this clusterfuck of a job is enough to lift my spirits. It doesn't take us long to get settled in.

The girls get their things put away in their room while I stash mine in the massive oak chest that doubles as a coffee table in the living room, before we work together to put the groceries and supplies away. Liv's a whirlwind as usual, learning her way around while we point her to various things.

Somehow, in a blink and a breath, it's evening. Liv and Em are sprawled out on the floor in front of a crackling fire, playing some card game with magic monsters gathering or something like that and completely ignoring the Lord of the Rings DVD playing on the TV.

I'm on the couch messing around on my laptop, using the wi-fi hotspot on my phone to run through the Enguard database's information on the Pilgrims plus anything I can find on Liv's old man.

It's harder than it should be to focus.

If I'm being honest, I'm watching Liv and Em over the top of the screen. It *does* something to me, to see how well they get along. Liv subtly takes on the role of the adult, but without stifling Em or repressing her natural enthusiasm, independence, and creativity. She takes real, genuine *interest* in Em, and I don't know if she's had experience with kids before or if it's a natural talent, but she seems to genuinely care if my daughter is happy and fulfilled, and if she grows into the wonderful person she's meant to be.

She treats my daughter like a person. Not a damn impediment or an annoying accessory.

And it's part of what makes me so stuck on her, when the one or two women I tried dating in the past couple of years treated Em like an obstacle to overcome if they wanted to score a role in my life, instead of like someone they could befriend.

Liv glances up and catches my eye, flashing me a little smile.

It takes everything to keep my answering smile minimal and preoccupied, when Em doesn't know about us – and she'll see through me in an instant.

I force myself to look back down at my screen and the data files I'm comparing to find any link between Alec Holly and the Pilgrims.

It just doesn't make sense to me that Holly senior

would order a hit just because some guys were muscling his daughter for drug money. Why not just pay them off exorbitantly?

A bribe still would've been cheaper than taking out a hit.

There must be something else at play here. Something driving the need to take out the Pilgrims by force and send a message, even if Holly clearly hasn't realized just how deep blood grudges run with these types of gangs.

Or just how deep the Pilgrims' connections run throughout the Pacific Northwest.

It's disturbing how much the gang has going on.

On the surface, they look like dirty punks, lurking on street corners. Beneath that façade, though, is an entire root system reaching its tendrils out into law enforcement and businesses throughout Washington, Oregon, and Northern California.

They own multiple shell corporations for laundering dirty money, maintain an entire distribution network for drug imports, have protection rackets set up as organized state-wide networks intimidating small businesses, keep multiple city and state police in their pockets.

About the only thing the Pilgrims don't do is manufacture their own drugs.

I'd known they were dirty assholes, but I didn't realize just how far the filth went.

Not that Alec Holly's much cleaner. He's exactly the rich, self-absorbed dickbag I thought he was.

Three messy divorces, backstabbing rise to corporate power, the kind of guy who somehow finds the money to award himself obscene bonuses in the middle of a recession and among waves of layoffs.

He's always jetting around, hosting fundraisers for nebulous causes that don't actually seem attached to any real charity, and I'm wondering where that money goes when he seems to have more than enough of his own between managing smart investments in Milah's career and a run of very successful stock trading. It's the foundation of an international business incubator that makes its money by buying promising fledgling startups for a song, nurturing them into global corporations, then selling them off for a seven-to-eight-figure profit.

Something doesn't seem right, though.

With all those corporations constantly changing hands, it wouldn't be hard to hide some pretty shady dealings in the transactions, burying them down in the fine details as a cover for something else. Something that might overlap the Pilgrims' business interests. Something where, if Lion saw an opportunity with Milah's drug debt, he could easily use Alec Holly's daughters as leverage to go after what he really wanted.

I think Alec Holly's in this mess even deeper than we thought, and this entire clusterfuck is his attempt to cover his tracks – and cover his ass.

Even if he has to sacrifice his own daughters to do it.

The only time I've ever felt this kind of black, bubbling hatred rising up from my gorge like bile is when I saw that man dragging Liv. I need to keep a lid on it, though.

I can't let Liv know I suspect her father of being this big an asshole or taking things this far. Despite their conflicted relationship, she clearly loves Alec Holly. She'd be even more devastated than she was that day at my house if she knew the naked truth.

I distract myself looking through a few more documents, then pause, frowning.

I've been through both the Holly file and the Pilgrims file before, and this data wasn't there last time.

Was it?

I check a few folders full of PDFs. Every last one of them has *CrownRecovered* in the file name. I can't help but grin to myself.

Landon's a smart, sly dog.

He's managed to seize the info databases from Crown Security, our old rival, after it was shut down by the FBI, adding their case files to augment our own.

It looks like there's an entire data dump of files no one's organized yet. *Good.*

It'll give me something to do to keep from going stir-crazy cooped up in this cabin, unable to even go to work. I love spending time with Em and Liv, but after even three days, we're going to need some solo time or we're going to be at each other's throats.

Em lets out a triumphant sound that I think means she beat Liv at arranging numbered cards with monsters on them until someone had the right number to win. Then she looks up at me, grinning. "Hey, Dad? I just beat Liv with an entirely green deck, even giving her all my black cards. Can I call Ryan to tell him about it?"

"Hm?" I look up from the laptop. Liv's mock-pouting, but I can tell she's trying not to laugh.

I linger on her for a moment, then shake my head at Em with a smile. "Sure, love. Just remember you can't tell him we're here. We're just out camping."

"What if he asks where?" she asks.

"Be vague. Change the subject."

She bounces up, already fishing her phone from her pocket. "Okay."

I'm not expecting her to retreat to the bedroom, and the fact that she does makes me arch a brow. Private conversations with boys, now?

When did my little girl grow up?

Chuckling ruefully, Liv pushes herself off the floor. "I haven't played Magic since I was fifteen, and she's whipping my butt with a basic deck. God, I need to relearn how to play."

"I have no idea what any of that means."

"Means girls like math, monsters, and magic battles. That's all you need to know." She settles down next to me, patting my arm, then follows my line of sight toward the bedroom door; Em's voice is a faint, excited murmur drifting from inside. "She really likes that Ryan kid, doesn't she?"

"Seems like it. He's a pretty good kid, even if I find his old man smarmy as hell." I look down at the tempting, beautiful woman sitting so close to me, yet still too far away. "I think he's her first crush."

"Her first crush *that you know about*."

I blink. "What? C'mon. Em tells me everything. She would've told me if she liked somebody."

Liv just keeps staring, a smile pulling at her lips.

I pause, frowning, stroking my beard. "Wouldn't she?"

"Oh, Riker." Liv laughs gently, shifting to tuck against my side and resting her head on my shoulder. "You're a great dad, but there's a point where men realize they have *a lot* to learn about raising girls." She pokes my arm. "Welcome home. You've reached it."

"Let me guess – you're going to teach me?"

Her smile turns sly, and she leans just a little more into me.

Just enough for that light pressure of her weight to turn from comforting to enticing, while the curve of her breasts mold to my arm and her waist fits against mine, her hip a soft roundness sliding against my side. "Seems fair. You've taught me a lot of things."

It's like she's flicked a switch inside me. I'd like to teach her a whole lot more right the fuck now.

My blood runs ten degrees hotter, my cock pulsing in time with the flutter of her pulse against her throat, and I lean in, drawn by her magnetism.

We hold each other's eyes in tense silence.

We haven't had a minute alone. Not with packing and getting the fuck out of dodge with Em always around, and the last time we kissed was a quick stolen thing while I was busy swapping the plates on the Wrangler with a loaner pair from Landon, just in case the Pilgrims had mine.

Liv's somehow become such a deep part of me that just a few days without her leaves me feeling like I can't breathe, but now those parted, soft lips are offering the very air I need.

But even as I lean closer, Liv breaks back, snapping the trembling thread between us. With a reluctant smile, she pats my arm, glancing over her shoulder. "We should behave. Em might walk in."

Right. Reluctantly, my chest heaves, and I sink back against the couch while Liv puts a little more distance between us, curling up in the corner of the couch and hugging a throw pillow to her chest.

I have to figure out what I'm doing here. I have to talk

to her about what *we're* doing, if this is going somewhere. If it's just a dalliance for as long as this assignment lasts or if Liv wants a permanent place in my life. In *our* lives, I should say.

Fuck. I can't keep sneaking around Em like this, but I'm not risking more chaos in my daughter's life.

It would kill her if I told her Liv was staying, that Liv and I were together, only for Liv to suddenly just up and leave.

Leave, just like Crystal.

I tilt my head against the back of the couch, looking up at the crossed beams in the ceiling, and drag my mind back on track. "So, you going to tell me what I'm not understanding about my own daughter?"

"Mm. It's about girls in general." Liv hugs the pillow tighter and looks away, into the fireplace, the flames flickering in her eyes in flashes of gold on blue. "One day, boys are just kids we play with like everyone else...and the next we're told they could be boyfriends, lovers, husbands. Even heartbreakers. They're going to touch our bodies. They might hurt us, too. Boys can bring heaven or hell, and there's no way of knowing which one it'll be until you're up close and personal. Two worlds colliding. We're told everything men do means something, mysterious as ever. And the only way we'll decode it is to act this way and dress that way and do this little dance of enticement, flirting, loving."

I stroke her arm, loving how thoughtful she seems. Her voice is soft, melancholy, her face half-hidden by the pillow by now, voice muffled. "It just...changes how we think about ourselves. It changes how we think about the men in our lives, and how safe it is to talk to them when they might speak this weird boy language we have no idea about, too." I can't see her mouth, but I can still hear the bitter smile in her voice. "Including our fathers."

I want to say it's not true. I want to say that won't happen for Em, but can I really?

"I never wanted it to be that way with Em," I whisper. "Never wanted that kind of thing to hold her back from being who she is."

"And you did great with that. But now..." Her gaze shifts to me, something dark and hurting in her eyes, old and buried deep but slowly rising to the surface. "You can't control how other people around her influence her, Riker. You can help, but it's hers to find out. At her age, she's probably dealing with it right now. All her peers suddenly focused on this crazy boy-girl dynamic, making her painfully aware of this imaginary difference between how we think and who we are."

I wonder at Liv when she was Em's age, now. Wonder at her life, her father, and the pressures placed on her to be just this way or that, to fit herself into the tidy little box her old man had already chosen for her long before she was even old enough to recognize the walls closing in.

I *hate* thinking of any walls closing in on Em, too. Knowing the only thing I can do is teach her to be strong enough and proud enough and certain enough to push those walls back until they break.

I just don't know if I can do it alone. Suddenly I'm realizing something insane.

Em may need Liv just as much as I do.

A woman who sees the things I can't, who knows everything I thought I knew but now I'm not so sure of. A friend who can tell her where the weak points in those walls are.

And someone who'll show her just where to strike to send them crashing down.

But Liv is quiet now, her lashes trembling, and even with Em just in the other room, I can't just leave her like this. I offer my hand, beckoning.

"You sound sad," I say.

"It's just something I think about sometimes. Heavy stuff." She takes my hand, hers soft against mine, small and slim and sweet, and after a moment she uncurls to tuck herself against my side again, nestling her head to my shoulder. "That's why I like you, though. You see me as a woman, but you don't treat me like this alien outsider. You don't lay on burdens. You don't expect games, and you don't play them with me. You read me well, and you let me do the same."

Fuck. That hits somewhere strange and deep.

I smile, rubbing her wrist. "Damn. Always thought I had this walled-off thing down."

"You're closed, but not enigmatic. That means a lot, Riker." She smiles, resting her chin on my shoulder, the tip of her nose nuzzling my jaw. "Or maybe I just speak your language."

I know it's not the right time for it, but I want to distract her from that ache in her eyes, to see the light come back to her smile.

Without stopping, I lean down and kiss her. Just a slow, soft collision, a melding, yet somehow I want to tell her through the kiss that I'm here. That I don't need her to squeeze herself into a box, that I don't need her to restrict herself or to be some imaginary person some strange, archaic rules tell her she should be.

I just need her to be herself.

As our mouths part, I nip her upper lip, teasing gently, before whispering, "What language am I speaking right now?"

Her eyes glitter warmly, and a gentle understanding I don't need words to decipher spills out. Maybe if there's some coded language between us, it's one only we know.

One only we understand.

"Something I can't say out loud with Em in the other room," she teases, then pulls away, tugging at my arm to pull me off the couch. "C'mon. Help me start dinner."

"Wait," I say, catching her hand. "I know we just got here, but…how do you feel about another trip into town?"

* * *

Sometimes, I don't know what the hell I'm doing until I'm already doing it.

And I'm not sure what's bugging me until I'm parking the Wrangler outside a Bed, Bath, and Beyond in Yosemite, and staring in through the brightly lit windows at the displays.

This late, we only have an hour until closing. I probably should've put this whim off until morning, but fuck.

I don't want to spend another night in a house haunted by ghosts.

"Dad?" Em asks. "What are we doing?"

"We're…" I fumble for an excuse. "The house smells a little musty. Don't want anyone getting sick. Figured we should replace all the linens, and that's a good opportunity to redecorate, right?"

Em perks. "Can we do blue?"

"Sure," I say, watching her fondly in the rear view mirror as she scrambles for the door. "Blue sounds great."

Liv watches me knowingly, then smiles and reaches over to touch my arm. "It doesn't smell musty in there at all."

I glance at her, grateful for her understanding. "Old then, maybe. You know what I mean. Why don't you and Em have some fun? Do whatever you want. Redecorate the place. Buy anything you need."

Her eyes glint. "That, sir, is a dangerous proposition." With Em looking away, Liv leans in and steals a kiss to my cheek, then tugs at my arm. "Come on."

I follow my girls inside. From there it's a total circus – and I think the shop staff would hate us with every fiber of their being for showing up this late, if we weren't buying so much.

I'm just along for the ride, while Em and Liv patter back and forth with everything from curtains to bedding to knick-knacks for the shelves. There's just something about seeing them together – how well they get along, how effortlessly they blend – that puts wicked thoughts in my head.

Ideas about family and impossible forevers that shouldn't be there.

It's worth every penny of the huge amount we spend in the store to see them like this.

Back at the cabin, though, it's all hands on deck.

I join in, stripping down the bedding, putting up new

curtains, laying out new throws and pillows on the couch, lining up decorations along the fireplace mantle.

By the time we're done, it looks like somewhere different. Never erasing the memories steeped into the wood grain walls, but simply quieting them to make room for something new. Something brighter, breezier, without pain and loss haunting every corner. It feels right, I realize, as I collapse onto the couch in an exhausted heap next to my tired but very satisfied girls.

It feels like home.

* * *

WITH THE WHOLE PLACE REDECORATED, it's surprising how well we settle into cabin life.

After a day or two of tension, constantly on the lookout for intruders, I start to feel safe letting Liv and Em go hiking as long as they promise to stay out of sight of the road and promise to come back if they spot other people – no matter how friendly they seem.

I've taken my own precautions, with weapons strategically stashed both inside and outside. Unloaded, of course. I'm not having a loaded gun around my daughter unless it's holstered on my person, and you'd better believe my ankle holster is strapped at all times, but there's always a hidden magazine close by.

We might be enjoying ourselves playing house.

The days drag on, shorter as the season burns away and the sun sets sooner.

Em makes a few new friends on our family hikes and shopping runs, local kids who hang around a park playground with their parents on the edge of town. You'd better believe I run a background check on all of them.

It takes three weeks before I let her go off bowling with Juanita McReynolds for a couple hours, and that's only because the girl's old man, Ken, retired from NORAD last year and doesn't have so much as a speeding ticket on record.

I'll pick her up soon. That leaves Liv and me blissfully alone, her humming this soft, seductive tune to herself when I come back to the cabin and find her in the kitchen.

She's just pulled a huckleberry pie out of the oven and placed it on the cooling rack.

It's a dangerous thing seeing her bent over, then turning around with a perky little smile and a sunbeam in her eyes that tells me she's glad to see me.

Dangerous, because for the past few weeks, we've barely had a chance to sneak out to my truck long after Em's asleep. We've had to fuck quickly, quietly, more like satisfying a savage animal reflex than taking the time lovers should to explore, to savor, to own.

The second we're alone, I'm not the Riker she thought she knew.

I'm more man than beast.

I need her the fuck under me *now.*

"Liv," I growl her name, nipping at her ear, then trail teeth and tongue down her throat until she gives up that sweetness, that whimper I need to safeguard my own sanity. "Still can't fathom what you do to me, can you?"

She shakes her head, shy as ever. Consider me slayed.

Something about her adorable aloofness just makes me throb that much harder.

"Bedroom, woman. Now." I lead her by the hand in a headlong rush.

We tumble into the darkness together, barely pausing long enough to switch on a lamp. I can't take this a second longer, so I push her onto the bed, hiking up the knee-high skirt she's had on since morning. "Riker...*yes.*"

Fuck, do I love my name when she announces it in that breathy half-moan.

Still, it's just half the reason I growl my approval in her ear, careful to rake my stubble against her skin. The rest has to do with what I'm ready to tear off her body with my bare hands, that flimsy skirt hugging her far too fuckable hips.

"This, sweetheart, I like. Want you wearing a whole lot more of these things. Going to buy you a whole damn new wardrobe if I have to for easy access." I'm fisting her skirt, pulling it up over her waist, meaning every word.

A soft, longing sigh slips out of her heart shaped lips.

Lucky for me, she's done me one better than the skirt. I'm expecting to find something lace up under it, inviting me to tear it right off, but instead my fingers brush her soft, bare pussy. Already slick and wet for every inch of me.

Fuck.

"Tell me you weren't commando all morning?" I smile, push my forehead into hers, unable to resist when I catch the spark of mischief in her eyes.

"Only if you tell me you aren't hard?"

Like hell.

She's too adorable, expecting me to form coherent words when I'm hard as granite.

I can't even think, let alone remember how to talk. My

hands go to my belt, undoing it, loving how she opens her legs before my belt is undone.

I need to fuck this girl. I need it bad. I need it because her black magic is turning every part of me inside out.

I also need to get a damn grip again. Time to remind her who's really in control.

That's why I drop to my knees, push her thighs apart, and ignore how sweet she moans my name again.

"Riker. Oh, God!"

That's what I hear echoing in my head when I hold her tight and move on her.

First Liv gets my breath, my lips, my tongue. My mouth works her swollen little pussy up and down, pushing her straight to the brink, knotting her up in that way I know she likes when she writhes, my licks fucking deeper in her folds.

She's tiny as ever. So delicate.

So small and tight and mine.

I savor every ripple, every taste, every low murmur in her throat when she begs for my cock. She does it wordlessly, bobbing her hips, her whole body wracked in a breathy swoon.

I'm so fucking hard it hurts. My dick jerks, my balls in full meltdown, seething like never before to empty their steaming contents deep, deep inside her.

So damn deep she screams.

But she's not ready for me. Not yet. I know this little pussy, and it needs to be trained to take me to her full, wonderful depths when I go *hard*.

So I take full advantage while she's like this. Turned over, thighs pushed apart, lush ass in my face, snarling as I drive my tongue deeper into her tight heat.

Deeper, faster, harder into everything I've claimed.

Everything I'll never give up

Come for me sweetheart, I think with a growl. *Come until it hurts real good on my tongue.*

Exactly eight seconds later, after I've sucked her throbbing clit between my teeth and smothered it with the tip of my tongue, she does.

My woman comes like the world's brightest, hottest, best firecracker.

Just a mess of flailing limbs and choked moans and convulsions. Face pressed into the mattress. Ass shaking, my hands holding her back on my face, demanding more, every ripple of her body for my tongue.

Liv comes beautiful for me while I eat her cunt alive.

When her gasping, mewling mess of an O finishes, I can't even see straight.

That goes double for her, so I rise, dick in hand, pushing my weight onto the bed. Her legs are still open, the backs of her thighs calling like two dangerous, flushed sirens.

I'm fisting her hair when I push in, mounting her from behind. Something feral leaves my throat the instant I'm engulfed in her heat.

"Gotta make the most of our alone time, gorgeous. Think you can come a few more times for me before we get Em?"

Liv makes a muffled sound into the sheets, but there's no mistaking it.

She's all heat. All want. All fiery, screaming need for my thrusts.

"Yes, Riker. Holy hell, yes..."

Holy hell. Must be one of her favorite terms, and it couldn't be more perfect when I throw my hips into hers.

We crash together frantically, all smoldering flesh and fire between her legs. I'm on her like a bolt in the night.

I slow my thrusts a few strokes in, marveling how bad she wants it.

Her sweet little ass rocks back against me, grinding every time she swings low, savoring the friction of my balls on her clit.

"Holy hell. Yeah, sweetheart," I echo back. "Fuck me like you really want it. This is you."

I add a crisp palm when she bends into me again and slow my thrusts. My hand flies over her ass cheek, leaving another apple blossom red mark, and I know she likes it rough because that gets her moving. She smacks back into me; faster, louder, harder.

I should feel like a dirty old man.

Here I am, with a woman almost half my age and millions richer, riding every inch of Riker Woods like it's what she was made for. And I'm holding back like a champ, barely keeping the fire in my balls from burning us both down.

Her pussy starts tensing on my dick before I give in.

Then I fucking bring it.

Melting. Snarling. Grinding. Thrusting.

Owning her from the inside out.

I level myself into her with powerful, long strokes that bring her over the edge. Her well tongued pussy opens nice and deep, accommodating my fullness, sinking to her depths.

It shouldn't be possible, but it is.

Liv comes even sweeter for me the second time. I'll

never forget it as long as I live, her blonde hair gone amber gold in the dull light, our bed creaking like mad, this lunatic tempo between us that's only broken when her O hits so hard her limbs go rigid and still.

I hold her up anyway. Spread her legs apart. Push one hand between her legs and frig her clit wild while I hammer twice as hard, balls deep, one frantic fuck after the next through her convulsions.

Holy hell indeed.

Now here's the weird part – there's nothing dirty or old or wrong about this.

Not when we're in the heat of it, racing each other to find out who burns down first.

Not when I'm buried to the hilt, mastering every inch of her, knowing I'll die before I ever let this pussy belong to anybody else.

Not when I've found the first woman in my life who makes me feel more alive than I did when I was eighteen years old.

Not when it's Olivia Holly I'm fucking.

And Olivia Holly's the only one worthy of pulling the come from my balls until I draw my last breath.

"C'mon, Liv. Holy fuck," I snarl a minute later, never giving her a chance to come down, driving down into her until she's sandwiched between my weight and the mattress.

Something just sets her off again.

Something just ignites in my skull.

Something snaps.

My own release hits so hard I don't see it coming. My vision blurs, everything goes white, and then I'm just this frenzied pump of hips, this human jackhammer, desperate to break and ruin us both by spilling myself so deep in her sweet cunt I never come home.

Holy fucking hell!

The roar in my head fades into the stream of growls leaving my throat.

Then it's all just an animal blur.

Her pussy milking my cock like a vise.

My balls pumping, churning, flaming, urging me on.

Deeper, deeper, goddamned *deeper*.

Little Liv, throwing her hair back when ecstasy peaks, just a glorious mess of honey sweet fuckery I want to take all over again – even though I'm barely halfway through coming.

My dick doing things it's never done to my head before. Never, ever, as long as I've lived.

There's sex with the women I've had in my life before.

And then there's sex with Liv, this small, unassuming fae thing, who makes up for her size with every dirty, mad thing she does to me.

I'm still trembling, every muscle firing on its own, when I'm able to see straight again.

Then I pull out, admiring the mess I've left that steams out of her, flopping down on the mattress and bringing her into my arms.

We kiss real soft, real slow, too lost for words.

We kiss because we're lost in something neither one of us dares say out loud.

We kiss like we're gone, because holy hell, we are.

And fuck if either one of us can stop.

Before the alarm on my phone goes off as a reminder to grab Em, she's got her little fingers wrapped around my slick, throbbing dick again. And I'm rolling her over as I bite her bottom lip, ready to spend the next half hour mating this beautiful woman to my flesh.

* * *

I CAN'T LET myself forget this isn't a vacation.

I spend a few days sorting through more of the backlogged documents recovered from Crown Security, then settle into doing repairs around the house. There's a definite bite in the morning air now, a faint hint of winter approaching.

Even if Em's grandparents keep this place in pretty decent shape, things still happen, and we're here nearly a week when I realize the weather stripping on the windows is dry rotting.

It happens with the mountain weather, always freezing and defrosting over time.

We might be here through the winter, so I take the hike back down the slope to the car and drive into town to the hardware store in Yosemite. I pick up some groceries while I'm there, and take the time to get the lay of the land now that I'm looking around by daylight. Yosemite's a tourist town, so expecting anyone to notice strange activity or people who shouldn't be here isn't something that's going to happen.

But people still stick out like sore thumbs when they're here with ulterior motives. People move in patterns, and tourists have completely different patterns from the scum trying to hunt down the woman I need to protect with everything in me.

No one in Yosemite sets off alarms, at least.

When I pull into the parking lot down the road from the trail, though, I can't help but tense.

There are two new cars in the lot.

One's a battered Honda with California plates, the other a sleek black town car with Washington plates. Rich people vacation out here all the time, so it's probably nothing. Still...

I'm quick on the trail, pushing myself despite the thin high-altitude air, sucking in sharp breaths as I climb quickly to the house. Something doesn't feel right.

No one outside. Everything looks peaceful, the curtains open to let the natural light in, but as I approach the door, I can already hear voices. Not Liv's or Em's, either.

Male.

No one sounds upset.

There's laughter, and when I look through the window, I see Em sitting on the couch with a sandy head bowed near hers, Magic cards exchanging hands. Liv in the kitchen reaching into the fridge, and a man I don't recognize at first sitting at a barstool in front of the kitchen island.

This is wrong. *All fucking wrong.*

I fit the key in the lock and shove the door open. Everyone pauses, looking up at me.

I know the kid on the couch. It's Ryan, the instructor's boy, and from the guilty look in Em's eyes, I know exactly how he knew we were here.

And who brought him, when his father Mike watches me from the kitchen with his face frozen in a mask of nervous shame, beads of sweat brimming on his forehead.

I slump, closing my eyes and nudging the door closed behind me so I can set the bags down. "Emily."

"It's just Ryan, Dad!" she protests. "And his dad had to bring him!"

"I told you no visitors," I say, shooting Liv a look.

She should've put them out before I even got here. She winces, mouthing *I'll explain later* while I transfer my gaze to Ryan. He looks confused and a little scared, so I try to keep my voice gentle. "I'm sorry, son. This isn't your fault, but you can't be here."

"Can't he stay?" Em pipes up. "He already knows where we are. You let me hang out with Juanita. What can it hurt?"

"Everything," I say coldly, flicking my fingers to Mike. "You need to leave. I can't explain why, not right now. Just take your son and go. It's not safe for you to be here – either of you."

Mike frets his fingers together nervously. "I, um...I'm sorry. I can't."

Can't? Who the hell does this guy think he is?

I don't understand what's going on here.

"Dad, come *on!*" Em protests. "You always ruin everything, just when I'm starting to make friends!"

I hate that I have to be Dad right now, and not her friend, but there are lives at stake, including hers.

"Watch your tone, young lady," I warn. "You're already in trouble. Don't make it worse." Then I turn that same tone on Mike, watching him steadily, while he shrinks further and further into himself. "What do you mean, 'can't?'"

Mike winces, staring down at his knees. Liv is watching intently now, an odd expression on her face, something mixed between resignation and dread. Like she knows what's going on here, even if I don't.

I get a clue pretty damned fast when Mike whispers, "Shit, I'd never have taken the money if I'd known. If I'd known you were in real, true danger. He was just...he was so insistent, and the rent on the studio's bankrupting us, and just...just!"

It takes everything in me not to pull this sputtering worm up by his collar and shake him until his neck snaps. I take a single step closer, but it's enough to make him cringe and flatten himself back against the chair.

"Mike," I say softly. "You want to be very clear on who 'he' is. *Now.*"

Mike opens his mouth, but before he can answer, a light, almost mockingly polite knock hits the door. Three quick raps and done.

I go still, looking over my shoulder. Nothing but a hint of a shadow visible under the door, no line of sight out the window.

Dropping my voice, I grind through my teeth, "Everyone in the bedroom. Now."

Liv and Em immediately rush to comply, with Em dragging Ryan behind her. Mike starts to get up to follow them, but he stops when I plant a hand in the center of his chest.

"Not you. You stay."

The look he gives me is sheer dread.

I swear to fuck, if I open that door and Lion is on the other side of it, I don't know who I'm going to shoot first: Lion, or Master Mike Godart.

The knock comes again, more insistent this time. Impatient.

I drop to one knee and slide the same Ruger I'd taught Liv to shoot on from inside my ankle holster, rolling up my jeans briefly, then tucking them back down as I rise. Safety off, weapon pointed at the floor, I edge toward the door and press myself to one side of it, leaning out the window.

I catch a hint of a shoulder in a very crisply pressed and tailored suit. Not Lion, then.

I shift in front of the door, holding my gun hand behind my back just in case, and undo the latch, pulling it open.

Alec Holly stands on the other side of the door, as cool and calm as if his collar isn't drenched in sweat, fastidiously adjusting his tie clip. "Mr. Woods," he says, clipped and perfunctory and entirely condescending. "Quite the walk up here by the scenic route."

That black, ugly disgust I'd felt the other night comes boiling back up.

It's like the man coats everything with the slime of his presence. With an irritated sound, I drop down to slide my gun back into its holster, eyeballing him from under my brows. If I'm going to shoot anyone today, it's not going to be Alec Holly.

As much as I'd enjoy it.

"You paid Mike to find out where we went," I snarl, my disgust turning into sheer loathing. "You used his son's friendship with my daughter. You used my *daughter*."

"No one used anyone. I simply took the most expedient path to get what I wanted." Alec Holly's smile is thin, almost triumphant. "Now, speaking of daughters...I believe you have *mine*, Mr. Woods, and I very much would like her back."

XV: A LITTLE MORE TIME (OLIVIA)

The moment I hear my father's voice from the living room, I experience an emotion I don't think I've ever felt in my life.

Rage.

Pure, unadulterated rage.

Whenever I tried to write rage, I always thought of it as a red thing.

But it's actually white, flashing in my vision, eclipsing it like a nuclear explosion, searing through my veins like a flash of light. I can't believe my father's here.

And if he's here, and Mike and Ryan are here...then Daddy must've pulled something pretty dirty to find out where we are.

I thought it was strange when they showed up, but I'd tried to play along until Riker came back. I didn't know what was going on. I was afraid of tipping off anyone Mike was involved with if I sent him packing. I'd thought maybe the Pilgrims had tracked us here through Mike.

Knowing it's my father – and that my own father

might accidentally lead the Pilgrims here anyway with his arrogant carelessness, without a care for my life, or Riker's, or Em's – makes it so much worse.

Before I can stop myself, I'm stalking into the living room, Em and Ryan trailing behind me like confused ducklings. I barely get a "Dad, what do you think—" out before he's suddenly pulling me into a hug, catching me completely off guard with the tightness of his grip.

I go stiff, alarm prickling through my entire body. My father doesn't hug like this.

He's never been overly physically affectionate with me, just the occasional brush of his fingers down my arm or through my hair, fleeting and always leaving me feeling vaguely uncomfortable.

This is more than uncomfortable, the tightness of his grip possessive in a way that leaves me squirming and cold and thinking of Milah with her dress torn, crying over her skinned knees and elbows. I flick an almost desperate look at Riker over Daddy's shoulder, but he's glaring at Mike as Mike takes the opportunity to grab his son and bolt out the door, away from this situation.

I wish I could follow him.

"Darling Olivia," Dad says, the overwrought emotion in his voice practically dripping falseness. "I can't *believe* they have you living out here like this. Come home, baby girl. Please come home."

"*No.*"

That's what it takes to get me to thrust away from him, putting an arm's length of distance between us – but it takes all my strength and all my bravery not to put Riker between us, too, a solid wall of protection so that Daddy can't try to overwhelm me again.

It's disturbing how easy it is to *see* him, now.

To know he does things like this to throw me off guard so I'll be too spun around to question anything or do anything but let him maneuver me in whatever direction he wants me to go. It's controlling. It's abusive.

And I won't let it happen anymore.

I square my shoulders, lifting my chin. I don't need Riker to hold me up. I'll stand on my own. "I'm not going anywhere," I say. "I'm here because it's the safest place to be, but you being here is jeopardizing the safety of everyone in this house."

Daddy scoffs, smoothing his graying hair back and looking at me like I'm the little girl I know I still am in his mind. "Don't be silly, darling. How can anyone keep you safe in a rickety cabin like this? I've upgraded the security at my estate, and –"

"It's not the security that's the problem," I point out, interrupting *him* for once, and his eyes go flinty. "It's the people. I trust the people here. I don't trust the people at your estate. That..." I swallow hard. Bravery or not, it's hard to admit this out loud. "That includes you. Not anymore."

My father's mask hardly cracks, but that hardness in his eyes is impenetrable. "Now you're being ridiculous. Hysterical. Olivia, you *are* coming home. I'm your father, and I know what's best for you. All this madness, it's gone to your head. You aren't mature enough or experienced enough to be making decisions like this."

"Nice to finally know what you really think of me. But no." I never thought standing up for myself would hurt so much, but I guess the problem is when you get bigger than people think you should be, the first thing they want to do is knock you down.

I'm still standing, though, while I continue, "I'm staying here, Daddy. And so are you, until you start telling me the truth."

Daddy looks down his nose at me. "I don't understand what truth you think needs telling."

There it is. The *you're crazy* tone. The *you're a little girl, your imagination's running away with you* tone, but it doesn't work on me anymore. I shake my head.

"Em, go back in the bedroom," I whisper. She doesn't need to hear this.

Em bites her lip, standing awkwardly behind me. "But..."

"Please, Em. This is serious."

She nods quickly, already retreating. "Okay."

I don't speak again until she's gone, shutting the bedroom door with a soft click of the latch.

Then I meet my father's eyes, staring him down. "Tell me what's really going on. Tell me about your real involvement with this. This isn't all Milah's mistakes. I want to know what's really going on. With the Pilgrims, with the Runners...all of it." When I say the name Runners, that's when his expression gives him away, his eyes widening slightly, his entire body oddly motionless. "You've been acting strange since this started. Erratic. Changing your mind all the time. Like you're trying to hide something." I step closer to him. "If you really love me, Daddy...just give it up. Tell me what you're hiding."

He looks at me for a moment, a strange look like he's afraid *I* might hurt *him*, before he looks over his shoulder toward the door. But Riker's there.

He positions himself in front of the door, a grim and forbidding obstacle that my father isn't getting through. My dad's a tall man, but he's not Riker; over two hundred pounds of solid slab muscle standing with his feet planted and his arms folded over his chest and a look on his face that says if my father tries to force his way past, Riker will find a way to lay him on the ground very, very easily.

I catch Riker's eye. *Please*, I mouth.

I need him to let me handle this. I need him *here*, but I need him doing just what he's doing right now: backing me up wordlessly, letting me do the talking while he sends his own message with silence.

His jaw sets as if he's about to argue, before he sighs and nods subtly.

It gives me the boost I need, to know he's trusting me to take the lead.

I wait until my father finally looks at me again. There's a wariness there, careful, and I can tell from the way he watches me that he's trying to figure out how to talk his way out of this.

That's all he's ever had besides money. Words.

Hollow, slick lies and meaningless bait.

He's calculating how to get off free, without consequences, if he can just snowball me into accepting whatever he says. I plant my hands on my hips, glaring at him, just waiting until he stops with his mental gymnastics. Finally, he settles on a smile.

"If it will ease your mind, darling, of course we can talk things out. I had no idea you were fussing and worrying so much."

He's patronizing me. I don't care. I point at the couch. "Sit."

He folds himself ingratiatingly onto the couch, even if he curls his upper lip at the crocheted throw and plucks at it as if it might get his fine wool suit dirty. He crosses his legs, lacing his fingers together, and gives me with a plastic smile. "Really, dearest, all this because I asked you to come home? I never –"

"You never ask anything. You just phrase your orders a bit more politely."

Dad raises both brows. "Do I? And where's this coming from now? Who's been feeding you this sort of nonsense?"

"No one's been feeding me anything!" I let a bit of my frustration out, flinging a hand out, before taking a deep breath and calming myself. I can't fly off the handle, or he'll just treat me like a little girl throwing a tantrum. "It's normal for adults to want to make their own choices, instead of having them dictated and following along passively. And you seem to have missed the fact that I'm an adult now. Just because you couldn't stop Milah from growing up too fast, doesn't mean you can keep me as your little girl forever to make up for it. I'm not a damn bird in a cage."

Briefly, Daddy's face crumples. It's the first honest expression I've seen out of him in a long time.

Then it closes over in a look of icy offense, flung right at Riker. "Is this your doing, Woods? Making Olivia think she can survive without my help?"

"Don't," Riker says softly.

It's just one word, barely heard, but it's as heavy as a sledgehammer.

I fold my arms over my chest. "Do you really think I'm that incapable of independent thought? Like I can't come up with these ideas myself? Do you think I don't know *what* to think, without you to tell me?"

"Now, dearest, that's a bit –"

"Don't. You heard him. You're going to say something that makes me feel silly and foolish and small, so you can dismiss everything I think and feel," I bite off bitterly. "Don't you get that's *why* I don't want to come back? You think I can't survive in the outside world, but you'd be surprised how well I do when people trust me to stand on my own. Riker's trusted me to pull my own weight, and damn it, Daddy, I've been *pulling*."

My father blinks, leaning back against the sofa, looking between me and Riker, before his eyes widen with an offended gasp, his brows lowering. "You've got to be damn well fucking kidding me."

Finally.

There's *real* Daddy.

Not fundraiser Dad, mild and charming for the masses. It's controlling, angry Dad, tongue all sharp barbs and foul words. "You've defiled my daughter," he flings at Riker. "You're actually sleeping with her, aren't you? Animal. I should sue. To think I'm paying you to take liberties you have no right to!"

"Technically," Riker points out grimly, eyes flashing with cold green steel and edges sharp enough to cut, "you aren't paying me at all. Enguard is."

"Well, they won't be able to pay you a penny after I sue your entire company into bankruptcy," my father hisses, glowering at Riker, ignoring that I'm even in the room. "My daughter is not something you can paw over, some toy, you maniac."

"Your daughter," I say, lips trembling, throat tight, eyes

stinging, "is not some *thing* at all. That's what you can't seem to figure out. I'm a person. Not an object. And my life is mine. Not your business. Nothing's your business except what you've done to *fuck up* my life with whatever it was you did to get us in this situation in the first place."

The entire room goes still. My hand flies to my mouth, to my burning face.

I don't think I've ever said *fuck* in front of my father in my life, but it just drops out. I'm that angry, but also that ready to breakdown crying.

This is so messed up. I wanted to be strong in front of Daddy, but all he had to do was talk about me in that mortifying, horrible, dehumanizing way to reduce me to tears.

Maybe I really am a little girl after all.

He starts to open his mouth, but Riker stops him with a single cold word. "No."

A chill runs up my spine. He's looking at my father with that same blank, deadly expression he'd had when he'd taken that Pilgrim down and made him talk one careful, precisely applied bit of pain and terror at a time. "I don't think you need to say another word to Liv if you're going to speak to her that way." His voice gentles, just for me, but that hard, razor-wire stare is just for my father. "Liv, go wait with Em. Tell her everything's okay."

I know I shouldn't run away, but I need to go right now.

I need to be anywhere but within my father's sight, when he's looking at me like *I've* somehow betrayed *him*.

Of course I have. I've refused to be his perfect, docile little doll anymore, empty and quiet and sweet. I've refused to live up to the image he's painted of who I should be. I've let him down by daring to be my own person.

But not nearly as much as he's let me down, by showing who I really am in his eyes.

I turn and run before the tears can come.

And I don't feel sorry for my father at all, as the bedroom door closes on Riker's steady murmur of, "Now, Mr. Holly...you and I are going to have a talk."

* * *

When I step into the bedroom, Em looks as miserable as I feel.

She's slumped on the bed, her knees pulled up to her chest, and from the wet tracks on her cheeks, she's obviously been crying. I kind of want to curl up and cry next to her, but I have to be the adult here.

Realizing that Em needs me helps me pull myself together a bit, out of my own shock and upset.

I put on a smile for her and sink down on the edge of the bed near her feet.

"Hey," I offer softly.

Em sniffles, rubbing at her nose and returning a tremulous smile. "Hey."

"You okay?"

"Not really," she mumbles and buries her mouth against her folded forearm. "Dad's kind of a jerk, you know?"

"Dads can be like that," I murmur.

"Your Dad's not so great either, huh?"

"My Dad's...got issues. Big ones. But Em..." I don't want

to make her feel like what she's feeling right now is wrong.

I can't do that to her, not when people do it to me so often. But I know she's a smart girl, and it might help her to understand that her Dad's on her side this time. Unlike mine.

Riker's her everything, her rock, her best friend and her worst enemy, her role model and her chain, all those confusing things a parent is going to be at this age when she's just figuring out who she is...but he's not trying to hurt her, and I think with a little nudging, she can see that. "You know your Dad made Ryan leave for his own safety, right? And for ours?"

"He made Ryan leave because I'm not allowed to date boys yet and Dad figured out I like him," she bites off, her cheeks coloring with anger and mortification. "And now he's humiliated me so bad, Ryan will never talk to me again!"

"Are you kidding me? Ryan probably thinks you're a cool super spy now. Totally Kim Possible. Later, when this is all over, you can tell him how you helped your dad take down those bad guys at the airport. Not a lot of twelve-year-olds can say they've been in a shootout."

I bite my tongue. For a second, I feel sick that our mess put her in one, but we lived. And Em just sits up with a look that says something different.

Her eyes light, but warily. "Really, Liv?"

"Really." I find another smile just for her, reaching out to lightly nudge one knuckle against her cheek. "I know it feels like your dad's being a massive jerk right now. *My* dad's being a massive jerk, too. But all these rules...they're bigger than school, and crushes, and parents being mean. People are trying to kill me, Em."

"I know. And they're trying to kill us, too."

I hate that she has to say this so calmly, so matter-of-factly. But I'm also proud of her that she's learned from the lessons Riker's laid down. "Yes. And if they'll hurt you, then they'll hurt Ryan, too. That's really what this is all about. Your dad wants your friend to be safe, and he wants you to be safe. Once this is over, you can see Ryan again, and I'll bet your dad will even be glad to chaperone you on a few dates."

Her face flames, her eyes widening. "Ew, I don't want to *date* Ryan! We're friends!"

"No?" I grin. "That's okay, too. Having friends who like the things you like is the best. And you deserve those kinds of friends, Em."

She bites her lip, watching me uncertainly. "Are...are we friends, too?"

I don't know if my heart wants to break or explode with this warm, sweet fullness, but I do know I can't resist hugging her any longer. I reach for her and she tumbles against me. Then I remember being a little girl tumbling against my older sister just this way, clinging for the kind of comfort words just can't bring. I hug Em close, and run my fingers through her hair.

"Of course we're friends, sweetie," I murmur. "Of course."

She just clings to me. She's quiet, so quiet about it, but I can tell she's crying.

I let her, holding her close, and repress the urge to cry myself. There's no one here to tell me that my dad really means the best, because he doesn't.

He means what's best for *him*, and I hate that the blinders I've been wearing for over twenty years have been stripped away this way so I can see my father for the complete and utter bastard he is.

Honestly, the fact that I need almost an entire hand to count his wives really should have tipped me off sooner.

When that many women can't stand you, the problem isn't the women.

I've been so naive. So sheltered. This twelve-year-old girl is more worldly wise than I am, but I gotta say...I could pick worse role models than a brilliant little thing like Em Woods.

She subsides before long, and after a few sniffles suddenly breaks the silence with, "I know about you and Dad." She blinks owlishly up at me through the tear-spiked fan of her lashes. "You're not as sneaky as you think you are."

I wince, but try to tease, "Hey, I'd like to think we're pretty sneaky. You're just too smart for us." But it feels fake and forced, and I let the act drop with a sigh, looking at her ruefully. "I'm sorry, Em."

"Why are you sorry?" She shakes her head, confusion flitting across her face. "Dad's happy when he's around you."

She nearly stops my heart with that one, then starts it again when she admits shyly, "I'm happy when I'm around you." She rubs at her tear-pinkened nose. "It's...it's okay if you're gonna be my new mom."

For a second, I'm in shock. Then I'm in this daze of emotions, trying to speak too much at once, this rush of words and feelings and fears that I'll screw this up bad.

"Oh, Em! Sweetie, no." I gather her close again,

cradling her head against my shoulder. "No one can be your new mom, because your real mother loved you very much...no one can take her place. Your mom will always be your mom, even when she's gone. But me? I'm still your friend. And your dad's." I press a gentle kiss to her forehead. "Even if your dad and I don't work out...I'll always be your friend, okay?"

She searches my face, questioning if she can trust those words, before a sweet smile seems to offer her acceptance. "Okay," she says, and burrows down against me again.

I'm content to stay like this. Em is just as much a comfort to me as I'm trying to be to her. But still, I can hear voices from the living room, Riker's steady and calm, my father's raised and agitated, and I wonder.

How many times can my father lie to Riker Woods before Riker loses his patience?

XVI: A LITTLE TOO HARD (RIKER)

I've never broken a rich man's fingers before.

I'm very tempted to now.

But I won't have to lay a hand on Alec Holly to break him. He's not that kind of man.

He doesn't need blood and pain to make the fear of what can and will happen to him real. All he needs are words – words he believes with absolute certainty, because I mean them just as absolutely.

I fucking mean it when I say I'll break every finger on both hands until he talks just to make it stop, saving the thumbs for last because they're the thickest and hurt the most to snap.

I mean that by the time that's done, I won't let him speak because I'll tape his mouth shut, gagging him with a cloth that barely lets him breathe, and then force him to write what I want to know by hand with those broken, mangled fingers. I mean that I'll find new ways to make him bleed, if the Pilgrims or the Runners or anyone else threatens Liv in this house because of him. I mean that I'll murder this shit in the most exquisite, horrifying way possible if anything happens to my Liv or my Em because of him.

I mean that he has everything to fear from me.

And nothing – not his money, not his companies, not his power, not his connections – could ever make me fear him.

He stares up at me from the couch, eyes wide and wild and pale. He's trying to maintain some hint of that aloof composure, but it's the chain on his tie clip that gives him away. It's rattling ever-so-subtly, this quiet chime of fear that gives away his faint full-body shaking.

I haven't even taken a single step toward him. I'm leaning against the door, arms folded over my chest, ankles crossed. All I've done is talk to him.

"Wh-what the hell's wrong with you?" he stammers.

I arch a brow. "It's amazing the things you learn you're capable of in service to God and country. So. Let's get a few things out in the open." I unfold my arms. He flinches as I lift a curled fist, but all I do is begin ticking points off on my fingers. "One. You're an asshole. You're also not in control of Liv's life anymore. She is. That's not up for negotiation."

A second finger. Middle finger. Satisfying finger. "Two. I know you hired the Runners to take a hit out on a few Pilgrims. Stupid ass move, by the way." My third finger flies up. "Three. I also know you do a lot of under the table business using the startups you buy to conceal it. I'd bet that business has crossed paths with the Pilgrims' operations, including their little indentured servitude racket with their traffickers across the border." Last finger. "Four. You're at the center of all of this. Not random chance. Not Milah's drug habits. So you're going to tell me what's really happening, and then I'm going to tell Landon Strauss and the FBI."

Holly starts to open his mouth, then thinks better of it when I count off again on my thumb, his mouth snapping shut hard enough to make his sallow cheeks wobble.

"Fifth and final," I add, "you're not going to argue with me, asshole. Because believe it or not, I'm trying to keep your greedy, shitty ass alive, and the only way to do that is for you to come clean so the people trying to protect you *and* your daughters and my family aren't shooting in the dark."

He actually has the nerve to look offended, drawing himself up with false bravado. "You think I don't care about my daughters? I would do anything to protect them."

"As long as you can protect yourself first. I bet you'd cry crocodile tears at their funerals if their deaths got the Pilgrims off your ass. You'd be partying in Milan by morning."

"I most certainly would not!" He sniffs. His angry face falls, and he rubs his temples. "Look, Mr. Woods...this was all a misunderstanding. A domino effect that ran out of control. I never intended for my girls to be hurt. Not for anyone to –"

"Shut up. Tell me about the first domino that fell."

Alec Holly licks his lips, then pulls the neatly folded pocket square from his coat's breast pocket and dabs at his sweat-dewed brow and upper lip. "Well. You see, I was quite worried about Milah. She's been through this song and dance before, you know. And she always backslides. She always finds a new supply for her nasty habit, but her primary supply lines run through this gang. The Pilgrims."

My eyes beam hot death at him. I nod slightly. "Go on."

"I only wanted to make them afraid to sell to her. Milah's skeletons are piling up so deep the closet simply won't stay closed much longer, and I suppose I just..." His voice cracks dramatically, and he looks off into the distance. I sigh deeply while he continues, "I don't want to see her bring any more harm to herself, or this family. So, yes, call me guilty. I hired a few men to intimidate a few of the Pilgrims' drug runners. Murder was never supposed to be involved, but they went too far – and it was only terrible luck my Olivia was there. Don't you see? A misunderstanding. A truly awful one."

I stare at him blankly.

The disgust is too thick in my mouth to even speak, and my tongue weighs a hundred pounds when I finally say, "You don't play the martyr act very well. Nor do you know anything about the criminal underworld, or how seriously a gang like the Pilgrims takes blood vendettas. And you're leaving something out, Mr. Holly." I survey my nails. "Are you right-handed or left-handed?"

He cocks his head like a puzzled cocker spaniel. "Right...why?"

"Because I'll start with the fingers on your left. I'm generous like that. Let you keep your dominant hand to jerk off when all this is over or whatever the fuck."

He goes pale, actually hides both hands behind his back. "All right, all right!"

I glare at him, undaunted. But we might be making progress.

His face is all grimacing, hateful lines as he stares me

over. "You're a disgusting brute, Woods. I don't know what my daughter sees in you."

"I'd say that's between me and her, isn't it?" I push away from the door, just the slightest movement to straighten, but it's enough to make him flatten himself against the sofa. "Talk, Mr. Holly. Or I'll find more things to break than your stubby fingers."

"You've made your point, Mr. Woods," he snaps frigidly, before sniffing and adjusting his collar. "Very well. I was telling the truth when I said I wanted to protect Milah from any additional scandals, despite what you wish to believe. But I'll admit an ulterior motive in protecting my business holdings as well. You see, I...ah..."

He clears his throat, then speaks in a mild, dismissive tone, as if discussing the weather on a balmy day, nothing of particular importance. "A few years ago, I was involved in several land prospecting and investment opportunities tied to a stock trading deal. What I didn't know at the time was that the land rights were tied to a project the Pilgrims were working on with developing a strip mall for less...ah...*entitled* business owners. They needed their labor cheap and undocumented, the same as their tenants. The Pilgrims were happy to provide. Once it was legally binding, I couldn't pull out without involving my lawyers, audit transparency, a few other things...and considering the fact that tying stock values to this sort of deal is highly frowned on by the SEC, not to mention fiscally supporting the Pilgrims' less than legal ventures..." He loosens his tie.

I wonder if it's choking him more than his conscience. "Spit it the fuck out," I snarl.

"I have a vested interest in not being discovered,

considering it would be prudent to avoid jail time. And considering Milah's connections to the Pilgrims could lead to my connections to the Pilgrims, it was in my best interests that they be *suppressed*."

You little idiot, a vicious voice stabs at the back of my brain.

My leash is fraying. I can feel it, popping one thread at a time as the tension in me pulls tighter and tighter on it. "Did you tell them where we are?"

"Not this time," he answers glibly—then freezes, teeth half-bared in a frightened grimace, as he realizes what he said.

This time.

My hands slowly curl into fists. "I want you to be very clear on what the fuck you mean by *this time*, Mr. Holly. You get one chance to answer. Take a second. You don't want to know what happens if you answer incorrectly."

"I-I-I didn't have a choice!" he blubbers, scooting back along the couch. "They were going to shoot me! They were going to shoot me if I didn't give them your address to find Olivia!"

Sneaking suspicion feels almost like dread. "And the night they tried to kill us at the Vancouver airfield? How did they know we'd be there, Holly?"

He can't meet my eyes, and his voice is barely a whisper. "They swore they would just take Liv and Milah...not that they'd hurt anyone. And that they'd give them back once we'd...negotiated a suitable settlement. The girls were only supposed to be collateral! To make things fair and even!"

I can't speak.

If I do, I'm going to say every hateful, cruel, murderous

thing inside me – and then I'm going to kill him with my bare hands.

I thought I was a monster.

Fuck, no. I'm nothing compared to a demon-man like Alec Holly.

I'd never turn my kids over to animals like the Pilgrims. I'd never consider sacrificing Em to line my own pockets.

Hell, Em's why I *took* this job, to make sure she had a future, and yet now I feel sick at the idea that this foul bastard's money will trickle through Landon to Em when it's as tainted as he is. Alec Holly claims to love his daughters, but all he really loves is himself.

To him, his daughters are an extension, an expendable one he can live without if need be as long as he doesn't have to sacrifice his power, his position, and his luxury.

No wonder Milah's tried to drown herself in drinking and drugs with a shit like him controlling her life. No wonder Liv's learned to make herself small, invisible, so at least she can find a moment to hide where she's not jerked around on his string. His need to control everything for his own benefit has come one hair short of killing them both – and they're not out of the woods yet.

All because of this selfish, stupid, shameless fucking prick.

I don't even realize I'm moving until I am.

Until he's small and gray in my shadow, until he's looking up at me like a sparrow just before the hawk dives down to catch it in its claws. I snare his hair in one hand, gripping up a thick handful of it, and drag him to his feet.

Higher. *Higher*, until he's practically squawking in pain, clawing at my forearm, struggling, his toes dragging on the ground as he dangles from my grip, his face stretched out of proportion as my grasp and the full force of his weight pulls on the skin of his head and skews it into a warped mockery of a scream.

"You have two choices, little man." The black shroud is wrapping me up again, sucking away all emotion from my voice, my thoughts. I can't feel if I'm going to keep myself under control.

But I can't feel if I'm going to kill him without conscience, either.

And I can't quite trust myself not to do that right now.

This is the monster in me. The one not even Liv or Em have truly seen.

They've seen me kill in self-defense, seen me threaten and hurt men for a purpose, but never seen me willing to kill someone simply for threatening the people I love. Simply for being the scum of the earth.

I give Alec Holly a rough shake, just enough to stop his screaming.

He stares at me, practically blubbering. I hold him dangling for several long seconds more before I bite off, clear and cold and slow, "Time to make a choice. You can either confess everything – to the police, to the FBI, and to the Pilgrims – and take full responsibility for this mess. I don't care if hell rains down on your head. I don't care if the Pilgrims kill you, as long as they leave Liv and Milah out of it and stay away from my family. You take responsibility for your shit, and you deal with the fallout. That's option one." I give him another shake, and he makes a gagging sound of pain. "Option two is that you mysteriously disappear while traveling for business. Maybe in two or three years, some hikers will find your bones in the bottom of a ravine, if the coyotes even leave enough to pick over in a forensics' lab."

It's not Alec who answers.

It's Liv.

Just a sharp, shocked sound, strangled in the back of her throat.

It's enough to tear me from the black and shadowed place and dump me into the harsh, garish light of reality, where it's all too clear to see her standing in the doorway, staring at me with her eyes wide and filled with tears. Em's behind her...and for the first time in her life, I see fear on her face when she looks at me.

Just like her mother.

Fuck.

What am I doing?

I let Alec Holly go. He crumples to the floor, half-sagging against the couch, moaning and rubbing at his reddened scalp and hairline. I can't meet their eyes. Not Liv's or Em's.

I just turn around and walk out, heading out into the deepening afternoon sunlight.

* * *

I don't go far.

I can't go far. Not when I know there's not even an illusion of safety in the house, and even if I need a moment apart, I also have to stay close by in case anyone trailed Alec Holly here. Or in case he tries to drag Liv out by force.

So I only make my way out into the garden, surrounded by sprays of flowering milkweed, clematis, daisies, and vine blooms left to run wild and untended until the garden is a burst of bright color too sweet and soft for my dark, brooding mood.

That look on Em's face was familiar.

Just like Crystal.

I've made my own daughter afraid of me, and that's something I can't live with.

I drop down heavily into one of the green wire patio chairs out near the rock-lined garden pond, just staring at nothing, my hands limp against my thighs. I thought I was in control.

I thought I knew myself, thought of this other side of me as someone else who wasn't the real me. But now I wonder if he's more real than the Riker who tries to be a good father, tries to be a good role model, tries to be a good protector.

More real than the Riker who's learned over the past few weeks that it's okay to let the cracks in his armor show to let someone else in.

Maybe those cracks were what let this darkness out and gave it more space to grow.

I never should've tried to be anything besides Em's father. That was who I threw myself into being after Crystal died. That was how I tried to honor her memory, and tried to fill in that gap in Em's life by being two parents in one.

As long as that was the only role I had to play, I could balance between myself and whatever this black, cruel thing is inside me.

But the second the chaos of Liv's maddening, beautiful, wonderful sweetness, fragility, and odd inner strength entered my life, I was fucked.

That's when I started losing control.

I don't know how long I sit out there. Long enough to watch Alec Holly go slumping out of the house, alone. He casts me one furtive look, but I hardly even glance at him.

Just long enough to watch him make his way toward the paved trail that will take him at least a couple of hours to walk in those shoes, and I wish him many raw, bleeding blisters along the way. But at some point I realize there's something on the table as reality begins to filter through my numb, bitter haze of self-recrimination.

Liv's notebook, with that chewed-up pink pen clipped into the rings.

I shouldn't read it.

But I need something to take me out of *me*, just for a little while. Maybe something to remember her by, when I know the awful decision waiting for me, the only thing I can do if I really care about keeping Liv safe instead of being no better than her father and keeping her to myself.

So I flip the notebook open to where the clip of the pen makes a bookmark, landing on a single messy paragraph scribbled and crossed out and rewritten on the page.

I skim it, adjusting to her looping, slanting handwriting – she could've been a doctor with writing like this – and pick up that apparently her hero is in the hospital.

The scratched-out parts have him in a car accident, but in the new writing it's different. He's suffering from chills, weakness, because he was brave enough and deeply in love enough to dive into the frozen waters around a small town lighthouse to save his nanny-turned-lover and his daughter from the deadly waves. The moment I see the word "daughter," a prickle starts on the back of my neck, one that turns into a full-on tingle as I recognize the description of green eyes, of silvering brown hair, of a man shut off from the world by grief, of a cold and ruthless side used to protect those he loves. Of layers peeled away to show a warm and loving heart underneath.

She describes him as a dark knight who wasn't meant to live, but found a way if only to give his life, his last breath, for everything he loved. His daughter. His beloved.

A dark knight.

And even as I read the last line about him promising to always be with her, even as he slips into a coma...

I realize that this truly is how Liv sees me, because somehow Liv has managed to fall in love with me, and love is more than just blind.

Love is careening toward a cliff, and when the crash comes, there can be only tears and ruin.

This isn't just a fling to her. It's not just incredible sex.

It's not catharsis, experimentation, self-discovery, running out of control with this new and wild and unnamed thing. Not for her, and not for me.

What is it but pure self-destruction for both of us?

And if I don't put an end to it, I'm going to get her killed.

I drop the journal, pressing my face into my hands. If I care about her at all, I know what I have to do.

I fish my phone out of my pocket and dial Landon's number.

XVII: A LITTLE BIT SOFTER (OLIVIA)

I promised myself I wouldn't let this mess break me, but I'm not so sure that's a promise I can keep.

Not when I'm sitting on the couch numbly with Em limp and quiet against my side, watching my father scuttle out of the house like a frightened turtle without even a glance back to say goodbye.

I thought I knew what betrayal felt like.

After the number of times Milah stole from me to feed her habit.

After the number of times she said *I swear I'm done this time* only to show up on the front pages of the tabloids the next morning, coked up and half-naked.

After the many times my father dismissed me as if I was nothing.

After...after I realized he was manipulating me, realized he was just using me to soothe his own ego and somehow couldn't even hold his fragile self-image together without me around to be his dutiful, pretty little prop.

After realizing my father screwed everyone so bad ordering that hit on the Pilgrims.

But it's nothing compared to the betrayal of realizing that my father is the one who *put* me in this situation, that it goes so much deeper than an attempt to protect Milah gone wrong, that he left me and Milah to be hurt. And rather than doing the right thing, all he's cared about is covering his own ass so he doesn't look bad in the Monday headlines.

My own father. My own *father*.

How can he even claim to love me, to love Milah, but then do these things?

What pulls me out of myself isn't my own willpower. It's Em, who's finally coming out of her daze with a soft whimper, her face crumpling. She's been put through too much today, and even if she's a smart, wonderful little girl, she's still a little girl.

If I'm overwhelmed, I can only imagine how she must be feeling.

"Em?" I coax, offering my open arms. She immediately dives in, wrapping her arms around my waist so hard she nearly chokes the air from me.

"Liv, I'm scared," she whimpers.

I hug her tight. "Baby, it's okay. You don't have to be scared." I rub her back. "Your dad was just a little angry."

"I'm not scared of Daddy," she whispers with utter faith. "Daddy's a hero. Sometimes heroes have to hurt the bad guys."

"Oh, sweetheart." I wish the world was that black and

white. That simple. I smile faintly. "Your dad is so lucky to have you. Then why were you scared?"

She peers up at me. "I thought my dad was going to kill your dad, and I was scared you'd be sad."

Oh.

What scares me the most?

It's the fact that right now, I don't know how I'd feel if Riker hurt my father.

That shakes me even deeper, but I can't let it show. So I just kiss the top of Em's head, and lean into her, offering every support I can.

"Yeah," I say numbly. "Me too."

* * *

Eventually, Em dozes off. I guess today took a lot out of her, and I ease her to rest on the couch with one of the throw pillows under her head, then drape the crocheted quilt over her before slipping out to look for Riker.

We need to talk about what I overheard, and then plan our next move.

I thought I'd have to look for him, but turns out, he's right outside.

The sun's setting, the light slanting blue and twilight purple, falling over his motionless form in the garden. He's sitting at the patio table, elbows resting on his spread knees, clasped fists pressed to his mouth, staring at nothing.

God, he's gorgeous. This huge, somber bear perched in all his imposing splendor.

The events of the past few hours must have taken their toll.

I hadn't realized just how open and expressive his face had become when we were together until I see him like this, completely closed off behind the same impenetrable wall that masked him when we first met.

Somehow, that frightens me more than everything else.

I drift closer, starting to reach toward him, then drawing back, curling my hand against my chest. "Hey?"

He doesn't look at me. But that doesn't mean he's not aware, when he goes hard as stone in an instant from head to toe. There's nothing of Riker in this statue in front of me. Especially in the clipped, cold voice that says, "Pack your things. I've already called Landon. Skylar and Gabe are on their way."

My stomach sinks like a bag of rocks. "Your crew? Why?"

"Because you're being escorted to a new safe house. I can't protect you anymore. The Pilgrims know who I am. Your old man knows how to track me. It's time you wind up in someone else's custody."

"What? Someone else's *custody?*" I stare at him, but he's still just this motionless block with his gaze trained somewhere distant.

I thrust myself into his line of sight, anything to get him to look at me. To *see* me the way he did before. This can't just be about the argument with my Dad. There's something else. Something darker.

"Riker, this isn't just custody, obviously. I mean, we're in this *together*, I thought..."

"Doesn't matter what you thought, Liv. What matters is keeping you alive. Anything else is second to that." Finally, he looks at me – and I really wish he hadn't. It's like being stabbed in the chest by icicles, the blank way he stares through me, the affection in his eyes frosted over. "They'll be here by morning. Get moving. Don't argue."

"So this is it? Just like that?" I can't believe it.

I'm so thrown, I can't even find it in me to argue, to process this, to defy him.

I'm just standing still. Frozen. Stunned.

This is the second time today a man I loved tossed me aside like trash, and I can't freaking stand it anymore.

I don't know when I start crying. I just know that suddenly the world is wet trembling crystalline prisms and Riker's just a mess of dark color so I can't see that awful empty way he's looking at me. "Talk to me...please. We can make this work. I want to stay with you. I only feel safe with you."

"Just because you feel safe with me doesn't mean you are." Grim resignation. There's a hint of emotion there, lost and heavy, but it's not enough. It's not enough to ease this ripping, terrible feeling inside. "You have to go, Liv. Someday, you'll understand."

"Understand *what*? This crappy goodbye, all of a sudden? That it's done, just like that?" It comes out wavering, choked. "That you never cared at all?"

There's a brutal pause. Then he looks at me, and my whole world goes hot and sad and white.

"If I didn't care," he says softly, "I wouldn't be doing this."

But he is, and I can't hear it anymore. I can't hear him telling me he's breaking my heart and shutting me out for my own good.

It's like being thrown from summer into the bitterest winter. I'm freezing inside-out.

I turn, run from him, into the house, stumbling blindly through my tears, through the shattered feeling in my chest. Then I'm brushing past Em, past this amazing girl I've come to love like family, past the illusion that I could ever be a part of *their* family.

I should have known all along it was just pretend.

I just never knew reality could hurt so bad.

* * *

They let me have the bedroom to myself tonight. Riker sleeps on the floor while Em takes the couch. One of them, probably Em, leaves a forlorn wrapped sandwich on a plate outside my door. I ignore it.

I just shove my things into my bag, then curl up in bed and sob myself to sleep, trying so hard to empty this feeling out of me so I can leave it behind in this cabin and forget it once I walk away.

* * *

It's not until days later that I realize my notebook is gone.

Ugh. I must have left it at the cabin with Riker and Em, when Gabe and Skylar showed up to shuffle me off with my head down so I wouldn't have to see Em's miserable look or the fact that Riker wasn't there at all.

But I almost burst out crying again when Em glued herself to my back with a whispered, tearful *goodbye* before running away without giving me a chance to respond. For days, Sky and Gabe have been all gentle voices and careful space and sympathetic looks.

All while I pretend to appreciate the tactful handling. Honestly, I can't stand being around them when that *connection* vibrates between them. Their love is so tangible, so full of everything I thought I'd had with Riker and somehow lost in the blink of an eye.

So I stay in my room in this weird little two-bedroom shack off in the woods on the Oregon coast, watching the day turn into night.

There's sleeping. A lot of depressed, heavy sleeping.

I've gone full Ophelia, and getting out of bed to take care of myself is my most impressive feat of the day. But I'd been thinking about throwing all of this into my book, killing off the hero after last one valiant struggle to wake from his coma, his last words a tearful promise of forever love before he's gone, and the strong heroine has to stand alone. Fend for herself. Survive.

Except now my book is gone, too, and I...God.

I can't stand the idea of going back to get it, let alone asking. Not when Riker would look right through me, and Em might be upset for betraying my promise to always be her friend, even if it isn't really my fault.

How can I be her friend, her anything, when her father shut me out of their life like nothing?

I'll just have to start over, I tell myself. *With everything.*

With my life, looking for my independence on my own.

With my book, with a new draft.

Maybe one of the last things I'll buy with Daddy's credit card is a laptop, so I can save my novel in a better medium plus start looking for jobs. I'll find somewhere to work, somewhere that can teach me better skills than I learned with a liberal arts degree that focused mostly on the type of secretarial work my dad expected. Maybe I'll have to start off in like a women's shelter or something like that, but sooner or later I'll have a place of my own.

And I'll be okay without Daddy. Even without Riker.

Though my heart's telling me otherwise, right now.

My heart's telling me I'll never be okay again because I'll never know what could have been.

Before I enact this grand plan, though, I've got to enact my grand escape. There's one more thing I need to do with Daddy's money before I take the scissors to his AmEx.

I'm going to fix this. So that no one has to worry about the Pilgrims ever again.

I can't just sit here and mope until I waste away, waiting for someone else to wrap this up.

Not after Milah called this morning, shaking and afraid because she saw two black cars parked down the street from her house, and not even a double patrol by her security team scared them into driving away and settling elsewhere.

She's terrified. She wants to come see me, but she's scared to leave her house, scared to lead them to me, constantly pushing Daddy to turn himself in and falling back when he won't listen.

This has gone on too long, and I'm tired of being helpless.

If the Pilgrims want blood money, I'll pay them off out of Daddy's own pocketbook. However much they want.

Daddy might argue with them, maybe, but I won't.

By the time it's done, it'll be too late. He won't be able to stop me, the money will be in their hands, and this can all be settled. I have my trust fund, too, and the private account Daddy set up with a stipend for me. I couldn't access them before in case they might be tracked.

But it doesn't matter if I'm giving the money to the people tracking me, right?

I linger on my small notepad, the only thing I salvaged with a few stray story notes, and that list I'd been keeping.

Seven hundred sixteen dollars and eighty-two cents. That's the final tally I have written down.

It's weird to think that's how much my life with Riker cost him, down to the smallest latte or pack of gum. That's what my existence is worth, in the space of a few weeks.

That's how much I'll leave in my accounts. One way or another, I'll get it to him, and turn the rest over to the Pilgrims to end this. A bribe of that magnitude, seven figures...

It has to be worth more to them than revenge.

They're monsters, but they're business people. It wouldn't be rational to stay angry if I give them far more than they'd have ever made off those drug pushers.

By the time my resolve hardens, I've already worked out a game plan.

After dinner, Skylar and Gabe always go sit on the back porch and watch the sunset and talk about fishing and some old stories from New Orleans when he was a boy. While they're not looking, it's easy to slip away.

Out the front door, into the woods, a backpack with a change of clothes and a few personal items slung over my shoulder. Within seconds, I can't even see the house, but I know where the road is.

I stay in the trees, parallel to the small lane leading through the forest, and in another hour I'm coming out on the highway and can see the on-ramp for a small town nearby. Good thing I built up my leg muscles hiking through the hills with Em.

Just a short walk, a Greyhound ticket, and a bus ride to San Francisco.

I'm going to pay my last debt to Riker.

Then I'll end this insanity with the Pilgrims once and for all.

XVIII: TRY A LITTLE HARDER
(RIKER)

Let's count the ways one man can fuck up his own life.

One: take on a job you know you have no business taking, because the money's good enough to pay off your dead wife's chemo bills and make sure your genius daughter can afford to go to college. Be an arrogant shit. Think you can honestly protect your family from the hell that's going to come.

Two: blur the lines between professional and personal until a client job somehow turns into a fling, only for your coworkers to find out. It's just a matter of time before your boss finds out, your career is ruined, and you're lucky if you only take a pay cut instead of getting thrown out on your ass with a black mark on your resume and no references.

Three: let your daughter get so attached to your client-slash-fling that when you chase said client-slash-fling out of your life for her own safety, your daughter will never forgive you, still will barely speak to you, and will hold a grudge forever.

Bonus points if you also embarrass her in front of her crush and then forbid her from attending his scum-sucking father's classes ever again, making sure you'll be paying for this mortification until adulthood. Extra bonus points if your daughter pointedly takes over making breakfast each morning to remind you of who's missing, and why the house no longer feels like home.

Four: fall for a girl you have no business having feelings for, because she's too damn sweet and magical and vulnerable – too fucking good for you – and you're too much of a defensive, snarly asshole to ever fall in love.

It's incredible I'm able to keep the list down to four.

I'm tempted to write them in the back of Liv's journal. She left it at the cabin and never came back for it, and I keep thinking I should call her to tell her I have it.

Of course, she wouldn't want to hear from me. So it feels like writing those words in her journal would somehow bridge some connection between us, whenever I finally find a way to mail it to her.

Maybe because it's hers, she'd feel those words as if I'd inked them onto her skin and know that I never meant to hurt her.

It just wasn't meant to be.

Our fucked up almost-love is too much like her stories. Always meant for tragic endings.

I linger on those words she wrote. This story where somehow I live on the pages, but I'm a better version of myself than I could ever be.

I stare at those last few lines. They're wrong. All wrong.

And I can't help but uncap the pen she's chewed to hell and back, the imprints of her teeth scratching against my hand as I scribble those lines out.

Guess I hope if I ever have the chance to give this back to her, I'll also have a chance to tell her why.

So she'll forgive me this one thing, even if I don't deserve forgiveness for anything else.

* * *

I'M SITTING in the car, waiting for Em to get out of school, once again paging through Liv's notebook.

I've skipped over parts that aren't her book – parts that are personal, about her, about me, about us. She writes down everything.

How she damn near lost her mind that first day we brushed real close in the kitchen.

How she thought she'd die during our shootout in Vancouver, how I saved her, how she knew I always would.

How hard she came the first night I had her sweet cunt. How she'd always remember being deliciously sore, eager to repay me a thousand times over with dirty, indecent, dick-killing shit I can't repeat, much less continue to read.

I slam the book shut with a sigh, feeling even more hollowed out.

I can't bring myself to read more. I've already seen too much.

Hell, just reading her story feels like a violation of privacy, and now having her true, honest feelings about us carved into my soul that way...

Fuck.

I should be in the office, but the tension there has been stifling lately. I can just feel the other shoe waiting to drop. So I left early. Checked out.

Isn't that all I've been doing for the past few years?

Checking out, so I won't have to face the pain of losing someone ever again?

I glance up as the school bell trills, and students come spilling out of the building. Em used to come tumbling out like an overexcited puppy, ready to tell me about her day.

Now she's one of the last kids out of the building, shuffling slowly...and that Ryan boy is next to her, their pinkies linked while they lean in over a conversation that looks very private and miserable.

My jaw tightens. *You did this, you fuck. Wasn't just Liv you crushed that day doing 'the right thing.'*

It was your own stupid ass.

While I eyeball that kid hard any time he's up close and personal with my daughter, I'm actually glad she can still see him at school. I'm glad she has a friend.

I just don't want her anywhere near his old man, Mike, when I clearly can't trust him with anyone's safety. I wouldn't even trust him with his own.

At last, she reluctantly peels away from Ryan and straggles over to the Wrangler. Instead of climbing in the front seat, she climbs into the back – just another wall between us, more distance to remind me that I'm not her friend anymore, I'm just her father, and her father is an asshole.

My jaw feels like it might break as I look up, watching her in the rear view mirror as I pull out of the parking lot.

We've always had moments when I had to be the adult and the disciplinarian instead of her friend and confidant, but it's never been because *she* shut me out and shoved me into that role.

I wish being Dad came with an instruction manual.

It's a tricky line to walk when you have to be the adult, but also try to start off early respecting your daughter's boundaries and making sure she knows she deserves it.

So I breach the silence with a simple, "How was school today?"

"It'd be a lot better if you weren't picking me up," she bites back, glaring out the window with her arms wrapped defensively around herself.

Fucking ouch.

Okay. Whatever.

I probably deserved that. I try again, "Look, Em. I get why you're mad. But I think you understand why I had to take you out of karate class, too."

She shoots me a furious look in the mirror. "You think I'm mad about *class?*"

I blink, splitting my attention between the road ahead of us and her. "You're not?"

"Ryan still teaches me at school in PE. Big deal. Whatever."

I shake my head. "Then I'm lost right now."

"Of course you are." She rolls her eyes. "You're such a dad! No *wonder* Liv left. You were so stupid, and she ran away because you just don't get it."

That slams into me so hard, I almost hit the brakes, trying to keep my calm. "Em, love, Liv didn't leave. I sent her away for her own safety. Had to. Enguard has more resources than I do alone. We couldn't protect her anymore."

"That makes it even worse!" Em fires back, her eyes brimming with big, fat droplets of angry tears. "Don't you see?! We were *happy* with Liv here. You were happy for the first time in years, and I had a friend, a *real* friend who likes all the same stuff I like, and she's so cool and I want to be just like her, and you made her go away because you're too scared of being happy! It's like you wanted to die with Mom...you're afraid being happy forces you to remember you're alive!" She's glaring at me, her face blotchy and red with fury and hurt, tears streaming down her little cheeks. "Mom's dead, Dad. We've done nothing but dwell on it. We're not. I'm so tired. I don't want to be sad all the time, and I don't want you to be sad all the time, either."

I keep driving on pure instinct, focused on the road because I'm fucking gutted.

This is what having kids too smart for their own good means.

They're too smart for your own good, too.

Because while you think they're off in their budding hormonal clouds stabbing at mundane teenage stuff, they're seeing all the things you can't even see yourself. They're looking into you and understanding you and knowing you because even when they're rebellious and wild and hateful and angry, they love you and need you to love them. They need to understand you, because you're all they've got.

And my wonderful, amazingly smart, deeply hurting daughter clearly understands me better than I understand myself.

I wish I wasn't driving so I could hug her, soothe her, tell her it'll be all right. But I'm in the middle of traffic and can't pull over, and I don't know what to say.

I don't say anything for a while as she sniffles and scrubs at her face and pulls herself back together as the sparks from that explosion start to fade.

But finally, I admit quietly, "You're right, Em."

She's too damn brilliant for me to patronize her. What else can I do besides be honest?

"I've felt guilty all these years, love. Guilty for surviving when your ma didn't. Guilty helping you grow up because she didn't get a chance. So, yeah...you got me. If I was happy, if I had anything good, it wasn't fair. Because I got to live and she didn't." I sigh. "But, you know, even thinking that way...I couldn't help but be happy. I have you, Em, hands down the best thing in my life. Maybe I didn't show it well enough, but I've *always* been happy to be your old man. And I always will be"

She meets my eyes in the mirror, a bit resentful but softening. "But Dad...I don't get how feeling guilty is gonna change what happened. You can't, like...suffer Mom back to life. And making Liv go away isn't gonna do that, either."

I smile faintly. There's a hot, red pain digging at my eyes, but fuck if I let it show.

"Got a better question, love. How did you get so smart?"

She offers a smile back, tired but genuine. "Mom lives on. She was a marine biologist, remember? I definitely didn't get it from you."

"Okay, that was below the belt." But we're both

laughing – wearily, sadly, but suddenly we're both father and daughter *and* friends again.

More than that, we're human. We're allies. We're on the same side, locked in whatever this war of life is that we're struggling to fight our way through.

But we sure as hell could use another friend down here in the trenches with us, and goddamn me if I don't miss Liv with a physical ache.

I should have tried harder.

I shouldn't have let my fear get in the way – my fear of losing someone again, my fear of not being enough to keep them here, keep them safe, keep them alive.

No, Liv isn't Crystal – and I'm not the man I was when I was married to Crystal.

I'm someone new, someone better, someone stronger. And Liv was part of making me a new person as much as raising Em did.

The new man Liv taught me how to be wouldn't walk away from her the way I did, when I'm not myself if I'm not protecting her.

I've got to go get her.

And then I have to do whatever it takes to end this, once and for all.

I catch Em's eye in the rear view mirror. "Love, I need to fix some things," I say. "Would you mind staying with your grandparents tonight?"

She worries at her lower lip, then asks softly, "You're going to see Liv, aren't you?"

"Yeah." I smile. "Busted."

Her little face lights up, the first time I've seen her truly smile since that terrible day at the cabin.

"*Finally*," she says with exasperated amusement. "Sure. Let me just pack a bag when we get home, okay?"

"You got it."

The air's easier between us as I drive us home, and the moment we pull into the driveway she's upstairs, rocketing away to pack an overnight bag. I settle on the couch with my phone to call her grandparents and make sure it's all right to drop Em off on such short notice, but before I can pull up their contact, I see over a dozen missed calls and voicemails.

Damn. I'd fully muted my phone at work and forgotten to turn it off. But what starts as confused curiosity turns into hot, rushing alarm as I check the number on the calls.

They're all either Milah or Landon.

As I wander into my workshop and idly drop Liv's notebook on the table, I tap the voicemail button and lift my phone to my ear, heart cold and sick.

"Riker?" Milah gasps on the recording. "Riker, where's Liv? Is she with you? We can't find her. We can't find her and –"

I barely hear the rest.

The canned voice recedes down a dark tunnel.

All I catch are words like "missing" and then, as it rolls over to Landon's first voicemail, "whereabouts unknown" and "right under Sky and Gabe's noses" and "have to assume the worst."

The worst.

The worst is that the Pilgrims have Liv.

The worst is that she's already far out of my reach, and there'll be no protecting her, no saving her, no getting her back.

The worst is my stupidity sent the woman I love into mortal peril, and there may be nothing I can do.

No, that black and hateful thing inside me whispers, that beast of darkness that lives to hurt, to kill, anything to complete the mission at hand.

Its voice is all-consuming, drowning out the voicemails, rising up to pull me into its blackness and swallow me whole.

This time, I welcome it because its icy determination is the only thing giving me hope. *She's not gone. Not yet. You can find her.*

And no matter what you have to do, bring her back.

XIX: ONLY A LITTLE LEFT (OLIVIA)

It's just like me to forget to return Riker's key.

He's not home yet, at least. It's funny how I know all his schedules, when he picks Em up from school, what days she has practice. It's funny how I even know when her next math competition is, and what weekend he's going to be away until late evening running the Enguard crew through their annual firearms re-certification. It's funny how they told me these things like I'd be around long term, and I was part of the family who needed to know.

Funny.

Only, it's really not funny at all.

It's gut-wrenching.

Stepping into this house feels less like trespassing and more like sin. A sin against my own memories of the happiness I found here. A liar for believing those memories could ever be true. And a ghost, haunting the hallways of a place that for just a little while, felt more like home than a dozen massive, sprawling mansions staffed with people who were only paid to be nice to me.

Unlike people who genuinely loved me.

I can't think about this, or I'm going to stand here and start bawling in the middle of Riker's kitchen. I just need to leave him a check for the money he wasted on me.

Knowing him, he'll be too stubborn to cash it...but I have to try anyway.

And while I'm here, I might as well look for my notebook. He probably threw it out in sheer loathing, but it can't hurt to check. Maybe he saw it in the cabin and brought it back.

At least the familiar house makes a search quick and easy. I'd like to think the man I met before he closed away behind that terrible wall wouldn't destroy something that meant so much to me – and I'm right.

I find the journal in the small room off the living room that he uses as his workshop. The walls are lined with little shelves supporting bottles as small as my hand and as large as my forearm, each with a meticulously built ship inside. I remember standing in the doorway and watching him work.

I'd meant to call him for dinner, but instead I'd found myself frozen, fascinated by his utter focus, the look of relaxed, serene calm on his face. I'd tiptoed away without saying a word, leaving him to his peace.

I'd give anything to see his face that way again.

But there's my notebook, next to his latest half-finished project. Only the notebook is flipped open to the last page, and the last paragraph's final sentence has been scratched out in a jerky hand, with something new written in bold, masculine letters that are definitely not my handwriting.

Leave the tragic endings to tragic pages.
Why are these words so easy in fiction, but I can't say them to you?
It's just three simple words.
Three simple words, to make them true.

Three simple words.

I press my fingers to my lips, a shock running through me. What's Riker saying?

Does he still care after all?

Is there something left between us to save?

I suddenly want to find out. More than anything.

But as much as I hate it, now isn't the time. There can't be anything between me and Riker as long as my presence is a danger to both him and Em. I have to settle this, so I can cast off the shackles of my old life and my father's problems to start over again, fresh and new. I want to come to him without baggage, without dependency, and say *please*.

Please, can we try?

For now, though, I rip a page out of the notebook and scribble a quick message.

I'm sorry I came and left. I'll give your key back next time I see you, if you want it...but I really hope you don't.

Please take the check. It's everything it cost you to look after me.

Maybe when I get back, we'll talk about your three simple words.

-L*IV*

I WANT to sign with *love, Liv,* but I'm just not that brave yet.

So I tuck my notebook under my arm, clip the pen to the spine, and head outside, already tapping at my phone for an Uber. I've had enough highway walking to last a lifetime.

And that Greyhound here smelled like a porta-potty.

Broadening my horizons, right?

But I'm good with narrower horizons now, like a heated, private car.

I head down the block to wait. I don't want Riker coming home and finding me standing on his walk.

I'm just reading the confirmation that a driver is on the way, checking the license plate, when a compact, battered Honda eases up toward the curb next to me. My entire body instantly goes on sizzling alert.

Last time a car pulled up to me on the sidewalk, a man was shot to death in front of me.

The window rolls down. I instantly scowl when I see Mike leaning over to look out at me with a pathetic hangdog look on his flat, sallow moon face. *Not this guy again.*

This jerk who let my father buy him off, who shattered everything, who was willing to put Riker and Em and me in danger just to help my father control me. All for a pathetic bribe, too.

I fold my arms over my chest, eyeing him.

"What do you want?"

"Liv, I know you're upset," he begins. He's almost sniveling. "I don't blame you. I won't ask your forgiveness —"

"Good. Then you have no reason to be talking to me."

"*Please*. Wait." His voice is broken, raw. He looks like he's been crying, but the redness and puffiness look a little like he's been knocked around a bit, especially with a drying bloodied scrape on his temple. "It's about Ryan, or I wouldn't ask."

My heart starts to beat a little faster. I don't like the look of this. Not at all.

I know I should just walk away. But Ryan's a good kid, cursed with such a sleazy father, and Mike's crimes aren't Ryan's fault. I sigh, eyeing him warily. "What? What happened?"

"I can't find him. Anywhere." He twists his hands nervously against the steering wheel. "Oh, God, I'm such a fuck-up! His phone's at home, but he...he fucking disappeared after I picked him up from school. He's not at the studio, either. If anyone will know where he is, it's Em, but Riker won't let me talk to her. He'll let you. Please, Liv, I just need your help to find my son."

"You're sure?" I mutter, but deep down, I know it's true. When it rains, it pours bad luck on everyone. "Sorry, Riker and Em aren't home. I don't know where to find them."

"They're probably on their way to the studio for practice! Ryan's been trying to talk that girl back into my class." He leans over and pushes the latch on the passenger's side door, pushing it open. "I can drive you there."

Something about this is making my hair stand on end, but I can't risk the chance Ryan might really be in trouble...can I?

I check my phone, making sure the 9-11 app is ready in case I need help, and then carefully slide into the Honda, closing the door and strapping on my seat belt.

"Oh, thank you, thank you! You have no idea how much this –"

"It's fine," I say, just wanting to get this done. "But I can't stay long. I have some stuff to take care of."

Mike nods, saying nothing.

He's just eerily silent as he pulls the car out into the street again.

But he reaches down into the little door compartment on his side and fiddles with something, and for some reason that makes me nervous.

I lean my shoulder against the window, watching the traffic flow past.

Somehow, I'll need to get back to Seattle without either my father or Milah realizing, if I want to make contact with the Pilgrims – unless I can find a local chapter here.

From late-night conversations with Riker, I know they have a few smaller chapters in San Francisco, Portland, a few other cities up and down the coast. The guy I need to talk to, the one in charge, is Lion.

He's the one I'd have to negotiate with. I'll just have to get in touch with someone local and arrange a meetup in person, somewhere safe. Somewhere crowded and brightly lit where I can make a cash handover and get some kind of binding agreement that it's enough to buy our safety and freedom from this vendetta of theirs.

I jerk out of my thoughts, though, as I realize we've been driving too long.

Sitting up straighter, I glance out the window. This isn't a neighborhood I recognize, all run-down buildings and abandoned factories and shops, trash in the streets, hardly any cars around. I frown, glancing at Mike.

"Hey...aren't we going the wrong way for the studio?"

He still doesn't say a word.

But his eyes are bulging, fixed, staring straight ahead. That hideous unease turns into an outright bolt of fright and anger striking through me.

I reach for the door handle.

I don't care how fast we're going, I'll jump right out of the car.

But he reaches over, pushes the master lock on the driver's side, sealing me in.

"Please," he whispers, voice shaking. "Don't make this harder. D-don't struggle."

Struggle? I freeze, cold sweat soaking my skin. "Mike...what did you get roped into? Did my dad pay you to kidnap me?"

He shakes his head jerkily. "Not your father."

He swallows hard, his Adam's apple practically jumping. "Fuck, I'm so sorry. I'm really, really sorry, I'm such a goddamn coward, but...Ryan. He's my *son,* and they said they'd hurt him if I didn't bring you. You have to – fuck! – you h-have to understand what it's like to be willing to do anything for your kid. And you don't bargain with these people, Liv. Not on your own terms."

"Who?" I press, every muscle in my body keying up and ready to run.

Like I don't already know.

I can't do this again.

I can't be trapped and scared with a hand against my mouth and darkness sinking over me. The second I see my chance, I'm going to use the same techniques Mike himself taught me, punch him in the balls, and *run*.

"*Who*, Mike?" I demand, though I'm afraid I already know.

Still no answer.

He just kills the engine in eerie silence, letting the Honda coast to a halt on the curb. The doors unlock, and I kick mine open and scramble out into the street.

I don't make it more than two steps before several black cars come screeching around the corners from the streets on all sides, blocking me in. I bite back a scream and try to think smart, diving for a gap between two of them, grabbing at my phone and frantically mashing the screen on my app.

The door to the van in front of me slides open.

A tall, brutish man with a wild mane of hair leans out, his body cutting across my path. He snatches me around my waist, yanking me off my feet, knocking the air from my lungs and rocketing my phone from my hands to clatter to the ground. His leer fills my vision, fills my world, as he drags me into the van, his words falling around me like pure, cold horror.

"Hey there, little girl," he growls. "I've been looking for you a long fucking while."

XX: A LITTLE BIT OF HELL (RIKER)

I missed her.

Somehow, in the hour it took me to drop Em at her grandparents', I missed Liv.

Just like that.

She was right here in my house, but a slip in time, in fate, and we passed each other right by, flirting on the edges of each other's lives but never quite touching.

I stare down at the note on my work table. The note and...a check?

I don't understand the check. Can't fathom how she can think this number could ever represent everything losing her has cost me. But I can hear her voice, her sweetness in the note, and that strange maturity, too. The things she's not saying. The warmth, the kindness, the hope.

The faith she still has in me.

It's a fucking killer.

I just have to find her, because without Sky and Gabe

watching over her, there's no telling what kind of trouble she could fall into.

I just need my gear.

Fortunately, the old habit of a soldier helps me now, always having a go bag ready.

It's come in handy for security gigs, too, and the Enguard Security branded duffel bag I keep on the top shelf of my bedroom closet is already primed to go with weapons, ammo, burner phones and infiltration devices, rope, plus a few other practicals. First aid kit, cash, a couple fresh shirts.

I sling the bag over my shoulder and nearly vault down the stairs, heading for the door, which rattles with a knock just as I put my hand on the knob.

The half-second of sharp alertness vanishes when a head of sandy hair bobs just below the door inset. That kid Ryan again.

Shit, I don't have time for this. I just hope his father's nowhere nearby.

I pull the door open and step through, gently nudging him aside so I can lock up.

"Hey," I say, trying to keep my voice calm. No point in scaring him. "Em's staying at her grandparents' tonight. You can come back and see her tomorrow. I gotta run."

I hadn't even really been looking at him, preoccupied, ready to be on my way, until I see it.

He stops me in my tracks when he suddenly tries to get one word out and can't.

Not when it breaks off in a sob, and I turn from the door, watching as he bursts into tears. Full-on gasping, gulping, red-faced despair, shaking his head and burying his face against his palms.

"Mr. Woods...y-you...you have to...help..."

He's falling apart, panicked, frightened, can't even get sensible words out. I've got my own issues to deal with, but fuck, I can't be heartless enough to leave him here like this, especially when he might be in real trouble. I step closer, resting a hand on his shoulder.

"Breathe, son," I say. "Slow, deep breaths. Calm down. Clear your airways, then try again. Tell me what's wrong."

Ryan nods quickly, rubbing at his cheeks and taking several heaving breaths, sniffling and swiping his forearm across his dripping nose. He opens his mouth to speak again.

Instead of his voice, I'm treated to the sound of tires screeching as a car pulls up to the walk outside my house, a little Honda that jolts to a stop so fast it rocks forward on its wheels and then bounces back.

The driver's side door opens, and Mike angles himself out, raising his voice to carry across my lawn.

"Ryan, get in the car!" he orders. At first his voice sounds sharp, commanding, but what's really driving it is a sheer edge of raw terror.

Ryan flinches, but turns back and glares at his father. "No," he retorts, and for all that he's shaking, voice trembling, it's the clearest thing he's managed so far. "He has to know. He has to know or she's going to get hurt!"

I go stone-cold.

The only *she* either of them might have to tell me about is Em or Liv...and either of them being *hurt* is not an option.

Not unless someone wants blood today.

Mike comes scrambling through the gate and up the

walk toward his son. I look between them both, then settle on Mike.

He deserves the sick, frozen dread that crosses his face as my gaze lands on him. His kid doesn't.

"I want you to be very clear," I say slowly, forming each word precisely to be certain neither my words or the threat riding silent between them is misunderstood. "What do I need to know, who's going to be hurt, and by who?"

Ryan starts to open his mouth, but Mike catches his eye and shakes his head, before catching his son by the arm and dragging him behind him. Mike flashes me an ingratiating, practically shit-eating grimace that looks less like a smile and more like he's trying not to piss himself.

"It's nothing," he babbles. "It's nothing, nothing, I'm so sorry Ryan bothered you, we'll just –"

"Ryan?" All I have to do is say the boy's name for dread silence. I meet his eyes over Mike's shoulder and ask softly, "Is your old man lying to me?"

All it takes to prove Ryan is more of a man than his father will ever be is a single wide-eyed, determined nod.

"Thanks," I growl, nodding.

Then I catch Mike by the collar, whip him around, and slam him against the front door of my house.

Four things happen simultaneously.

Ryan yelps. Mike outright screams. The door rattles on its hinges. And I drop my grip on Mike's collar so I can slam my palm in the center of his chest, pinning him there with my hand spread, pushing just hard enough that he'll be able to feel his sternum strain.

Not one of his karate techniques will get him out of this, but he tries. He twists, he grabs at my arm, he whines

– and all he ends up doing is kicking his feet against the porch, making the door rattle even more.

"Hold still," I command. "You're upsetting your son."

Mike freezes, save for the heave of his chest under my palm as he breathes in slow, swift gasps through his teeth, mouth open on a clenched jaw like a frightened animal. He stares at me, wild-eyed.

I look back flatly, calmly.

"Simple questions, Mike," I say. "Simple answers. Who's going to be hurt?"

He's shaking wildly now, the stink of terror rising off him like vinegar. He shakes his head frantically, but suddenly he's quiet as a mouse.

I sigh, shifting my hand so the heel of my palm presses against a precise spot on the center of his chest. "You know about the human body, Mike, being an instructor and all. Do you know about the xyphoid process?"

He nods rapidly, chokes, his sweaty skin going pale.

"Sweet. Then you know that if I apply just the right pressure, that little spur of bone will break right off your sternum. If you're lucky, it'll just hurt. If you're not so lucky..." I shrug. "It could lodge in your heart and kill you. I don't want to do that. Especially not in front of your son. It's really up to you if that happens or not, and you have a choice to make. Start deciding." I lean in just a little harder, just enough that he'd feel bone *creak*, and he lets out a horrid little whimper. I'm careful to hide it from Ryan, make it look like I've just got him pinned.

If Mike has any functioning brain cells, he'll fucking thank me for that later. "Now, tell me what's going on. Why your son's here crying on my doorstep over something you don't want him to tell me?"

"It's the Pilgrims!" Mike blurts out in a high, cracking screech, arching against the pressure of my hand before going limp as an empty sack, shoulders sagging. "They said they'd take Ryan...said they'd kill him if I didn't –"

"If. You. Didn't. *What?*"

"*If I didn't give them Liv!*" he screams, before bursting out in muffled sobbing.

Liv.

Part of me wants to give him a better reason for those tears.

Part of me wants to break him apart right here, right now, and leave him to suffer and bleed.

But I can't. Not in front of Ryan, and not when I don't know what I'd be driven to do if I was forced to choose between Em and a stranger's life.

And now that I'm coming down from the original shock, it registers that Mike's left eye is a pulped and swollen mess of red and purple and bruise-yellow, probably from a fist. *Not mine.*

I can't pity Mike. I just can't, not when he's already shown himself a coward willing to sell people out for money.

But I can have mercy. Mercy, yeah. That, I can do.

Besides, I'll need to conserve every ounce of my rage and darkness to get Liv back.

I step back, letting Mike go. He crumples in a mewling heap on the stoop, curling forward and wrapping his arms around himself. He's small in my shadow, but not trying to run. He won't look at me, cutting his eyes to the side, keeping his head bowed and hunched like he's just waiting for the final blow to come.

"Enough," I say. "Stand up and tell me exactly what

happened. Then take your son and go home, and make sure I never have reason to see you again."

Mike curls up, pulling his knees to his chest. Ryan starts to edge past me, glancing at me warily, almost as if he's asking for permission, and I nod subtly.

Fuck, I don't want this kid scared of me. He's a good kid, brave, smart, and I trust him to understand what's happening right now.

He returns my nod, and then rushes to his father's side, sinking down next to him and wrapping his arms around his shoulders. Mike latches on hard, clinging, burying his face in Ryan's hair, and for all that I loathe this cowardly piece of shit, I can recognize something else, too. The familiarity of holding your child close just to remind yourself that they're safe in your arms; just to comfort yourself with the weight of their *being*.

He takes several deep breaths, calming, and then speaks more steadily. "I don't know how the Pilgrims figured out I was connected to you. Probably thanks to Mr. Holly. But they cornered me. The big one, Lion, the one in charge, he...he made sure I understood how much he could hurt me. How much he could hurt Ryan." He gathers his boy closer, looking up at me with a mixture of fear, shame, and defiance. "And he told me I had to find Liv and bring her. So I...I thought she'd be at your house, and I was on the way there when I saw her walking. I had to lie to get her in the car, and then I texted the signal to the Pilgrims and took her to the designated pickup. They came in black cars. Lion took her, and they drove away." He fumbles in his pocket, then produces a dirty, scratched up pinkish gold iPhone with a cracked screen and thrusts it at me. "Sh-she dropped this."

I feel as cracked as the screen as I take the phone and stare down at it.

It's Liv's.

Fuck. There goes any hope of tracking her by GPS.

Looks like we'll have to do this the hard way.

I shove her phone into an outer pocket of my bag, then pull my own phone from my pocket, striding toward the Wrangler.

Throwing the back door open, I shove the duffel bag into the back seat, then slam the door and point at Mike. "Take him home. Lock your doors. Don't answer for anyone. I'll tell you when it's safe."

He stares at me, though I'm half-ignoring him, already dialing Landon's number. Mike makes an odd noise, then says, "How can it be safe? How can any of us ever be safe again?"

"Because," I say, hefting myself behind the wheel of my car. "By the time I'm done, there won't be a single Pilgrim left alive."

XXI: A LITTLE FEAR (OLIVIA)

All my life, I've never known pain.
    I've known loss.

I've known the quiet little hurts that come with everyday life, the bumps and wounds that cut deeper and deeper until somehow, sooner or later, they become a gash on your soul that never quite heals.

I've known the emptiness of a pointless life that seems as though it'll never become something true, something real. I've known the betrayal of realizing your father is a sniveling, self-serving coward who would let you die to save himself.

But I've never known the true pain of heartbreak.

Not until I realize I really might never see Riker again.

And I've never known the pain of a body exploding on itself.

Not until a fist goes crashing across my face, whipping against my jaw, knocking my head to the side.

My whole face is on fire, my skull ringing, my brain jounced inside my skull.

Savage pain throbs through my entire body like that blow was the epicenter of an earthquake and it sent its full force through me. I stare blankly at the rusted metal wall of the tiny room I've been locked in, stuck in this chair with my ankles tied to the legs and my hands locked behind my back by cuffs that bite my wrists.

Everything feels upside down and nauseating. It's not just the slow rock and sway of the floor under my feet, telling me I'm on a boat.

My vision wavers, and I'm too fucking angry to cry, but I think I just might pass out. I can taste my own blood, and it's metallic and salty and terrifying.

It's also a comfort. A grounding point, a thing to hold onto, to center myself so I don't fall apart.

I may have lost my freedom, but I still have my will, my determination, and it tastes like that coppery hot rush of blood in my mouth.

"For the last fucking time," the man standing over me says, a low and guttural snarl, "I want the info on your Daddy's offshore accounts, and I want it fucking now."

Lion.

He's all beard and mane and vibrating, dripping malice, wrapped up in a bulk of aged black leather and solid muscle. His knuckles are red from how hard he hit me. His fist is clenched with the dark and terrible promise that he'll do it again.

I lift my head, glaring, squinting until my vision focuses and there's only one Lion instead of overlapping blurs of two or three.

"I told you already," I force out. Talking hurts, my jaw on fire, my lips aching, but I make myself speak anyway. "I'll pay you. Between Dad's charge accounts and my trust fund...I can offer you a little over a million dollars." I look him over with complete loathing.

Heck yes, I'm afraid, but I can't seem to hold back my contempt, even if it might get me killed.

This man may be large and intimidating, a demon wearing a man's face...but it takes someone small and weak to think terrorizing people like this makes him powerful. "Just take it and be done. Done with all this."

His nostrils flare, and he snorts.

"You're goddamned adorable. You really think a million's enough to compensate for two lives?" He sinks down into a crouch, bringing himself in close until I can feel the heat of his breath on my skin. His teeth are large and hard, bared in a snarl. "You think a shitty million makes up for everything your daddy's done to me? He's worth half a billion dollars – and you insult me with this fuckin' pocket change?"

I refuse to flinch, meeting his eyes without blinking. "No. But it's what I have. Me, Lion, not my father. And it's more than you'll ever get from my dad. His pride won't let him negotiate with you."

"It's an insult! Far, far less than what he owes me." He rises to his full towering height, leering down at me. "Daddy dear's been a very bad business partner, little girl, and he's got to honor his contracts."

I frown. "Contracts?"

His hand hits the table next to me so hard, I jump. He leans down, making this weird coughing sound. It takes me a second to realize he's laughing. Then he looks up.

"Fuck me with a jackhammer. You really are a naïve little princess, aren't you?" He captures my jaw in one brutal hand, jerking my head up, holding so tight I feel like my jawbone's going to crack like an eggshell. "You have any idea how much money Daddy took from me before he bailed on his promises? How much I busted my balls shuttling those fuckers up here to build his goddamn mall so he could turn a nice little profit? How we took all the fuckin' risk, all the fuckin' screaming and whining and dead assholes the cartel killed on the way here before we bought 'em, fair and square, only for Daddy to piss his pants real bad and worm away at the last fuckin' second?"

My throat hurts. I can't believe my father was involved in something like this, even if he tried to get out. Something that used human trafficking and *killed* people.

I try to shake my head, struggling to speak around the fingers digging into my flesh and holding my jaw in place with bursting points of pain. "It was just a mistake. An honest, screwed up, really horrible –"

"It was a knife in the goddamn back!" Leaning in, Lion lets out a deep snarl. His breath is foul, his spittle flecking on my cheeks in hot little spatters.

His eyes are brown and wild and crazed, a little too wide, the stare of a psychopath who's no less dangerous even though he's in complete control of his insanity. "He cut and run too late. Left me with a lot of debt, and thought just because I couldn't take him to court, he'd get away with it." He jerks my chin hard enough to make my neck twinge in a whiplash snap, and I bite back a cry of pain. "He was wrong. Your daddy took my men *and* my money. Then he tried to cover his braindead ass and killed my boys. There's no forgivin' that."

It's not hard to tell he's enjoying this.

He wants to see me cower, see me cry, see me trembling and begging for mercy. And honestly, he might.

I don't know how long I can be strong in the face of pure evil.

He takes his time slipping a knife from his pocket. It's a long jackknife that he flicks open with a terrible, ominous *snick*, the edge gleaming in the low white light of this cold, awful, echoing room.

Pointedly, he runs his thumb along the edge, the lightest ghost touch. But it's enough to raise a thin line of blood along his skin, the edge keen as a razor and ready to bite into me.

My stomach quakes, turns, but I hold my silence.

"Sorry, little girl. You're not getting out of this in one piece no matter how much he pays." He smirks, solidifying his grip on the knife, holding it like he's about to start carving a Thanksgiving turkey. "You're gonna get him to return my goddamned money – double, with interest – and then I'm gonna leave your limp, broken body bleeding on his doorstep. I owe him two corpses. No fuckin' money ever trades blood. Not in this world. Not ever."

Somehow, I find it in me to smile.

It's a fierce, terrible smile, but like hell am I going to die sobbing and begging. "Funny. Doesn't really give me much incentive to help, if you're going to kill me anyway. Dunno, Lion...this plan doesn't sound very well thought out."

"There are many different ways to die. That's your bargaining chip. Be a good girl, and I'll make it quick. You won't even feel it. You'll be dead before you even hear the gunshot...right...*here*." He lightly taps the cold, wicked point of the knife between my eyes, and my heart lurches.

"Be a bad girl, a royal bitch, though..." His voice drops,

purring with sadistic pleasure as he traces that mocking, horrid point down the bridge of my nose to the tip in a ticklish threat. "And I'll make you watch me carve your sister up into slices of thin red deli meat before I do the exact same thing to you. How the fuck will that go down when it hits her Instagram? They'll talk about it till the end of time." *Tap-tap-tap*, the blade pricking at my nose.

A slow, scared breath heaves out of me, even though I try to stop it. Lion pauses, looks me over, his eyes twisting with mock sympathy.

"Aw, you wanna live? Thought you might. So, here's option two: maybe instead of you and Milah the Whore, I give your old man that hard-nosed daddy-fuck you've been clinging to like a damn life raft. Him and his pretty little girl. I could have a lot of fun with a soft, sweet thing like that, don't you think?"

I swallow a lump like a boulder. *No!*

The fear and horror I'd been staving off are like a slow acid drip on my soul. It sinks in.

He's going to kill Riker and Em.

He's been watching me for that long, and he knows about Riker, about Em, how much I care about them, how to get to them. I know Daddy and Milah can keep themselves safe as long as they keep throwing money at security and pulling strings until the problem goes away, one way or another. But Riker and Em...

They don't deserve this.

I *have* to keep Lion's attention on me, dammit.

I don't even know the magic info he wants. I've never had access to Daddy's offshore accounts, never even knew they existed.

But I have to make him believe I do, and that he can't

afford to mess with me if he wants more money. I have to stall him out. Every minute I'm alive is one more chance that something, anything, will come along and end this horror.

I'm just tired. So tired.

I want to lie down and let this be over. But as long as I can stay conscious, as long as I can endure this, my silence gives me power.

He can't force me to say anything, and as long as he has me, he won't go after Riker, Em, or Milah.

I need to keep his cruelty focused on me, and only me. Need to take all of the pain, and all of his hate.

If I can do that, maybe I can keep them safe.

It's that thought giving me the strength to lift my head, look up at him, bare my teeth against a smile. Animal against animal. I'm going to find my claws and my wildness and my strength no matter how deep down I have to dig.

"Sorry," I say. "Guess I'm going to make you work for it. I'd start with small cuts. You don't want me to bleed out too fast, after all. There's something you don't know."

Lion arches a brow. He actually looks interested, curious, a challenging light in his eyes. "Yeah? What's your ace in the hole, little girl?"

"If you kill me, you'll never get the money you want." It's a bluff, but I'm betting he's greedy enough to buy it. "My father can't even get to his accounts without me. It's part of his security. I'm the only one who knows the wire info for his Swiss bank accounts. Kill me and you might ruin him when he's cut off from his money, but you won't get a damn thing."

He stares at me. I glare back defiantly, jutting my

aching jaw forward, bracing myself all over. Lion throws his head back, belting out a roaring, deep laugh.

"So you've got a spine," he sneers, stepping closer, laying the blade against my throat, against the wild, hot flutter of my pulse, the metal warming against my skin. "I fuckin' love it. That'll make it so much more fun to find out if you're lying."

His thumb strokes along my cheek, coarse and loathsome. I turn my head, lean into the touch.

Then I sink my teeth into the soft webbing between his forefinger and thumb.

He jerks back with a ragged, furious growl, but not before I can draw back and spit in his face. I barely have half a second to see murder flashing in his eyes before his fist comes crashing down again, and everything goes bright and dark. Then red and horrible and starry with pain as he backhands me.

I'm not going to survive this. *I'm not.*

But if I can make him believe it's all useless with me dead, he might leave the people I love alone.

I won't break. I can't.

But all I have to hold on to, as I steel myself for more, is remembering Riker's lips.

The memory of his sweet, reassuring kiss, and the desperate wish to see him again. To taste him. To love him deeper than ever before and sink into the safety of his arms.

Does he know where I am? Is he looking for me now? I hope not.

There's too many Pilgrims. I woke up in this room with Lion, but I've seen enough men come in and out, heard enough noise to know there are at least a dozen of them here, maybe more.

They'd kill Riker and all his friends in an instant. Even two dozen of the best Enguard personnel won't stand a chance, and all of this would've been for nothing.

Riker, I think as Lion's shadow falls over me, the edge of the blade sharp, white, and hungry. *Stay safe. Please don't come.*

XXII: A LITTLE BIT LIKE HEAVEN (RIKER)

Please, God, let Landon's intel be right.

We've parked over a mile down the road from an abandoned dock that's been converted to a junk and scrap yard. Landon's files from the Crown Security servers says this is the Pilgrims' main base of operations in San Francisco, barricaded inside an old oil tanker they've turned into a hideout.

I have to hope they've brought Liv here rather than taking her all the way back to Seattle.

If not, then we've just wasted precious hours putting together a strike team.

And one worthless minute could mean her life.

We took the last mile on foot – me, Landon, James, Sky, Gabe, plus over a dozen part-time grunts from our lower ranks, all of us in utilitarian black that lets us blend into the night, connected by mic collars and radios.

But we're communicating by signals now, shadows in the dark moving to flank the entrance to the junkyard, each of us armed with SAR 80s and a dozen spare clips.

I've got mine braced to my shoulder, with several other handguns stashed on me, the Ruger at my hip. *Liv's gun.*

I've promised myself it's the one I'll use to put a bullet through Lion's skull.

Landon catches my eye. He's nothing but a glint of cold blue eyes caged by a mask and black grease paint. There's a warning in his gaze, but he's asking, too, if I'm ready.

This is my mission. My call.

And yeah, I'm about to raise hell.

We don't have much time. The police are on their way, SWAT en route. We had to report this to the police, but they're too loud. Not subtle. They'd tip the Pilgrims off from miles away, giving them the chance to get away clean.

I'm not letting that happen.

Stopping, I scan the interior of the junkyard through the chain-link fence. It's dark save for a few small mounted lights, hulking heaps of scrap metal and dead cars and ships making it hard to see the few Pilgrim guards patrolling. The shadows give us cover, too.

Our target: a ship floating at dock, so old and broken down, it's listing half to the side, lit up from inside, gold illumination shining through the portholes. I sweep our team with a glance, then give the signal.

Go in quiet. Don't make a sound.

Together, we swarm forward in a carpet of seething black, barely a rustle of gear and tread of feet.

I can taste imminent blood in the air, as salty as the brine off the sea. I can see sweat beading around the eyes of a few of the grunts, but I'm cold as ice inside my gear.

Every terrible thing I've ever done, every moment

when I've become a monster, has been preparing me for this. I've always hated the dark, ruthless thing inside me.

Right now, I'm grateful for it.

It's the only thing that'll give me the strength to save Liv.

I catch the first guard from behind. He doesn't get a chance to make a sound.

My hand clamps over his mouth from behind, and I drop him with a quick twist and a *crunch* of the vertebrae in his neck. To my left I hear the muffled *thump* of a silenced bullet striking flesh, and the *thud* of a dropping body.

I let the limp man in my arms crumple to the pavement and dash forward, arrowing toward the ship. All around me the Pilgrims drop like flies, my team lethal and swift and closing in at my back. We're too good at our jobs.

In seconds, every last one of the guards is on the ground, and there's nothing between us and our real target.

We hit the ladder on the side of the ship hard, vaulting up over the rail, onto the deck.

There's only one entrance. We can't risk going in shooting, not with Liv possibly in there.

On my signal, the team rings the upper cabin, while I press myself to one side of the door. Below the hardened shell I've wrapped around myself for the sake of the mission, I'm struggling to breathe.

Fear hits hard and fierce.

This terrible knowledge it could end like Liv's book, with nothing left but her dead body in my arms and the pained keen of grief and loss rising up in my throat, only I'm not going to Nicholas Sparks this.

I'm not going to go on with my life lessons learned and my heart opened and her memory driving me forward day by day to live every moment to its fullest.

Fuck that.

If I find Liv's body in there, I will break.

I'll have to find Em a babysitter.

And then I'll personally slaughter every man with a Pilgrim tattoo from Seattle to San Diego.

But I can't let that happen. If she's alive, if there's even a chance, then fuck...I know what I need to do.

I hold up three fingers, catching a dozen eyes, then fold them down neatly one at a time: *three, two, one.*

Then, weapon on my shoulder, I kick the door open before dodging out of the way of any retaliatory gunfire.

There's nothing.

No blowback.

Just mad, eerie silence.

Only the faint slapping sound of water on an empty hull, and the echoing hollowness of quiet.

Carefully, I lean around to look into the room. There's nothing. Just a chair with a pair of bloody handcuffs swinging from the back. Blood spattered on the floor.

And a pretty little woven straw sandal, speckled in red and lying forlorn on the bolted steel. Unmistakable.

Fuck!

Landon sees my panic and takes over. Quick hand gestures split the group up into teams.

I recover, just in time to start barking orders.

"Search the ship. Top to bottom. Check every closet,

every room. Turn out the fucking galley cabinets if you have to."

I'm not giving in to despair yet.

Not until we've turned this ship inside out.

Even as the team peels off, footsteps storming over the ship, I step into the cabin, sweeping my gaze left to right, searching for clues. I drop to my knees next to the chair and press my gloved fingertips to the spatters of blood drying there. It's still wet, just barely, soaking into the thick weave, the smell hot. Fresh. Not enough for a kill shot or fatal cut.

She was just here, dammit. She was alive just minutes ago.

"Hold on, Liv," I murmur. "I'm coming."

Just as I push to my feet, I catch the sound of tires squealing and an engine revving close by. I throw myself to one of the portholes and look out.

Just in time to see a black car pull out of its hiding place in the piles of junk, taillights flashing red as it careens toward the gate. I don't stop to think, to hesitate, to calculate.

I kick through the door and stagger out onto the deck, catching myself against the railing and bracing as I lift my SAR 80 to my shoulder.

Half a second to aim.

Just a touch of pressure as my hand tightens.

Then that calm I've honed over the years settles, takes over, and time stops. I have one chance.

One chance to stop them. One chance to save her. One chance to get her back, and I can't afford to miss.

I pull the trigger, and the automatic slams back against my shoulder with recoil force.

Time jumps forward again. The bullet zings out, a furious hornet, and finds its target for a fatal sting.

The rear tire of the car punctures with an explosive retort, and with a scream of rubber on pavement the vehicle spins out, slamming violently toward a tower of junk.

I'm over the railing before it can even hit, leaping down to the dock and taking off running. A vicious impact bursts over the night as the car crashes into rusted heaps of metal.

Then the entire tower of broken, jagged parts comes tumbling down in an explosion of dust, the roof of the car caving in as a broken crane arm stabs into it. It's the last thing I see before the car disappears into a cloud of debris.

"*Liv!*" I roar, my chest constricting, and dive into the billowing dust cloud.

I can't see. Can't breathe, but I don't let that stop me, forging through the choking puffs of rust and dirt toward the dim shape of the car.

I hear coughing – soft, feminine, and call again.

"Liv?"

"H-here!" she calls. "I...I can't get out, my wrists –"

The sound of her voice lights a fire inside me. "I'm coming!"

I fall against the side of the car and wrench at the rear passenger door. It's crumpled inward and won't come loose. I can see several shapes inside, struggling in the front and back seats, one slumped over the steering wheel, but the only one I care about is the slim figure kicking at the very door I'm yanking at.

I have to get her out. I have to get her away from them, especially when I can hear the creak and moan of more scrap getting ready to tumble down on us. Especially when the hood of the car is crumpled in, billowing smoke, and I can smell gasoline.

Fuck, gas!

"Get back," I say. "Now!"

Liv scrambles backward. I catch a glimpse of wide eyes and her shoulders working clumsily with her arms behind her back before I reverse the SAR 80, flick the safety on, then bring the butt crashing down against the car window.

The glass shatters inward, and I quickly sweep the jagged shards aside with my Kevlar-lined sleeve before reaching in for her.

"Come on." My fingers hit soft flesh, and I manage to snare her around the waist. "Come on, I've got you."

Quickly, I haul her out. She slumps against me, her full weight in my arms.

Being able to feel her whole and alive and safe is everything I could ever call heaven.

She's bloody, bruised, torn, her hands tied behind her back with plastic zip ties...but she's *here*.

She's safe. She's mine. And now she stares up at me with her eyes wide and confused and frightened, as I drag her fully free from the car and stagger back until we collapse on the pavement together on our knees.

"R-Riker?" she breathes. "I told you not to come..."

"Think you were dreaming, sweetheart." I rip my mask off, then stroke her hair back from her brow.

It's a relief to see her, but it also makes me furious. I want to savage the animal who did this to her.

A strip of her sweet hair is matted with blood. There's

a deep, narrow gash above her eyebrow that looks like it came from a blade, rather than the crash.

I can't stand that look of fear in her eyes. I'd do anything to soothe it, holding her close, cradling her against my chest. "I'm here. There's no world where I'd never come for you."

With a broken sound, she buries herself against me, shaking and pressing closer.

I take a step back, starting to stand with her in my arms, when a heavyset, gasping shape struggles free from the car. A snarling man I recognize from the dossier photos, clawing his way out of the wreckage, bleeding but whole.

Not for long.

Carefully, I set Liv down. "Sweetheart, stay here for me for just a second," I say, pausing only to slip the utility knife from my belt and slash through the zip ties cutting into her bloodied wrists.

Every scratch on her builds my itch for vengeance.

Then I rise to my feet and stride forward. Lion is still pulling himself through the shattered window.

He doesn't get far.

I slam my elbow down on the back of his head with a satisfying *crack!*

The raw impact twists up my arm, and I take deep, *deep* pleasure knowing as much as it hurts me, it's hurting him ten times more. He falls with a furious howl, hanging half-in, half-out of the car, cursing wildly.

"Surprise, asshole! Not so tough when you've got a trained man at your throat, yeah?" I'm snarling, barely forming words.

I grip up a handful of his wild hair, pull back, then

slam forward with all my strength, grinding his face into the car door. He's big, forceful, desperate. Trying to fight, trying to lash out, but I've got him in the worst position possible, and I'm not letting go.

Instead, I keep him trapped as I bend to scoop up a long, deadly shard of glass broken off the car window, my gloves protecting my hands so I can grip it at the wide end like a knife.

I'm smiling, grinning something feral when I press the point to his throat.

Asshole immediately goes still. I jerk his head up just enough so I can meet him eyeball to glowering, resentful eyeball.

"If you die," I say, "every problem you've ever caused goes away. Everything you've worked for. Everything you've built. All the fear people live in thanks to you. I can't bring back the people you've killed, but I sure as fuck can make sure you never hurt anyone else. Ever."

I can see something new in his eyes, something that hasn't ever been there before – terror.

Still, he's a piece of shit to the end. He grins, a heart chomping leer.

"Go the fuck ahead. Even if you kill me," he slurs, his mouth swollen with a split lower lip, "I still fucked your bitch up. No taking that shit back. I'll take her screams into the next world."

Kill him, that black thing inside me whispers, and it feels right and perfect and pure.

Kill him, kill him, kill him now!

But even as I tighten my grip on the glass shard to drive it into his throat, fingers gaining their hold, Landon's voice rings loudly out over the yard.

"Riker!" he calls. "That mess is about to collapse! Get Liv out of there. Now! I'll get Lion and the rest of his trash into custody."

The beast I am in this moment strains at its leash. I could do it anyway.

One push into his throat. End this scourge. For an eternity, I can't move.

Not until Liv whispers my name. "Riker."

Then her voice reminds me who I am. Reminds me that I'm human. Reminds me who I'm not. Not anymore.

Reminds me I'm the man who loves her, a father and a lover, and not a cold, remorseless killer.

I drop the shard of glass. Then swing the stock of the SAR 80 around hard enough to crack across Lion's skull. He lets out one last, angry growl, then slumps forward unconscious.

That'll do. Let the justice system deal with his demon ass.

I hope he rots for the rest of a very short life that ends in a syringe in his arm, but that's not my call to make.

Murdering him isn't worth putting Liv in danger. Not for a second more.

And even as Landon and the others come sweeping in, I sling my automatic on my back, then turn back to Liv, lift her up against my chest, and duck through the wreckage to get her out of there. She's soft and small and so warm even through my Kevlar.

I hold her close, reminding myself over and over again that she's safe. She's really safe, I found her, I have her.

But after everything that's gone wrong, after how terrible I've been, there's one question still weighing on my mind.

Will she ever let me call her mine again?

* * *

She's pulled away from me when the authorities sweep in.

Suddenly she's wrapped up in an emergency thermal blanket and sitting in the back of an ambulance while an EMT fusses over her, dabbing away the blood and checking her bruises, cuts, and scrapes, wrapping her wrists in bracelets of gauze.

In the meantime, I'm with the team, debriefing the police, recounting what happened.

This is going to get rough. We killed people.

Even if they were bad, murderers and criminals, we still killed people. We'll have to justify it as protection and part of our jobs, but that's for another day and another court date.

For now, it's all about getting the details out while they're fresh in our minds. I feel like I'm in shock as the adrenaline comes down and I slip out of that cold, numb battle fog.

I'm able to at least recount the sequence of events leading up to this point enough to satisfy the officer taking notes and looking between me and Landon.

Finally, the cops leave us to go start taking inventory of the scene. I can't help watching Liv and the EMT, but I feel like there's an invisible wall between us.

Landon drifts to my side, watching Liv as well.

"If that was my girl," he says, "I wouldn't be standing over here watching her."

I stiffen, darting a startled glance at him. "My girl? You know?"

He smirks tiredly and scratches at the edge of a bruise on his cheek. "How stupid do you think I am?"

"Yeah." I sigh. "Sorry, Landon. It just –"

"Happened. Yeah. I know how it goes. You're not fucked. Not yet." With a weary chuckle, he claps a hand on my shoulder. "Get over there and talk to her. Then we'll have our chat later."

I give him a brotherly nod.

I should move, yet there's still an invisible force field holding me back, whenever I remember how she looked at me at the cabin.

How must she see me now, after witnessing the violence I'm willing to commit to keep her safe?

How much does she trust me, to believe that the animal inside me lives only to protect her and Em?

I scrub my hands against my thighs, then force myself to take that first step. It's the hardest, and after that, it's suddenly like the gravity of Liv has me, drawing me in.

As I approach, she looks up, watching me with wide, sparkling eyes that don't have the slightest bit of fear in them. They're warm, soft, and fuck, I hope that light in them is hope.

I stop in front of her, fumbling for something to say.

"Riker," she says, offering a shy smile. She reaches up to touch the line of medical tape stretched over her eyebrow. "Five stitches. I don't think the scar's ever going to go away."

"I hope it doesn't." I can't help myself. I need to touch her, to feel her, and I rip my gloves off before offering her my hand. "Badge of honor. So everyone can see how brave you are."

Slender fingers slip so trustingly into mine.

"I don't feel brave," she whispers. "I feel like a mess."

"Liv." I use that grip to gently draw her to her feet, then pull her into my arms. "I don't know what he put you through, but you need to know – you're here now. Here with me, and you endured all of this, and you're the bravest person I know."

"*Riker.*" She clings tight against me, her arms around my shoulders, her body trembling against mine. "God, I thought I'd never see you again."

"I know. That's my fault. I'm so sorry, Liv. So damn sorry I let my fear take over. I'm sorry I pushed you away. I'm sorry I shut you out. I'm sorry I didn't *listen*." I hold her tighter, curling my fingers in the back of her ripped, dirtied dress. "And yeah, you'd better believe...I'm sorry as hell I ever let you go."

She looks at me then, assessing my litany of regret, this small, soft thing wondering if she should let me in. Give me a second chance.

Liv, come on, I think to myself, clenching my jaw.

Then she speaks.

"Riker...just...never again. I need you to stay."

Stay? She shouldn't have to ask.

I'm on her, wrapping her up so tight, saying more than words ever could in every touch.

"Shhh." I stroke my fingers through her hair. She's shaking so hard, and I'm afraid she's about to collapse. "Not here. We'll talk at home. If you'll come back." My heart's never been in my throat this way, so big I can barely breathe or swallow it again. "If you'll come home with me. Back where you belong, I mean."

She looks up at me once more, and Christ...how could I ever think this woman feared me?

How could I have been so incredibly blind, so stupid?

There's so much trust in her eyes, and in the way she holds me close.

"Of course," she whispers, offering a shaky, but sweet smile. "Nowhere else I'd rather be."

"Then let's go home, beautiful. Together." I bend down and sweep her up against my chest, lifting her off her feet, savoring her low, startled laughter as she fists handfuls of my shirt. "Hold on tight."

I don't put her down for the entire mile walk back to my Wrangler.

When a man has his whole world in his arms, he knows.

When a man has a second chance, against the odds, against even death itself, he knows.

When a man has the woman he's meant to keep forever if he wants to hang onto his own damn sanity, he knows.

And I know it now, I know it all. Just carrying her, loving how her eyes never break from mine for a single blink.

We don't say a word, just move together under a silent night sky that once smelled like blood.

Now, there's just reflected sea and stars.

It's like communion, this insane moment when we've found each other again.

And I don't need to say a thing.

I only let her go to settle her into the passenger seat and stow my gear in the back. On the drive home, she stretches the limits of the seatbelt to lean against my shoulder.

I risk one-handed driving to wrap my arm around her. The only time I speak is when I call Em's grandparents and ask them if they can meet me at home and give them an ETA.

They're just parking in the driveway when we pull up. A sleepy Em climbs out of the back seat of the car, followed by the slim, slightly stooped figures of her grandparents. Crystal's parents.

I haven't seen them much in ages, shutting myself off out of some strange sense of guilt even though they've always said I'm still welcome. Still *consider* me family.

In some ways, they're the only parents I have left, with mine passed over two decades ago – my father in a work accident, my ma from sudden illness. It was strange, even after Crystal passed, for her parents to still include me in that familial warmth I'm so unaccustomed to.

Maybe that's why I'm completely unprepared for Grandma Em to pull me into a surprisingly strong hold the second I get out of the Wrangler, hugging me tight and murmuring "Riker, my dear boy!"

While at the same time, my daughter launches herself at Liv, nearly flattening her back into the Wrangler. They bang into it together with an audible noise, the door almost denting from the force.

"Liv!" Em cries. "You're back!"

My little girl clutches at Liv hard, almost overbalancing them both. Her face is hidden against Liv's stomach, but I know what it sounds like when my daughter's screwing her face up, trying not to cry. "Please don't go away again...pretty please?"

Liv stands there helplessly, looking at me over Em's head. There's a question in her eyes she never should've had to doubt, waiting for an answer.

Am I going away again?

Then she folds her arms around Em, bowing over her, hugging her tight. "Em...oh, Em."

That's when it happens.

Something builds inside me, something pushing to a breaking point.

Something that almost snaps at a soft, wizened hand on my arm. I jerk back into myself, looking down into Grandma Em's kindly smile and warm eyes.

"And who's this nice young lady?" she asks. There's something knowing in the way she looks at me, something amused and sweet.

It's like the question's just a formality. She already knows.

It's like everyone knows, and I'm the last fool to figure it out, the last one to know this is right.

Now that I do, it's choking, overwhelming.

My voice strangles. "Em, meet Liv. My –"

Little Em pulls away before I can finish, proclaiming firmly, sniffling the whole time, "She's my friend!"

I flash my daughter a smile. "Where's my hug?"

Em shakes her head fiercely, wrinkling her nose at me in a mock scowl and clinging even harder to Liv. "Not you, Daddy. Not now. You need a shower."

Everyone bursts into laughter, and I can't help but join in.

This is so right. This is so us.

My family, my love – all here, together.

And even if I'm a mess and covered in hurt and grime and the scent of gunpowder, I feel less like the killer I once was and more like a *man* than I ever have before.

A son, a father, a lover. One warmed by the sweet, naked emotion in Liv's eyes when she looks at me. This is what I fought for. Everyone I care for, together, safe, home.

Forever? I'm looking at it.

Everything I need to hang on to.

And I need to do it now, before those walls of fear and doubt and loss slam down to choke me off again.

Maybe it's the adrenaline ramping down. Maybe it's something crazier.

Fuck, I'm not questioning it anymore as I step forward, closer to Liv.

"Em's right. I do need a shower," I say firmly, no hint of what's next. "Which probably makes it a bad time to do this. I still haven't gotten a ring. It's not what I pictured, but damn if I could live my life wasting another second not in the know." I sink down to one knee, looking up at her. "Liv, listen..."

Liv stares at me, her breaths catching audibly, and she covers her mouth with both hands. "Riker? Riker...what are you doing?"

"The right thing. Everything I should've done weeks ago." I hold out my hands for hers, and after a shaky moment, she slips her fingers into mine, gripping so tight.

I hold hers just as strong, a solid, concrete reminder that she's here, she's safe, and I want so much to make her mine forever. "Tonight I almost lost you, and not just thanks to the Pilgrims. I never should've let you go in the first place. I can't bear the thought of letting you disappear from my life again just because I was too damn afraid." I glance at my daughter. "Can't bear you being out of *our* lives, and if it's all right with Em..."

Em lets out a nervous little giggle, blushing. "Oh my God, Daddy, you're so embarrassing. *Ask her.*"

At my side, Grandma Em lets out a fond, indulgent chuckle. "She's right, dear."

Liv laughs. "I think the popular vote has it."

She leans in toward me, as if sharing a secret, all dramatic stage whisper. She's smiling so bright, her cheeks flushed pink, and even though we're both filthy and exhausted and disheveled, I've never seen her more beautiful. "Quite an audience. You'd better get it out."

"All part of the show, Liv." An unplanned show that couldn't be more perfect, now that it's here.

I grin, stroking my thumbs over her knuckles. *Here we go.*

"Olivia Holly." I pause. No – Olivia's that girl who belongs to her father. Liv's the woman who belongs to herself, and who I'm hoping soon belongs to me.

"Liv," I correct myself. "Will you marry me?"

Just like that.

The whole damn world tilts on its axis.

It's not rational, it's hardly prime optics, and it's *right.*

I can barely get out the words *marry me* before she's exclaiming "*Yes!*" and throwing herself against me.

I catch her, then wrap her up in my arms and hold her so tight, there's hardly room to breathe between us.

Yes. Fuck. She said *yes.*

That one word was the key to unlock everything.

I've been shut away inside myself for so many years,

and every emotion goes flooding through me with the force of the raging waters coursing over a shattered dam. It's overwhelming, building up inside me until I'm ready to burst my skin, my blood burning, my smile so wide, it hurts my face.

Little Em's half laughing, half crying. Her grandparents are both smiling, looking at each other with the kind of love that can only come from decades together.

The kind of love I hope to have with Liv for the rest of our lives.

I pull back to look at her, stroking her cheek, threading my fingers through her hair. "I love you, Liv," I whisper.

Her smile only widens, and she leans in, resting her brow to mine. Just me and her in our own little world.

"Most people," she teases softly, "say the love part *before* the marriage proposal. Those three simple words can do an awful lot."

I beam like the sun, remembering what I wrote in her notebook.

"So you're not going to say you love me too? Bull."

"If I have to say it..." She touches her lips to mine, just the sweetest promise of what's to come. "Then you haven't been paying attention, sir." Then she laughs, a happy silvery sound that lights up the night.

"I love you, Riker Woods. With all my heart. I can't wait for you to be my husband."

XXIII: A LITTLE BIT LIKE HOME (OLIVIA)

I finally know the ending to my story.

The world has enough tragedies. The life we live right now, the way every day is full of little pains and ugliness and constant disappointments, is enough tragedy for anyone.

I should know. I've lived my share of it all.

But I've come through the other side to my happy ending, and I think my Eden deserves the same.

As does anyone who might read her story and see a little bit of themselves in the many pieces of *my*self that I put into her tale.

So maybe the story turned into a bit of a thriller, and my heroine gets her happy ending.

Her beloved hero wakes up from his coma as if she's willed him back to life with her strength and dedication to stay by his side, no matter how long it takes. And me?

I get my happy ending, too.

And I'm looking at it across the altar right now.

I'm looking at *him*.

It's a small wedding, just like we wanted, but it's full of big presence.

Milah in the front row, smiling through bursts of tears, surrounded by the entire Enguard team. My idol Kenna Strauss is even there, next to Landon.

I mean, she should be, we're at her house, getting married on the gorgeous beach outside their estate, the sea wind blowing through my hair and threatening to send my crown of flowers sailing.

Em's my matron of honor, standing close by in an adorable knee-length slip dress in spring green to match her eyes. And she can't stop smiling at Riker's best man, none other than Ryan Godart – even if his father, Mike, is conspicuously absent – with security alerted to escort him off the premises if he even shows his face. Ryan's back with his mom now.

My father's conspicuously absent, too, though it's not entirely deliberate.

In a perfect world, I'd have possibly forgiven him just enough for him to attend my wedding, if he'd shown real, on-his-knees honest remorse. But there wasn't even a chance.

He's currently in police custody after spilling his guts. After losing ninety percent of his fortune.

Life's nothing like he imagined, at least temporarily, until his plea deal for ratting out several other big names in his industry goes through.

Maybe the past few months in jail will teach him the things he never seemed to learn about being human.

I'm surprised how much I don't miss him. But it's been hard to miss my old life when my new life keeps coming together so wonderfully.

Riker finally got me a ring. I finally finished *Eden in Alaska*, and my literary agent is in final negotiations with a major publisher for an advance and publishing deal.

Busting Lion gave the FBI what they needed to bring down the entire multi-state Pilgrims organization. That shadow isn't over us anymore, leaving our days and our lives bright and breathless and perfect.

Every moment led us up to this day, when I can finally look at Riker so handsome in his suit and realize in just a few moments, in just a few words, this man looking at me with his heart in his eyes will be my husband for the rest of our lives.

When I first met Riker Woods, I never could've imagined that he'd be so warm. So open.

So expressive, the love written on his face for everyone to see as he clasps my hands tight and we listen to the priest reading us through our vows. *Those perfect words.*

Those sweet, perfect words that I'm hardly aware I'm speaking, when my entire world narrows on him.

His smile.

That spark in his vivid green eyes.

The way his lips shape every syllable of to have and to hold, for better or for worse, in sickness and in health. And then the priest asks me, there are only two words I could ever say.

Two simple words to go with his three.

"I do."

And then it's Riker's turn, and his small, warm smile turns into a full, dazzling grin, teeth white against the silver-and-brown trim of his beard.

"I do, Liv. Always. Now and forever, I do."

My heart nearly rockets from my chest.

The priest gets maybe half a second more to tell us we're officially man and wife.

Then we're in each other's arms, fused together as we share our first kiss as forever. He tastes like the promise of every future I've ever wanted.

Like the independence I've fought to have for myself as I cut myself loose from the last strings tying me to my father and a life that was never my own.

He tastes like every dream I've ever had, and I lose myself gladly in him, in the firmness and heat of his mouth, in the way he turns me inside out with every sighing stroke and whisper of my name.

We might have stayed that way forever if not for Milah's voice rising over the laughter and applause. "Hey, you two. Save some for the honeymoon."

Flushing hotly, I break back, looking up at Riker. I can't stop smiling, and he's just as bad, grinning from ear to ear. Leaning in, he whispers against my ear. "So is this the perfect wedding we talked about?"

"Any wedding would be perfect as long as you're here," I tease, curling my fingers against the back of his neck. "For a minute, I was afraid you'd get cold feet."

"Never. You're what I've been after for years, Liv." He steals another kiss, leaving me warm from the inside out. "You're the reason I learned how to live again."

I don't get a chance to answer when the entire wedding rushes in on us.

Everyone wants to congratulate us, hug us, from Riker's coworkers to Em's grandparents. Somehow the wedding tumbles into a small reception party around Landon and Kenna's pool, with Milah up on a dais built just for her and belting out her latest single while people eat, dance, stroll together.

Riker and I have our first wedding dance, and it's mostly us laughing and him holding me up while I trip over my train and then finally just give up and tie it around my waist like the heathen I am so that he and I can swirl in and out of each other's arms and let the whole world fall away just a little bit more, once again.

I've never been this happy in my life.

Even when we're pulled apart again.

What no one ever tells you about weddings is that *everyone* wants a piece of you because everyone wants to touch a little of your happiness, like it's starshine that can rub off on them in magic, glittery dust.

I'm happy to share that with them with laughter, with hugs, with shared gifts, with warm and friendly conversation. Sometimes I feel like I never truly knew what family was, but these people feel like family.

These people feel like home.

Once the pool is ringed with wrapping paper and the tables piled high with gifts and everyone is pleasantly tipsy, we're about to make our grand, melodramatic escape for our honeymoon when James intercepts us.

He offers a dark maroon whiskey gift box with the name Glenfiddich on the outside, wrapped up in a pretty gold ribbon and bow.

"I nearly forgot," he says, smooth as always. He doesn't creep me out anymore, but he still manages to be cold as ice even under the summer sun. "Your wedding gift, my friend."

Riker snorts a laugh as he takes the box, eyeing it

appreciatively. "It's not a gift if I won it fair and square, you cheap bastard."

"You didn't win," James points out coolly. "Remember? The condition was three catastrophes to win the bet. I dare say this?" He glances around the reception, then stops with a pointed look at me, one brow arching. "Hardly qualifies as a catastrophe."

"I'll give you that one,' Riker admits dryly.

"You shall." James sweeps a mocking half-bow. "Now, as I'm the only sober one here, I'll bring your car around so you can make your escape."

Rolling his eyes, Riker fishes his keys from his pocket and tosses them at James. James catches them out of the air, then melts through the crowd and away. I watch him for a moment, then give Riker a puzzled look.

"What was that about?"

Riker actually blushes. My big, rugged, stoic man actually *blushes*.

"James and I had a bet. He thought the Enguard run of disasters was over. My father taught me good and bad things come in threes, so I was ready for one more." He looks down at me then, his smile warmer than the sun. "But I lost, and I'm glad. Because you've been the best thing to ever happen to me, and to Em."

I can't even find the words to tell him I feel the same.

So I just pull him down into a kiss, and let my lips shape every emotion I don't know how to say, trusting he knows me. He knows *me*.

And he feels everything I feel, down to the depths of both our souls.

* * *

STILL NOT YOURS

It takes longer than expected to peel away from everyone and finally make our escape. The Wrangler is already loaded, packed with weeks' worth of camping equipment.

I've never been properly camping before, even with that week at the cabin, so our honeymoon is a long drive down the coast to Baja, spending every night sleeping under the stars.

I'm almost sad Em will miss this, but she's happy with her new Russian Blue kitten and a few weeks with her grandparents. The new cat, Toby, is totally adorable.

She's been obsessed with them since a visit to Landon's house introduced her to his Velvet and Mews.

Fine by me. Right now, frankly, I don't want to share Riker with anyone.

The sun is just setting over the Pacific when we pull off the road for the first night and find a secluded beach cove to set up camp. Riker shows me how to do all the little things.

He's never once patronized me over needing to learn things others just know as part of growing into adulthood, and everything he teaches me I take in, use it to build myself up stronger.

Everyone has to learn some time, right? There's no shame in learning a little later in life. Riker taught me that, too.

So freeing.

Yeah. That's a good word.

It's freeing, to know I can explore and discover and grow into who I want to be without anyone shaming me for it, least of all my new husband.

We settle in front of our tent to watch the stars come

out over the ocean, framed by the silhouette of an old shipwreck on shore, left to fall apart and pulled to pieces by the wind and waves.

Dinner is kebabs roasting on skewers over the fire, filling the night with savory scents of grilling meat, mushrooms, vegetables, then plenty of wine to go around. With a contented sigh, I rest my head on Riker's shoulder and look up at the sky, tracing the dark outline of a leaning, half-broken mast.

"Hey, Riker?"

He stirs from his silence next to me with a murmur. His arm is warm around me, sheltering me from the faint chill and damp bite of the night breeze. "Yeah, sweetheart?"

"You never told me...why model ships?"

He blinks, then chuckles, the rumble of it vibrating straight through me.

"Because they let me build something that's almost impossible to take apart again." His hold on me tightens, fingers gently stroking down my arm. "I spend time putting all these tiny parts together. And once that ship's in the bottle, it's there. Secure. Whole. Nothing can touch it. Nothing can change it. Nothing can ruin it." He looks down at me, that easy, warm smile lingering on his lips. "Just a quiet, beautiful little bit of forever."

I lean into him with a gentle nudge. "Is that what you've been looking for? A quiet, beautiful little bit of forever?"

"Guilty." He brushes his fingers under my chin, tilting my face up to his. "And now I've found it."

He kisses me as though he could keep me tucked in this moment forever.

As if I'm a fragile thing he wants to hold and preserve and always protect. And even if I've grown stronger all these months, even if I've learned to stand on my own, I still can't help but melt into the delicious feeling of him.

All his manly strength enveloping me, sheltering me, reminding me that every time I ever feel small and afraid, he'll always be there. My bulwark and my shield.

My love, my life, my husband, my everything.

He guides me again as I push him back onto the sand-strewn blanket and look down in the light of the stars and the flickering flames.

God. I love how his body feels between my legs as I straddle him, his thick bulk spreading my thighs until they ache and I feel so *open* and ready for him.

Even when I'm on top, he's in full control.

His tough, strong hands on my body shape me.

He caresses me out of my clothes, stroking over every inch of me until I know his touch with every fiber of my being.

I don't feel vulnerable, even fully naked on top of him, bared to the moon and the stars, while he's beneath me.

I just feel beautiful. He touches me with a hunger, a lust that can't get enough and makes my entire body shiver with sweet anticipation.

I'm dying for him. Aching for his touch, melting wet, burning down every second he isn't lighting me on fire.

"Riker, yeah!"

His name purrs softly on my lips, a single sensual word as our mouths mate and part and mate again.

Our bodies tangle together and fuse hotter and hotter, fires into infernos.

Then I whimper, a little louder, sweet for him in the way I know he likes. "Please. Fuck me, please."

It's the first time I've begged for him as his wife.

The first time I've called his name as my husband.

Riker always was my first in everything, and now this night marks one more new beginning.

Another first, as finally he gives in to my coaxing touches, my begging lips, my grinding hips, and lifts me over him.

The better to free his cock, pressing up against me, ready for the conquest.

I don't know if he rocks up into me or I sink down onto him first, but suddenly we're just caught in each other's tide.

Rolling with the ebb and flow. One rhythm. And he's moving so deliciously inside me, filling me in that way only he has, an aftershock of sharp, gliding pleasure that tunes my entire body to his frequency until we're trembling and gasping together.

"You'd better come for me, sweetheart. Come so fucking hard."

Like it's even a choice.

I throw myself into him, riding his cock, all drifting ass and lungs crawling up my throat. My pussy clenches him so hard, I think we'll both break. He thrusts like mad, hurling himself into me, throwing his full, glorious bucking weight at my hips.

And I'm gone.

Coming!

Somewhere in the white hot eye-rolling heat, I just know how much I love him.

Love and adore him more than I could ever love

anyone else, and it fills me as deeply as the thrust and taunt and surge of his cock as I give myself over to the fire building between our bodies.

He doesn't stop for my release. He only flogs it harder, higher, splitting me open with long, deep strokes, a feral growl deepening in his throat.

The animal glare in his eyes brings me off faster again than should even be humanly possible.

Nothing could break this moment.

Nothing could ruin it.

Alone against the sea, alone against the sky, alone with each other, trapped in something sacred and profane and forever binding. Riker will always be a part of my body, a part of my heart, and it feels as though we trade breaths, trade hearts as the writhe and flow of our bodies reaches fever pitch.

I almost can't tell pleasure from pain, love from heartbreak, with the intensity of emotion rushing over me. My body turns into fire, then bursts into sparks, as waves of need and blazing release surge through me.

My awareness narrows down to the wild, searing sensation as my flesh convulses around his cock, forcing me to be aware of his thickness, of the way he throbs inside me, the way he pulses and swells with a tortured groan.

"Liv, fuck!"

That's when I let go, and so does he.

He fills me so good.

My husband fills me like no other man ever can.

There's a single moment frozen between us as our bodies lock. Timeless, breathless perfection.

Then we're spiraling away, still tangled together as we come crashing down.

His pubic bone grinds my clit, his hands dig into my ass, and I couldn't hold back if I tried.

We come together with a force that's almost scary. Twitching, screaming, clutching, groaning, and totally, forever undone.

My body doesn't want to hold me up anymore.

So I just sink down on Riker with his cock still inside me, snuggled close, content to let his body keep me warm against the night chill.

He holds me tight, his heaving breaths slowly stilling until he's quiet underneath me, and I can lull myself nearly to sleep by just the faint rumble emitting from his throat and the pure, deep contentment that's fallen over me.

Here I am. Mrs. Riker Woods.

It's like I'm a completely different person from the girl who, at the beginning of this strange and sordid path, stood frozen and afraid while a man died at her feet.

There's no more death in my future. Only life, however I want to make it.

However *we* want to make it.

You really don't know which day will be the last day of your life.

But you never know which day will be the first, either – and the start of something more amazing, more real than you ever could've dreamed.

You don't know when you'll meet the man worth calling yours.

XXIV: EXTENDED EPILOGUE (RIKER)

Five Years Later

"Shit, you're kidding me. It's today?"

I've just gotten through apologizing up and down to a very impatient Liv over the phone. I should've been home half an hour ago, right before Em steps off her NASA chartered bus with a whole new summer of memories behind her, and a leg up on the career in actual rocket science ahead of her.

"You knew, big daddy. Oh, and if you have a spare minute while you're racing home, we could really use a few more diapers."

"Got it, Liv. Give me fifteen minutes." I hang up, grinning at the two men next to me at the bar.

"Sounds like somebody's gotta move sweet time to get across town in this traffic if he don't want to catch hell. Rain check on the next round?"

"You know it, Gabe. You'll get me next time." I slap his wall of a shoulder.

"A real shame, my friend, but there's no arguing with family duty." James looks over his spectacles, straightening his tie. "I understand perfectly. I'll have an extra drink in your place, Riker."

"Bull. Like you weren't *already* planning to get full on shit-faced with your woman out of town."

He gives me a crooked smile. "You know it calms the nerves. After the way I put a ring on Faye's finger, you know what being apart can be like for us."

I can't roll my eyes hard enough. They're damn near inseparable.

I throw down an extra crisp fifty and slide it over to Gabe. "Here. Get him something strong from the top shelf. You know, before he has a chance to tell that story about the lodge again."

"Aw, shitfire, not the goddamn lodge!" Gabe grins bitterly, shaking his head, throwing his giant arms over both of us. "You boys know I still hear Sky saying how lucky we are to be alive about once a week?"

"Well, after that –" James starts in.

"After *that*," I growl, cutting him off. "I don't think any of us ever need another reminder to count our lucky stars. The boss knows it, too."

"A story for another time, I suppose." James says matter-of-factly. "We'll wait for the entire crew before I grab you by the balls again with my little tale of love and terror."

"We were both there, man. We were there," Gabe says like a broken record, summoning the bartender over with a wave of his hand. "Go get your little girl, Riker. And you, get us something nice and smooth. Whatever the hell makes a man's brain too buttery to feel all nostalgic and hankering for a story."

James gives me that look again as the bartender smiles and nods. *Another time.*

He's serious. So I just clap his neat pressed suit on the shoulder one last time.

"We'll all catch up at Kenna's birthday next week. Then you can remind us how you were the big hero."

I turn, finally making my way out.

We've all had our moment to shine over the years, every last senior part of the well oiled Enguard machine.

After what went down with James, Gabe, Skylar, Landon, and too many more than I can count, yeah, I guess I should feel lucky.

After that night I put Lion away, and came home to make Liv my wife, make her part of our family, our forever, I should feel like the luckiest damn fool on earth.

Some days, I do.

But I'd be lying if I said there weren't something better.

Like getting to live my good fortune every day I come home to my wife. I'll take family reunions a thousand times over bullets and blood.

How James won his woman, saving everybody's day, has nothing on every new day I get to live with mine.

* * *

Sometimes it feels like children grow up too fast.

Yet, no matter how fast Em grows, she'll always be my

little girl. Even if she's almost as tall as me now, minus a few inches, at seventeen.

I don't know where the last five years went. I've been caught up in this happy haze of family and warmth and togetherness.

Somehow in that time, while Liv and I were growing closer and closer, Em grew up.

And she's grown up enough to watch me kill that Ryan boy if he doesn't get his hand off her hip as they step off the bus from the NASA summer camp they attended together.

Fucking hell. I never should've let her start dating. She's still too young for this.

Liv leans into me, bumping me with her shoulder and giving me a knowing, amused look as she bounces the rather fussy, teething baby in her arms.

"Hey, stop glaring like that. After they've been together this long, you'd think you'd be used to it."

"It's not Ryan I can't stand. More like Em growing up too fast," I mutter. "Oh, yeah. And the thought of his asshole father as an in-law someday."

It's been years, and I still want to kick Mike's ass. Sure, he's gotten his shit together.

He's hung up the martial arts credentials and he's teaching yoga around town now. A far more successful business, judging by the new sports car in his driveway, and one that's less likely to show the whole world he's a coward.

Whatever. At least it made sure Ryan's got a ticket to college. Not that the kid doesn't have scholarships pouring out his ears. He's plenty smart, or else my Em would've dropped him like a hot potato.

STILL NOT YOURS

Laughing, Liv arches a brow, snapping me out of my growly thoughts.

"They're seventeen, Riker. It'll be at least another whole year before they're talking about eloping."

"Over my dead body." I'm totally serious.

If that boy tries it, I'll get Landon on board to send a whole strike team after his eloping ass.

"You probably shouldn't be saying that when your daughter's a black belt." Her soft whip of a tongue flicks out to tease me.

I suppress another growl, too many inappropriate thoughts invading my brain. Have to hand it to my wife – even after all these years, she knows how to distract me just right.

Then she breaks off as Em catches sight of us and belts out an excited cry. Liv's just as excited, lifting her free arm in a wave and calling, "Em, hey!"

Em and Ryan exchange a glance before she clasps her boyfriend's hand and practically drags him over to us. Only to stop mid-step, both hands flying to her mouth as she stares at the sniffling bundle swaddled in Liv's arms.

Em stares, eyes huge, and asks in a hush, "Oh my God. Is that really...*her?*"

"Your baby sister Eden," Liv murmurs, smiling so brilliantly it could make the sun jealous.

She pulls the swaddling back on baby Eden's red, scrunched-up face. "She's a little cranky right now because she's teething, but...want to hold her?"

"Um, are you kidding? *Yes!*" Em's enthralled.

It takes me back to the day I rushed Liv to the emergency room.

Milah talked her into this natural birth business. I

thought she was out of her damn mind at first, pushing out a kid with no meds and a midwife. Especially considering how Milah seemed destined to be the cool wine aunt until she finally shacked up with her boy, Jake, last year.

It didn't take them long. The tabloids can't shut up about the Holly baby, coming to a gossip rag near you in just a few more months.

I've never been happier knowing I'll never be famous.

I'm sure Milah will give our little family a lovely niece or nephew when the time comes. Still, the best Holly baby was the one born on a bright sunny day just a few months ago.

I'll never forget how Liv looked in my eyes the first time we held her.

There's something perfect about a baby looking back. Little Eden had our whole world in half a heartbeat, her sweet eyes the same color as mine, green and sharp enough to cut this world to pieces.

I swear she gave me a look that said she knew we were a family from the very first time her eyes opened. That look said mama, daddy, family. That look tore my heart out in the best ways, and made me fall a little more in love with Liv. The kind of love that should be illegal.

Almost the same way Liv and Em are looking at her now.

I can't help but smile, forgetting my fretting over Em and Ryan. My heart swells with love and pride as I watch my little woman gently take Eden from Liv's arms, looking down at her with utter rapture and adoration.

"Oh, I wish I'd been home, Daddy. Can't believe you guys went and had her while I was gone."

Liv laughs. "She's a little impatient. Too much like her dad, maybe. She didn't want to wait a few months until you came home."

Eden's fussing immediately quiets in Em's arms.

Hell if I'm not going to fucking explode with all these feelings.

This perfection, this warmth, this content.

Even Ryan grins, extending his hand for a firm handshake.

What the hell? I can't be pissed, even when he keeps his other hand draped over Em's shoulder, so I return his respect like he deserves. I shake his hand with the same happy energy I've fought for all along. Had to chisel out of this life piece by piece.

"Congrats, Mr. Woods. She'll be a beauty someday, just like her big sis."

Em gently elbows Ryan and shoots him a sassy look. I can't help but chuckle.

"Seems like she already knows you, Em," I say. "She hasn't stopped crying all day."

"That's because she knows her big sister's going to take good care of her." Em gently strokes a fingertip to Eden's little button nose. "Don't you, little Eden? I'm going to take you everywhere with me, and teach you about the stars and planets and Falcon Heavy rockets. Everything under the sun."

Eden opens her eyes and smiles a sugary, lopsided baby grin. Em and Ryan laugh themselves silly.

Liv leans into me while they're busy, watching our girls with a fond expression on her face. "You did good with that one, Riker. Let's hope number two turns out just as well," she teases softly.

"*We* did good," I correct, squeezing her so tight it almost hurts. "And we'll do even better with Eden, sweetheart. And better still with every new kid."

"Every *new* kid?" She lifts both brows, giving me a mock-stern look. "I'm still recovering from our first, you know. And I'm already late on my publisher's next deadline. They only give you so much leeway for being a bestseller superstar before they start getting mad. Don't start planning a tribe yet."

"Operative word being 'yet.'"

"Behave." She swats my arm, but I can tell she doesn't mean it.

Not when there's such joy in her eyes, such peace, as our little family – and I'll include Ryan in that just this once – clusters close.

Not when she leans on me so trustingly, and even now, after years, her touch is a comfort and the spark that ignites a fire inside me.

I can't think of anything more perfect than this moment. I don't even want to try.

This is like a ship in a bottle, perfect and eternal. I'll always hold onto it as an unchanging, beautiful memory.

I've found my quiet, beautiful little bit of forever, all right.

And it's in Liv, in Em, in Eden.

In the love of my family, now and every last minute of our happily ever after.

THANKS!

Want more Nicole Snow? Sign up for my newsletter to hear about new releases, exclusive subscriber giveaways, and more fun stuff!

JOIN THE NICOLE SNOW NEWSLETTER! - http://eepurl.com/HwFW1

Thank you so much for buying this book. I hope my romances sweeten your days with pleasure, drama, and all the feels! I tell the stories you want to hear.

If you liked this book, please consider leaving a review and checking out my other romance tales.

Got a comment on my work? Email me at nicole@nicolesnowbooks.com. I love hearing from fans!

Nicole Snow

THANKS!

More Intense Romance by Nicole Snow

ACCIDENTAL HERO

ACCIDENTAL PROTECTOR

CINDERELLA UNDONE

MAN ENOUGH

SURPRISE DADDY

LAST TIME WE KISSED

PRINCE WITH BENEFITS

MARRY ME AGAIN

LOVE SCARS

MERCILESS LOVE

RECKLESSLY HIS

STEPBROTHER CHARMING

STEPBROTHER UNSEALED

Enguard Protectors Books

STILL NOT OVER YOU

STILL NOT INTO YOU

STILL NOT YOURS

Prairie Devils MC Books

OUTLAW KIND OF LOVE

NOMAD KIND OF LOVE

SAVAGE KIND OF LOVE

WICKED KIND OF LOVE

BITTER KIND OF LOVE

Grizzlies MC Books

OUTLAW'S KISS

OUTLAW'S OBSESSION

OUTLAW'S BRIDE

OUTLAW'S VOW

Deadly Pistols MC Books

NEVER LOVE AN OUTLAW

NEVER KISS AN OUTLAW

THANKS!

NEVER HAVE AN OUTLAW'S BABY

NEVER WED AN OUTLAW

Baby Fever Books

BABY FEVER BRIDE

BABY FEVER PROMISE

BABY FEVER SECRETS

Only Pretend Books

FIANCÉ ON PAPER

ONE NIGHT BRIDE

Made in the USA
Middletown, DE
19 February 2023